THE WAKING

T. M. JENKINS began a professional career in
newspapers, wrote a column for the *Evening Standard*,
was a newscaster for Thames TV and a reporter for ITN
before going behind the scenes to produce and direct
documentaries for the BBC and Channel 4.
T. M. Jenkins now lives in Hollywood.

'A startling, original novel. A provocative,
credible story that grips, fascinates and disturbs
right to the very last page'
Peter James

T. M. JENKINS

THE WAKING

PAN BOOKS

First published 2006 by Macmillan

First published in paperback 2007 by Pan Books
an imprint of Pan Macmillan Ltd
Pan Macmillan, 20 New Wharf Road, London N1 9RR
Basingstoke and Oxford
Associated companies throughout the world
www.panmacmillan.com

ISBN 978-0-330-44032-5

1 3 5 7 9 8 6 4 2

A CIP catalogue record for this book is available from
the British Library.

Typeset by SetSystems Ltd, Saffron Walden, Essex
Printed and bound in Great Britain by
Mackays of Chatham plc, Chatham, Kent

Visit www.panmacmillan.com to read more about all our books
and to buy them. You will also find features, author interviews and
news of any author events, and you can sign up for e-newsletters
so that you're always first to hear about our new releases.

To Juliette,

for all of it

Acknowledgements

The idea for *The Waking* came while I was attending a conference about the brain in Jamaica. I was led there by the science writer and friend, Rita Carter, whose excellent book *Mapping the Mind* became my landscape for many months. While there I met the neuropsychiatrist Peter Fenwick, whose fertile imagination was able to take the leap into fiction and he came up with many ideas that I gratefully plundered. First-draft red-pen markers who made an indelible impression are Paul Reizin, Helen Fielding, Billie Morton, David Hirst, Gary Humphreys, Harry Leech and Clare Alexander. The professionals who helped along the way are Dr Victor Amira and Dr David Drake. Much-needed enthusiasm and encouragement came from Suzan Crowley, Robin Maxwell, Cameron Spencer and the late Daz Spence.

One of the most vigorous edits came from the novelist and friend Juliette Mead. I am most grateful to A. P. Watt, notably Sheila Crowley, Caradoc King and Jo Frank, who not only believed in the book but were assiduous in knocking it into shape. And now to my editor at Macmillan, Stefanie Bierwerth, who is up for the adventure. And then there is Derek Penn from UCLA, who became the final mapquest through the maze of the science. Last, but not least, there's G.B., who stuck around until the last words were written, but unbeknown to me, had already run out of lives.

PROLOGUE

The future enters into us, in order to transform us,
long before it happens.

RAINER MARIA RILKE (1875–1926)

The best prophet of the future is the past.

LORD BYRON (1788–1824)

Death is the dark backing a mirror needs if we are
to see anything.

SAUL BELLOW (1915–2005)

LOS ANGELES / 2006

1

In the moments before his death, Dr Nate Sheehan was able to see clearly how the shooting had unfolded. He was driving home with his wife Mary when they turned on to La Brea, a shabby, wide-berthed boulevard that ran from Hollywood down to the tar pits and beyond. Nate idly took in the crazy debris washed up on the forecourts of the retro furniture stores: the lime-green sofa in the shape of a pair of lips, the eight-foot-high stainless-steel palm tree from some 1980s' nightclub and the tawdry electric organs from long-closed lounge bars. Thinking back on it, as he lay in a pool of his own blood, if only he'd been more tolerant. Mary had made him angry. If he hadn't been angry, he might have seen what was coming.

'Do you know what, Nate – if you don't tell me stuff – how can you expect us to be intimate? You did Psychology 101. You know the score,' she said, looking out of the tinted window. Mary was in her bullying mode, a mode reserved for getting things done. It was what made her effective at work, but if she ever turned it on him, it got him riled.

Mary was quizzing him, as she often did, about his involvement with Doctors for Justice, a radical support group set up to help patients fight the medical establishment when the court system had failed them. Right now, Nate was extremely nervous. He was sitting on a piece of information that would be dynamite to any news organization and he wasn't quite sure what to do with it. The information was almost too big for the media to handle, and what was more, he couldn't tell his wife. He glanced sideways. Mary was giving him one of those looks.

'I can smell trouble,' she said.

'Look, we talked about this before and we agreed, the less you know about what I'm working on, the better.'

'OK, Capo,' she said, and saluted him, which irritated him even more. She wasn't taking him seriously.

'Hey, look at that!' she exclaimed as they sped past another fenced-off parking lot called Nicky Metropolis. 'It's a Zulu warrior's shield. We could hang it in the stairwell.'

'We don't need a Zulu warrior's shield,' he muttered darkly, and accelerated.

Shopping was another minefield between them. Mary had a habit of dawdling in shops and becoming hypnotically oblivious to his impatience as she sifted through endless piles of junk. Nate was an A to B man, charging along the shortest route from departure to destination with no stopping in between. There just weren't enough hours in the day.

'OK – but we do need cilantro,' she said. 'There's a Trader Joe's up here on the right.'

Nate saw this latest need to stop as another diversion designed to test his patience to the limit. He yanked the wheel of their SUV into the car park and braked.

'Go ahead,' he said.

'Are you staying in the car?'

'Yes, I'm staying in the car.'

Mary sat back, folded her arms, crossed her legs and banged her shin against the dashboard. He could see her gold anklet, her little token of sartorial rebellion, looped over her red suede trainers.

'How long are we going to be on this earth together?' she said, searching his face with her intelligent hazel eyes.

He picked at the bottle-opener on his key ring.

'I'm asking a serious question. Don't hold out on me.'

'It's *not* a serious question.' His voice sounded petty and mean.

'Yes it is. We've got maybe forty years, fifty years – tops. We need to *eat*, Nate.'

He said nothing. He didn't want to get into it.

'So every time I want to shop for something like *food* I have to placate you? Because that just isn't going to work.'

She scraped her thick dark hair back as though she was about to tie it in a ponytail, then let it drop back over her face.

'It's just this constant need to *browse*!'

She looked at him, one eyebrow raised. 'You better watch those glucocorticoids.'

'If I'm producing more stress hormones it's because you're always in my face!'

So this wasn't going to be a serious argument after all, but a kind of facsimile of an argument that could so easily go either way. Sometimes, Nate saw the pair of them as a couple of seals on a beach, lazily slapping each other with their flippers. Sparring. That's what they did a lot of the time. They sparred – just for the hell of it. But sometimes it got nasty and that's when the damage got done.

'You're such a dud,' she said as she opened her door and hopped down from her seat.

Nate watched Mary walk towards the entrance of Trader Joe's, taking long, purposeful strides, her hands dug deep in the pockets of her linen shirt.

At that moment, he realized how much he loved her. He loved her for many reasons, but right now he loved her because she was never intimidated by his temper. As he watched her wrestle with the cart and disappear into the store, he wondered what her lean, almost boyish body would look like six months from now. She was the physical type that wouldn't put on much weight, except around the belly. And he couldn't wait to feel that belly taut like a football and their baby somersaulting inside. He knew Mary felt agnostic about motherhood. But she had decided to go through with it anyway, for his sake. Maybe that's why she was leaning on him about Doctors for Justice. She was frightened of his involvement in anything risky. All these thoughts sent another great surge of love through him. But he could never tell her, not when he was supposed to be in the middle of a funk.

Nate followed Mary inside the store and sure enough, she found dozens of reasons to dawdle. The cilantro, the original purpose for the trip, soon disappeared under mounds of herbs, vegetables and fresh pasta. She became a little dreamy by the meat counter, unable to decide if they needed Italian herb sausages or rib-eye steak, so he grabbed both, threw them into the basket and marched off towards the checkout. If only he'd let her linger. Then someone else could have taken the bullet.

The kid was no more than fourteen. He was running towards them across the parking lot. Nate saw him out of the corner of his eye, noticed it when he realized it was the wrong kind of run. It was a sidle, and if the kid kept it up he was going to crash right into them. Nate half turned to brace himself for a collision, but the kid stopped just short of them and hovered. Nate saw the gun then, a decrepit little thing with a distended barrel and a brown plastic handle. The kid was holding it in both his filthy, tremulous hands.

'Dinero, dinero.'

The kid had a high hook to his Mayan nose and his nostrils were flaring as he breathed in and out. His rapid heartbeat was almost visible through his ragged T-shirt and there was a bluish tinge to his lips. Nate could tell, just by looking at him, that he was probably suffering from some kind of congenital heart disease. He decided to use it to bargain with the boy.

'*Pienso que estas infermo. Soy un doctore – tengo un clinica para los povres en Huntington Park. Venga com migo. Permita me ayudar te.*'

'What are you saying?' said Mary, swallowing. Her mouth was dry, her voice high and reedy.

'I'm telling him about the clinic,' said Nate, still looking at the boy. 'I'm asking him to come with us – so we can take a look at him. I think he's got mitral stenosis.'

The boy shook his head and motioned to Nate's pockets.

'*Soy un doctore. Permita me ayudar te,*' Nate repeated. 'Let me help you.' He held out his hand, but the boy shied away and wielded the gun to let them know how deadly it was.

'*Dinero, dinero.*'

Nate wanted Mary to run but couldn't take his eyes off the kid. Forgetting his Spanish, he ploughed on. 'Don't hurt us – OK? Our family needs us. They depend on us. Just like your family will depend on you some day. *Dinero*? I'm just putting my hands in my pockets to get it out.' Nate fumbled around, trying to be casual. 'I'm not doing anything else – OK?'

Mary, still frozen to the spot, was clutching the bags of groceries to her chest as though they were her brood of imaginary children.

A little way off, a cart rattled across uneven concrete and the kid's eyes darted. An old couple in ice cream-coloured casuals were heading towards their car. Nate seized the moment and tried to grab the weapon.

A 'parp' sounded like the retort of a toy gun, but so close, it flung Nate back against the SUV. The kid staggered back and tripped, letting off another round into the sky. It was so unexpected that Nate laughed, thinking it wasn't for real, then he saw Mary looking blankly at his chest. His legs buckled and he slithered down the side of the car.

Mary dropped the groceries and in a terrifying fit of rage wrenched the gun from the kid's hand and started pounding his head with it. Nate's own head was slackening on its pivot, but he tried to raise an arm to stop her.

'Don't, baby,' he whispered.

The kid scrambled to his feet and raced off down the street. Then everything went slow. There seemed to be an inexorable destiny about the shooting: his impatience, his arrogance, his foolishness for thinking he could get the gun from the kid. And here he was, unable to speak, trying to get his wife to press down on his aorta which he knew was bleeding out. Mary yelling for help and pressing down, her fist pressing against the tiny, deadly hole in his chest. Her teeth chattering in shock. People running and shouting. His legs getting colder.

'I love this street,' said Mary as they turned on to La Brea.

'We don't have time,' said Nate. He knew that hungry look.

Mary reached across the front seat and ran her fingers through his hair. Now you give me a kiss, he thought to himself, and in the routine of their affection she leant her face towards him and kissed him on the side of his mouth.

'Keep your eyes on the road,' she said. 'So what is the latest thing you're working on that's making you so tense?'

And all he could hear now was the deafening pump of his own blood leaking out. Blue lights flashing. A siren and an ambulance coming to a halt. People rushing over – a black guy – huge – lumbering. And Nate was floating like a piece of driftwood on a calm, black sea. Mary – Mary. It wasn't a voice, only a thought, a useless strand of a thought. He could feel no particular pain, wet numbness, but very little pain. Maybe it was too great for him to register.

So this is how it feels, he thought, over and over. *This is how it feels.*

Someone was shouting, 'Stay with us, Dr Sheehan!' and now the big guy, his charcoal angel, was wheezing and lifting Nate on to a gurney and delivering him into the ambulance like a big, wet fish being propelled down a chute . . . only it felt like levitation . . . weightlessness, and Nate was high, high up over the scene. Mary was leaning across him now and there was blood all over her face. A mask going on.

'Yes, I am a doctor – at UCLA. Christ! Don't use the defibrillators – you'll give him a reperfusion injury. We need to drop the temperature. Do you have any cooling packs?'

It didn't sound like Mary but a choked-up, ugly voice. 'Hang on, Nate, just hang on for me, baby.'

Mary . . . my Mary . . . flashing blue . . . keep breathing . . . cold creeping up . . . keep breathing . . . so cold . . . a cool rush like ice water down the side of a glass . . . glacial blue . . . like the time we caught the Amtrak train across the Glacier National Park in Washington State . . . do you remember, Mary? . . . screwing like frenzied adulterers against the toilet wall . . . only it was our fifth wedding anniversary . . .

There was no chance of saying that he loved her now . . . and he'd been so horrible . . . that short fuse of his . . . he hoped she would understand. A soft pillow . . . that's all he wanted . . . a beautiful white, cotton pillow like a cool hand on his cheek . . . her hand moments ago . . . her hands were always cold . . . like the tip of her nose. So tired. Sorry, Mary . . . I know it's wrong but you just have to let me sleep . . .

2

'Are you guys carrying Alcius catheters or anything like it?'

'No, ma'am.'

'Medivance cold packs?' Mary was screaming.

'We don't carry anything like that,' said the black guy, ' – yet.'

'I've got to give him a – I've got to get him to—' Mary couldn't find the words. Her thoughts were stumbling. 'I need microparticulate ice slurry. Do you know about that?'

'Excuse me?'

'His temperature needs to be cooled, right now, to preserve the tissue.'

The crew looked at each other. It was the kind of look that said she was cuckoo.

'Ma'am – your husband is dead,' said the paramedic slowly, 'and now, we need to hand the body over to the police. Do you understand? This is a crime scene now. They will want to examine the body to see what happened here.'

'No! We can save him.'

'No we can't, ma'am. He's dead and this is a crime scene and the medical examiner is coming. Do you understand?'

'You called him already? Who called him?'

'My partner.'

The paramedic was good at calming people, but this was no time to be nice. Mary had less than eight minutes. She flicked open her cell and with shaking fingers found the number.

'Greg. Are you at work? Thank God. Do you have an ambulance? Nate's just been shot! I've only got the cryo-protectant. I don't know. Do they have the hydrogen sulphide on site yet? Where am I?' She looked around. She couldn't remember. 'In the parking lot at Trader Joe's on La Brea. Can you come?' Mary turned to look at Nate. His eyes were still open but unseeing and glassy. 'I think he's dead.'

The emergency crew began to lever the body back down into the car park.

'Wait, wait,' said Mary, trying to pull herself together. 'I'm taking his body for organ donorship.'

The ambulance men looked at Nate's chest.

'He won't be much use.'

'Yes he will. The corneas. Brain tissue. Pituitary. There's a lot we can save. But I have to do it now! An ambulance will be here in a couple of minutes.'

She felt like a madwoman. Totally insane.

'You can't take a body from a crime scene.'

'I can and I will.'

'This will get you into a lot of trouble.'

'I know the medical examiner. He'll understand.'

The big guy squared up to her. 'Do you have his donor card? And your doctor's licence?'

'You cannot be *serious*!' She couldn't believe he was thinking of procedure at a time like this.

'If you want to break the law, go right ahead, but we got to release liability.'

Shaking like a leaf, Mary rummaged around in her car. Miraculously, she found both cards.

'OK – but you got to sign for him,' said the guy, shaking his head.

Mary signed with a wild signature, getting blood all over the paper. She heard a siren. She looked up and saw Greg's ambulance turning out of 3rd Street. A miracle. He made it before the police. Greg looked completely unmoved as he swung his long, gangly body out of the driver's seat.

'OK, Mary,' he said calmly. 'What do you want to do?'

'Let's go to Pasadena.'

A crowd was gathering now. The checkout girls from Trader Joe's were screaming and the security guard, who'd missed the entire shooting, was running around and shouting. The manager pushed through the crowd.

'Help me,' hissed Mary, and the three of them heaved Nate's floppy corpse into the second ambulance, then Mary turned to face the throng.

'You're all witnesses to this crime. My husband was shot by a young boy who ran down that street. My husband's name is Dr Nate Sheehan and I'm his wife – Dr Mary Sheehan. I'm taking my husband's body for organ donorship.'

Her hands were still trembling as she wrote down their names and handed the slip of paper to the manager. 'Tell the police that I've taken the body and will hand it over as soon as we've farmed it for what we need.'

The manager took the paper, utterly bewildered. Mary leapt into the back of the ambulance and held Nate's limp hand while Greg hit the accelerator. They raced through the streets, sirens blaring.

'Greg, stop!'

'I thought we were going to Pasadena.'

'It's been ten minutes – stop!'

Greg pulled over to the side of the road. She looked at him.

'We can't do it here,' he said.

'Yes we can.'

'This is demented,' protested Greg, turning off the siren. 'What if the cops find us?'

Her look silenced him. He jumped out and slammed the door. Mary took one last glance at Nate.

'I'll see you again,' she said as she finally closed his eyes and kissed his bloody lips.

Greg joined her in the back. 'What do you think?' he said.

'I think the head is the only thing we can save,' she said.

Greg prepared the instruments while Mary positioned the body. She leant against it to stop her hands from trembling as she cut neatly below his Adam's apple, then made a clean incision through the neck to the spinal column, leaving the top two vertebrae in place. Greg turned into the master of calm, as she'd seen him do many times before, delicately attaching tubes to the carotid arteries in the neck, closing off the other blood vessels and checking the ice slurry as it pumped through the vessels and into the brain cavity. It was gruesome, messy work, but the routine of the procedure was holding Mary together, making sure she did a good job of it.

'It's a shame we're not working with hydrogen sulphide,' Greg said sadly.

'This is good enough for all the technology that's coming,' she said quietly.

Within five minutes they were able to start dropping the temperature of the head. Another couple of minutes and they would be able to put it in the dewar and carry on to Pasadena. Mary knew she was about to be in deep trouble for taking her husband's body, especially as the ambulance crew would confirm that Nate was already dead. But she didn't care. She'd seen too many times what happened to murder victims once the crime scene investigators arrived. She remembered with horror the aerial shots of the Santa Monica farmers' market when an old man ploughed through the stalls in the heat of midsummer, killing ten people. The corpses had been left out on the road for most of the day while forensics did their work. She didn't want her husband decomposing under a tarpaulin while helicopters buzzed overhead. If that happened, she would lose the one chance she had of ever seeing her husband alive again.

VENICE CANALS, LOS ANGELES / 2006

3

As she came to, the dull ache across her temples and the iron smell on her shirt made Mary remember. She got up and pulled on a cardigan. Her whole body ached. She could see through her bedroom window that a marine layer of dense cloud had descended over the canal during the night. The moorhens and the ducks were pecking at weeds. A neighbour was walking her dog. It all looked impossibly normal.

She dragged herself upstairs and reflexively turned on the gas to heat the water. She looked down at her shirt. The blood had dried crisp and rust-red and there were streaks of dark matter, Nate's matter, splattered across the front. She ran a finger across the stains. How his face had crumpled and gone slack. He had apologized to her with his eyes. She could tell that he was only thinking of her as the fury and the vitality of his stare turned into a deathly glaze.

She wasn't going to wash today. Or any other day. She wasn't going to do anything to get rid of his blood. She was just going to stand there, rooted to the spot for ever. She realized that she ought to get some medication or she might just lie down and die.

A pelican, with its huge, ungainly wingspan, see-sawed past her window and made a crash landing on the canal. The big old seabirds were coming in from the ocean. They would hang out, catch what fish they could in the canals before relaunching themselves in the spring. She had seen more birds every day during her early-morning power walks down Venice pier. She couldn't imagine ever taking that walk again.

The pelican started to stab at something on the bottom of the canal. It was a momentary distraction before the stupefied face of Nate's killer came flooding back to her. He was an idiot, incomplete, and the squint in his eye and the snot around his nose had told Mary that he did not know how to look after himself. He had nothing to lose by shooting a rich man in a car park. She'd hit him hard, but he'd got away and would probably never be found. The futility of it made Mary forget to breathe. She hugged herself and shivered involuntarily. She felt the tautness of her belly and remembered that she was expecting a child. It made her realize just how deeply she must be in shock to forget the baby.

'What am I going to do?' she said out loud. She became aware of the phone ringing. She didn't answer it. No one could bring Nate back, so what was the point? She looked at the message machine, a battered old contraption that Nate had insisted they use instead of paying for voicemail. He could be so tight like that. There were thirty messages. She wondered how she could have slept through them all. She played Nate's message. He was more sociable than she was and insisted on leaving his own greeting on the machine.

'You've reached the Sheehan residence. You can leave a message for me or Mary and we'll get back to you. Thanks.'

The voice was warm, friendly, sage, with a hint of wit at being confined to the conventions of an answering machine. She wondered with sudden panic if she had any other recordings of Nate. She couldn't bear to forget that voice. Mary raised the linen shirt to her face. At least she had Nate's head. Fuck his wishes not to be frozen.

'I'm sorry, but I'm not letting you go,' she said to the empty room.

Nate had always derided Mary's interest in cryonics. She knew it embarrassed him if she ever got talking about it with their friends, but she didn't care. Her 'obsession', as he called it, was fostered partly because of her work fertilizing frozen eggs and later, her fellowship studying a line of foetal stem cells at UCLA. Nate never understood why she got so embroiled with the tiny band of fanatics who were dedicated to cryonic resuscitation.

'*You're all a bunch of nut jobs,' he would say to her.*

'*It's my hobby,' she would say back. 'What did my dad say? The key to survival is outside interests. Well, indulge me, Nate – cryonics is my outside interest.*'

What Mary actually believed was that she was the one who was indulging *Nate*'s scepticism. Every day, she was witnessing the extraordinary advances that her colleagues were making in the field of nanotechnology. They were already developing a micron-sized camera. Within a few years, they would be using micron-sized computers to repair diseased hearts and other damaged organs inside the body. Mary was convinced that physical reincarnation would be possible. It was only a matter of time.

She watched the blue flame of the gas buffeting the bottom of the pan and tried to piece together the chaos of the day before; her fumbling for her medical licence and Nate's donor card, grabbing the cryoprotectant that she always carried in her car and turning into a tyrant with the paramedics. She remembered how angry the black guy was, insisting that she sign a liability form with her bloodied hands.

She pictured the old couple by their car, the husband comforting his wife who was in shock. Mary hoped the woman was OK and that they would be able to tell the police what had happened. She ought to get hold of her lawyer.

She ladled fresh coffee into a plunger, then wiped the tears and spittle from her swollen face. She wasn't superstitious, but as she looked at the way things unfolded, it was like a dream, as though it was all *meant* to happen. She could see from the hole in Nate's chest that his body wasn't up to a median sternotomy. The bullet had already shattered the chest wall and done so much damage going in that accessing the arteries was going to be pointless. And then Greg had happened to be at work at the veterans' hospital around the corner with an ambulance at his disposal. If that wasn't fate, she didn't know what was. Her legs suddenly felt wobbly. She held on to the kitchen counter and waited for the faint to come.

'When did I last eat?'

She lifted the lid of the breadbox. There was a loaf. Nate had bought it with the money in his pocket. She pictured his arm, those beautiful arms of his, finding the money and handing it over. The fact that his warm, vital body was now lying in the cryogenic centre in Pasadena made Mary retch. She twisted a corner of bread from the loaf and tried to chew, but her mouth wasn't working. Neither was her ability to swallow. The bread stayed at the back of her throat, lodged there like an impossible burden. She drank some water to get it down.

She replayed the terrible journey in the ambulance, cutting into her own husband's throat with a scalpel. It felt like a piece of lunacy in itself, but his life was over, so what else could she do? Mary could tell that Greg thought she was insane. She half thought it herself, but she knew she had to do something or there was nothing left to live for.

She heard a sound. It was the handle of the back door. Someone was rattling it. Trying to get in. Mary's mind went blank. *Answer it*, she thought to herself. *That's what normal people do, they answer doors.* She drifted downstairs and saw a darkened figure standing in the doorway. The sun was behind him and she couldn't make out his face.

'Nate?' she said, bewildered.

'Mary?'

'Nate – is that you?'

'Mary – it's not Nate. It's Martin. Martin Rando. Remember me? I roomed with Nate at Harvard.'

The disappointment to learn that it wasn't her dead husband almost made Mary sink to her knees. It made her leery too, that she could be capable of such crazy thoughts. She opened the door and wandered back upstairs to the living room.

'Are you on your own?' asked Martin.

Such a stupid question. She could have clawed his small, closely set eyes out. He was the least favourite of Nate's college crowd. That he should be the first on the scene was somehow an insult to Nate's memory.

'I don't know – my sister's on the plane today, I think. And my dad,' she said, genuinely confused.

'Have you eaten anything?'

Mary bent her head. Words were not possible. She noticed he had something in a bag. Coffee and muffins. He gave her a coffee and put the muffins on a plate.

'I thought you might need something. Meds,' said Martin hesitantly. It wasn't like him to make a mercy call. He didn't know how to behave. 'Then I got to reading about paroxetine withdrawal syndrome. The study from Morristown. Four neonates presenting with narcotizing enterocolitis—'

'I saw it,' she interrupted. 'I don't want any drugs.'

'That's what I thought. Anyway – I brought you some Tylenol,' he said ruefully. He held the bottle out to her. She didn't take it. 'In case you have a headache.'

Great. Extra strength for the grief.

'Have you slept?'

'I don't know.'

Martin knelt down beside her. Mary noticed his pale, freckled skin stretched tightly over his large nose and his wide-lipped mouth. Though plain, with receding crinkly red hair, he was much younger-looking than the rest of them – like a moody student, though she knew he was over forty. He registered the bloodstains on her shirt, but said nothing. Mary wondered why he had come.

'Who did this – do you know?' Another stupid question.

'Of course I don't,' Mary said bitterly. Her ears felt so clogged and tender that her voice sounded as though it belonged to someone else.

'Are the police doing anything?'

'I think so.'

'I'll give them a call. Push them. We've got to get this guy.'

'Don't call them,' she said suddenly.

'Why not?'

In that instant, she realized that she didn't trust Martin at all. 'My lawyers are dealing with it, thanks.'

'OK – but we really need to find this kid. Drink up,' he said, gesturing to the coffee. Mary took another sip.

More than any of Nate's college crowd, Martin Rando was destined for huge success. He'd made great strides in business since moving to California, buying up small biotech companies for their potential and tapping into the deep well of Government grants and private trusts to provide their running costs. Mary had gone to him for funding once and he seemed to have taken a certain amount of pleasure in turning her down. She had wanted nothing to do with him after that.

Her mind drifted and she watched her coffee cup slowly skid off the arm of the sofa, the liquid spraying out across the floor. She was vaguely aware of Martin catching her and steering her downstairs to her bedroom.

At one point in her long sleep, Mary could have sworn that someone was in the bedroom going through their things, but she felt so drugged that she just turned over and drifted off again. When she did finally wake up, it was dark. She could hear the trampling of feet and the whispering of voices upstairs. She lay there, terrorized, until she could make out female voices, then Kate, one of her closest friends, came into the room followed by Miranda, Carl and Bob.

'Is Martin Rando still here?' she asked them.

'Rando! God, no. Was he here?' said Carl, outraged. 'Is he the one who left your back door open?'

'Did he?'

'What did he want?'

'To help.'

'There's always an angle.'

'Mary,' said Kate, tears welling up in her eyes, 'there's a lot to do and we're going to share out the immediate stuff and . . .' She hesitated.

'Tell me,' said Mary.

'Bob is going to organize the funeral.'

All at once, the house seemed to be full of people. Her friends formed a barrier between her and the outside world. 'We'll deal with it,' they kept saying as she wandered trance-like through the house. There was also a strange, almost surreal visit from Albert Noyes, who Mary knew was involved with Nate's campaign group, Doctors for Justice. He leant in to kiss her, his aristocratic nose looming large in his small, chinless face. He was a dynamo lobbyist in Washington and Mary respected his goal to reform health care.

'Albert,' she said, clutching his hand. He was like a long-snouted mouse with pink-rimmed eyes. He'd been crying too.

'Count on me, will you?' he said.

'I will.'

Albert frowned and whispered: 'Did Nate say anything to you about what he was working on?'

'He never told me anything.'

'Did he have any files or discs that he left in the house, the office, the car – anywhere?'

'I have no idea.'

'Mary, I need to see the car.'

'The police must have it.'

'They do?' He looked worried.

'Why are you asking me these things?' she said with growing panic.

'I can't – I can't say anything right now.' It obviously hurt him not to confide in her when she looked so desperate. 'I will, Mary. I will – but right now – it's impossible. You *have* to trust me.'

Just then, Kate brought the phone over to Mary.

'It's for you. He's very insistent.'

'Who is it?'

'Martin Rando.'

Albert blanched visibly and backed off while Mary took the call.

'Martin – you left the back door open.'

'I'm sorry. I thought you needed to sleep. How are you?'

'OK.'

'Mary, listen to me. It's terrible now, but we are going to get through this.'

Martin sounded more bullish now that he wasn't standing awkwardly in her kitchen. Mary resented his use of the word 'we'.

'Everyone's here now, Martin. I have to go. Thanks for helping.'

'Since when did Martin Rando become part of the Sheehan household?' asked Albert.

The very mention of the name Sheehan, the name that Mary took when she married Nate and the name her baby would take, brought back to her where she was and what had happened. She began to cry. Albert looked crestfallen that he had caused a new wave of grief. He hovered in the background and left soon after.

The calls kept on coming and soon there were dozens of press gathering outside. They'd heard that Mary had taken the body from the crime scene and wanted to interview her about it. At one point, a reporter turned up in the kitchen and Carl had to physically eject him. Mary felt like a stroke patient, unable to respond. She sat in a dazed torpor, going through the motions of being alive. Just before midnight there was another knock at the back door.

'Jesus Christ!' said Carl. 'Don't they *ever* give up?'

He went bounding downstairs and returned almost immediately with two men. Mary didn't need to be told who they were. Their dress and demeanour gave them away.

'Mary – I think we do need to get in touch with your lawyer,' said Carl. 'It's the LAPD with a warrant for your arrest.'

4

That night Mary was charged with 'tampering with evidence' under section 141 of the California Penal Code for taking her husband's body from a crime scene.

She had very little coherent memory of the events that

unfolded: the arrest, the fingerprinting, the retrieval of Nate's headless body from the Cryogenesis Research Institute in Pasadena so that a formal autopsy could take place. The police were determined to make an example of her, to deter anyone else from doing the same. They wanted to turn it into a high-profile felony case. At one point, it looked as though they were going to win the right to confiscate the head too, but after a plea from Mary to the medical examiner and intense negotiation between her lawyer and the district attorney, the crime scene investigators were allowed to view the head in its cryonic state so that no further damage could be done.

In those first dire days Mary hadn't even begun to comprehend what it was like to be without her husband. She sat on the sofa for most of the time, doing nothing except drifting in and out of the world she used to inhabit. She thought she saw Nate constantly; the back of his head disappearing through doorways or along the street. One night, a bad one, she was convinced that she saw him sitting in the backyard. She peered into the blackness for an hour, watching his head turn towards the house. But it was the branch of the pine tree that towered over the yard, the needles catching the silvery light of the moon and flickering into a profile of his face.

The murder had an immediate impact on the media. *Dateline* wanted to do a special. *Today* wanted to talk to Mary via satellite. She even got a call from the production staff of *Oprah*. They wanted to know how, in the middle of the crisis, she had had the presence of mind to decapitate her husband. After a bombardment of calls and uninvited visits, she agreed to an exclusive interview with Katie Couric, thinking that if she spoke about it once, the issue would be settled.

When Mary played back the recording, she barely recognized herself. She was not in the least bit vain, but was horrified at how strained, awkward and traumatized she had become. 'It's lucky Nate's not around to see me,' she said to Miranda, who was watching the tape with her, 'I think he'd walk out on me.'

She shared a lot of grim jokes with friends these days, but inside she felt utterly desolate.

Katie Couric had skated around at first, asking a couple of compassionate questions, but very quickly honed in on the big one: 'How could you do that to your husband?'

Mary had gone into professional mode. 'At that precise moment in time, I didn't have an emotional attachment to his body, but I did to his soul. I could see my husband was clinically dead, so I knew, because I've cryonically frozen fourteen bodies, that his best shot was decapitation. To save the head, which had suffered minimal damage.'

'Mary, I know you are still grieving for your husband and I understand that you are expecting his baby, but I have to say that we have spoken to a number of doctors who say that the damage done to a body during the freezing process, when the ice literally expands and ruptures individual cells, means that it's impossible for that body or head *ever* to be revived. How can you, as a doctor and scientist, go on believing in cryonics, when the rest of the medical profession disagrees with you?'

'The rest of the medical profession does *not* disagree with me. They're using hydrogen sulphide to hold mice in suspended animation, and it works. The technology is too young to use on humans yet, but our own cryonic practices are improving all the time. Right now, we're working on a micro-particulate ice slurry or human anti-freeze where you can achieve vitrification or freezing with very little cellular damage.'

'Tell me more.'

'As we drop the temperature of the body, the chemical complexity changes, allowing the liquid to seep inside each cell and lock the molecules in place instantaneously. There is very little water seepage or rupturing to the individual cells that you mentioned.'

'But there are no technologies to bring your husband out of cryonic suspension, are there?' It was more a statement than a question.

'Not yet,' said Mary, 'but if you come to UCLA, I will show you how far we've come with nanotechnology. We will be able to work on repairing single cell damage with microscopic computers in a matter of years. When you see that kind of work going on, you *know* that physical reincarnation is going to become a scientific reality.'

'I think we *should* pay you a visit,' said Katie.

'My colleagues are developing micron-sized computers that are one hundred times smaller than a human hair and they will have encoded instructions to lock on to a single cell and work like microscopic engineers repairing any faults.'

'And when can we hope to see that?'

'Realistically? Mid to late century.'

'Not within our lifetime then.'

'No – but our children's lifetime.'

'But the whole point of your action was so that *you* could see your husband again, wasn't it? So that you could be reunited with Nate?'

'I *will* be seeing him again,' said Mary resolutely. 'And so will my unborn son.'

'I hope for your sake that you're right,' said Katie.

Mary switched off the TV. 'Well,' she said to Miranda, 'that made me look like a loon.'

'Do you think you will be seeing him again?' said Miranda. Her question went unanswered.

5

The criminal case against Mary receded into the background when the baby was born, a boy weighing in at 7 lb 2 oz. He had a startling triangle of red hair like an upturned goatee beard on his forehead. Mary called him Patrick after Nate's father and felt overjoyed that he had her dead husband's colouring and eyes. The maternal feelings she was so worried she wouldn't have came gushing in on the tide of her milk. She was inseparable from her baby, fiercely overprotective and highly unstable. She hoped she would calm down as she slowly recovered from Nate's death, but she felt more frightened and out of control than ever. And always at the back of her mind was the fact that she was about to go into battle with the police.

As it turned out, the criminal charges against her never reached court. Her lawyer went to work undermining the police motivation and raising the bar on the exceptional circumstances of the case. He got the charges reduced to a misdemeanour and negotiated a 1,000-dollar fine. Mary cried with relief and hugged him when the case was settled. Now she could finally get on with her life. That night, she celebrated with friends and even talked about going back to work.

When the celebrating was over and everyone had gone home, Mary opened up the trapdoor that led down to the crawl space underneath the house. The torch illuminated a torpedo-shaped canister that she and Nate had hidden among the foundations soon after they were married. They called it the 'love missile' and used it as a repository of all their precious mementos. Mary unlocked the lid and rifled through the photographs of her and Nate, the amateurish tape of their wedding and the passes to the conference in Arizona where they had first met. She added an envelope of photographs of their baby and the bloodied linen shirt that she was wearing on the day that Nate was shot.

'Just because you're gone doesn't mean I'm going to neglect the love missile,' she whispered. 'There you are, Nate, the first pictures of your baby boy. I hope he turns out to be just like you.'

She could hear little Patrick cooing from the baby alarm that she carried with her everywhere when she wasn't actually in the same room as her son. She wondered how she was ever going to leave him with anyone else when she returned to work. She wasn't really sure if she could go back just yet. If she was honest, she still felt utterly distraught.

'Who am I without you, Nate?' she said in the darkness. 'I don't even know myself any more. I never realized just how much you defined me.'

She was on the point of closing the lid of the capsule when she noticed that the floor of the container was spongy. She pressed the layer of plastic and felt it give way. Underneath was an extra compartment containing documents. Tentatively, she opened up an envelope and pulled out some papers. They were written by a Dr Lew Wasserstrom. Mary knew him. He worked at Caltech and had recently been found dead in his car near La Jolla, a pipe leading from his exhaust to the interior of his car. It was supposed to be suicide, but everyone in the scientific community was outraged. He was not a depressive and was well on his way to being eligible for a Nobel prize. Dr Wasserstrom was one of the scientists studying Cyclin D1 – a protein needed to activate two cancer genes present in breast tissue. Having lost her own mother to breast cancer, Mary was watching Wasserstrom's work like a hawk. She glanced through his research notes. Although it wasn't Mary's subject, she quickly identified tests involving the Neu and Ras cancer genes and learnt that they were already testing a vaccine to suppress Cyclin D1. She had no idea that Dr Wasserstrom was so far down the road. She turned another page and found a handwritten note from Albert Noyes:

> Nate –
>
> I don't want to risk sending you any more e-mails. Enclosed are the notes from Wasserstrom's assistant. I don't know how many copies there are in existence, but I suspect that Martin Rando has one. Also included are the memos from Rando wooing Wasserstrom to come and work for him. This may be the evidence the police are looking for to secure a search warrant. I must talk to you. We have to work out a coherent plan or the whole thing could blow up in our faces. I have a friend in Washington who can advise. Keep them safe.
>
> – Albert

Mary's head began to swim. The letter seemed to implicate everyone. Was this the reason why Martin Rando made a peculiar appearance after the shooting? He certainly wasn't a good enough friend to come over to the house like that. Was he looking for the documents? And is that why Albert Noyes interrogated her about them so soon after Nate's death? Dank-smelling air wafted through the crawl space, making Mary shiver. She took a deep breath to steady herself and looked at her watch. It was three o'clock in the morning in Washington. And in a few minutes, Patrick would be waking up for the first of his night-time feeds. As soon as she'd finished with her son, Mary was going to call Albert and find out what the hell was going on. She didn't care what time it was.

CHIHUAHUA, MEXICO / 2006

6

The bus was sweltering and stinking. But the blockage in Javier's nose kept the foul smells at bay. He felt in his pocket for the wad of notes that he had stashed down by his crotch. He looked suspiciously around him. He was sixteen years old and scrawny for his age, and he knew full well that any one of a dozen of the guys on the bus could overpower him and take his money: he was convinced that a couple of them were looking at him oddly. Javier tried to be nonchalant and hide behind his poverty and anonymity.

The front of the bus was dressed up like an altar with all the comforting images of home: a beautiful, romanticized picture of Jesus, a metal-framed mirror, rosary beads and family photographs belonging to the driver. The mirror swayed violently on its hook as the brightly painted bus lurched along the road, which was deeply rutted from the last rains. There were around two hours of the journey left before they would reach Chihuahua, then a long walk after that. Javier thought of taking a taxi but decided against it. If he played rich, he might draw attention to himself.

The only thing to mar the satisfaction that he had 4,500 dollars in his pocket was that he wasn't feeling well. He never did these days. He was always slightly dizzy, especially when he stood up. He'd complained to his uncle that he was short of breath, but his uncle had just looked at him and shrugged.

'You look OK to me,' he said, patting him on the back. 'Hey, you did a good job. You're a hero.'

Javier had stayed in a tiny room in the shadow of the big

buildings in Los Angeles after the shooting. He had been told that he'd have to lie low for a few weeks before he could cross the border and go home. Sometimes Javier got a terrible feeling about what he'd done, but his uncle said the man was a bad man, turning immigrants in to the authorities and sending them back to countries they had risked their lives to escape. Dr Nathaniel Sheehan was an enemy to immigrants and had to be stopped. It was the only thing that gave Javier inner peace. The money helped. He'd be able to buy his grandmother a proper bed and a new stove and make sure she was comfortable. She was often sick too.

The border had been the worst part of the journey and he made that walk under the covered archway over the bridge from El Paso with wavering steps, feeling as though he was going to faint. He did faint on the other side, and when he came to, the first thing he thought of was the money. He fingered the tumorous wad of cash wedged down by his groin. It was still there.

He saw himself in the reflection of the dirty window and touched the blotted scar on his cheek where the woman had hit him. He'd nearly taken a whack at her too but his uncle had warned him to get the hell out of there once he'd shot the doctor and run down to Wilshire – not on La Brea, but through the back streets. He couldn't run very far, so he walked, passing all the luxurious apartment buildings where the rich people lived. It made him feel small and insignificant, walking through those beautiful, lawn-lined streets. And a couple of people had stared at him. He wondered if they could sense that he had just shot a man. He had found his uncle spitting with impatience by the stop where the blue bus came. And that was that. Finito. Job well done.

But sometimes, especially in his dreams, he was filled with doubt. The man he was paid to kill said in Spanish that

Javier was ill, and that he could help. That confused Javier. The man seemed so kind, and Javier had almost forgotten what his uncle had told him to do. He wished the guy hadn't reached for the gun. In truth, he wished that he hadn't done the shooting at all. But he desperately held on to the fact that the guy was a political agitator, who needed to be eliminated, and that he was a hero for stopping his evil practices. Funny that no one had mentioned the political work in the news-paper stories. They'd only talked about the doctor running a free clinic in some poor neighbourhood in Los Angeles and how his crazy, eccentric wife had cut off his head in an ambulance. Javier told himself that it must have been a cover for the doctor's double life. Maybe he was a spy. Javier was fond of James Bond movies and had seen six of them in an open-air cinema on the outskirts of Chihuahua. His favourite James Bond was Roger Moore.

He looked out at the scrubby brush that lay beyond the road and the jagged peaks of the Sierra Madre mountains in the far distance. Not long now. One more hour and he would be back in the land he considered the most beautiful place on earth, tending to his grandmother's chickens and watching the crazy growth of traffic going by in the valley below their shack. The area was yellow with pollution now. Maybe that was why they got sick all the time. But at least they had money. And he would pay for them both to go and see a doctor, now that they had the money.

BOOK ONE

INCARNATION

The future is purchased by the present.

DR SAMUEL JOHNSON (1709–84)

LOS ANGELES / 2037

7

The jacaranda trees that lined Madison Avenue in Pasadena shielded the street from the merciless sunshine that beat down on the San Gabriel Valley. The temperatures in this north-eastern corner of Los Angeles had grown as hot as the Mojave Desert over the past thirty years, sometimes reaching as high as 125 degrees Fahrenheit during the summer months. The tree-bowered boulevard managed to screen out some of the more punishing rays and a dappled light fell across the once lavish houses and scrubby, dirt-patch gardens, giving the street an air of faded, breathless gentility.

Mayor Jose Villaloboz owned a red-brick colonial mansion at the eastern end of the street. Everyone knew the house and his four boys who ran in and out and tried to sell lemonade to passing motorists. Pasadena had suffered in the great earthquake of 2012 and the mayor's house was one of the last domestic brick buildings left standing in the city. It needed a lick of paint, but paint was exorbitant and the mayor, though wealthy, had other priorities.

He was a big man in size and spirit, with wide spatula hands and jet-black caterpillar eyebrows that he combed each morning with a toothbrush. As he watched his wife usher their youngest son Marco towards his chauffeur-driven Mercedes, he smiled. How serious little boys could be at that age, especially if they were told they were serious. The boy leapt on to the back seat of the limousine. The mayor gave his son a hug. He felt grateful that Marco still had that unbridled affection of eleven-year-olds. All too soon it would be replaced by teenage defiance.

'So what are we going to do today?' he asked Marco as they cruised up the avenue, the sun sending a Morse code of signals bouncing off the Mercedes' hood.

'We're going to see the Head,' said the boy.

'That's right – we're going to see the Head and it's going to look very strange but it's nothing to be frightened of.'

They turned from the tranquillity of Madison Avenue into the pandemonium of Colorado Boulevard. The electric Mercedes wove in and out of the scooters, bicycles, horse-drawn carts, rickshaws and electric cars being driven by people lucky enough to live off solar generators at home. The mayor could have walked the two miles to his destination quicker than battling through the traffic, but he believed in the formality of these occasions and the car was part of it. To be calm and relaxed in the face of this quickly imploding city was one of his major contributions as mayor.

Transferring from oil to other forms of power had turned out to be a long reign of chaos for LA. However much the city had tried to prepare, it was never enough. For months now, there had been severe shortages of electricity. Lines of cars were backed up around every recharging forecourt and people's lives had become much more localized. Those who could afford the water had resorted to horses to get around.

Great dumps of petrol-driven cars and other obsolete machines formed huge, mangled pyramids of glinting metal all across the landscape. In spite of threats from the authorities, people were still abandoning their cars long before the cranes could catch up and remove the metal carcasses to official dumping grounds.

It pained the mayor to see the old pictures of Pasadena in the days when it was a garden paradise. Publicly, he pledged to return his beloved neighbourhood to its former glory. Privately, he knew it could never happen. And now there was an even bigger environmental catastrophe looming in California. With so little snow to fill the upper reaches of the Colorado River, the levels had never been lower and the state had been propelled into a rushed programme of building desalination plants all along the coast.

The mayor heaved a dispirited sigh. All dignitaries like himself could do was to ask for an acceptance of a reduction in the quality of life for the time being. The message wasn't exactly a vote catcher for any politician, but Villaloboz believed the time had come at least to acknowledge the seriousness of the crisis. So many politicians were still in a complete state of denial.

They rounded a bend into a horseshoe driveway and pulled up before an impressive Art Deco building with neo-gothic frescoes. The media were already waiting for them. A tall, rake-thin man with a strangely twisted face stepped forward to greet them.

'Mayor Villaloboz, welcome to the Pasadena Cryogenesis Research Institute. I'm John Blake, the director. If you'd like to follow me.'

Villaloboz paused briefly for the image-makers, then held his son Marco's hand tightly as they walked up the steps.

'Mr Mayor, why did you choose to pay a visit to the Institute today?' asked one of the reporters.

'I've always been fascinated by cryonics,' he replied obligingly.

'Does that mean that you intend to freeze your own body when the time comes?'

'It's under serious consideration,' he joked, then looked down at Marco. He could see a certain terror growing in the boy's face. 'Don't worry, Marco,' he whispered, 'I'm not going to die for a very long time and while I'm still alive, you will *always* be safe.'

The party entered a darkened chamber.

'Gather round me if you will,' said the director. 'Welcome, everybody, to the Chamber of the Head. He's something of a mascot here at the Institute. Most of the heads and bodies that we have here lived for a full life span, but the Head is very different in that he died young and was frozen instantaneously, so there is very little decay.'

'I'm curious – how does cryonics work exactly?' said the mayor, letting go of his son's hand for a moment.

'Well, as you know, Mr Mayor, from your giant food business, freezing is a delicate process. With cryonics, to preserve tissue, we have to act fast, ideally while the major organs are still functioning or have just ceased to function. What we do with bodies today is rush them to a chamber filled with hydrogen sulphide so the metabolic rate drops instantaneously. Core body temperature and oxygen phosphorylation drop concurrently. Once the metabolic processes have come to a halt the body is effectively in suspended animation. Then we exsanguinate the body, or drain it of blood, and flash-freeze it for long-term storage.'

'Is that how the Head was frozen?'

'No, the Head was vitrified in the old-fashioned way by taking out all the bodily fluids and replacing them with a human anti-freeze, then dropping the temperature of the body to −107 degrees Fahrenheit. The organ was then exposed to nitrogen vapour and the temperature was dropped down even further, to −320 degrees. After that he was immersed in liquid helium. The technology was much more cumbersome then, but we have remained committed to looking after our patients, as we like to call them, and will honour the contracts that they and their relatives signed.'

While they were talking, Marco walked around the display case. The Head slowly came into view, distorted by the rainbow prisms of the moulded glass. Marco could see that it was suspended by dozens of glimmering, silken threads as it floated in the viscous liquid.

'Tell me – what are the chances of him being revived?' asked his father.

'Well, Mr Mayor, many of our historical patients suffered a major cellular destruction during the freezing process, so our nano-machines, those tiny micro-dot computers that we use to repair very localized damage to the heart or the brain tissue for instance, cannot cope with larger, multi-cellular body parts. But the technology is coming. And we like to think that the Head, because of the way he was frozen and impeccably preserved, has a good chance of revivification.'

Marco was mesmerized by the entity in the glass case. The forehead was tipped so distortedly over the eyes that he had to bend down to see what lay beyond the matted eyelashes. There was milky grey matter between the two slits but no irises. The lips were thick and swollen and the texture of old rubber. The mouth was gaping. Inside, Marco could just make out a brown tongue and yellow-stained teeth.

'Can we take him home?' asked Marco.

Everyone turned towards the boy.

'He looks sick, Dad.'

'Our house is like an animal hospital,' explained the mayor. 'My son brings home all kinds of injured creatures, but no heads – at least, not yet!'

Villaloboz joined his son and cupped a protective hand around the boy's neck. 'Will you look at that,' he said. 'Are you OK, Marco?'

The Head held them all in its thrall for a moment.

'Yes,' said the boy.

'I have to say that I find it impossible to believe that this thing—'

'The Head,' corrected the director.

' – that the Head could ever wake up,' said the mayor.

'We've taken scans and there's very little necrotic material or decomposed tissue in evidence,' countered the director, 'which is remarkable considering the methods of freezing.'

Marco wasn't really listening but tracing a finger through the air, drawing an outline of the Head's tragic face.

'We know we can bring an organ out of cryostasis. We've done that many times. But it's very much our intention to revive the *soul* of a human being. We're training a dog right now, and when she passes over, we intend to freeze her and revive her two years from the day she died to see whether she has retained the personality and training that she had when she was alive.'

'What if you go broke in between times, like all the other cryogenic companies?' asked the mayor. 'I mean, the whole industry crashed, didn't it?'

'It did go through a period of difficulty many years ago,' said the director defensively, 'but we are the oldest cryogenics institute in the world and there is no way that we will be going broke any time soon. We are assured of funding right up until the turn of the century. How many companies can promise that? Can you?'

'I can't even determine my company's future beyond the end of the year,' the mayor gave in warmly. 'Do we know who this man is – or was?'

'Oh yes,' said the director, relishing the question. 'His name is Dr Nathaniel Sheehan and he lived in Venice, California. His is a classic Romeo and Juliet story. He was shot thirty-one years ago, and his wife Mary, who was with him at the time, happened to be involved in cryonics. She couldn't bear to part with her husband so she severed his head and froze it right there in the ambulance on the way to this very institute. She always believed that she would join her husband one day.'

'Is she still alive?'

'No. Unfortunately, she was killed in the great earthquake.'

'Was she frozen too?'

'No. We know she wanted to be frozen, but her body was never found and neither was that of their son.'

Marco looked anxiously at his father. He knew the very mention of the great earthquake would bring on a reaction, maybe even tears. He held his breath. He couldn't stand to see his father cry.

'So many were lost,' said the mayor mournfully.

'You lost someone too?'

'My mother.' The mayor breathed deeply to exorcize the sadness. 'So – Romeo and Juliet. They have been reunited in one way.'

'In death? Yes, I suppose they have,' said the director.

'But what if you do bring back the Head? You'll be parting them again.'

'We have to assume that he would want a second chance on this earth.'

Marco reached up his hand to touch the display case, trying to smooth away the frown lines that were deeply etched into the frozen man's forehead.

'Tell me,' said his father, 'will you keep him as a disembodied head? Or will you graft him on to another body?'

'Oh, he would have to have a new body.'

Marco removed his hand, leaving a perfect palm print on the glass. Each groove could be seen through the light. He hoped, in his young imagination, that the print would somehow connect with the Head and soothe its chronically tortured brow.

'And where would you get a body from?'

'At this point in time, Mr Mayor, we have absolutely no idea. What about yours?'

There was something utterly humourless about the joke, but for the sake of diplomacy, Mayor Villaloboz found himself managing a smile.

'All in good time,' he said genially, 'all in good time.'

GAMMA GULCH SUBTERRANEAN PENITENTIARY, CALIFORNIA / 2069

8

Convicted killer Duane Williams shuffled into Room 3105 in the medical wing of Gamma Gulch Penitentiary. The tiptoe steps that he made were a giveaway to any neurologist that he was suffering from some kind of brain damage.

Dr Persis Bandelier had been waiting to interview Duane for more than an hour. She noticed his odd gait straight away. She reckoned that when she looked more closely at Duane's brain on her 3-D imager, she would find some kind of damage to his frontal lobes. It meant that he was more likely to splash straight through puddles rather than sidestep them, or bump into things. She'd read in his files that he was unable to cope with unexpected events and was prone to unprovoked violence. Mentally, he was a sorry specimen. And a killer too. But providing that no damage to the brain had impacted the body, she was prepared to pay a good price for him.

Dr Bandelier had been tracking bodies across the United States for two years now. She kept in regular contact with emergency rooms and local morgues, hoping to find the right kind of cadavers, but it was virtually impossible. The old organ donor network had ceased to exist after stem cell regrowth and nanotechnology had started to repair damaged organs, and nearly all the bodies that they were being offered were in terrible condition with multiple fractures or severe internal damage. They had been useful at first, when the unit's needs were so basic, but now the experiments were becoming more sophisticated, the bodies had to be in better condition.

In desperation, Dr Bandelier had turned to the prison system, figuring that Death Row would have an unlimited supply of healthy cadavers and that it was simply a matter of negotiating a price. She'd been right about that as it turned out. Most prisons were financially stretched to the point of bankruptcy and were only too keen to sell off the newly departed inmates for substantial sums of cash. In no time at all, Dr Bandelier's unit was being offered dozens of corpses from all across America. The man standing before her now was due for execution in less than a month.

'Take a seat,' she gestured to a chair opposite.

Duane Williams shuffled forward. His expression was presumptuous and intimate. She had read in a description by one examining psychiatrist that the prisoner could be 'grandiose with an unshakable belief that every woman was available to him'. Persis knew when she looked at his blood work that she would find elevated levels of cortisol and testosterone, but she held off taking any samples for now. She wanted the prisoner to relax before she started in on the physical exam. At each stage, she had to get his permission.

'My name is Dr Bandelier and I'm here to carry out some simple tests, if that's OK by you?'

Duane Williams shrugged and raised both hands, which were welded together with plastic stays. 'They better be simple. I can't do much in these,' he said in a deep, throaty voice.

Persis looked long and hard at the man's face. When he walked the streets a free man, he would have attracted a lot of attention. Facially, he was uncommonly beautiful, with sleepy eyelids and flat, carved cheekbones that slanted down to a full, sensual mouth. The face could have been regal in another life, showing the traces of his Native American ancestry, but there were scars that upset the symmetry, one cutting through an eyebrow, another forming a ragged frown line and a fish-hook snag at the corner of his mouth. The stress of Death Row had taken its toll too. There was a tautness to his skull, and although he was just twenty-six years old, Duane's closely shaven hair was snow-white. He stared resentfully at Persis with the haunted look of a much abused dog.

'Are you my corpse collector?' he asked. His voice was surprisingly authoritative. 'Come to measure me up for body parts?'

Persis had been told by the prison authorities that under no circumstances was she to admit her intentions in case it made Duane frightened or difficult in the last weeks of his life.

'I'm just here to carry out some tests.'

'A Death Row tourist.'

'A what?' said Persis, feigning distraction as she wrote something down on her screen.

'You know, one of those psychs who come in here and try to find out why us creatures do the things we do and then scurry back to your cosy little lives in – where are you from?'

'Phoenix.'

' – Phoenix, and write a book about whether evil really exists. Did they tell you I can read minds, Phoenix?' He tapped at his temple with a long and elegant finger. 'I'm a mind-reader.'

'Is that so?' said Persis flatly.

'You know what I'm picking up in you right now?'

'Mr Williams, we're not here to—'

' – that you are one unhappy woman. You're married,' he nodded towards her wedding ring, 'but you're not right for each other. It was that sex thing that people get up to when they're young. And he's so handsome, just like you, Phoenix.' He finished the word off with a slight hiss. 'And you're a genetic. Don't tell me you're not, cos you are.'

Duane Williams had been her most talkative prisoner yet. The others had been quieter, more broken.

'You know what? That's none of your business,' she said, trying to keep the hostility from her voice.

'Call me Duane,' he said, and smiled, showing a brown front tooth.

Persis hated being called a genetic, particularly as she was one. Both her parents were doctors and had made sure that Persis got every advantage in the womb, including the maximum genetic alteration allowed by law. Offspring who had received the full package of adjustments did have a generic look about them; tall, slim, fit, no adolescent acne to contend with, no quirks in appearance that would set them apart. She had come from the first generation of 'genetics' that were picture-perfect. Now they tended to leave the physical appearance alone to give the embryo more individuality. Yes, she was a genetic and had suffered much for her all-American-girl good looks.

'You look like a robot, did you know that?'

Persis said nothing. But it hurt.

'Now you tell me. Have I been wrong about anything I said so far?'

This wasn't how the interview was supposed to go. The prisoner was the one in control and mocking her. And what's more, he was right about pretty much everything.

'And if you're waiting for my execution, you can forget it,' he added. 'I choose when I'm ready to go and I ain't ready.'

Persis had already checked with the State who confirmed

that it was 99 per cent certain that Duane Williams would make it to the death chamber on schedule.

'So – what do you want with me?' he said eventually.

'I'd like to start by measuring your head.'

'Sizing me up for the noose?'

He was almost jocular. His reaction was so unexpected that it would stay with Persis a long time. She produced an electronic headband which she fitted over Duane's skull. Two standard deviations below the normal circumference and there might be retardation; two deviations above and he might have hydrocephalus – an accumulation of water in the cranial cavity, another deficiency that might explain his peculiar walk. The measurement came out normal.

'Can you spread your hands for me, please?' Persis held up her own hands, palms towards him, fingers apart. 'Like this?'

Duane followed her instructions and she checked him for choreiform movements, little tremors, to see if his gross motor coordination was unstable. Duane's hands were steady.

'This may sound like an unusual request,' she said, 'but it's to test your balance. Can you skip on one leg for me, please?'

'Only if you will – Phoenix.'

'It would help with my examination,' she said.

'And I volunteered for this meeting. Like I said – I will if you will.'

Persis didn't want to interact with him on a personal level, knowing that he would misinterpret it as flirting, so she looked away. Round two to him.

'I need to do one more physical test,' she said. 'It won't hurt and it's nothing to be concerned about.'

Persis got up and walked around the table. When she was

behind Duane, she reached over his head and began to tap him on the nose, watching for his reaction in the reflection of the observation window.

Duane blinked. 'What the fuck are you trying to do to me now?' he stammered, and leapt up, the chair falling back against her. The guard grabbed Duane's arms and twisted them cruelly, forcing him to sit down.

'I wanted to see what your reactions would be to something unexpected.'

'With this guy standing around?' he said, pointing two double-jointed thumbs at the guard. 'Do you have any idea what he can do to me when you've gone?'

Any normal person would have received a message from the logical-thinking frontal lobes that there was no threat and would have stopped blinking. Duane kept on blinking and overreacted, another sign that the right messages were not reaching his left orbitofrontal cortex. He clearly had trouble working out the difference between threatening and non-threatening behaviour.

Persis opened her case. She pulled out a rubber cap with hundreds of tiny sensors moulded into the fibre.

'Would you wear this, so we can take a closer look at your brain?' she said politely.

Dutifully, he took the cap and put it on.

'Thank you,' she said, and flipped open her computer.

'No – thank *you*,' he said mockingly, and smiled another crooked smile. There was a grim charm about him now, a gentlemanliness in contrast to the outburst of a few moments ago.

Duane's brain appeared on the screen. Persis had never grown used to the wonder of the technology that she worked with. It was like watching a living, breathing, oscillating planet with millions of tiny aircraft carrying dispatches from country to country. Her eyes travelled over the brain's bulges and down its infolds, through its nodules and along its millions of neuronal pathways as she followed the vastly magnified and slowed-up images of neurotransmitters navigating their way over the synaptic gaps between neurons.

'Do you know what I'm thinking now?' he asked.

'I'll be with you in a minute, Mr Williams,' she deflected as she moved her cursor. The brain tilted on its axis and rotated at her command. She pressed her keyboard for magnification and a window opened up. Duane's brainstem came into view. It looked like a number of liverish folds of tissue wrapped around the top of his spinal column. It was the oldest part of the brain and controlled the basic impulses like breathing, heart rate, blood pressure and erection. But it was so much more than that: the *seat of the soul* as neurologists liked to describe it, with crucial pathways linking it to every region in the brain. Without a brainstem, no man or woman could physically function or have consciousness. It was vital that Duane's should be in perfect condition. She inspected it from every angle. Her spirits lifted as she found nothing wrong.

She moved her cursor up to Duane's limbic system, the second-oldest part of the brain, which dealt with the fundamentals of the personality like emotion and long-term memory. She could see the outlines of the chestnut-shaped nodules buried deep in the grey matter. She pressed her keyboard and brought the right brain amygdala into close-up. Shaped like a golf ball, the amygdala modulated Duane's responses to threatening stimuli. It came as no surprise to Persis that Duane's was white-hot with activity, stimulated by his rage from the nose tapping.

She moved on to examine the frontal lobes behind the forehead. She magnified them as far as the technology would allow and thought she could see a number of lesions or tiny nicks in the tissue. She took several freeze-frame pictures.

'Did you spot the devil down there?' said Duane.

Persis jumped. She was so engrossed that she had forgotten his presence.

'Is he wearing Government ID?'

She managed a smile, then moved her cursor back down to Duane's hippocampus, the paw-shaped nodule which acted like the brain's librarian by collecting, indexing and consolidating long-term memories before sending them off to the storage shelves in the depths of the brain. She could see immediately that Duane's was undersized. She froze the image, drew a black line across it and confirmed that it was 5 millimetres under the norm in both hemispheres. Her 3-D imager also told her that there were abnormalities in the dendritic morphology of the hippocampus due to too much activity from the amygdala. She decided to test his memory to see how impaired it was. Chances are he would be able to recall old memories, but would have difficulty forming new ones.

'Can you tell me something about your childhood, Mr Williams?'

'I'm done talking about it.'

'I understand, but I just want to examine your spontaneous brain activity. Memories light up specific areas. It would help me.'

A cynical expression flitted across his face. 'OK – how about my daddy taking a pop at me in the backyard? I had to dance to dodge the bullets. He was a crazy guy and thought that shooting his kids like they were monkeys in a barrel was a joke that we would all find amusing.'

'How old were you when that happened?'

'Five or six. My brother actually took a slug in the leg. My father thought it was the best way to turn us into men.' Duane chewed at the flesh on the inside of his cheek. 'Or how about the time he said we had to find out our limitations, so he set us on each other like a pair of fightin' cocks?'

Persis could see the faint glimmer of activity spread out through Duane's brain but it was like searching for dock lights across a black lake.

'Is that the kind of thing you're looking for, Phoenix? Is that what turns you on?'

'Do you remember being thrown down the toilet?' continued Persis.

'No.'

'But you've got a scar on your head from that incident.'

Duane automatically reached up and touched the white worm that ran from his forehead and disappeared under the sensor cap.

'How do you think you got that scar?' she persisted.

There was something missing from his expression now – a dull, unlively look in his eyes.

'Who cares? I got me a lot of scars.'

'Do you remember being beaten with a spade by your mother?' she pressed further.

'No.'

His long-term memory was worse than she had anticipated.

'Do you remember anything about your mother?'

'I remember her face – pig-ugly – like my sister.'

Persis had seen images of Duane's mother. There was some digital recording of her in the file. She was not ugly, but rather beautiful in a debauched, undernourished way, with the sinewy neck of someone who was highly strung. She was smoking with her hand swung high and she was saying something to whoever was filming her, but the roar of the city drowned out her voice. Her skin was paper-thin and dry, with lines leading down to a cruel, down-turned mouth. Duane had inherited that mouth.

'Why do you say that she was pig-ugly, Duane? She looked attractive in the images that I saw.'

Persis noted that his amygdala was getting busy again. She looked up and saw his face contorting.

'You got a cigarette?' he said.

'No smoking in here and you know it,' warned the guard.

Duane let out a mean laugh. 'She was pig-ugly to me. What are you looking at anyway?'

'Your hippocampus.'

'My what?'

'Your hippocampus. It's the part of your brain that collects and redistributes long-term memories.'

'Where is it?'

Persis tapped the base of her skull just behind her ears.

'I bet you smell like freshly cut grass right after a shower,' he said, breathing in.

'When was your last act of friendship?' she continued, ignoring him.

Duane paused and looked at the ceiling, then squinted one eye at her. 'All the time – every day.'

'Do you remember anything specific?'

'Do you?'

'When was your last act of kindness?'

In a flash the anger arrived, clouding out the softness. 'When was yours?'

'I'm just testing your recall.'

'I remember things, but I'm not going to tell you.'

There was a sulky, recalcitrant little boy in him that she'd not seen yet.

'Pussy,' he said, looking right at her.

There seemed to be no core to him, no stability to his personality. She glanced at the guard standing by the door.

'He ain't gonna help you,' said Duane, quick to respond to her look.

'How would you describe your personality?' she ventured.

'Pussy. Pussycat – yeah, that's right. I'm a pussycat.'

'Do you remember jumping from a moving car five years ago?' Persis was honing in on the crime that got him the death sentence.

Oddly, he perked up. 'Now that I *do* remember. They had to scrub my face while it was raw, all the way across here.' He touched the bridge of his nose. 'Never felt pain like it. They said if they left the grit in the wound it would stay black and I'd end up looking like a Dalmatian.'

'Why did you jump?'

'My brother was doing something.' He hesitated and shook his head. 'I don't remember. There was some bad shit going down. He drove right on and left me there in the middle of the night. It was lucky that a ranger found me.'

But they didn't find the girl in time, thought Persis. She had to ask him, though she didn't want to, knowing it would make him mad. 'They found you, Duane – but they also found a young woman – Jenner Sommers – down by Pebble Creek Canyon and you were convicted of her murder.'

His whole body stiffened. The guard tensed too but stayed where he was. Persis glanced at her screen and could see the amygdala turning into a mass of activity.

'I don't know anything about no murder,' responded Duane.

Persis remembered how watertight the evidence was, how Duane's DNA was mingled in a cruel twist of the girl's fate and how he had been caught on the roadside by the ranger. But she believed Duane. With all the brain damage that she could identify, it was highly likely that he couldn't recall the *actual* murder.

'You remember nothing about that night?' she pressed.

'Fuck you!' he said, and yanked the sensor cap from his head, breaking the strap. He threw it at her and the flap of her computer slammed down on her fingers. The guard leapt forward, yanking Duane's shoulder back.

'I know you. Coming in here with all this cute talk, asking me about my memories. You're collecting evidence, you fucking fake!'

Before Persis could see how it was done, the guard had twisted Duane's tethered hands behind his head and slammed his face down on the table. 'I think this interview's over for today,' he said, dragging Duane towards the door.

'I'll be seeing you, Phoenix,' shouted Duane as he was dragged along the corridor, 'and don't think I won't remember you!'

Persis sat there, breathing hard. She listened to the clanking of the prison doors as the two of them disappeared into the bowels of the prison.

His words sent a chill right through her and she shivered. She lifted up the computer. Duane's brain remained in a frozen image on the screen, the amygdala white-hot and the brainstem strangely animated. If this was evidence of his soul, then it was a sorry picture of half-remembered truths and synaptic dead ends.

In the gloom of the windowless room, a depression overwhelmed her. How macabre her professional life had become. But she couldn't go back, not now that they were half-way through a programme that could make medical history. And she was going to be right there, right at the heart of it.

9

The mind-reader was wrong about one thing. He did not choose when to die. Just as the prison had said, there was to be no reprieve for Duane Williams, and on the morning of his execution, he heard footsteps marching towards his cell. Their clipped formality let him know that they were coming to get him. He drew heavily on his cigarette. They'd allowed him a packet in the deathwatch cell where he'd eaten buttermilk-fried chicken-approximate and said goodbye to his sister, Bobbie. That hurt more than anything. He was touched that Bobbie had come, but accepting her tenderness had been tougher than dealing with any cruelty that he'd suffered at the hands of the Gamma Gulch guards.

He looked up the shaft of concrete which led to the square of wired glass fifty feet above him. It was the last time that he would see the sky.

Gamma Gulch was gouged out of the rock in the Mojave Desert and boasted proudly that no prisoner had ever escaped from its brutal, earthen labyrinth. It was constructed around a central quadrangle with tentacles spreading deep into the rock. The poor ventilation and abysmal sanitary conditions meant there was always a gagging smell of rotting vegetables and urine. The corridors were always cool and dank and lit by dim lights which ran off the prison's solar generators. There were frequent outages and when they happened, Duane had to sit there in the dark and talk himself down from the claustro-phobia that overwhelmed him. The only mercy Gamma Gulch bestowed on the inmates was a consistency in temperature, which was why the facility had been built in the first place, to save on power. It had been like doing time in Hades and, in that respect alone, Duane was ready to kiss the world goodbye.

A commander and five prison officers strode into view, halted and turned to face him. The extraction team. He didn't know them. Officers switched duties for executions so they wouldn't have to look a known prisoner in the eye. This detail had come from the North Quad.

'Approach the force field. Put your hands through the meal slot. Step back and kneel on the bed,' barked the commander, his dead eyes staring straight ahead.

Duane looked at them each in turn and held up his cigarette. 'I'm giving up today. What do you reckon my chances?'

They did not register the joke. They drew no eye line. Duane raised himself up to his full height. 'I'm not going to give you any trouble, OK?'

He put his hands through the meal slot and they tied his wrists with plastic rope, fusing the ends so he would never be able to break free. He fell back on the bed. The guards swiftly deactivated the force field and swept inside, pulling a gurney behind them. They lifted him on and secured his hands and feet. No rough handling today. They were on their best behaviour. He tried to connect with one of the guards. 'You should get another job,' he said. 'This one's gonna kill you, just like it's killing me.'

The guard looked straight through him. *The final humiliation*, he thought to himself. *Make sure I feel utterly alone.*

They wheeled him along the corridor. He watched each light pass by overhead, tried to count, but his mind was fogged. A guard had slipped him an extra toilet roll with some dope in the tube and he'd smoked the last leaves a couple of hours before. He'd refused a sedative. There wasn't much he could control in his life, but whenever they presented him with a choice, he always opted for what would make their lives more difficult.

The door to the anteroom burst open. There was another shaft of light coming from a concrete funnel which fanned out into a dome above them. A simple wooden cross was hanging on the opposite wall and a cartoon image of Jesus with a curtain of flowing brown hair and a saintly expression. Everything in the room was green: the cart of monitoring equipment, the line of web cams on the wall. He looked at the faces around him. The chaplain was holding a Bible and his lawyer, Jim Hutton, blinked back tears from his eyes. Duane could tell by the expression on Jim's face that he was a dead man.

'We've told the clerks at the US Supreme Court to go home,' said Jim, lowering his head. 'No more stays.'

'Come on, man, look at me,' spat Duane. 'You're all a bunch of cowards. Who's got the guts to look at me?'

No one said anything, then Jim raised his eyes. 'I'm sorry, Duane. I did everything I could.'

'I know you did, man. I know you did.'

The commander stood to attention. Duane tensed. Each stage of the proceedings sent a fresh stab of terror through his gut.

'By the State of California District Attorney, we are empowered to carry out the death warrant issued for Duane Williams on 5 May 2065 by the administration of a lethal infusion. We're taking you through, Mr Williams. Prepare yourself.'

'Look at the cross. Just look at the cross,' said the chaplain. Duane yanked violently at his stays. From somewhere deep in his body came a great cry like a strange animal's moan.

'Do you want your sister to see you like this?' said the commander, trying to calm him. 'Bobbie came all this way to be with you, Duane.'

'Fuck you,' he snarled, but his physical strength, the very thing that he had relied upon for all of his life, felt tantalizingly out of reach.

The guards wheeled the gurney through to the execution room, secured it to the floor and left. Duane was now positioned in front of a hexagonal window, his view blocked by a plastic curtain. He craned his neck and saw three hooded executioners standing to attention through a hole in the wall.

'Fuck all of you,' he slurred.

It had been explained to him that the chemicals would be delivered by three tubes which were dangling on a ledge through the hole. Each executioner would open a single valve but only one would deliver the poison. The other two tubes would carry a harmless saline solution which would be syphoned off into a bucket. That way no one would ever know which executioner delivered the fatal dose.

'*So this is it,*' thought Duane. '*One turn of the valve and my life is over.*'

He realized that he hadn't quite taken in what was about to happen to him. He suddenly felt flooded with self-pity. An IV team in white cotton hoods entered the room, pushing a cart of medical supplies. One of them was a woman. She was squat and thick-set, but he could see the outline of her breast through her surgical scrubs. The last breast he would ever see. How he had cherished those curves in his lifetime, fought bitterly to hold them, nuzzle them, cling to them as though he was literally holding on to an absent mother's love. His body felt so numb and peculiar that he wondered if he was dreaming.

'Oh, man, I'm walking into that long tunnel and I'm *stoned,*' he said, and laughed. No one responded.

He heard the clink of metal objects on a tray just behind his head and he knew that another procedure was about to begin. The female medical officer walked around to his left side and signalled to her colleague. They tied rubber tourniquets around his biceps and swabbed his elbows. In unison, they began attaching intravenous tubes to both arms.

'Now *that* hurts,' said Duane to the junior medic who was trying fitfully to find a vein. Blood spurted out, daubing the white surgical gown with a streak of scarlet. His lawyer made a note. After an exchange of furious glances, the female officer walked around the gurney, pushed her colleague out of the way and inserted the IV with no further trouble. When they had finished they took up positions on either side of the bed and the plastic curtain was drawn back.

Duane peered out of the hexagonal glass window. He could see three rows of witnesses straining to get a glimpse of him. He searched among the faces for his sister Bobbie, who was seated next to her husband. Tears were streaking down Bobbie's face. Duane gave her a signal; a nod, which meant I love you. She signalled back, making the letters I, L, U with her fingers. His eyes moved across the room and he saw her. The mother. And her sons, all three of them, and in that moment he remembered Jenner Sommers, the girl he had tried so hard to block from his mind.

'Come down to the water,' she'd said to Duane and his brother Keith. '*I've got something to show you.*'

She was strange. Everyone in the kit park knew she wasn't right in the head. He could see the creek and the girl crouching in the mud and his brother standing over her. And he went nuts over what they did.

'*Stay calm, brother,*' said Keith. But he couldn't stay calm. How could a woman have a life after that?

'Do you have anything you want to say?' barked the commander.

Duane took a deep breath and looked out at the rows of rapt faces. 'To my sister Bobbie, I love you with all my heart.' His voice cracked and sounded strange to him. 'To my brother Keith, may you rot in hell for deserting me now. I forgive the State of California for murdering me for something I did not do, and to Casey Sommers, I forgive you too, for helping the State to murder me.'

Through the glass, he saw the girl's mother mouth something that he couldn't hear. He saw his sister's face scrunch up with an ugliness that he had seen so many times in their mother and shout something venomous back, and a guard step between them. He saw all this with absolute clarity. But he could hear nothing through the glass.

He remembered being told that when animals in rescue pounds were carted off for extermination, all the other animals could sense something wrong and would start to howl. No one, not Keith, not his fellow prisoners, not even a dog, had howled for him.

Then the music started. He'd requested Elvis Presley because he couldn't think of a better person to play him out of this world. Elvis, a mythical pop star from the twentieth century, meant everything to some people, including Duane's grandmother, who said she was born on the day that Elvis died. As the music played, breath suddenly became crucial. He drew deeper and deeper gulps and his panicked ribcage began to seize up. He could smell the sweat from the men and women around him and the chemicals from the executioners' room: a sharp, deadly tincture about to flood his veins. Fighting the bodily weakness of panic, Duane yanked pathetically at his stays.

'Don't kill me. Please don't kill me.'

He had never begged for anything in his life. Except as a kid. But he was begging now.

'Let me live. *Please.*'

The medics stood back and the senior officer gave the 'go' signal by holding up two fingers. The three executioners made formal tight movements as they opened the three valves. Duane squeezed his entire body to try to shut off the deadly sweep of poison as it crept up his arms. But he couldn't stop it. It was seeping into him. It felt creamy and cool inside his arms, like melted ice cream. Then everything began to relax. His chest, his breathing.

He could just make out the fuzzy outlines of a cross on the wall when a crushing vision came to him. It was the girl and she was smiling and telling him something.

'*Jesus loves you,*' she said.

They were the same words that she'd said that night down by the creek.

'Jesus loves you.'

That made him so crazy at the time, that she could feel compassion for *him* after all that they had done. It was her tenderness that made him despise her.

'Jesus loves you,' he murmured, and his eyelids flickered and his jaw grew slack.

10

Standing by the door, so she wouldn't be seen by the prisoner, Dr Persis Bandelier watched Duane's head flop to one side. The curtain was drawn back across the window and a voice announced: '*Ladies and gentlemen, this concludes the legal execution of Duane Williams. Time of death, 9.35 a.m.*'

After her initial interview with Duane, Persis was hoping that her immediate boss at Icor Incorporated would fly to California to collect the cadaver, but he cried off at the last minute and she was left to carry out the grisly task herself. She'd done it a number of times now, but it was just as gruesome every time. There'd been a nasty exchange between the condemned man's sister and the victim's mother. The sister was rocking and whimpering, while the mother was sitting completely still with a serene expression on her face. But Persis couldn't allow herself to become emotionally involved. She needed to keep her wits about her.

She hoped the medics would not waver from their commitment to make the dose of sodium pentothal much lighter than the criminal's relatives or the victim's relatives would ever know. Just enough to put Williams into deep anaesthesia and block the nerve transmissions to the brain. That's what they'd agreed.

A prison guard came into the witness area and searched for Persis among the faces. She followed him into the anteroom.

Duane's body was being prepared for surgery by Monty Arcibal, one of Icor's most trusted medical technicians who had flown in to Gamma Gulch with Persis the previous day. Monty had already accessed the femoral vessels in the leg and was pumping a sluicing fluid through the prisoner's veins. Blood was seeping out through another tube. Everything looked neat and tidy.

She looked at what was left of Duane. His features were sunken and his handsome face was free of all the anxiety that had made him look so old before his time. She closed his half-open eyes.

'Did we remember the diode for the blood?' she asked Monty.

'Yes.'

'We'll have to run it through dialysis. It's going to be full of dope.'

'Was he stoned?'

'Stoned and angry.'

'Ready to open him up, boss?' he said.

Monty, a Filipino, was a dedicated and meticulous worker. Persis felt she needed his warmth and good humour today.

'Ready.'

She took the scalpel and made a clean incision in the chest. Monty yanked back the ribcage and applied the clamps. They looked at the slow, rhythmic flump of Duane's heart.

'OK – let's go,' she said, and cut open the organ's outer wall while Monty inserted a canula. He turned on another valve and the cryoprotectant started to leach into the organ. They were up on time.

'I wish we didn't have to use these methods,' she said. 'I feel like an Ancient Egyptian prepping a mummy.'

'But it works best on the old heads, right?' said Monty.

'Yes – we seem to do better when we stick to the same technology.'

Persis peered at a mobile fluoroscope, where she could get a microscopic picture of the cryoprotectant's percolation through the veins and capillaries. The liquid had to maintain the body at a consistent temperature or parts of it might ice up and decay. Right now, water was the enemy.

'OK, let's try to get it right this time.'

'Don't ice. Don't ice,' pleaded Monty.

'Any ischaemia?' asked Persis.

Monty checked another monitor. 'Nope.'

'Brain swelling?'

'Not yet.'

'Then it looks like we have our next donor body.'

Persis and Monty nodded at each other and smiled.

'What are we going to do about the tattoos?' said Monty,

running a gloved hand over Duane's knuckles where the name A-N-N-A was crudely etched.

'I never knew he had so many,' said Persis.

They were daubed all over Duane's torso like graffiti. There were burlesque lap dancers that had been split in half by the chest cavity, the gothic letters spelling 'Gamma Gulch' laid out in an arc across his stomach, and the self-inflicted ones – the spiders, skulls and blue and green letters spelling out the names of people he used to know.

'All those people he tried to love,' said Monty.

'Well, if this body lasts longer than a few days, we'll need to get rid of them,' she said, making a cursory inspection. 'I don't want any identifying marks.'

'I think we should leave the dove.'

'What dove?'

Monty lifted one of Duane's shoulders. 'Right there. Like a peace offering to the gods. Everyone wants to feel that they did some good in their lives, however bad they were.'

'He was a killer, Monty. Not a priest. I don't think goodness was ever part of his agenda.'

Persis expertly jiggled the tube that was leading into the heart to make sure it wasn't about to come lose.

'You don't know that,' said Monty.

'Don't go getting all sentimental on me now. Personification is a dangerous thing. It's flesh and bone and that's it.'

'Whatever you say, boss.'

Over the next two hours the cryoprotectant began to harden. As the temperatures dropped, the viscosity of the liquid turned the flesh from the texture of hot tar to cold tar and finally to glass. They could have taken a hammer to Duane's arm and shattered it into tiny pieces.

Persis had taken the decision not to remove the head at

Gamma Gulch. She'd done it once before at another prison and there was a constant stream of guards and officials taking a curious peek through the observation window. The last thing she wanted was for the details of their operation to get out. All Gamma Gulch needed to know was that the body was being frozen for transportation and that it was going to be used for medical research.

Once vitrification was complete, they inserted the body into a titanium dewar and wheeled it to a lift shaft which cranked into action and took them to the surface. When they reached ground level Persis blinked in horror. She hadn't expected any media. Executions were so routine, they barely attracted a single reporter, but there was a large group of journalists and onlookers standing beyond the force field fence.

'Are they here for us?' she asked one of the guards in alarm.

'No – Norman Powell is coming in today.'

Persis vaguely remembered the name. Norman Powell was a minor movie star who had just been convicted in a seedy murder case.

'I hope it isn't going to be a problem.'

'I don't see why.'

The air ambulance lifted off the ground and the scrubby sprawl of the Yucca Valley came into view over an outcrop of jagged rocks. Persis looked down and saw a reporter turn his camera towards them. *Why is he filming us?* she wondered. *Does he know anything?* A news blackout was essential right now or the whole project could be jeopardized. Persis thought for a moment. The chances of someone knowing about it were so unlikely. They'd been so careful. She slumped in her seat and allowed herself to be tired for the first time in quite a while. An almost perfect donor body was on its way back to Phoenix and they had secured another chance of moving the project forward.

11

When TV reporter Fred Arlin saw the huge metal sarcophagus being wheeled through a side door, he felt a punch in his gut.

'I bet that's Williams's body on its way to the morgue,' he said to no one in particular, and swivelled his micro-light camera on its harness to capture a few seconds of the casket being loaded into the air ambulance. The swordfish craft took off vertically, lowered its snout, rotated 45 degrees, then sped off towards the east.

Why would they spend so much money airlifting a body? thought Fred. Normally, they brought up the most ancient ambulances from Yucca Valley.

Fred had been waiting along with the press corps for more than four hours for the arrival of Norman Powell. They were wearing coolant body suits, but the heat was killing and they were all huddled under a makeshift shelter set up by the Government network.

Fred had routinely asked for a digital implant detailing the executions of the month. He inserted the readout into his sunglasses and the information appeared before his eyes. The only one of note was Duane Williams, mainly because he had killed a girl in Fred's hometown of San Luis Obispo. The story wasn't going to make much in any bulletin, but if Norman Powell didn't show up then Fred might get mileage out of it. He didn't want to return empty-handed. Not since he'd only just recovered his Government licence. He looked up and saw

Gamma Gulch's media relations officer approaching them across the gravel.

''Bout time,' said one of the journalists.

'I know you're all waiting for Norman Powell, but we had an execution this morning. Duane Williams. The mother of the victim has said she's prepared to give a statement. 'Anyone interested?'

The journalists grumbled but prepared to go inside. Fred sighed lazily, switched off the camera and trailed after the press pack. He knew that no self-respecting reporter would file such an interview, but it was better than sweltering outside.

'We have our lives back,' the mother kept saying, her voice echoing in the cavernous, windowless room, her strange, hypnotic blue eyes shining challengingly at the crowd. She held up a pocket screen and played images of her daughter Jenner at her sixteenth birthday party. A sad-looking girl with a bewildered expression. Fred extended the jib arm of his camera and pressed the zoom lens, but the mother's hand was jerking around.

'Keep it still,' demanded one of the reporters.

'Our daughter has been honoured today,' said Casey Sommers. 'We had to endure, over and over, what happened to Jenner down by Pebble Creek Canyon. Well, we don't have to hear it any more. Our sentence ends today.'

Sound-bite perfect, thought Fred as he finished off with a close-up of the mother hugging her three sons. He rushed outside to the parking lot where someone said Duane Williams's sister was giving *her* statement.

Bobbie Williams's quaking chest heaved asthmatically as she delivered her set piece of anguish. 'May God forgive the State for what they did to my brother. I believe him to be totally innocent of this crime. He had the hardest of lives, which he tried to overcome, and this is how he has been rewarded.'

Bobbie's husband put his arm around her and ferried her to their truck.

They've all got this down to a fine art, thought Fred. *It's like they go into a trance and deliver the exact same text.* He doubted such clichés would ever make it to air, but he was going to try anyway. He flicked open his wristwatch. 'Dan – you there?' he asked the producer in Los Angeles.

'Powell arrived yet?'

'Not yet.'

'Jeez – what's going on?'

'They won't tell us.'

'Are you sure you're asking the right people?' The producer was playing hardball.

'Yes,' Fred said defiantly. 'Look – an execution just happened. I got shots of the air ambulance leaving with the body. I'm the only one who got that and the parents of the girl who was killed. And the sister of the murderer. You interested?'

'Anything special about the case?'

'It was the Jenner Sommers murder. There was a lot of controversy about it in San Luis Obispo.'

'Yeah? Well, it never got as far as Los Angeles. Send it if you like. And Fred, your visual must be no more than twelve seconds or you don't get on.'

Fred swivelled the camera away so the producer wouldn't see his sneer, then ran back to his BMW Speedway, looked around to make sure no one was watching, and flapped down the sun visor where he kept his powder and brush. He dulled the sheen on his nose, flipped the camera so it was facing him, flattened his hair and stood to attention in front of the prison entrance. He transmitted a perfect twelve-second link. The producer grudgingly thanked him.

'Need an update?' he asked. 'I think I know where the body ended up.'

'I'll take it,' said the producer, 'but find me Norman Powell!'

Fred contacted the morgue to confirm when the Williams body had arrived. It hadn't. He checked with two other morgues. No body there either. That was odd. He called media relations and asked the guy what happened to Williams's body. He was told that Duane had stipulated that his body be given to the willed body programme and they couldn't disclose any more information.

'Why not?' Fred asked peevishly.

'Policy,' came the reply.

Impasse. Fred thought for a moment. 'It's not what I'd expect.'

'What isn't?'

'I don't know – a prisoner opting for the willed body programme. Convicted killers aren't exactly known for their community spirit.'

'Well, I guess we'll never know what his motivations were,' said the officer, and hung up.

Fred's mind was buzzing. An idea was coming to him. Why not write a landmark article for *The Metropolitan*, the country's most respected journal and the last to be published on paper? He would call it 'The Anatomy of Life after Death' and trail the Williams body through its journey to the frontiers of medical science. He would go into great detail about the nether world of the people who worked with cadavers, with character studies of the doctors, the morticians and the scientists, nothing sentimental, but spare, muscular writing that would put him on the map.

He sighed. How many ideas had he come up with to advance his career? How many had he acted on? He felt a young man's bitterness that he was too preoccupied with simply paying the rent and recharging the batteries on his overly expensive car. But he filed the Williams execution at the back of his mind. A friend of a friend knew the entertainment editor on *The Metropolitan*. Maybe there was a possible way in. Breaking into these exclusive journals was tougher than breaking out of Gamma Gulch.

He stared across the desert, dotted by crazy Joshua trees which looked like mad clowns with their spiky cuffs. Apart from the abandoned shacks pockmarking the valley floor, it was still a primaeval landscape, and easy to imagine the foot of a dinosaur stepping over the crenellated hills.

Nearly everyone who lived in the Mojave Desert had some kind of underground home these days. Whole towns and malls had gone subterranean to withstand the heat and the wind. Only a few cities like Palm Springs valiantly fought on above ground, its community braving the tornadoes and the hurricanes that whipped sand and debris down the main street. Fred wondered what it must have been like to live there before the real weather arrived. There used to be more than 180 golf courses in the region, all fed by an underground aquifer. Now there wasn't a single one.

He saw a plume of dust rising up from a line of vehicles in the far distance. It had to be the convoy bringing Norman Powell to Gamma Gulch. Fred flipped open his watch.

'You'll be pleased to hear that Norman Powell is on his way,' he said to the prick of a producer at the other end.

'Oh, Fred – they want you to do a story about the debut of a male cheerleader in Palm Springs,' said the producer.

'No,' moaned Fred. 'What about Norman Powell?'

'After you've shot the arrival.'

THE WAKING

He really was being punished.

'And by the way, we're not running the Williams story, but thanks for your effort.'

As Fred drove away from Gamma Gulch, he glanced at his clean, handsome face in the rear-view mirror and felt an empty longing. He definitely deserved better than this.

ICOR REGROWTH PROGRAMME, PHOENIX, ARIZONA / 2070

12

'It's too early to invite the President,' said Dr Garth Bannerman, feeling the twitch return under his left eye. He hoped his boss wouldn't notice. 'I've only just got the EIS off my back. I'm not ready.'

'It's too late,' said Rick Bandelier, the managing director of Icor's Phoenix division. 'He's already coming.'

It was a great privilege, but Garth felt torn. He knew a visit from the President of the United States would throw too much attention on the regrowth programme. And if there was any further trouble at Icor, the Epidemic Intelligence Service had hinted that they would shut down the laboratories altogether. They had the power to do it and they had shown, time and time again, that they weren't afraid to use it.

It had been five years since the EIS forcibly marched through Icor's gates after a dozen people had died from a mystery virus having received infected organs from the regrowth centre. Everything that the staff were using had been bagged and swabbed, right down to the coffee cups and toothpicks in the canteen. The EIS had made Garth feel like a criminal for the accident and Icor had to pay a hefty fine, not to mention huge settlements to the families of the victims.

It had become more difficult for Garth to get licences for his work after that, let alone regain the trust of the Center for Disease Control. The EIS, an arm of the CDC, had returned to Icor frequently, sometimes arriving at dawn when no one was expecting them and always bringing the National Guard for protection. The pressure had been intolerable and Garth had taken to lying low in the scientific world. He'd even created his own private laboratories in the basement of the building that no one but himself could have access to so that he could carry on his work without the disease detectives breathing down his neck. For a while there, he felt like a wanted man. He wasn't alone. Every scientist who'd ever come under the scrutiny of the EIS had been forced to set up secret laboratories. The agency's excessive powers had literally driven the scientific community underground, which, to Garth, was much more dangerous than the old practices of sharing knowledge.

The EIS had more jurisdiction than any other group within the National Institute of Health and could enter any building by force at any time, hermetically sealing structures and testing for infection. The agency always defended its position, saying it was a product of its time, where viruses and bacteria had devastated populations and bioterrorism was always a threat. But they were hated by the professionals they hounded, and Garth knew that the fatuous executive sitting at his overblown desk on the top floor of Icor had no experience of how the agency operated, let alone what they were capable of.

'Why is the President so interested?' said Garth.

'He saw the Head as a kid apparently. It used to be on display in Pasadena where he grew up.'

'You see – that's precisely what I'm talking about, Rick. If it gets out that we've used some kind of famous relic as part of our experiment, we're going to have every anti-interventionist group bussing into town and waving their banners outside. Do you see what this could do to us?'

'And his father's cryonically frozen,' said Rick smoothly, ignoring Garth's outburst.

'The President's?'

'Apparently. He wants to revive him.'

'I hope he hasn't been misinformed.'

'About what?'

'I don't want the President to think that we're about to bring his father out of the cooler.'

'I understand,' said Rick. 'That's why I stipulated that this is a totally private visit. No media. No EIS. No false expectations. We simply reacquaint him with the Head. Show him the donor body. That's it.'

'We don't need *anyone* sniffing around, trying to find out where the bodies are coming from either,' said Garth, breathing hard. Usually he was a mild-mannered man who hated confrontations, yet always seemed, somehow, to get involved in them.

'I *know*,' said Rick, bristling. 'Let me explain how this is going to go. We let the President see the unit . . .' He was talking slowly now, as though he was addressing a child, in spite of the fact that he was fifteen years younger than Bannerman. 'Your job is to explain as much science as you can. And remember, Garth, he's a layman, not a scientist. Give him hope about his father and let him go on his way. The result? We have ourselves a big friend in a very high place.'

'But I'm concerned that—'

'I know you are,' said Rick. 'But I – we – need the President's support on this. There's nothing that gets the chairman of Icor more fired up than having the spotlight thrown on to one of his divisions! Think about it.'

'Why can't he come later – when we're further along the road?'

Rick looked at him. 'You think we have any way of manipulating the President's schedule? This visit will do useful things for all of us.'

It'll do useful things for you, thought Garth. How could someone like Rick Bandelier end up running Phoenix? Stem cell regrowth and body part replication had always been a quagmire of legal grey areas and licences which was clearly beyond the man's expertise. Garth was convinced that Rick Bandelier had advanced so far so fast simply because he was a genetic, just like his wife Persis. Genetics were always swamped with opportunities while other mere mortals had to languish in the backwaters and bide their time for promotions.

Rick spread his beautifully manicured hands over his huge oak desk, as though he needed to touch something he admired.

'What do you want me to do? Turn him away?'

'And the EIS?'

'We're not doing anything illegal – so what's the problem?'

Garth raised an eyebrow. 'Aren't we?'

'Let's just stick to what we agreed,' said Rick, agitation ruffling his satin delivery.

Garth was simmering. The ball was in motion. The President was coming, and while he too desperately wanted recognition for his work, this was not the best way to get it. A high-profile visitor was likely to draw unwanted attention to the unit and you didn't get much more conspicuous than the leader of the free world.

13

The black and gold aero car was cruising at 300 feet above Phoenix. The driver had put his vehicle on to automatic pilot and had fallen asleep. Everyone in the car was asleep, except for Marco Villaloboz, the 55th President of the United States.

He looked down at the urban sprawl beneath him. Through the pollution cloud, he could see vast stretches of tract housing, mostly abandoned, and the odd saguaro cactus with its arms raised up to the heavens as though it was pleading with God for mercy. And mercy was what was needed in times like these.

The President watched acre after acre of derelict houses pass by beneath him until he could look no more, then turned his attention to his entourage. Even his private secretary, Charlie Preston, had drifted off. President Villaloboz felt neglected and in that mood he wanted to punish someone, so he gave Preston a sharp nudge in the leg. Charlie jumped to attention. 'Are you cold, sir?'

'Hand me some of that water, would you?'

The President could have reached over himself but he wanted Preston to share his loneliness. Now that the man was awake and attentive, the President stretched out and looked through his briefing notes:

> 9 a.m. – Depart Los Angeles. Fly to Icor
> Incorporated, Phoenix. Meet the Chairman of Icor,
> John Rando, and the Medical Director of the
> Regrowth Programme, Dr Garth Bannerman.
>
> 9.30–10.00 a.m. – view 'the Head'. Private visit.

Good. No media. He was glad to have a few hours off. He closed his eyes and remembered. He was clutching his father's hand and they were walking up the steps of the Cryogenesis Research Institute in Pasadena. He searched the notes for the man's name: Dr Nathaniel Sheehan. That's right. Irish. They were called the Romeo and Juliet of the cryonics industry. The President could see the man's face; the skin repulsively bloodless and waxen, the hair floating like seaweed in a rock pool. And it was on that very day, during the visit, that the

President's father had decided that he wanted to be frozen himself. Marco had forgotten all about it, but when the old man suffered a brain haemorrhage, Marco's mother had repeated his father's dying wish. The family had gone along with the plan at the time, but the whole process had become an embarrassment, not to mention a huge financial burden, costing them hundreds of thousands of dollars. And, infuriatingly, it was *the* thing that the media always mentioned about the President in character profiles:

> Marco Villaloboz's love for his father is so great, that he keeps his body in suspended animation, hoping that one day he will be able to bring him back from the dead.

How could the President cancel the contract now? But he so longed to end the charade. All the Villaloboz family griped about was the cost and two of his brothers had stopped contributing altogether. Maybe this doctor had the answer. The scientist was one of the few men in the world who could make resuscitation possible. If he succeeded, they could bring the President's father back, and if it failed, the family could bury the old man once and for all.

'Mr President?'

Villaloboz craned his neck to look at Charlie's earnest face.

'We're almost there.'

The building loomed up before them, a black glass obelisk against the clear blue sky. The driver lowered the aero car with expert precision, and before the vehicle had even settled, one of the aides was out of the car and running to the passenger door to let the President out. The jets blew him wildly off course but he fought valiantly to recoup his dignity, his trouser legs flapping.

'Someone should tell Steve that he doesn't have to try so hard,' said Villaloboz, and they all laughed with the casual disregard of important men.

A delegation was waiting to meet them at the grand but sterile entrance and a square-jawed, military-looking man stepped forward. The President knew him from functions in Washington. It was John Rando, the chairman of Icor Incorporated. Rando peered out from under his mudslide eyelids like a toad emerging from a pond. He was once a redhead, though the colour had faded to dusty strawberry, and his mouth was set in a narrow line. Rando was hard, bullying and secretive, and the President had seen him intimidating his caddie at the club where they played an occasional round of golf together and swapped insider information for the sake of their mutual advancement.

'President Villaloboz. Welcome to Phoenix. How's the handicap?' said Rando.

'Better than yours. Where have you been? No one's seen you at the club for six months.'

'Someone has to keep the empire going.'

Rando gave the President a quick, savage smile, a concession to Villaloboz's importance on the world economic stage, and guided the delegation towards the building.

'Now we can breathe, let me introduce you to the genius behind all this – Dr Garth Bannerman,' said Rando.

President Villaloboz grabbed the hand of a kind-looking man with a head of greying, curly hair. 'I hear you have a friend of mine in custody,' he said to the scientist. 'You've been keeping him incarcerated for way too long.'

The doctor smiled but was too shy to speak.

'Lead the way,' said the President gently.

The party hurried through endless corridors before stopping to see the regrowth laboratories where rows of organs were being farmed for people all over the United States. The President had visited stem cell production lines before, but was always impressed that such insignificant-looking offal could relieve so much human suffering. Then, at last, a metal door slid back and they were in the nerve centre of the building. Lights glowed in a gantry and there he was, the Head, immersed in isotonic fluid. They were all silent for a while.

'And so we meet again,' said the President at last. 'It's been some thirty-five years and you haven't changed a bit.'

There was a ripple of appreciative laughter. As Villaloboz grew accustomed to the lighting, he could see that the Head's eyes were open and half a dozen tubes were pumping liquids through the neck opening.

'I saw this very head in Pasadena when I was a little boy,' he said.

'So I understand,' said Garth shyly.

'He's got brown eyes. I always wondered what colour they were going to be. When I saw him before, he didn't seem to have any eyes.'

'We had to regrow the corneas. That's one of the things that don't survive the passage of time.'

'Is he conscious?'

'No, though there is some neural activity in the brainstem – that's the ancient part of the brain that controls basic impulses. We can switch that on like a reflex and it does inform other areas of the brain, though in this state, not significantly. It turns out that the Head's brainstem was damaged in transition.'

'But it looks like he can see through the liquid.'

'His sight *is* registering in the brainstem and he can see us, but not as a conscious thought in the upper cortices. It's much like the responses of someone who is brain-dead. The patient's eyes will follow a visitor around a hospital bed. They seem to be responding, but there is no consciousness. It's disconcerting because relatives and loved ones believe the patient is "present" when actually they're not. If you stand in front of him, then move, his eyes *will* follow you.'

Garth gestured for the President to take up position. The President got a jolt as the Head's eyes flickered and focused on him. He took a step to one side. The eyes followed. He took another. The brown, emotionless eyes darted again. The President walked to the edge of the Head's peripheral vision, the pupils still fixed on him.

'So when are you going to wake up our sleeping prince?'

Garth looked from the President to John Rando and on to Rick Bandelier, wondering what the President had been told.

'We're attaching the Head and the body at two,' he said, 'but it will be a long time before he wakes up – if at all.'

'Then thank God for President Clinton!' said Villaloboz bombastically, wanting to assert that he knew *something* about the subject.

'President Clinton?' said the doctor.

'You know about him, surely.'

'I'm afraid I don't recall, sir,' said the doctor blushing.

The President realized that he must refrain from being a bully. He often used information to sideswipe people and impose his authority.

'He was president at the turn of the twenty-first century. He allocated the first serious money towards nanotechnology. And look at us now.'

'Indeed,' said Rando.

'So tell me – how is this all going to work?'

The doctor started in again. 'We have circulated a fluid that contains an army of microscopic nano-machines. What they do is unlock all the human anti-freeze that's wrapped around each molecule and . . .'

'Well, he's going to have one hell of a hangover,' said the President with his customary impatience, but just as he said the words, he felt a profound loss of energy, as though a life force had been sucked out of him.

'Are you OK, Mr President?' asked Garth presently.

'It must be the change of temperature.'

'It often gets people that way,' said John Rando.

The President shivered. 'It's funny. My father and I concocted so many stories about the Head. We built up a whole life around him. I just had the strongest feeling that my father was standing by me just then.'

'Maybe he *will* stand beside you again one day,' said Rando.

Garth held his breath. This was exactly what he didn't want to happen; that someone in ignorance would set up absurd expectations. He decided to intervene before Rando made any other false promises.

'The face has three thousand meaningful expressions. We can electromagnetically stimulate groups of muscles to give the face a workout. Would you like to see that?'

'It won't terrify me, will it?' said the President.

'Oh, no. It's purely a mechanical reaction.'

Garth gestured to a technician sitting behind a bank of computers. 'Can you give a 3.3 to risorius, the zygomatic major and the depressor labii, please?'

The technician typed an instruction and the Head's lips peeled back over its teeth like a monkey grimacing just before a fight. The expression was inhuman. Revolting.

'He has to be registering this, surely,' said the President.

'It's electronic stimulation. There is no consciousness.'

'I'm wondering what my father would have made of all this.'

'He was a gracious man and a champion of progress,' said Rando.

'Yes, he was,' agreed the President. 'Treat the Head well, will you, Dr Bannerman? He's come a long way.'

'We will,' interjected Rando. 'We have the body ready too, would you like to see that?'

The delegation moved into the next chamber. The cadaver, now headless, was lying suspended in a huge tank of fluid with dozens of electrodes attached to muscle points and a confusion of clamps and wires protruding from the neck. Two large tubes were pumping blood in and out of the cavity and at small intervals, electrical impulses were stimulating the limbs. Every now and then they would jerk or levitate.

'Where did you get the body from?' asked the President.

Garth gave a quick, furtive glance towards the chairman. They had agreed on complete confidentiality about the source of the bodies.

'He was in a road accident.'

'One man's death gives another man life,' said Villaloboz, pausing for effect. 'How old is he – was he?'

'Twenty-six.'

'And our friend?'

'Thirty-seven.'

'Will that be compatible?'

'We have found a body that has seventy per cent genetic compatibility with the Head and the same blood type. The rest we correct by inserting a forty-seventh chromosome which, as you know, can deliver a huge amount of genetic information to individual cells. The fact that the body was younger is a good thing. It has more chance of withstanding the trauma.'

The body's left knee jerked as though it had been tapped by an imaginary hammer. The President searched for the kind of question his father might have asked.

'We can regrow internal organs, skin tissue, whole limbs. I'm wondering how useful will this be to the march of science – honestly?'

'This is an interim stage, Mr President. I hope my growth accelerator will be able to reproduce an entire brain in a matter of years, and limbs, and one day in the not too distant future an entire body, and we won't have to rely on finding donor bodies to match our subjects. The current supply is unreliable, much like the time when people had to wait months, even years for suitable donor organs to become available. Sometimes the wait cost them their lives—' Garth stopped talking when he saw the chairman looking at him.

'It's wonderful what you're doing, Dr Bannerman. Quite wonderful. But how do you see this advance being applied now?'

'We can clone a copy of *you* from a single cell. That's been done many times. But we know about the ramifications. Not only is that body more prone to hundreds of defects which show up in later life and are prohibitively expensive to correct, but whoever is created has none of your emotions, behaviours or cellular reactions connected to your memories. Your clone would never feel any reaction on retasting the South African Chablis that was served at your wedding. He would never have felt your sorrow on seeing the last family of tigers roaming free on your state trip to India. He would never have experienced elation while dancing with Princess Magdalena at the White House . . .'

'I take your point,' said the President.

'Imagine if you were assassinated. It might be crucial to have *you* brought back. You might be the only person to have some secret code or information that is vital to the survival of the United States. Your head is uninjured, but your body can no longer sustain life. There are no donors available. This way, we could create a new body for you in a matter of weeks, maybe days if my growth accelerator works quickly enough.'

'Or someone might *care* enough about me to want to keep me alive.'

Garth blushed again. 'Well, of course. That is *always* the imperative at Icor.'

Villaloboz patted the doctor on the back. He was in charge and enjoying himself and grateful not to be taking on another caseload of woe from the outside world.

'But I still have no sense of how great the demand is going to be for this kind of thing,' he said.

'Neither do I,' said Garth. He'd honestly never given it a moment's thought. He was only ever interested in the science.

'There's going to be a huge demand!' said Rando.

'And here's a man who should know,' announced the President, clapping a hand on Rando's shoulder. 'This is the man who, along with his father, cured many of the major cancers and built up the most successful medical corporation this country has ever known.'

There was a ripple of spontaneous applause. 'John – we thank you and your father, and all the people who could have suffered from that terrible disease would like to thank you too, I'm sure of that.'

John Rando twitched a smile. 'And we at Icor thank *you* for coming all this way to see our small but significant operation, Mr President. I'm sure you're on a tight schedule.'

'You're so right, but I'll take one more look at the Head if I may.'

'Be our guest,' said Rando, guiding the President back into the first chamber. 'Take as long as you like.'

President Villaloboz walked up to the tank and raised his hand to the glass for the second time in his life. 'See this, Dad,' he whispered to himself. 'Everything you predicted is coming true.'

The eyes of the Head flickered and focused. Marco shivered. The chamber had chilled him to the bone.

14

'That was tricky,' said Garth.

He was sharing a coffee with his colleague Dr Persis Bandelier after the President's visit. It was a ritual they often enjoyed in her office.

'Oh – I think you charmed the President,' she teased, 'particularly the bit about his assassination.'

'I know!' Garth slammed his forehead with the palm of his hand. 'I thought he was going to ask me when we were going to bring back his dad. I didn't know what I was saying half the time.'

Persis tilted her head to one side. 'I think it went really well,' she said, and looked back down at the science paper that she'd just downloaded.

'What's it about?' he asked, leaning over.

'Macrophages.'

He could see she wanted to read rather than talk, but he lingered just the same.

'Sometimes I think they should lock me up and throw away the key,' he muttered.

Persis smiled. Garth enjoyed watching his colleague. She

was a true genetic with everything in perfect proportion. She had long blonde hair which she had tied back today in a formal French plait, dark brown eyes and an appealing Roman curve to her nose. He envied her many things, not least her disposition to robust good health, a life expectancy of maybe 150 years if she kept out of harm's way, and so far she had managed to survive the plagues and outbreaks of disease that had wreaked so much havoc in her home town of New York.

But it was something of a mystery to Garth as to why Persis had accepted the job at Icor. Her husband Rick had been drafted in to run the Phoenix division and he had in turn recruited Persis to take up the deputy director position in the regrowth programme. Garth was grateful to have someone so talented working on his team. Persis had been a rising star in neurotechnology at New York University, but he wondered why she didn't want to stay where she was and have a commuter marriage. A lot of people at their level did it, and her husband would probably be back in New York within a few years anyway. Garth couldn't quite believe that anyone could love Rick Bandelier that much to give up their precious tenure for him.

It was tough working between a married couple, one as the boss and the other an employee. Garth thought it would never work and he said so. But it had been made very clear to him that he had no choice.

So when Persis arrived, he'd been distant and defensive, keeping her out of the decision-making loop for months. But she had never fought him on it or even pushed him to be included. She seemed to have more self-containment than to get embroiled in office politics. Very soon, he began to depend on her professionalism. She was inventive and impeccable and never mentioned Rick. Not once. And she'd shown real poise when given the grim job of interviewing Death Row prisoners to secure their cadavers and bring them back to Phoenix.

'Was a visit from the President exciting enough for a New York socialite?' he asked, trying to keep the conversation going.

'It was OK – I guess,' she said, pretending to be nonchalant.

More than anything, Garth enjoyed her company. She tended to be aloof, but she had a good sense of humour and they had locked into gentle ironic banter that drew them closer together, and her presence had definitely created a buzz in an otherwise sterile and rather gloomy working environment. Garth's reverie was interrupted when John Rando strode into the office with a delegation of Icor executives.

'I think the President was happy, don't you?' said Rando, looking at Garth from under his amphibian eyelids.

'I hope so.'

'So, this is body number—'

' – thirteen,' said Garth. 'The thirteenth attempt.'

'So many,' mused Rando. He had a penetrating, disconcerting stare. Garth thought he was probably ruminating about the cost of it all.

'It's an ongoing programme, sir. Each time we get a little closer to understanding the workings of the growth accelerator.'

'I know – I know, but some of us can't wait for ever.'

'I understand,' said Garth.

The chairman grunted and left, his entourage following like a pack of grinning mutes.

'What did he mean: "some of us can't wait for ever?"' asked Persis when they were out of earshot.

'His heart is failing.'

Persis looked surprised.

'It's not common knowledge in the company.'

'But that's OK – isn't it?'

'Not really. He was born with a hole in the heart, so they fixed that. Then he got an artificial heart in the prototype phase. That didn't work for very long. Then one of the first generation of pig's hearts. I think he's on his eighth heart.'

'Now I'm really beginning to feel sorry for him.'

'It's a miracle he's still alive. Left to himself, he wouldn't have survived much beyond childhood. So the President is not the only one with great expectations.'

'Well, we can't go any faster,' she said.

'I know it.'

15

A second aero car descended from the skies to the front steps of Icor's regrowth centre that afternoon. It was occupied by Dr Tim Boath, one of the West Coast's top spinal cord injury surgeons who had been drafted in to carry out the grunt work on the reconnections. Tim was an old college room-mate of Garth's and caught the doctor up in a bear hug that almost winded him.

They went down to the decontamination rooms where they showered, powdered and dressed in their lightweight biohazard suits, the uniform for anyone working directly with the cadavers.

The Head had been removed from its gantry and was lying immersed in an open canister of isotonic fluid. A few yards away, the body was lying suspended in another tank. Surrounding the body was a series of platforms so they could get up high and plunge their gloved hands into the freezing liquid to move the two body parts around when necessary.

'When did they freeze *this* one?' said Tim through his oxygen mask.

'2006,' said Garth.

Tim grabbed a long surgical pincer and began to tease parts of the neck opening.

'It's good that they left the C1 and the C2 intact. And the larynx. That's what I call foresight.'

'Well, they didn't exactly work with hacksaws and alcohol,' joked Garth. 'Like I said in the notes, this one is in much better shape, but if you take a look at the imager you can see that the brainstem and the larynx are damaged, so we're going to use the brainstem from the body.'

'I know, I've been prepping for it,' said Tim, an edge entering his voice. 'I have to tell you, Garth, that I think it's a waste of a good head.'

'You think?'

'Sure. He's a fine specimen. You should keep him for when you know more about what you're doing.'

'I can't swap him out now,' said Garth.

'Why not?'

'Too many people are interested in the outcome.'

'But if you take away the brainstem, what chance does he have?'

'What chance does he have anyway? I want to try it this way. If you look at what happened the last three times, there was so much damage to the stem's reticular formation that they had no chance of talking to the intralaminar nuclei of the thalamus. Let alone receive any afferent signals from the rostral brain structures.'

'True.'

'This way the brainstem is already connected up to the spinal cord, the solitary complex and the vestibular nuclei. Less work for the accelerator. I honestly think that, in the long run, it's going to be the only way forward.'

They both peered down at the Head, its sagging grey flesh flopping over the neck opening.

'How do you match the core consciousness of one human being to the higher consciousness of another?' said Tim.

'With a lot of prayer,' said Garth.

Tim laughed. 'You scientists. You get so bound up in your microscopic view of the world that you never see the bigger picture.'

'I just want the ribosome to inhibit the growth factor and the nanos to articulate some kind of binding activity,' said Garth. 'If I get that far, I'll be celebrating. Persis has brought in a new semaphorin stimulator from New York. She thinks we should see the first evidence of temporal organization, but I'm not holding my breath.'

Tim clapped his hands. 'OK – let's get to work.'

They joined up both tanks, raised the adjoining hatches and inched the Head into position above the body. Tim sat a little way off and gripped the joysticks. Four robotic arms plunged into the freezing liquid. He instructed the robots to sift through the layers of the neck opening. They unhinged the Head's remaining vertebrae and removed the damaged brainstem, then inserted the Williams brainstem into the cavity. They cleaned both sides and fused the vertebrae to the base of the skull with fibre clips, sending an eerie blue flame through the liquid.

'I'm getting way too good at this,' said Tim, breaking away from his 3-D imager. 'Pity we've got nothing to show for it.' He winked at Garth, but there was condensation on the inside of his mask. Tim always made flippant remarks when he was under pressure.

With great delicacy, the mechanized arms removed the tubes that had been feeding plasma substitute into the Head's carotid arteries and sutured the artery walls to the matching carotids in the neck opening. Tim repeated the instruction again and again, taking each vessel and fusing it to the Head's matching vasculature network. It was exhausting, detailed work, painstakingly attaching every millimetre of flesh from the inside out, then finally fusing the neck wall and suturing the skin. The join of the skin flap formed a primitive, engorged seal. For the first time, Garth noticed how different the two skin tones were; the head a greyish taupe and the body a sallow brown. Garth hoped that the skin of the Head would be a closer match once the blood was in circulation.

'It's all yours,' said Tim, in a trance after twelve hours straight. The two friends hugged. The temperature of the body was brought up to just above freezing and Garth took Tim's place, commanding the robotic arms to remove the solid plugs of tissue from the body's sternum. They attached a tube and poured in a liquid containing millions of cell-repair machines. Almost immediately, the micron-sized computers gushed through the body.

Garth turned to watch an enormous fluoroscope, one of the biggest of its kind in the world. He brushed the screen lightly with his fingertips and magnified a midsection of the patient's neck. He could already see the minuscule computers coursing through the veins and arteries and piercing cell membranes. How much the nano-machines looked like viruses, he thought, wrestling with cell walls, bursting through them and doing their agitated dance as they began to mend each cell.

While the microscopic software got to work identifying where the damage hot spots were, the body was tilted to a 45-degree angle and hundreds of tiny metal needles were inserted into the spinal column. At regular intervals they were programmed to pump stem cells directly into the neurons.

Within minutes, Garth could pick up their journey on the screen as they sped towards the Head. Their job was to grow new neurons between the Head and the body, taking with them the precious growth factor that Garth had been working on for his entire career. It was a chaperone ribosome that was encrypted with a genetic code to start rapid cell growth.

In earlier guises, the ribosome had successfully activated, but the protein programmed to block the cells from proliferating had failed. The results were extensive and uncontrollable tumours. At the cellular level, it was like getting a key stuck on a keyboard and watching helplessly as the same letters scrolled out across the screen.

Garth winced whenever he thought about the deformities that he had created. Huge, hard goitre-like growths all over the body, stretching the epidermis to the point of tearing. If any patients had recovered consciousness, they would have been in indescribable agony. He kept the worst examples refrigerated and out of sight of prying eyes. He knew how easy it would be to point the finger at him and call him a ghoul.

To stop the tumours, Garth had doctored a forty-seventh chromosome that they had been using to carry substantial amounts of genetic code to the new cells. Unlike the extra chromosome that showed up in Down's sufferers, an engineered chromosome could live alongside the normal forty-six like a gatekeeper, shutting down the ribosome at exactly the right moment. It also worked to bring into line the last remaining genetic incompatibilities between the head and the body. The only problem was the vector. The most common delivery system for the chromosome was still an adenovirus, which carried with it all the risks of bodily rejection. For the neurons they were using a polymer-coated herpes virus small enough to seep through the blood–brain barrier.

Garth knew that they were still tampering with all the complex delivery systems and that they were a long way from reaching their goal. That's why his expectations were so modest, but as he watched the stem cells scratch around by the severed neurons, finding all the right cellular ports to dock into and start multiplying, he couldn't help feeling a great surge of excitement. He turned and looked at the faces of his colleagues, all of them transfixed by their own screens. At that moment, it was hard not to believe in the presence of God.

16

'What's happening now?'

Monty and Persis were watching the tiny nano-submersibles floating through the brain tissue. The team had been working for twenty-four hours straight, but were still riding high on adrenaline.

'This programme is a miracle,' murmured Persis.

'Explain it to me,' said Monty. It wasn't his area of expertise yet, though he intended to make it one, particularly with one of the top neurotechnologists in the country on hand to explain it to him. And Persis always loved to be asked.

'The nano-machines are creating a complete map of the Sheehan brain and the Williams brainstem, where the damage is and where the connections should be. They feed that information back into the database and have already started to reconstruct all those complex connections, neuron by neuron.'

'That's awesome,' said Monty.

'It certainly is.' She magnified some brain tissue. A starfish shape appeared with an extended arm.

'Say hello to the perfect neuron.'

'That looks healthy,' said Monty. He was beginning to identify what the cells should look like.

'It is,' said Persis. 'As from – ' she checked her readout ' – four hours ago. It's completely thawed and has no residual damage, which is a remarkable achievement in itself. Now what would really be extraordinary is if this neuron started talking to its neighbours. See the long arm. That's called an axon.'

'I see it.'

'Well, it's already docked into the receiving portal, the dendrite, of another neuron. But we have no activity.'

'When can we expect that?'

Persis laughed. 'Who knows? Sometime never? They claim the programme can tell the nanos to activate the neurotransmitters at will, but I'll believe it when I see it. No one has ever achieved that in the upper cortices of a human brain before. Only in animals.'

'Then maybe we'll be the first,' said Monty.

'It's genius, pure genius,' said Persis, tracking the microscopic computers.

'Why?'

'It's mimicking foetal brain formation. Normally, when new neurons make connections in a foetus, the brain uses a variety of signals to guide the growth cone of one axon to the appropriate dendrite of another. In a foetus, some of these signals are called semaphorins. The programme is stimulating the same kind of signposting. I'll show you.'

She brought up another neuron which, as they looked, was blooming like the stamen of a flower.

'It's responding to a chemical gradient and searching for the correct dendrite.'

They witnessed the elongated axon make an uncanny left turn as though it was being bent by an invisible hand.

'That is just beautiful,' she said in rapture. 'That's what we couldn't do before.'

'And where are we in the brain?' asked Monty.

'We're in the language centre of the left hemisphere. But, according to feedback from the nanos, there are billions of neurons that are damaged in that region.'

'Can we mend them?'

'I don't know.'

'Oh,' said Monty, disappointed. 'I don't understand why we don't skip this phase and thaw the cadavers with the heads already attached. Then we wouldn't have this eternal binding problem.'

'Any brain that we thaw is going to go through this, but we decided to use the older heads to find out exactly how to create temporal synchrony and to see how Garth's ribosome can be manipulated to speed up and slow down cellular growth at just the right moment. We want to save the newer bodies for later on when we have a better idea of how the chemical processes interact with one another.'

Something deep inside Monty stirred; an objection to using people who had lives, families and histories as nothing more than testing grounds for experimentation. Persis had a clinical side to her that he couldn't relate to. Nor could he match the gleefulness in her expression.

'Another thing we've decided to do this time around is manufacture billions more neurons than we need, and then prune them like the leaves off a tree.'

'So what's the problem?'

'I don't know what I'm doing is the problem,' she said, smiling. 'We had to swap out the brainstem, so we have to re-create perfect communication between the Sheehan brain and the Williams brainstem, or no part of him is ever going to function. If you think of all the regions of the brain as instruments in a massively polyphonic and polyrythmic symphony, the reticular formation in the brainstem is the conductor of all those instruments. It's responsible for setting the tempo, modulating the levels of various regions of the brain and keeping everyone playing to the same score. Without proper orchestration from the brainstem, all the disparate regions would fall into a schizophrenic cacophony.'

'What would that feel like to Dr Sheehan?'

'Insanity,' she said simply.

'And that's what he's got to look forward to when he wakes up?'

Persis smiled a kindly smile that she might reserve for an ignorant child. The smile irritated Monty, partly because he knew he was ignorant and partly because he wondered daily how he would ever be able to catch up with these genetics and their enhanced intellects.

'Waking up,' she said, almost dreamily. 'Wouldn't that be nice? It's a wild ride that we're embarking on, Monty, so let's enjoy the music while we can.'

17

Fred Arlin could feel his bile rising. He could pick up the features editor's indifference through the speaker system in the walls of his office.

'Where do you work?' asked the man with a practised, affected air.

'SCTV.'

'Never heard of it.'

'It's an affiliate station that feeds CTV,' Fred insisted, trying to muster some pride.

'How long have you been there?'

'Five years.'

'You'll be ruined as a writer. TV ruins any talent that anyone ever had as a writer.'

'Does that mean you're not interested?'

'If you send it to me as a spec piece, I'll read it.'

Fred could hear a deep inhale and the familiar hiss of the oxygen assist at the other end. It must be a high-risk day in New York or the guy was asthmatic.

'What kind of length are we talking about here?'

'Three thousand words.'

'On spec?'

'Take it or leave it.'

'I'll take it, I'll take it.'

Fred saw *The Metropolitan* as his only lifeline. It was the last great printed magazine in America, and though it hadn't been profitable for most of the century, there was always a new proprietor prepared to take on the debt. It was as though if *The Metropolitan* died, so would the nation's last link to the bygone era of paper. Most readers received it electronically, but a privileged few who were prepared to pay a very high price still had it delivered in print. The articles were much longer than in all the other journals and there was a tremendous cachet attached to anyone who got published.

For Fred, there had been the slowest of introductions to the entertainment editor who had been surprisingly helpful with a referral. But now he had ended up with this shit of a features editor, Jamie Bower, and his elitist condescension.

'What are the odds of you publishing it?' queried Fred. He was determined to get at least a few answers.

Another bored wheeze. 'Four hundred to one. And remind me of this conversation in your covering note, or I won't remember.'

The line went dead. Fred opened his micro-organizer and found the number for Duane Williams's lawyer. He arranged to see Jim Hutton in Santa Barbara that same afternoon.

Soft light filtered through the sycamore trees that lined State Street as Fred leapt up a tiled staircase to a whitewashed Spanish office complex and came to a studded oak door. Jim Hutton opened it. Fred was taken aback. The man was completely bald.

'You're wondering why I'm bald,' said the lawyer, turning his back on Fred and wandering off into the gloom.

'It's so unusual,' said Fred.

Hair growth was one of the cheapest and simplest genetic alterations on the market.

'I have contact alopaecia,' said Jim. 'Just occasionally there's nothing they can do.'

'I'm sorry, I didn't mean to—'

'Believe me, so am I.'

Jim led Fred into his den, which was filled with old books, a rarity in any office. There was a Sherlock Holmes leather armchair for the clients and an eccentric collection of what looked like torture instruments on a dusty shelf, and a hand in a jar. Jim sat behind a Mexican leatherbound desk and motioned for Fred to sit down.

'Is that what happens to clients who don't pay the bill?' asked Fred, pointing to the severed hand.

'I like to tell my clients that it came from one of my most famous cases, but I know I wouldn't get away with lying to a man from the media. It makes me look more interesting though, don't you think?'

'For sure,' said Fred, who wanted to take a cloth and wipe his chair. He rubbed his hands and noticed that they sent tiny squalls of dust particles dancing in the shaft of sunlight.

'Actually, it's from a toy shop. My son insisted I keep it in the office. So,' he barked, 'what can I do for you?'

Jim spoke with a buzzy, rapid voice. Fred noticed his bulging blue eyes made him appear more angry than he probably was.

'Well, I'm doing a story about following a cadaver to the frontiers of medical science. I know Duane Williams donated his body to the willed body programme before he was executed, so I just want to find out what happened to him.'

Jim laughed. It was a cold, single sound, like a bark. 'I can't help you with that.'

'Any reason?'

Jim shrugged. 'The companies that need cadavers insist on complete confidentiality.'

'Why?'

'Medical science is so high-risk. They may be working on some critically competitive product that they don't want anyone knowing about.'

'So you can't give me a name?'

'Look, Mr Arlin, I don't even know who the companies are,' said Hutton.

'So – no one knows where Duane ended up.'

'Gamma Gulch will know.'

'They won't tell me.'

Jim Hutton raised his hands and shrugged. 'Then it's up to you to find out.'

'Can you help me?'

'Now why should I do that?'

Fred had no answer. 'OK – tell me about Duane.'

'But that's not your story.'

'It *is* my story. Duane was executed. That's a story.'

'Judging by the amount of coverage in the media, it isn't.'

'Do you think he deserved to die?'

'You're asking a lawyer that question?'

Jesus, the man was hardball. 'Why not?'

'I don't believe in executions. That's why I work for the defence.'

Fred felt suitably patronized. He could tell there was all the mistrust of a smart lawyer in those eyes and didn't feel quite up to meeting that intense, bug-eyed gaze, so he concentrated on a dead fly on the windowsill instead.

'I liked him,' said Jim unexpectedly.

'You did?'

'Duane was crazy, but somewhere in there, you know—'

'Who was he? I mean, where was he from?'

Jim retrieved a brimming file from a battered cabinet. He was definitely old school, preferring concrete things you could touch and hold. Some people refused to run their lives by the screen. Jim let the file fall heavily on the desk, sending out more squalls of dust.

'I think this contains all you need to say about a family

tragedy, American style,' he said, opening up the first page. 'OK. Duane Williams. Born in Bakersfield. Date of birth, 2043. Mother, Desdemona Williams. DOB, 2013. Registered alcoholic. Abuse persisted even after alteration to the D2R2 Allele gene. Dopamine receptors way out of whack. Father, Doug Petty. His continued presence in the family unit was possibly the worst thing that could have happened to the Williams boys. He terrorized them. Duane and his brother, Keith. The father had some kind of hold over Desdemona. They decided in their wisdom to abandon the boys in a motel room one night. Put them to bed and just walked away. Didn't even pay the bill. And that was that. There was a sister by then – Bobbie. The mother, Desdemona, made sure that her daughter was OK. Placed her with a sister, but she didn't seem to care too much about what happened to the boys. They never saw them again.' Jim closed the file.

'What happened after that?'

Jim shrugged. 'The Williams boys were shunted from one foster home to another until they found Barry and Kristin Leneman, who adopted them. But that was a disaster too. The Lenemans only wanted one kid apparently, and it turned out that it wasn't Duane. So the outcome is pretty much what you'd expect from someone who was shown absolutely no love and was treated like a dog by pretty much everyone he should have been able to trust.'

Fred could see the lawyer's hostility was the necessary front of an emotional man.

'Do you think he was guilty?'

'Off the record?'

'Of course.'

'The only person who really knows what happened that night was Keith Williams, his brother. They were together when the Sommers girl died.'

'And where is Keith?'

Jim let out another mean laugh. 'Where is Keith? Hiding out in a cave somewhere. If you find him, Mr Arlin, I'd act according to the directive from the FBI.'

Jim pushed a printout across the desk. There was a picture of Duane looking defiant in a mugshot.

'No, no, this isn't Keith,' insisted Fred. 'This is *Duane*, the guy who got executed.'

'That's Keith. They were identical twins. Didn't you know?'

'There was nothing in the release . . .'

'Call yourself a journalist.' Jim let out another contemptuous bark. Christ, the guy was cutting. It was Fred's turn to raise his hands in resignation.

'It says that under no circumstances should you or anyone else approach Keith. He's about as dangerous as they come. There are some people on this earth that you can feel sorry for, and my sympathy stretches a long way considering the job I do, and then there are people like Keith Williams. I, for one, cannot find a shred of pity for the man.'

Fred walked out into the bright sunshine on State Street. He didn't know which way to turn. He felt slightly queasy. He was more used to the safety of electronic courtrooms, where case histories were delivered with a structured coherency and reporters didn't even have to be in the same *city* as the trial going on. He could tap in to any court case in the land from his office, and as a man who erred on the side of laziness, that's how he preferred to do his work, at home, in front of the screen. A murky investigation involving a dangerous criminal was the last thing he felt qualified to get involved in. He headed towards the beach.

'If it's the beach, then I must be a hedonist,' he said as

he walked through the crowds of affluent-looking people meandering in and out of shops. At that moment, with the sun shining and the sea in front of him, he found it impossible to imagine the existence of someone like Keith Williams. But he still felt strangely compelled to find the man. It was as if he needed to show himself and the rest of the world that he wasn't just a pleasure-seeker with cowardice in his bones, but that he had the courage and tenacity to rank among the top echelons of his profession.

PHOENIX

18

Within two weeks, the nano-computers reported that 87 per cent of the cells in Body 13 had been restored to working order. It was a distinct improvement on the earlier experiments, but there was still too much necrotic material floating around. Garth weighed up the odds. If they let the body continue on its course of recovery, they could excrete more rotten cells, but they were in danger of inviting a chemical torpor, where all the processes would slow down. That in turn would increase the risk of decay and cellular atrophy. The timing was crucial. Garth decided to bring the body out of its protective bath.

They warmed the temperature of the isotonic fluid and switched the liquid being pumped through the body from plasma substitute to newly cultivated blood. They all watched as the blue lines formed just under the skin.

Once the blood was circulating, the only thing left to do was to winch the corpse out of the bath. They stood around as pulleys inched the body towards the ceiling. The fluid slipped and slithered away from the flesh like unset glue. As soon as the body was suspended above the tank, the team drained and sluiced the lungs and inserted a respirator down the trachea.

'Will you look at that,' said Persis from the other side of the room. Garth joined his colleague. 'We've never had this before.'

Together they witnessed a reflexive quiver in the heart.

'That's way quicker than all of the others.'

Normally, the heart needed the help of an artificial pump for several days.

'He's strong,' said Persis. 'All those workouts in Gamma Gulch really paid off.'

For the next two days, the body was held in suspension while pressure on the heart began to build up. The microscopic readings were indicating that it was getting ready to beat on its own. On the second day, the heart flipped into a spontaneous contraction, automatically shutting down the assist. Everyone on the floor cheered.

'Let's not get ahead of ourselves,' warned Garth. 'We're at the frontier again.'

They warmed the body to a state of anaesthesia and transferred it to a hyperbaric oxygen chamber to increase the blood flow to the brain. They gave the tissue a delicate prodding with transcranial magnetic stimulation, knowing that they could do no more than sit back and wait for the neurons to grow. The forty-seventh chromosome appeared to be working. There were no tumours showing up on the scans or signs of rejection by either body part.

But by the fifth day, there was still not enough neuronal growth. For some reason, which Garth couldn't quite understand, the neurons were the most sluggish of all the body parts to grow.

'I think the heart was a false dawn,' he said miserably as he scoured the fluoroscopes for signs of electrical activity.

They moved the patient from the oxygen chamber to the basement of the building where they planned to keep him in a small room at the end of a long row of abandoned sleep laboratories. The labyrinth of tiny rooms and observation suites was dreary and depressing and no one liked going down there if they didn't have to. Garth wanted to keep it that way. His own secret labs were on the floor below and he didn't want anyone getting curious.

The team existed in a kind of suspension, making microscopic adjustments to the equipment and playing the endless waiting game. They even ran a sweepstake on how many days Body 13 would survive. Garth knew about it, but never placed a bet. He kept a distance from the rest of the staff and wandered aimlessly through the corridors of Icor trying to think of things to do. He played Mozart in his office and attempted to catch up on his paperwork. It was always the same when a new body came on line. Excitement was replaced by an almost intolerable no-man's-land between success and failure.

John Rando called, and so did the President. Garth took the calls in his office. He had never seen the Oval Office from such an intimate position before and promised to contact the President as soon as there was any news. He felt thrilled to get the call but he was also angry that Rick had put him in a position where he would almost certainly have to disappoint the man.

After the calls, Garth realized that there wasn't much more he could do, so he decided to go home to his family, stopping by to take one last look at the patient before heading out. He found Monty sitting by the bed.

'You need to get some sleep,' said Garth.

Monty shook his head. 'One of my uncles died and none of us could get to him in time. I want to make sure the doctor knows there's someone here for him if he wakes up.'

Garth sat down. They were silent for a moment, staring at the bloated, barely recognizable life form they had just created.

'Do you really think that *this* thing is ever going to wake up?' said Garth.

'I don't know,' said Monty innocently. 'I was hoping—'

'Please understand that there's very little chance.'

Garth looked at Monty's round face framed by the hood of his biohazard suit. His usual good-natured, sardonic expression had been replaced by something stubborn and grave.

'Don't get too attached to him, Monty.'

'But we're doing things differently this time, aren't we?'

'Every time is different and I need your dedication across this entire project. I don't want you getting exhausted over one body.'

When Garth had left, Monty looked down at the patient and wiped his swollen brow with a coolant cloth. 'This isn't right,' he whispered. 'This just isn't right.'

19

The telephone became part of Garth's dream. By the third drone he reached out a hand and pressed the touch pad by the bed. It was four o'clock in the morning.

'Sorry that we had to wake you.' It was Persis.

'Tell me,' he said, instantly alert.

'His immune system is fighting the herpes virus.'

Garth's heart sank. 'OK – I'm coming in.'

Garth's wife Claire emerged from under the covers, her tired, handsome face looking bruised from sleep. 'What is it?' she said huskily.

'Something's wrong with the body.'

*

When Garth marched along the corridor towards the patient's room, he could smell the faint traces of liquid nutrients, human waste and sputum filtering through his mask. He found Persis and Monty leaning over the patient. The body was the picture of diabolical medical intervention. His lips were parched and split, his hair matted, and his skin was puffy and engorged. Around his throat the porous silicone bandage was stained with seepage from the graft.

'Jesus, you could have tidied him up a bit,' said Garth.

Persis eyed him defiantly. She clearly didn't like to be rebuked.

'We've been busy. Come take a look at this.'

She showed him an image on the fluoroscope. The herpes virus that they had used as a vector to carry the forty-seventh chromosome to the neurons was being attacked by the body's own immune system.

'OK – here we go. How busy are the antibodies?' asked Garth.

'Gearing up,' said Monty.

'White cell count?'

'Forty-one over five and rising.'

'The resistance is from the Head,' said Persis, trying to blink away tiredness.

'You're right,' said Garth. 'He grew up around a completely different generation of viruses. Those old rogue cells came into contact with the herpes virus and thought they were being invaded.'

'Why hasn't it happened before?' said Monty.

'Because we revived him too early,' said Garth. 'I let too much undoctored material get through. Certainly enough to be an influence.'

'What are we going to do?'

'We're going to clean him up and hope he can fight it,' said Garth.

They worked for the rest of the night, trying everything they could to make the patient comfortable. In a quiet, contained, almost ritualistic way, they bathed him, anointed his skin with aromatic oils and put antiseptic balm on his lips. In his weakened state, the neck wound was showing signs of turning septic, so they scooped spoonfuls of maggots into a special bandage to feast on the infected tissue. But their efforts couldn't stop the infiltration of a predatory infection. Within twenty-four hours, the patient had succumbed to bacterial pneumonia.

'Another souvenir from the turn of the century,' lamented Garth. 'And we were doing so well.'

Reluctantly, they put the major organs back on dialysis.

'I think we have necrosis in the left lung,' said Persis after examining the patient by the afternoon of the following day. Everyone knew what this meant; that pus was gathering in the cavities of the sponge-like alveoli. Too much of it and there was a risk of haemorrhage or complete lobal collapse. Garth took his stethoscope and listened. He could hear the rales; the crackle and bubbling of fluid through the sternum wall.

'You're right. It's pleural effusion. There's very little that we can do for him now.'

'What?' said Persis.

'We've done everything we can. It's up to him now.'

'But we should give him a thoracentesis at least!'

The procedure involved taking a long needle and inserting it through the ribcage to take a sample of fluid from the membrane between the lungs and the chest wall to identify the infection.

'If the pneumonia comes from the past, the Center for Disease Control may have an antibiotic match in their archives,' she added.

'We can't contact the CDC,' said Garth.

'But an old bacterium might still be receptive.'

'I know that!' retorted Garth. 'Can I talk to you, please?'

'What about?' said Persis.

'Outside.'

'I cannot involve the CDC or any other agency,' he whispered to a wide-eyed Persis. They had retreated to an empty sleep lab where the rest of the team couldn't hear them.

'I don't understand.'

'If the CDC is tipped off that the Head brought back infectious bacteria from the past, they will tell the Epidemic Intelligence Service and the EIS will confiscate the body and shut us down.'

'If we show them how careful we're being, they'll work with us, surely?' said Persis.

'You clearly know nothing about the EIS,' said Garth. He lowered his voice and leant in. This was no time to pussyfoot around.

'Five years ago, a number of people died after receiving virally infected organs from these labs. It almost ended my career. I'm not going to let them do that to me again. I've got good data on the ribosome. I think we should sedate the body and let him go.'

Persis's mind was racing. 'Well, I *don't* have good data. There's not a single neuron firing spontaneously. I think we should do everything we can to keep him alive. We're so close, Garth.'

'But the body's infectious. Right now, it's a danger to you, to me and to the outside world.'

'We can keep the infection contained.'

'Then what?'

'It's possible to get illicit supplies of antibiotics from the CDC. Or abroad. I've heard of doctors doing that. I've got contacts. Maybe we can find a match without tipping off the agencies.'

'OK, so we find an antibiotic and it works. If the body survives for any length of time, the EIS will want to see it and take biopsies. They'll find residual evidence of the antibiotic, confiscate the body and shut us down anyway!'

'What you're telling me is that if we present this body to them alive *or* dead, we're in trouble.'

'I hadn't anticipated this,' he said truthfully. 'I brought him out of the bath too early.'

Persis turned away from him. 'OK, so we hide the body from the EIS.'

'That's impossible,' said Garth. 'They'll find out.'

'If they come here, we simply prep another corpse and show them that instead.'

'Where will we get another corpse from?'

'They haven't inspected every single body, have they?'

'No. They did spot checks on all of them except numbers five, nine and ten.'

'OK – nine is a white male. We use nine as our substitute cadaver.'

'Too old.'

'So, we alter the file. Come on, Garth. We can do it. Let me keep this one going for now. I'll take responsibility for finding an antibiotic. If and when the infection clears up, we tell the EIS that he was simply the next body on the production line. If he dies, we register the corpse in the normal way.'

'I can't jeopardize the unit again.'

'You've jeopardized all of our careers with your past

record. And the credibility of the project. Why didn't you tell me? Or Rick?'

It was the first time that Persis had brought Rick up in any discussion between them. Garth looked at the raised vein in her forehead. It was the most angry that he had ever seen her.

'What about Rick? Would he agree to something like this?' asked Garth.

'I'll brief him,' said Persis.

'And the team? Can they be trusted?'

'*You* picked them,' she said, exasperated now. 'Everyone signed a confidentiality agreement with Icor, didn't they? I certainly did. I trust everyone here, don't you?' She looked at him evenly. 'We have our first chance of partial brain recovery and I, for one, am not ready to let that go. Are you?'

Garth didn't know what to say. Their agendas were very different. Persis waited, staring at him, forcing him to decide.

'Go talk to Rick,' he said, and returned to the patient's room where the team were waiting. 'OK, someone go get me a needle. Let's find out what kind of infection we're dealing with.'

The results were as expected. The bacterium didn't show up on the current database, so it must have been present in the Head all along.

The entire team was summoned and briefed about substituting Body 13 if the EIS came to investigate. To Garth's surprise, they seemed to take it well. They too had a lot riding on the success of the programme. After that, everyone, including Garth and Persis, took it in turns to sit beside the patient as he lay on the brink of death. His breathing came in fits and starts and the fever raged across his brow. But there were no tumours growing anywhere on the body, which to Garth was the professional triumph that he'd been looking for. All he had been looking for. Persis had crystallized for him that he was more interested in the control of the chaperone ribosome than the patient's actual survival.

In those first days, Garth couldn't settle on anything. His concentration was shot and he felt a desperate need to talk to someone a long way from the claustrophobic atmosphere of Icor. He decided to call his friend who carried out the reconnection.

'San Diego, Tim Boath, SCI Clinic,' he said to his computer. The camera blinked and within seconds, Tim came into vision.

'You're lucky to get me. I was just flying off to San Francisco. There's been a big construction accident up there.' Tim loved to boast about his heroic dashes to save the critically injured. 'So – does our monster live?'

'I don't think he's going to make it.'

'Another one bites the dust,' said Tim. 'Nothing I did?'

'No. The Head mounted an immune response to one of the vectors. We're playing the waiting game. Tim, I just wanted to say thanks. You're doing a great job.'

'All in a day's work. By the way, when did this one die again?'

'The Head was frozen in 2006.'

'Try and keep him going, will you?'

'Why?'

'I want to ask him how come his generation fucked up the planet for the rest of us.'

'As soon as he wakes up, I'll grant you an audience and you can ask him yourself, but it'll be like talking to a brick wall.'

Garth was grateful for their badinage. It was a release to indulge in some familiar black humour. Deep down he felt as if the whole project was spiralling out of control.

20

By the following morning the patient's condition was no different, so Persis decided she had enough time for her morning walk. Rick, who was still asleep upstairs, had agreed to go along with their plan. He wasn't happy about it, but they had already come too far to do anything else. She passed the security sensor by the front door. The monitor beeped.

'Deliver,' she snapped.

A female voice spoke back to her: '*CO 7 per cent, NO2 9.5 per cent, NOx 15 per cent, PCBs, 28 per cent, PM10, 3.5 per cent, PM2.5—*'

'Now tell me what you really mean,' she said, cutting off the information. 'Deliver,' she repeated. The computer voice spoke again. '*Hazardous Air Pollutants: High Risk. Oxygen advised for exposure of longer than fifteen minutes.*'

Damn! An air warning. Persis opened her coat cupboard and began searching for oxygen. She rattled one tank. It was almost empty. The next was full, so she attached the mask and grabbed an oxygen harness for Hunter, the wolf that she had reared from a pup.

It had been weeks since Persis had been hiking in South Mountain Park. She parked her car at the trailhead and looked at the layer of pollution hanging over Phoenix like a yellow-brown drape. She tilted the angle of the rear-view mirror. She looked like a malevolent insect in her wide-brimmed hat and oxygen mask.

'Is it worth it?' she said to Hunter. He scratched at the car door and whimpered. 'I know you think it is.'

Persis had wanted a wolf cub ever since she'd left New York. He was a magnificent specimen now, with a thick, speckled coat and a white diamond on his forehead, the telltale sign of domestication. He came from a long line of Great Plains wolves that had been bred in captivity for more than fifty years. Their brains had increased in size and they had developed slightly rounder heads.

'Hunter, stay close!' she called out to him as he trotted off up the path. It was illegal to run wolves off the harness, but this early in the morning there would be no one around.

She found herself panting more heavily than usual, a sure sign that she'd lost the edge on her fitness. The mask was making her hot and sticky so she yanked it away from her face. A sharp, sulphuric odour caught in the back of her throat.

In New York, they'd found a way to deal with the pollution and airborne diseases by covering the sidewalks in vacuum-sealed corridors. But Phoenix was different. The city had so few pedestrians that it wasn't economically viable, so people had to wear expensive mini-air purifiers while they scurried from the house to the car or the mall, and on high-risk days, the great outdoors was a luxury for those who could afford oxygen.

Hunter was way out in front of her now, but every few hundred yards he would swing his big head around to check on her progress. Persis wondered what Hunter thought about his life in Arizona and whether he longed for the mountains and the elk, the moose or the wild turkeys that his ancestors would have stalked. He was a great protector, which was necessary since the city had undergone so much upheaval. He was savage on the leash and more than once had scared off dubious characters hanging around the estate. One day, she promised herself, she would take him to Yosemite or Yellowstone, just to see what his reaction would be to the call of the wild.

As she climbed, Persis wondered if she wasn't projecting

her discontent on to her dog. Maybe *she* was the one who felt landlocked. In Manhattan, for all its health crises, she was at home with the struggle, but in Arizona she felt trapped and suffocated. And then there was the interminable year-round heat. It was just past seven-thirty in the morning and yet the rays would beat them back down the hillside in less than fifteen minutes.

They persevered, climbing steadily towards the Hidden Valley. She stopped to take a gulp of water and edged out on to a granite slab that looked out over Phoenix. The city was already shimmering through the haze. She could see Icor's towering headquarters about five miles to the north, wobbling like a line of belly dancers in the heat. Her own house was way beyond that up in the relatively stable community of Carefree. She looked at her watch. Rick would be taking his shower. Persis crouched down and started stabbing at the dirt with a stick. Tears welled up in her eyes. She let out a big cry. Hunter trotted up and nudged his head on to her lap. She tugged at his ears.

'It's just the exhaustion,' she explained.

Hunter looked at her inscrutably, his amber eyes registering her distress.

'If only you could talk.' She stroked the coarse hairs from the diamond on his forehead.

'You could tell me what to do.'

For once, she wasn't talking about work. She was talking about her disintegrating marriage. Hunter lifted his powerful paw and flopped it down on her leg. She sobbed even harder.

PHOENIX

21

It was on the twelfth day of life for Body 13 that the Epidemic Intelligence Service came to call. The delegation arrived unannounced. They had heard about the President's visit, as Garth knew they would, and wanted to check on the patient's progress. Garth had them sent up to his office, then, with jittery fingers, called down to Persis, who was working on the patient.

'Prepare the substitute. You've got twenty minutes.'

Garth shut down his monitors just as the officers walked through the door. There was the regular crew from Phoenix and three people from out of town. Their number and seniority meant that they were taking this visit seriously and would decide here and now if the labs needed further investigation.

'We hear that you have a new body, Garth,' said Dr Kim Andrew icily. She was a woman in her sixties who'd been running the Phoenix arm of the EIS for half of her working life. She still wore her hair in a neat bob, the same style that she had when Garth first met her, only now it was streaked with grey.

'I was just about to register it,' said Garth, trying not to appear nervous.

'Don't get too behind,' she said sternly. 'And I'm sorry we weren't invited to meet with the President.'

'So am I. But it was a surprise to all of us. The President's father is cryonically frozen and he personally knows our chairman, John Rando, who told him about the project.'

'So he stopped by to see it. Just like that.'

'On his way back to Washington.'

Dr Andrew kept a neutral expression, neither believing nor disbelieving. 'So how is the latest incarnation?'

'He didn't make it.'

'I'm sorry to hear that. Can we see the body?'

Can we was not a request but a command. Garth played along with the polite language for now.

'Absolutely. Follow me.'

They descended into the bowels of the building. The showering and suiting took a while. Garth dithered with his own equipment, stalling for time until they grew impatient, then led them towards the sleep laboratories where Persis was waiting. She caught Garth's eye. He looked away and gestured for the officers to inspect the labs. The replacement body was laid out on the gurney. The team began to examine the corpse.

'When did it stop functioning?' said Kim, opening up the mouth.

'In the night.'

'It's cold.'

'He's been in and out of storage.'

She frowned. 'Any advance with your ribosome?'

'Some. But not enough.'

'I can see the tumours. Pity. You'll get there, though.'

That was the odd thing about the EIS. One minute they advanced like a militia, the next they behaved like colleagues with a common goal. They were mostly qualified doctors and nurses but tended to be bureaucrats who longed for status and power, kindly or savage depending on the circumstances. Garth had a fragment of sympathy for the EIS. They were on the front line of fighting disease and had lost many officers to deadly infections. It was one of the toughest jobs in medicine. And the loneliest. Anyone who worked for the EIS had to put up with a wall of hostility from the rest of the scientific and medical communities.

'We need to take tissue samples.'

'Be my guest,' said Garth in a friendly tone.

After they'd bagged their swabs and biopsies and took a good look around the room, they appeared to be satisfied. Garth led them back along the corridor towards the decontamination rooms. Then something caught Dr Andrew's eye.

'What's going on in here?' she said, turning the door handle to another sleep laboratory. It was locked. Garth glanced furtively at Persis. The look on her face told him it was where she had hidden the body.

'Nothing,' said Garth weakly.

'You've got monitors in there,' said Dr Andrew, rattling the handle and peering through a small window in the door. 'Why is this door locked?'

'These are old labs. We have to spread the equipment around,' he said, evading the question.

'I think we need to see this, Garth. Have you got a key?'

Garth felt his insides give way. 'I don't have one on me at the moment. Persis?'

Persis's mouth was open. 'I think so – yes. I'll go find it.'

They waited. The longer Persis was, the more impatient Dr Andrew became, peering through the door window and rattling the handle.

'Why did you lock this?' she said.

'Sometimes it happens during the night,' said Garth. 'You know, security—'

'Hi!' a voice shouted from along the corridor.

The party turned.

'I'm sorry I'm late. I don't think we've met before. My

name is Rick Bandelier, the Director of Operations in Phoenix. Have you got everything you need?'

Even through the mask, Rick's wide, college-boy smile was noticeably handsome.

'I think so,' said Dr Andrew, releasing her grip on the handle.

For once, Garth was glad to see Rick.

'Do you have time to come to my office?' he said jovially, playing host. 'I'd like to discuss something with you. I've prepared brunch, if you're interested.'

'After we've seen what's going on here,' said Dr Andrew.

'Tell you what, I'll get security to find the key and you can take a look after brunch.'

Somehow, the forcefulness behind his invitation swayed them. Garth glanced at Persis. She looked as panicked as he did.

Rick did the full public relations act with the EIS, bombarding them with questions about their work and wondering what Icor could do to make their lives easier. He also apologized for not including them in the President's visit.

'We asked if we could invite the local agencies, including the EIS,' said Rick, 'but the President insisted that he wanted total privacy. He was only here for what—' Rick looked at Garth.

'Less than an hour?'

'That's right. He was in a hurry.'

Garth could see that Kim knew exactly what Rick was doing, but she was prepared to tolerate his charm nonetheless. What youth and good looks can do to smooth things over. She even forgot about the locked room.

Once they left, Garth overcame his innate hostility towards Rick and thanked him for his timing before going back downstairs to his office. He slumped in his chair. He couldn't take many more days like this. He turned on the observation cameras and watched the nursing staff moving the patient back into his room. He wondered just what kind of trouble Persis was leading them into. But there was no going back. Like she said, they were all implicated now.

22

Garth couldn't sleep at all that night, so after his wife had drifted off, he went to his study and opened up the computer file on Dr Nathaniel Sheehan. He felt he needed to build up some kind of attachment to the Head, to justify keeping it alive, deceive the EIS and put his career on the line for the second time in his life.

There was a reasonable amount of information on the man: two certificates, a letter and a collection of newspaper articles. It was a lot more than Icor kept on most of the early collection. Some of the heads and bodies, particularly the ones from the 1960s and '70s, before records were computerized, had no documentation at all. Maybe a name and a storage number, but that was about it.

For Dr Sheehan, they still had the medical degree from University College of Los Angeles, a certificate commemorating the day he became a Fellow of the American Academy of Family Practitioners and a letter confirming the start date of a PhD in community medicine at Cedar's Sinai Hospital.

'Busy guy,' said Garth.

There was also a newspaper cutting with a colour photograph of the doctor standing next to the Governor of California at the opening of a free clinic in a poor neighbourhood of Los Angeles. The headline read: GOV. DAVIS GIVES HEALTH CARE A BOOST.'

The Governor was tall and slim with a pin head, stately blue-grey hair and an over-cranked, corporate grin. He had his arm around Dr Sheehan, who was also smiling.

Garth thought the doctor looked handsome enough, with his sandy, spiky hair, warm, expressive brown eyes, straight nose and air of genuine humility. It was useful to have an image from the past. His face was completely distorted from all those years in cryonic suspension.

Then there were dozens of cuttings and articles detailing the doctor's tragic death at the hands of a teenage shooter in Los Angeles and the decision by the man's wife to freeze his head immediately after the murder, and a final cutting from a medical magazine printed in the 2030s when Dr Sheehan was known simply as 'the Head'. A group of scientists had carried out a forensic examination to discover how much tissue had been damaged during the freezing process.

'Fate is not satisfied with inflicting one calamity,' muttered Garth. He looked across the screen at the file of Duane Williams. It was a much bigger file, but he didn't want to go there. Not right now. He was about to turn off the light when the web cam buzzed on his desk. He hit the receive button so Claire wouldn't pick up in the bedroom.

'You're still at work?' he said, surprised to see Persis.

'The antibiotics arrived this evening. We've got him on a drip.'

'What's his condition?'

'His temperature is finally back to normal.'

Garth's mood lifted. 'Well, I wasn't expecting to hear that anytime soon.'

'There's more,' she said. She was calm but there was a twitch of a smile dancing around her lips.

'Tell me!'

'We've identified some activity in a number of axons

descending from the rostral spinal cord to a few millimetres beyond the graft.'

Garth hit the desk with his fist.

'And Garth, I know it's late, but there's a light show going on that I think you might like to see.'

Garth drove through the deserted streets like a maniac, slowing only to pass the armoured tanks of the National Guard. Their search beams followed his car, but he knew they wouldn't stop him. Their security readings would show that he had clearance to be out after curfew.

The building felt eerie as he charged through the decontamination process. When he reached the observation room, he found that most of the team were present. They dutifully parted when they saw him. He looked at the fluoroscopes and there it was, a weak shimmer of light flickering in the brainstem. It looked as ephemeral and vulnerable as fireflies in a moonlit meadow.

'No help from us,' he said.

'Totally spontaneous,' said Persis.

'I cannot believe it.'

'Neither can I.'

He forgot his composure and hugged Persis tightly to his chest.

23

No one had anticipated what to do beyond the most basic survival of Body 13. There was no programme of recuperation set up or existing course of therapy to refer to. But as each day passed, Garth observed that the team was becoming more protective towards the patient. They were showing incredible devotion, working beyond their normal hours to make sure that he was comfortable and keeping abreast of all the charts that marked his progress. It was the kind of loyalty that Garth had been looking for in his team from the very beginning. It had never occurred to him that the simple fact of creating a living thing would do the trick.

Every morning, either Garth or Persis held a meeting where they mapped out the cellular recovery of the patient and swapped suggestions over how treatment should progress.

'OK, if I could have some attention,' said Garth to the gathered assembly. 'Persis has some great news for us. Persis?'

'I am delighted to report that the stem cell infusions and my semaphorin stimulator have recovered whole sections of the frontal lobes, the corpus callosum and the limbic system in the Sheehan brain.'

The team cheered.

'And the brainstem has reached a stage where it can operate the homeostatic regulation by itself.'

'When are we going to let the brainstem run the body?' asked one of the staff.

'Today,' announced Garth.

'Then what happens?' said Monty.

'To restore cognitive function, I'm going to have to be the head gardener with my computerized pruning shears and cull the extraneous neurons,' said Persis. 'I worked on living brain tissue when I was at NYU and have had some spectacular results in neuro-regeneration in living patients, but only to specific areas. I've never had such an extensive amount of damage to repair before. What I do know is that there's going to be a lot of crossed wires and some very strange bodily reactions, so be prepared.'

*

THE WAKING

After the meeting, Persis sought out Garth in his office. There was a lot more that needed to be discussed and not in front of the team. She found him looking out of the window.

'Don't you think we should talk about it?' she said.

Garth spun around in his chair. 'Talk about what?'

'Duane Williams.'

Garth had known this conversation was coming and he'd been dreading it because he didn't have any answers.

'What's your thinking?'

Persis sat down. 'He has the locus of control first. My guess is, he's going to want to keep it.'

'Has it been total hubris on our part?'

They were silent for a moment.

'When you suggested we seek cadavers from the prison system,' said Garth, 'I had no idea we would actually be *reviving* them.'

'Then what they say is true,' said Persis.

'What?'

'That we really are in an era where the technology is outgrowing us.'

'I'm wondering if we should terminate him,' said Garth.

'I don't know how you can say that.'

More silence.

'But what are we getting ourselves into?'

Persis frowned. 'The Williams brainstem is working.'

'Go on.'

'He is going to recover core consciousness in a matter of days.'

'What would that be like? Do you have any comparative data?'

'No. He will be alive and he will be conscious, in the sense of being aware of what is happening to him and of having a *self* that things are happening to, but he will have no intellectual capacity to process that information. He will inhabit a world that is sightless, soundless and wordless.'

Persis looked at him then, the sun glinting in the corner of her hazel eyes.

'An automaton?'

'Almost.'

'What was Williams's mental condition when you met him?' said Garth, leaning back in his chair. He really didn't want to hear it.

'Wastebasket category – diagnosed with every hue of the anti-social personality spectrum. Childhood socialized into brutality, head injuries, damage showing up in the limbic area, episodic aggression, manipulation, severe memory disorder, abnormal sexual behaviour. Significantly, there were no abnormalities in his autonomic nervous system and he showed normal levels of anxiety, so he wasn't a psychopath.'

'That's something.'

She didn't smile.

'In spite of the diagnosis, the brainstem was pretty much unscathed, which is why I selected him.'

'What did he do to end up on Death Row?'

'He raped, sodomized and beat a young girl to death.'

Garth put his head in his hands and moaned. 'I don't feel qualified for this.'

'I feel as concerned as you do.'

'*Concerned?* I feel a little bit more than concerned at this juncture.'

'I don't think we should be pessimistic, Garth. Maybe the Sheehan brain will have the power to control the body once the intellect has been recovered. Maybe the brainstem will have no residual influence. And maybe we'll lose him before we even get that far.'

'That's a lot of maybes.'

THE WAKING

'You *are* qualified to take care of the body, Garth. Let me take care of the mind. I think we should carry on. I *definitely* think we should carry on.'

Garth's mood was sinking fast. If only they had been more cautious about their choices, but they were so wooed by the idea of using fit, younger bodies to take them further than the older, worn-out cadavers could ever do. He cursed himself for agreeing to use the prison system. But then maybe, another maybe, they would never have reached this point in the project if they hadn't.

LOS ANGELES

24

Like so many stories that Fred dreamed would win him a major award, the Duane Williams execution still amounted to no more than a few lines in his ideas file. He put in the occasional call to the FBI to check if there'd been any sightings of Duane's brother, Keith, but when they came back negative, he'd all but forgotten the landmark article that he was going to write for *The Metropolitan*. Then one night, while he was cruising the Internet, he came across a list of the FBI's most wanted. And there was a tape of Keith Williams. The file included an interview with Duane's sister, Bobbie. It jolted Fred out of his screen-induced torpor. He would give Bobbie a call. No harm done. It was just a call. She agreed to see him immediately, almost sounded as though she expected it. He arranged to see her the following day.

Fred felt distinctly uncomfortable as he drove into Bobbie's neighbourhood on the outskirts of San Luis Obispo. She lived in a 'kit park', where rolling hills of scrubland had been covered by clip-together housing. The parks spread out over the edge of most Californian towns and cities like filthy checked tablecloths. They were supposed to provide temporary housing for the millions of people flooding into California after the first outbreaks, but many were still in use after forty years.

A battered sign saying '*Welcome to Sunnygrove*' gave Fred no comfort. He parked his car and fretted about leaving it unattended as he picked his way over the detritus of a scavenger's front yard. The ragged screen door swung open and the hefty woman greeted him. Bobbie Williams waddled over to a sofa and sat stout and wheezing, waiting for him to say something. She had the same bruised and pouting down-turned mouth as her brothers.

'Where are you from again?' she said, looking dazed and incoherent.

Fred felt sorry for her. She was wearing a shapeless dress that looked like a number of pieces of material crudely stitched together.

'CTV.'

'That's right – CTV.' Bobbie shifted in her seat as though it would make a difference to his impression of her.

'I covered Duane's execution and it always struck me that there was much more to this case,' explained Fred as he made his way round the frayed furniture and found a free space on another sofa. 'You said your brother Duane had a tough life. Can you tell me about that?'

'I don't like to go back there too much.'

'I understand, and I don't want to push you, but I'm looking to do a sympathetic piece,' offered Fred, and waited for her to speak.

'It is my belief that Duane was never really wanted by anyone.'

'Why didn't anyone want him?'

'He was strange.'

'In what way?'

'He got hurt as a kid and he was never the same, you know?'

'No, I don't know,' said Fred. 'How did he get hurt?'

She looked out of the window. Her chin began to wobble. 'All I remember is Dad laying into Mom one day. We hid under the bed to stay out of trouble. When Dad finished with Mom, he came looking for us. We was whimpering but trying to stay quiet. Duane kind of fell on me to protect me. Daddy saw his foot poking out from under the bed and pulled Duane's leg and started up. Duane got this lump on his head. I remember touching it. We called it his second head. He never smiled much after that. Later, much later, when we was all grown up, he would just sit there looking at nothing. He was kind of smart as well as dumb. Called himself a mind-reader and reckoned he could see things about people. But he never saw the outcome of things about himself. He never thought ahead of hisself and that's what got him into trouble. He wasn't bad in the heart, he was just – impressionable – you know? If someone said, "Follow me," he would tag along after them like a puppy dog. Keith knew it and took advantage.'

Bobbie dabbed her eyes with a tissue, as though she was wiping away tears. But there were no real tears. It was the most curious of gestures. Fred figured that she had told the story so many times that she had cried all the tears she could cry. He might even use that as a line.

'Your brother – is it Keith?' Fred left it as a casual aside, as though it was of no particular interest.

'Keith,' she said, neither confirming nor denying the fact of her other brother.

'Did he want to come to the execution?' Fred said the word *execution* in a quiet, respectful tone.

'I don't know and I don't care.'

'Where is he now?'

'He's on the FBI's top fifty most wanted list. That's all I know. Last year he was in the top ten. I don't know how they work these things out,' she added, as if Keith was a key figure in the world of entertainment.

'What's he wanted for?'

'Murder, rape,' she said, as though she was listing his attributes.

Fred took a brief look at his surroundings and saw several holes in the wall where someone had put a fist or a boot through the sheet rock.

'Does he ever come by here?' he said, trying to sound fearless.

The very thought drew an asthmatic wheeze from Bobbie's chest and he could hear the invisible cobweb constricting her bronchial tubes. Her mouth closed around her breath like a bite. Maybe she'd suffered at the hands of Keith Williams too.

'If my husband saw Keith anywhere near this house, he would take that gun and do whatever he needs to do. The only place where Keith deserves to be is taking a dirt nap in Sunnygrove cemetery.'

Fred followed the direction of her gaze and saw a gigantic F140 rifle by the door.

'So Keith dominated Duane?'

'He put a ring through his nose and put a chain on it. Do this. Do that. Duane would do anything for his brother.'

'Including murder?'

'He didn't kill nobody.'

Fred heard rustling from a cupboard. Terror seized him as the door creaked open a notch. Inside the recess he could see soft dark shapes climbing and tumbling over one another. It was a litter of kittens.

'Who did then?' ventured Fred, breathing out.

She stared at him, mistrustful. 'None of my brothers was down at Pebble Creek Canyon that night,' she concluded, and for a moment they sat in silence. Fred glanced furtively at the pile of undulating fur in the cupboard.

'You like kittens?'

'Sure.'

She waddled over and opened up the cupboard. 'Three weeks old.'

A mother cat stared out at them ruefully, her belly being kneaded by a dozen tiny paws.

'Want one?'

'I have a no pets thing where I live.'

'Oh,' she said disapprovingly.

Now it was Fred's turn to shift in his seat. He wanted to keep the interview on track and get something useful after coming all this way. 'It struck me as unusual that Duane would sign up for the willed body programme and give his body to medical science. Did you know anything about that?'

'Like I said – he had a kind heart.'

Is that so? thought Fred. *So kind he raped and throttled the life out of a young girl.* He was getting irritated now.

'Do you have any mementos of Duane?'

'I have his letters from Gamma Gulch, if that's what you're talkin' 'bout.'

At last. 'Great. Can I see them?'

She padded off to another room, knocking into bits of furniture as she went, and returned with a shoebox full of letters.

'This is unusual,' said Fred, sorting briefly through the treasure trove. 'No one writes letters any more. Only people over a hundred.'

'Or people with no access,' said Bobbie.

'True,' said Fred.

The letters were written in a sorry scrawl on tissue-thin prison paper. Fred picked out the first letter and began to read:

THE WAKING

Dear Sis,

I am sitting here in T-shirt and shorts and it's like a boiling hot day down here in the dungeon. The coolers have broken down and we all have to sit here. We're all dying slowly. There isn't no windows and so when we can, we stand under these shafts that got glass up at the top and look at the sky. Yesterday was my first time to stand under there. I saw a bird sis. It felt so good to see the bird. What we would all give to see a green blade of grass or a stream. Some guys go nuts in here and we hear them screaming, especially when the power goes off. There was an outage last week and two guys never stopped screaming all night. It sure shook us all up.

I'm in a bit of trouble sis. There was a fight in the canteen and I went to help Johnny and I got ground into the floor by a guard. I have been in isolation for four days now. Inside of me is this tension and I think about that single blade of grass. That's me and it's green and shiny and ridged like the first grass of spring.

I mustn't fight them. Or they will mow me down. So we do stuff to make it OK. Last week, which seems like so long ago, we had a scar competition of who had the worst scar and I won sis. It's the only competition I ever won in my life. It was the chunk out of my butt that got me first place – you know where Pappy's pit bull bit me? It's funny – but a lot of my friends turn the scars into tattoos. I was thinking of having a snake tattooed on my forehead to cover up the scar there – maybe you remember it – under my hair – but I don't want to get them done in here cos the needles are dirty and I must be the only one left on Death Row who doesn't have Hep P.

I know my life has been a disappointment to you sis – many things I have done have been unbecoming – but I want to tell you that I love you and always have. Death is all

*around us all the time and makes us full of hate and
despair. Some fight it, but they get beaten for it. I don't
because I've seen what happens. I am optimistic that the
people that made my head this way is going to be known by
the American public and that I will be venerated [crossed
out] vindicated. One of the guards found that word for me
and I like it. We have to read our letters to them out loud,
which took a long time. Pray for me little sis. I am an
innocent man and this is no right what is happening to me.*

 Your loving brother,

Duane

'Do you ever wonder, Bobbie, what *did* happen that night
down at Pebble Creek Canyon?' asked Fred.

The late-afternoon sun was sending unkind shadows
across the folds of Bobbie's flesh.

'Like I said – none of my brothers was there – so why
should I think about it?'

'OK,' said Fred, getting up. If she was going to toe the
family line, he wasn't going to waste any more time.

'May I borrow these and copy them?' he said.

'Is this the last time I'm going to see them?'

'No, I'll get them back to you, I promise,' said Fred,
smiling with practised charm but remembering all the times
he'd forgotten to return precious mementos to interviewees.
He *would* be good this time. After all, he was an investigative
journalist now.

As he shook Bobbie's hand, he realized that it had been
seven months since Duane had been executed and the body
might already have been disposed of or stored as tissue
samples in a freezer somewhere. He resolved to hit the phones
the very next day and get back on the trail of Duane Williams
as soon as possible.

25

'What was it Abe Lincoln said?'

Dr Kim Andrew's face looked pinched, her expression haughty on the web cam. Garth could read instantly that this wasn't a social call. It was late at night and she'd worked hard to find him in his office, even calling his home, which he thought was out of line.

'I don't know. Abe Lincoln said a lot of things,' said Garth warily. Her approach sounded like a verbal entrapment and he wasn't sure how to play it.

'Abe Lincoln said, "You can fool all of the people some of the time—"'

'"Some of the people all of the time—"'

'"But you can't fool *all* of the people *all* of the time." Tell me, Garth, just who do you think you're fooling?'

'What's on your mind, Kim?' Garth hated games, especially when he was on the losing side with the Epidemic Intelligence Service.

'Our tissue samples were *interesting*.'

'I'm glad to hear it.'

'We dated the head back to the mid-1960s.'

'You're exactly right,' said Garth. '1966 to be precise. I'm impressed.'

'I didn't know you had many cadavers left from that era now.'

'We've got a handful. It's useful to have them at this stage in the game.'

He wanted her to get to the point.

'You work in ice and we don't, so we borrowed a new machine from forensics.' She was watching for his reaction.

'And?'

'You'll be glad to hear that it's inconclusive . . .'

Garth relaxed. She had nothing. This was a fishing expedition.

'But it's our reckoning that your reconnected body died a good while before you said it did.'

'You're right,' said Garth. 'It didn't get beyond the first few days.'

Her mouth narrowed. 'So why did you lie to me?'

'If you want to know the truth, Kim, we wanted to look good in front of the President. His expectations are extremely high, so we said the latest body survived for a few days longer than it did. You got caught up in our exaggeration. I'm sorry.'

'That's a strange thing to do.'

'I agree. I think it was a mistake and I apologize.'

'You make my job very difficult, Garth. I don't want to have to come back with a warrant.'

'I'm more than happy for you to come back,' he bluffed. 'I think we'll be doing the next reconnection in two to three weeks and I'll show you everything I've got. There's nothing to hide.'

'Garth, I want you to know one thing. I am only *ever* concerned about the health of the nation. You've done nothing to make me take any further action so far – except lie.'

They both knew that if she did return to Icor with a warrant, she and her colleagues would be obliged to shut the unit down, temporarily at least, which in the long run could set his progress back months. Garth could tell she was reluctant to take such a dramatic measure. He was also convinced that the keen interest shown by the President was another reason for her caution. Rick had been right. Like Rick said, he was an important friend in a very high place.

'Everything is above board here, Kim. Our progress is

slow and that head was a no-hoper from the start. Too old. Too weak.'

'I don't ever want to come across another divarication like that. It makes my own reports look incomplete. And should anything ever happen and I was the one who overlooked it . . . do you understand what this could mean for us both?'

'Perfectly.'

After she'd gone, Garth switched on the cameras to look at the patient. They had brought in a mechanical suspension cradle, an elegant contraption of wired pulleys and old-fashioned canvas slings that held the body in a state of levitation, lifting, turning and rolling the limbs at regular intervals to simulate movements while the patient was sleeping. It was the best way to prevent external infections and get the body used to movement once it was fully functional. It was normally used on people who'd suffered major strokes and couldn't move.

Garth felt calmer as he observed the slow, delicate adjustments the cradle made. But he still couldn't quite believe what was happening. Every time he thought about the consequences of keeping the body alive, he felt a tightening in his chest. It would have been so much easier to let the body go when it contracted pneumonia. But he had deferred to Persis, which he felt was a weakness in his leadership. On the other hand, if they handled it right, the breakthrough was undoubtedly going to make him a household name. And Persis too. Garth wondered if he was up to coping with the changes that would inevitably come: the attention, the plaudits, the lecture tours, the fame. While he was lost in his thoughts, he hadn't heard his door open. He looked up. Persis was standing in the doorway with two cups of coffee.

'Do we have home lives?'

'I wonder.'

'You watch him too.' She nodded at his screen.

'It's my meditation.'

'It's like he's falling through water.'

'The EIS just called. Witchfinder Andrew.'

Persis tensed. 'What did she want?'

'She knows that we lied about the body.'

'Are they coming?'

'No. I think I got away with it. I told them we exaggerated the body's length of survival time to impress the President. I think she accepted it. I also told her that we had a new body coming on line in a matter of weeks and that she could come and see that.'

Persis breathed out. 'Well, I think we're near the waking.'

Garth couldn't help but smile. 'Tell me more.'

'There's just about enough activity between the Sheehan brain and the Williams brainstem to finally activate all the neurotransmitters that we can. He has full sensory function and today, I set him a number of habituation and dishabituation tasks. He managed them all without help from the nanos. I'm getting ready to take all the props away and see how he does on his own. I just want to make sure you're fully behind this. Because I think beyond this point, it will be a huge problem to dispose of him.'

Garth looked at her lovely oval face. He could see dark rings under her eyes.

'Of course I am,' he said. 'We'll do it first thing in the morning.'

He stood up and reached for his coffee. He felt a familiar ache in his knees. The project was taking its toll on all of them.

LOS ANGELES

26

The tallest cup of coffee imaginable. That was the promise
Fred made to get himself out of bed. He would make a special
trip to the mall, come back with a tower of coffee, then hit the
lines of communication on the Duane Williams story. That's
what he was going to do, no shilly-shallying around. But
when he did eventually return from the mall, he considered
cleaning the place up a bit. Though he knew it was just
another diversionary tactic.

'You lazy faggot,' he said as he finally sat down at his
desk and began to punch in numbers. He contacted all the air
ambulance services in the Yucca Valley and quickly found the
one that carried bodies from Gamma Gulch State Penitentiary.
He asked the service where they had taken Duane Williams.
The young man at the end of the line said they weren't
supplied with names, so Fred gave him a date. He confirmed
that the airline *had* transported a body from Gamma Gulch on
that day but refused to tell him where it had been delivered.

'Who was your client?' pushed Fred.

'If we're not gonna tell you where we took it, we're not
gonna tell you who the client is,' said the guy, and hung up.

Fred called a contact in air traffic control and asked if
there was any record of the flight. The contact came back
immediately. The air ambulance had flown to Phoenix.

'You can be very good at this game when you try,' he said
to himself. 'Only a morning's work and you've already got a
destination.'

Fred trawled the Internet for medical companies who

operated out of Phoenix and called every single one, asking them straight up what kind of medical research they were working on. Sometimes he used other company names to suggest he knew more than he did. Some were forthcoming. Some were not. No one would admit to working with cadavers.

Fred got back to the air ambulance service and when a different person answered, he said he was from lost baggage in Phoenix and trying to return a bag to a pilot. He explained that the bag had been lost in the system for seven months. Fred gave them the date of the flight and his number and pretended to read out a reclaim number. When they asked him if he had a name, he said he couldn't read the writing on his message board and that he'd just come on duty. Playing lazy and disinterested came easily to Fred. The air ambulance company said they would pass his message on.

The following day, the pilot, Jay Ruby, called back and said he couldn't remember losing any bag in Phoenix. Fred confessed immediately that he'd made the story up to ensure that his message got through. People usually took that kind of confession two ways; either they thought he was honest for owning up to a lie or they rejected him out of hand. Jay Ruby stayed on the line. Fred told Ruby that he was writing an article about private aviation and he knew that Jay was one of the most experienced pilots in the region (a calculated guess including a little flattery usually worked) and he wanted to talk to Jay about his job.

That afternoon, Fred pulled into a dust-ridden, palm tree-lined street on the outskirts of Riverside, a town which could still lay claim to a presence above ground, when so many other inland empire cities had gone underground. The inhabitants were clearly trying to maintain some kind of landscaping, in spite of the winds that drove sand drifts into every nook and cranny.

A certain gloom settled over Fred. It was the kind of street where he could envisage his own destiny being played out in the slow lane, his feet up on the verandah with not too much to think about than maybe taking a trip to Cabazon or Palm Springs when the winds weren't up.

A small, squat man with a grey buzz-cut answered the door.

'Jay Ruby?' said Fred.

'I recognized your name from the TV,' said Ruby. 'Come on in.' He showed Fred through the house to a shaded courtyard. The blistering heat stilled the air. Fred spotted what must have been Ruby's wife taking shy peeks at him through the screened kitchen window. Ruby didn't offer him anything to drink, so Fred got straight to the point. And lied.

'As I told you, I'm writing an article about private aviation.'

For fifteen minutes they discussed the kinds of journeys Jay made: the regular run that a businessman took to San Diego; the antique dealers who flew between San Luis Obispo and San Francisco. Excruciatingly dull stuff and Fred felt like screaming, but he kept an eyebrow raised in a facial display of sincerity and interest.

'Do you ever carry any unusual cargo?' he asked.

The pilot droned on about some animal emergency. Fred pretended to find the story both fascinating and amusing by turns. When he saw a gap, he homed in.

'You travelled to Phoenix last year. What was that for?'

The pilot ran his hands over his cropped hair, enjoying the friction. 'Phoenix – Phoenix.' He clicked his dry, cracked fingers. 'That's right. It was real peculiar. It was a body. Why didn't I remember this before?'

'Memories are strange things,' said Fred blandly.

'The body was stored in this big metal coffin. We had to take out some seating to get it in.'

'Is this a regular run?'

'Nope. Single order. Never done it before nor since.'

'Do you remember who was travelling with it? Maybe I can get in touch with them.'

'It was a man and a woman. I don't remember much about them. They were pretty quiet.'

Fred had shortlisted four of the biggest medical companies in Phoenix so he had a one in four chance of being right about the body's destination.

'Was it for Medicorps?'

'Don't think so.'

'Hoffman La Roche?'

'Definitely no. I do work for them but up to the Bay area.'

'Adronium Industries?'

'Nope.'

'Icor Incorporated?'

'Could be.'

'That's interesting,' said Fred, 'because this company is part of my story. They ship a lot of farmed organs around the country, hearts, kidneys and livers, that kind of thing.'

'I keep a record of all my clients. Do you want me to go check?'

'Sure,' said Fred.

The pilot disappeared and Fred found himself examining a petrified, leafless bougainvillea nailed to the wall. He glanced at the kitchen window and saw Ruby's wife disappear into the shadows, then he heard a muffled conversation from inside. When Ruby returned, Fred could tell instantly, by the nuance in the man's expression, that he was about to be shown the door.

'I can't help you, I'm sorry,' said the pilot.

'That's OK,' said Fred, standing up, 'it's been really useful.'

The pilot blew air into his cheeks.

'Was it Icor?' said Fred, feigning nonchalance. He couldn't resist another prompt.

Although Jay Ruby shook his head, Fred could tell that he was lying and was a man who didn't like to lie. And now Fred had a name.

PHOENIX

27

As they strode towards the patient's room, they could hear
the hum of conversation welling up from the observation
room. It sounded as though there was a party going on. The
entire team had turned up to watch the waking. Even in his
biohazard suit, Garth could sense the moisture forming in
his palms. He didn't feel comfortable about having an audience, but he thought that it would be churlish to dismiss
everyone, considering the amount of hours they'd put into
care for the patient. He greeted his colleagues warmly and
gave the go-ahead. The nano-machines that had been rebuild-
ing and supporting the brain structures up until now were
switched off, gang by gang, and the neurotransmitters were
finally activated. Almost imperceptibly, the body shivered and
the breath faltered.

'What's happening?' pressed Garth.

'It's OK,' said Monty, checking his readings. 'He's adjusting to the change.'

Silence fell as everyone scoured the face for signs of
movement. Persis kept her eye on her 3-D imager. The shut-
down had momentarily lowered brain activity by more than
half, but now she could see the polyrhythmic interplay of the
different brain regions start to fire up again, this time on their
own.

'He's preparing to do something – possibly move his
hand,' she said as she studied the temporal patterns. But for
several minutes he lay there, completely inert.

'Maybe I spoke too soon,' she said.

THE WAKING

Then, just as everyone was giving up hope of seeing any physical reaction, the patient tried to swallow. In what looked like a titanic effort, he licked his lips and struggled to open his eyes. Only the muscles on one side of his face appeared to be working under the autonomy of the new nervous system.

'We need to moisturize the mouth,' said Garth.

'And someone should have combed his hair,' said Persis, looking sideways at Monty.

'I keep doing it,' said Monty, 'but it has a will of its own.'

'Let's hope that extends to the rest of him,' said Garth.

They stopped talking when the patient's hand rose up to touch the bandage around his neck.

'So I was right,' said Persis.

'And we've just made history,' announced Garth, his voice sounding strange to him. 'With absolutely no prompting, a message has travelled from the brain through the graft to the hand, and the hand moved of its own volition. Finally, I can say that we have a waking.'

Suddenly, the mouth was stretching wide in a rictus of agony and a hideous guttural sound could be heard from deep down in the throat, like something heavy being dragged along a wooden floor. The patient's eyes bulged and his back arched as the body went rigid. No one who saw it would ever forget that first awful, silent scream and the terror in the eyes. Then his arms and legs began to jerk uncontrollably.

'He's having a seizure,' said Persis.

'He needs an ENG inhibitor,' said Garth.

Persis reached into the patient's mouth to catch the tongue. He bit down. She screamed and sprang away. It took four men to hold the body while Monty administered a shot.

'It's OK,' Monty comforted. 'You're not ready for us yet. You will be. But you need our help for a little while longer. Sleep now.'

'Let me see that,' said Garth, grabbing Persis's hand.

She had tears in her eyes. 'I think he broke through the suit.'

'And the skin. You better go get that checked right away.' She hovered.

'Now,' he ordered. 'And, Monty, put him in stays.'

Garth leant over the patient. 'Welcome back, Dr Sheehan.'

There was a flicker of half-closed eyes, but no response.

BOOK TWO

REINCARNATION

In everyone there sleeps
A sense of life lived according to love.

PHILIP LARKIN (1922–85)

28

'MARY!!!!!!!'

Nate prised open one eye. Horrible scratching lids scraping at his eyeballs. The light above him, a frosted-glass tub surrounded by a metal grid, had a pearly blur around it. He felt a searing pain in his left knee. He tried to lift up his leg to relieve it, but it wouldn't budge. He tried other parts of his body and with all his might he managed to turn his head an inch towards the observation window.

'MARRRYYYY!!!!!!!'

No sound. He felt his whole body ache as though it was trapped inside an iron cage. '*Locked-in syndrome*,' he'd heard the doctor say. When – yesterday? A week ago? He had no concept of time. He knew what the guy meant. The brainstem controlling his movement had been killed off by a massive stroke and he was like some creature before human beings crawled out of the slime. Every part of him felt poisoned and his heels hurt.

'HELP ME! SOMEBODY PLEASE HELP ME!!!!'

He was trying to recall how he came to be lying in this windowless room. The words came to him again: '*Locked-in syndrome.*' How dare the doctor say that in front of him? It was the worst prognosis you could give to anyone, especially a doctor, who would know what it meant. It left people incarcerated in their own skeletons, unable to move anything except their eyelids. They didn't last long either. And why was everyone wearing biohazard suits? Was he contagious?

Nate lifted his arm and let it fall on to his chest. Great. If he could move, his brainstem was working and he definitely wasn't '*locked-in*'. With numbed fingers, he felt a scar through the bandage; a raised mole-track of smooth, hard flesh coursing down his sternum. Had he had a heart attack followed by a stroke? Christ! He was only thirty-seven!

Maybe he didn't have long to live. Or maybe he *was* actually dead and lying on a slab somewhere and the residue of his soul was conjuring up this room, these thoughts.

'Is my toe tagged?' he said to himself.

He tried to lift up his head to take a look, but he knew there was a stab of pain in his neck, only the pain itself felt strange and faraway, not in his own body.

He heard rustling close to his ear, but he couldn't make out what it was. Slowly and with colossal effort, he moved his hand from his chest to his neck. He felt a huge bandage and an engorged lump underneath. After a while he could discern movement under the bandage. Something was alive under there! Terror welled up in him and he tried shouting but nothing came out.

After what seemed like an age, a young black woman strode in and positioned herself at the bottom of the bed. If he'd had a voice, he would have balled her out for neglecting him. If she *had* been neglecting him. Maybe she was an angel of death come to float him up and out of this place.

'Hi there, Nate. I'm Harmony,' said the woman in a smoky voice. She looked far off in the corner of the room. He wanted to reach out and touch her, just to make sure she was real.

'I'm a physical therapist and I visit you every morning to get you warmed up for the day.'

Nate was convinced he'd never seen her before.

She deposited a group of bottles on a metal tray and began to rub oil into her gloved palms. She pulled back his blanket and raised a knee. Blessed relief. She began to massage oil into his skin and at the same time pull his leg straight and bend it again. He had to be alive to experience this, surely, but his leg looked so alien to him, so much thinner than he remembered it. He must have lost a lot of weight. The skin was different too, more sallow. Was he jaundiced on top of everything else? His poor liver.

He tried to stay focused and thought about her name. Harmony – the spirit of cohesion, the perfect blend of notes in music. Concord. *'What is the discord of this concord?'* The sentence hung there. Where was it from? Shakespeare? Words were like scattered things, a meteor shower tumbling through the galaxy of his consciousness.

Harmony. With a gap in her front teeth so wide he could slot a dime through it. He began to dream of ice melting, and wolves in raincoats, and rubies dripping on to a pavement; strange, weird, hallucinatory images floating in and out. But he was wide awake. How could he be seeing these things and thinking these things and still be awake?

Harmony grabbed his right hand. 'Try to squeeze for me,' she said.

He imagined himself throttling her hand but their meshed fingers turned into a nest of writhing snakes. He clamped his eyes shut to try to rid himself of the hallucination.

He realized that large parts of his body had little or no feeling. When she touched his skin, it felt coarse and scratchy. His teeth clenched. He couldn't stand things scratching on other things, like chalk on a blackboard. They made him feel hysterical.

Now Harmony was working on his left side, grabbing his left hand.

'Squeeze for me, Nate.'

He squeezed.

'It works,' she exclaimed. 'We have a functioning hand.

Oh yes, this hand will be able to prise open a tub of ice cream in a couple of weeks. Now you can let go.'

The hand stayed clenched.

'Let go,' she said. 'Dr Sheehan, let go.'

The hand refused.

She had to pull his fingers open. 'OK – so we know *that* hand is functioning.'

She pulled some kind of tunic over his head. He didn't recognize the clothing or the material, which was coarse yet soft. Then, finally, she ran her wide, flat thumbs across his forehead, then down around his cheeks, and curled them expertly under his chin.

'I bet you were a fine-looking man in your day,' she said.

'What is she talking about? This *is* my day!' he railed silently.

A huge black guy came into the room and helped Harmony turn Nate's body over. They were tending to his bottom, wiping and drying and chatting. It was bizarre, gossiping over his buttocks, but medicine was like that. Nate remembered all the times that he had casually talked over the heads of stroke patients as if they weren't there. If he ever recovered, he promised himself he would be more attentive. He learnt that the tall guy's name was Okorie Chimwe. He was from Nigeria and was studying to be a nurse. Harmony congratulated him for getting out of Africa.

'You got to be some kind of Houdini,' she said.

He could sense pressure on his backside as they worked on him but he could only hear the sounds they were making. His skin barely registered the sensation.

'Will you look at that?' said Harmony.

'I guess they didn't zap everything,' said Okorie. 'That is one hell of a tattoo.' And they were both laughing as they flipped Nate back over.

'This is the part I really hate,' said Okorie, coming in close to Nate's face. He began to cut the bandage on Nate's neck. 'Ugghh – Harmony. Will you check this out? I can't even look.'

Harmony squinted at Nate's neck. 'There's only one infected spot now. Be clear in a couple of days.'

'I don't know how you can look,' said Okorie.

'After what you been through? Don't be such a baby,' she said, scooping a spoonful of maggots into a bag. She pretended to throw the bag at Okorie, who leapt out of the way.

'Baby,' she said, laughing.

She applied a fresh batch then resealed the bandage.

Nate tried to think. Maggots eat infected flesh, leaving healthy flesh alone. But treating wounds with maggots was a practice dating back to the Middle Ages. And what was he doing with an infection in his neck?

'You got the suit ready?' said Harmony.

'Right here.'

They raised up the bed and Nate was staring at what looked like a medieval suit of armour.

'I'll go get the doctor,' said Okorie.

'You do that,' said Harmony. 'Nate, you've been in the suit a number of times. It's a full body-stroke recovery suit. The doctor likes to be here when you put it on.'

A man came in. Nate recognized him. It was the doctor who said he had 'locked-in syndrome'. There were others too, but he didn't have the strength to turn his head. He so desperately wanted to talk, to be briefed on what was happening, but he couldn't muster the words, let alone say them.

'Good morning, Nate,' said the doctor. 'Can you hear me today?'

Nate tried to communicate with his eyes.

'He's beginning to look more normal,' said the doctor

cheerfully, examining Nate's face. 'The swelling has gone down and the skin tone looks more like bruising. Nate, can you hear me?' The doctor looked over to a blonde woman who was sitting in front of a fluoroscope.

'Registered,' she said.

'Nate, scans of your auditory cortex tell us that you *can* hear us. You have been unconscious for a very long time and have suffered the equivalent of a series of major strokes and some of your brain areas aren't working yet. But as you know, great strides can be made in a short space of time if we work on it. And we *are* working on it at the cellular level. We just want to work on you now.'

The only thing that Nate could do was wiggle the swollen fingers of his left hand. The doctor noticed it and smiled.

'Thank you, Nate. I take that as your first greeting.'

Two technicians began to unstrap the coat of armour.

'This is a titanium stroke recovery suit,' explained the doctor. 'It's lined with its own electromagnetic vasculature system of graphite fibre bundles that can pick up electrical pulses from your brain and translate them into movement. Basically, you can *think* of something like walking and the suit will do it for you. Don't worry, we will operate the suit until you can control the body movements yourself.'

He felt nauseous as they helped him into a sitting position and strapped him in. He heard someone typing, then the suit let out an electronic wheeze. Nate felt his legs being parted and hauled into standing position. There was a pause while they adjusted the catheter attached to his penis.

'Nate?' said the doctor.

'He heard that,' said the blonde woman.

'OK, Nate,' said the doctor, 'the suit is going to act like your skeleton until your own muscles are strong enough to move you independently. The suit will only compensate for what you can't do by yourself. You may remember from yesterday that I told you it works like a dream on stroke patients who've got locked-in syndrome.'

That prognosis again. How could he go on saying it when Nate could move his hand?

They programmed the suit and Nate was forced to take a step forward. Each hiss of air thrust one foot in front of the other in a cruel mimicry of a puppet. After half a dozen steps, they turned Nate around, walked him back to his bed and sat him down.

'He hasn't taken a single breath,' said another voice.

'Nate, can you breathe?' said the doctor. 'Open your mouth and inhale.'

Nate couldn't understand the instruction. He seemed stuck in a moment of suspension between life and death. His lungs were bursting, then someone yanked his mouth open and he sucked in air.

'How's the brainstem?' said the doctor.

'Normal. It's the connections,' said the female voice.

'I thought he was going to need CPR for a moment there.'

Just then the catheter got dislodged and everyone was sprayed in urine.

'That's enough of a workout for today,' said Garth, dusting himself down. 'Well done, Nate. Each day we take one step forward and today you took a dozen steps, so that has to be good.'

Nate vomited all the way down the front of his suit.

He was grateful to be put back into bed. It was a place where he felt safe and could conjure up the illusion that he had some privacy. He felt so sick in every cell of his body, a leaden feeling of indescribable awfulness, that he wanted to die and hoped that it would come soon. *Locked-in syndrome.* Who needed it?

A little while later, the blonde woman returned. She barely acknowledged his presence but went quietly about her business, changing programmes and cleaning up the software on her computer screens. When she'd finished her chores, she came over and pressed down on the bandage around his neck, which sent a shockwave of pain through him.

'So where are you, Duane?' she whispered. 'Did we really say goodbye to you at Gamma Gulch or have you been hibernating?' She peered deep into Nate's half-open eyes. He tried to focus on her, to get her to take her hand away.

'The mind-reader. Well, you're about to live under the autonomy of another man's impulses. Don't come back to haunt us, OK? We've got enough problems as it is.'

Nate couldn't understand what she was talking about. She was still leaning too hard on his bandage and an ache shot right through his skull. How could she be so insensitive?

'Is that a tear on your cheek?' she said. 'It must be a leaking tear duct.' She fetched a cloth and wiped his face, then her face screwed up in disgust. 'I can't wait to get rid of those maggots!'

Nate could hear a faint hiss as they fed on the residual infected tissue that was lodged in the folds of his neck graft.

'I know I shouldn't be squeamish, but I just can't stand them.' She turned to leave, then lingered by the door. 'Have a peaceful night, Nate, and we'll see you tomorrow.'

LOS ANGELES

29

Fred's home office was like a cockpit, with a scrim of screens banked up on all four walls around a circular desk. He was plugged into every national news network in the country so he could plunder their archives at a moment's notice. Some days, when he was editing a story, he felt like a wild composer, flipping from one news source to another and slamming the keyboards with a maestro's flourish.

He'd been trawling the networks for information about the use of cadavers in medicine, but had got distracted by the red flash of a health alert in Louisiana, so for the last few minutes he'd been tracking the progress of an outbreak of dengue fever that had crept into the Mississippi basin, its tendrils spreading up through the swamps and beyond. He watched the little red dots marking all the new cases as they were being recorded, thousands of dots filling the screen like blood clots blotting out the map. There were frightening images of riots as a mob set fire to a tip where contaminated medical waste had been illegally dumped. Thank God he lived in California, which was relatively clear of epidemics right now. When it got too depressing, Fred flipped back to his research.

If he'd read the pilot Jay Ruby's expression correctly, Icor was where the body of Duane Williams ended up. It didn't take much trawling to discover that Icor was one of the biggest medical conglomerates in the world. He chastised himself for not even knowing. Considering he was trying to become an investigative reporter, he could be shockingly badly informed.

He found footage of the chairman, John Rando, attending the 121st World Economic Forum at Davos in Switzerland and looking deadly and inscrutable as he made a speech. Fred felt envy for people like Rando who clearly had the clarity and the focus to become extraordinarily successful, travelling the world in their hermetically sealed cars and planes, beyond the legal restrictions of the rest of the population.

The Center for Regrowth in Phoenix was a tiny operation compared to the size and global might of the company. According to one story, the regrowth programme was kept going for prestige. It was barely profitable, but it saved thousands of lives every year. Fred found a medical digital library with images of the medical director, Dr Garth Bannerman, giving one or two hesitant lectures to various institutes.

Fred liked to familiarize himself with photographs or recordings of people he was about to interview. He conjured up how the conversation would go, always leading, in his imagination, to a positive outcome. Dr Bannerman was a modest-looking man with a bookish, intelligent face. As Fred watched his lecture, he felt it would be easy to charm the doctor with the promise of some kind of media exposure. The medical profession were just as anxious for recognition as anyone else for all the years of underpaid work that they had to put in to keep their demanding jobs.

When Fred felt ready, he tapped in Icor's number. He always preferred to call people direct, rather than going through public relations. All they ever did was waste his time and put up reasons for not cooperating.

'*We thank you for calling, but Doctor Bannerman is not available at this time,*' said the automated secretary on the web cam. '*Would you like him to contact you?*'

'No thanks,' said Fred. He didn't like leaving messages. Then he had an excuse to call again. He put in a dozen or so calls over the next couple of days and each time the message-blocker came on. Then he tried early in the morning, a good time for catching professionals, and the doctor appeared on the screen, looking every bit the academic that Fred was expecting.

'What can I do for you?' asked Dr Bannerman.

For a moment, Fred's brain went blank. It was a nasty little trick that his mind played on him when he was anxious for information.

'I'm doing a story for *The Metropolitan*,' he blurted. 'It's about what happens to people who donate their bodies to medical science. I've been tracking a cadaver that was transported from Gamma Gulch State Penitentiary to Icor in Phoenix. I have a very simple request, Dr Bannerman. I just wanted to ask you what the body is being used for.'

The doctor sat up so suddenly that the top of his head disappeared from the screen before the camera sensor could follow the doctor's iris and swing upward.

'The body belonged to Duane Williams. I reported on his execution. He signed up for the willed body programme and I understand that his corpse ended up with you. It's really a feature story, Dr Bannerman. All I want to know is what you are working on that involves Duane Williams's corpse.'

The web cam shut down. Fred violently prodded the retrieve button. He tried calling back, but the message-blocker was back on.

Maybe Fred had come at it too bluntly. He should have arranged to see the doctor, gain his trust, and then allow the man to open up in his own time. Fred felt green for revealing his true mission. He was great at lying to people who didn't threaten his intellect and yet when someone smart came along, he was easily flummoxed.

'Why are people so reluctant to talk about cadavers?' he

said to his blurred reflection on the screen. They'd probably raided the Williams body for tissue samples to identify some obscure neuropeptide. So what was the big deal? Money. That's what it was usually about. Money. Maybe the secrecy itself could be the story.

In his stark, empty office Garth's finger remained poised above the disconnect button for quite a while. He fumbled on his keyboard and called his boss's emergency number.

'Rick, I've just been contacted by a journalist,' said Garth, his voice sounding annoyingly shrill. 'He knows about Duane Williams. How the hell did he get hold of the story?'

'Was it Fred Arlin?' said Rick.

Garth looked for the name on his screen. 'Yes. Do you know him?'

'I got a message from head office about him last night. The public relations department have been watching him.'

'Why?'

'He's been asking a lot of questions about where cadavers go after they leave Gamma Gulch.'

'This could be a disaster!' spluttered Garth. 'We can't afford to have any – anything get out about this.'

'I know that, but according to Jeffrey Chatham, we've got nothing to worry about.'

'Why didn't you tell me?!'

'I *was* going to tell you,' said Rick. 'I had an early morning conference call. Look, why don't you contact public relations yourself? Talk to them about it.'

'Believe me, I will,' said Garth. In a rage, he found the number of Icor's head office in Savannah. The chief executive of public relations, Jeffrey Chatham, sat down. Garth knew him to be a devious strategist with a ferocious reputation.

'You have nothing to worry about,' Chatham assured

Garth. 'He covers court cases and executions out of Los Angeles. Believe me, this man's story is going nowhere.'

'He said he knows the body ended up in Phoenix,' said Garth. 'That's not *nowhere*.'

Chatham's eyes narrowed. 'The reporter knows it ended up in Phoenix but that's all he knows. We've asked around and he's a second-rate TV reporter. He's trying to sell some kind of medical feature to *The Metropolitan*, but so far he has no story and no commission. It's our reckoning that he'll make a few more calls and that will be that. The last thing we should do is overreact.'

'Why the *hell* didn't you tell me—'

'I told Rick Bandelier.'

' – directly?' Garth knew he was sounding petulant but he blundered on all the same. 'Messages don't always get through to the people who need to hear them most. I could have made a serious breach of confidentiality.'

'Well, it's a mark of your capabilities, Dr Bannerman, that you handled it as well as you did.'

'You made a serious error of judgement, not coming to me first.'

'Did I?'

Chatham's mouth set and Garth felt in his bones that he'd just made the kind of corporate enemy that could damage his career. Chatham was the classic personality type who could bear a grudge for thirty years.

'What's to stop him publishing what he already knows?'

'What's the story? Bodies go to Icor for scientific research. I don't think so. And if he tries to make moves on *The Metropolitan* we will discredit him and squash whatever comes up. He's already had his licence revoked once. We can make it happen again. Dr Bannerman, I come across journalists like this all the time. Every day. Look how calm I am.

We're going to throw this guy a bone this afternoon and put him off the scent and that will be the end of it.'

'What kind of bone?'

'I'll let you know in a couple of days. If he calls again, say casually that he needs to contact me. Now, is there anything else I can do for you?'

Garth felt dismissed. He retrieved the image of the journalist and looked at his handsome, fatuous face with its conventional square jaw and sincere tweak of an eyebrow, honed to suggest curiosity and seriousness. He could see that all the reporter was really thinking about was himself and the impression he was making. And that rather strange tan infusion that so many people were using. He did look slightly ludicrous. Chatham was right. This man was no threat. He was just looking to hustle a reputation.

From his office window, Garth looked out at the scorched earth of the Arizona Desert. Suddenly, he felt like a small ripple in a very big pond. In the labyrinthine workings of the corporation, physical reincarnation was a rich man's pipe dream, a project personally supported by an ageing chairman and the President, but that still wasn't enough to garner the respect of the public relations department. Garth watched his computer blink messages as they came in from the journalist. He wondered what hellish impact there would be if the story ever did get out.

Fred was still wondering why Dr Bannerman didn't want to talk to him when another call came through on the web cam. It was Duane Williams's lawyer, Jim Hutton.

'How're you doing?' the lawyer said, his rheumy eyes peering intently into the lens.

'Keeping busy. You?'

'It's all good, Mr Arlin. All good. Now, I *know* you will

want to hear *this* piece of information,' said Hutton with goading emphasis.

'What is it?'

'I've always wanted to say this and now I'm getting my chance. We've found the body.'

'Whose body?'

'Duane Williams's body.'

'How the hell did you do that?'

'I got a call.'

'Who from?'

'The University of San Diego.'

At last, a real lead.

'He ended up there?'

'In the anatomy department. But the question is, Mr Arlin – are you man enough to go see it?

PHOENIX

30

A fly landed on Nate's nose and he made a gallant effort to pucker his lower lip, pull the upper one back and blow. The fly didn't move. Wretched fly. Arrogantly sliding its legs over one another. Legs that were fully functional. Nate crossed his eyes, a feat in itself which he knew instinctively he couldn't manage days before. He could see that the fly was idly enjoying its full potential as an insect, while *he* could scratch nothing to relieve the intolerable burden of his itching skin. How did the fly get in here anyway? Wasn't this supposed to be a hermetically sealed unit?

Nate must have drifted off because he jerked awake to the beep, beep, beep of one of the monitoring machines. The feeding tube had come adrift and he was soaked, although he could only sense the wetness. His skin was still too numb to actually feel it. The bandage across his stomach was curled up and peeling after being saturated by the nutrient bag.

'*NURSE!!!!!*' he shouted silently.

Very little equipment surrounding Nate was recognizable to him, or the casual single-piece uniforms the nurses wore, or the hologram screens they worked with, or the silence of the machinery and the eerie rooms he inhabited. It was like a space station and it made Nate anxious, particularly as not one visitor had been to see him, not Mary, any of his friends, his mother, father or sister. He just couldn't understand it, and when he wasn't feeling exhausted and confused, it filled him with terror. He could only imagine that he was in some experimental stroke unit and that, for some reason, no visitors were allowed.

Nate was beginning to recognize his carers and he was already dividing them into two camps: those who regularly checked to see if he was OK after they had done their chores and those who didn't. He resented the way some of the staff, including the blonde woman, never looked at him, but dealt with his body as though he wasn't there. He wanted to grab them and tell them that he was human. Just like them.

'*NURSE!!!!!*' Another silent wail.

He craned his neck an inch towards the observation window. Who was behind the reflective grey sheen this morning? And how could they neglect him like this?

A few minutes later, Okorie stormed in, clucked at the mess, reattached the nutrient bag and changed Nate's urine sack without uttering a single word. At least the maggot-infested bandage around his neck had been taken off. He heard them say that the infection had cleared up. When he touched the wound, it felt like a huge hillock of scar tissue, as if his throat had been cut from ear to ear. This made him even more fearful. He was trying to remember what the hell had happened to him, but he couldn't recall a single thing.

His speech therapist, Karen Mackie, arrived a little while later. She was the opposite of the indifferent camp. If anything, Karen had compassion overload.

'There you go,' she would say after everything he did. He figured that he could defecate all over the bed and she would smile lovingly and say, 'There you go, Nate. Right on target.'

It was hard to tell Karen's age, but Nate reckoned that she was probably in her mid-fifties. She must have been very beautiful once with her big, expressive mouth and sad grey eyes. She was pure West Coast stock, inquiring, empathetic, liberal and slightly spacey. He knew for sure that she'd grown up in Northern California.

As she was preparing for their morning session, by rigging up various screens, Nate let his mind wander. He hoped he had been eligible for a tissue plasminogen activator within three hours of the strokes. It would restore blood flow to dead or dying tissue in his brain. The drugs were a newish generation of clot-breakers that had come on the market, but were only useful in a minority of stroke patients admitted to the ER. He was relieved that those kinds of details were coming back to him. And his heart. He wondered exactly what procedure they had carried out on that. Was it a triple bypass? Or, heaven forbid, a transplant? He thought about his wife. He couldn't believe that Mary would desert him now. She was his life. He was her life. They had been inseparable ever since they met, so why had she not been to see him?

What devastated Nate was that he could not picture her face. He could recall individual features – her eyelashes when she was reading, the curl of dark hair around her ear, the mole on her neck – but he couldn't make them whole.

Karen raised the headrest so that Nate was in a sitting position. She opened his mouth and placed a flat spatula at the back of his tongue.

'OK – we've done this many times,' she said sweetly.

Have we? thought Nate. He knew Karen. She'd been in his room and he'd made judgements about her, but he couldn't remember anything else.

'I want you to press your tongue against the spatula and close your throat. This is a workout for your swallow reflex.'

She pressed down on his tongue. Nate found it surprisingly hard to work against the pressure.

'Every day, I'm seeing a little bit of improvement in you,' she said brightly. 'You've got some weakness, but it *will* come back and then we can put you on solid food. Our resident neurotechnologist, Dr Persis Bandelier, tells me that you have language comprehension now, so you can understand some of what I'm saying but you don't have language production. They're two dissociable processes in the brain, as I'm sure you can remember, Nate, so I'm just going to talk at you and hope that you're taking in the information. Don't feel the pressure of having to respond. I'm going to repeat everything I say many times over. Oh, and next week, we're going to give you a new epiglottis, larynx and vocal cords. How about that, Nate – a whole new voice?'

And how were they going to do that, he wondered. Did they have synthetic replacements now? He'd never read about it.

'We've got quite a bit of work to do, but I know your mind is working. I can see it and feel it. Keep on thinking, Nate. Thinking is healthy.'

Karen brought up a picture on the screen. Nate could see it was round.

'This is the human brain. If you were well educated, which I reckon you must have been way back then, you would know that a right-handed heterosexual male carries ninety-five per cent of his language receptors in his left brain, unlike women where it's less, maybe eighty per cent. The language areas in your left hemisphere got badly damaged.'

She highlighted areas in blue on the picture.

'*Voilà* – all the damage that we have recorded in your brain.'

There seemed to be a lot of blue.

'If you can't see this image clearly, Nate, it's because there is some damage to your visual cortex too. But, as each day passes, the blue spots or damage will *decrease* and your brain map will end up with no colour at all. Your cerebellum will be as active and productive as any normal brain, possibly even better. We could be producing a genius here,' she said, and laughed her tinkling laugh.

'I just want to remind you of the list of qualities located in each hemisphere.'

Writing appeared on the screen. Karen read it for him.

Left Hemisphere	Right Hemisphere
Analytical	*Dreamier*
Logical	*Holistic – sees patterns of behaviour*
Time-sensitive	
Precise	*Emotional hunches*
Detail-oriented	*Pessimism*
Breaks down patterns into parts	*Fearful*
	Mournful
Left side cannot see wood for the trees	*Sensory perception*
	Abstract cognition

'If you understand the lists, then you can see where you are deficient in the left brain,' said Karen.

Nate was looking intently at the screen, trying to make sense of it. The written lists were replaced by another indecipherable image.

'Personally, I love the right hemisphere and the work it does. All those hunches and intuition. It's the stuff of life. But as a highly emotional female, I would say that.' She smiled. 'The two hemispheres are connected by a neural bridge of eighty million axons called the *corpus callosum*. You've got some damage there too. All this may sound scary, Nate, but we're not worried. There's a lot of cellular repair work going on and in no time at all, you will have recovered your integrity and you will barely remember these days. We've just got to get the left hemisphere up to speed, that's all.'

Karen called for help and two medical workers arrived to strap Nate into the recovery suit. He flinched as he heard the electrode insert into his neck and plug itself directly into his nervous system, but it didn't hurt, and to think of some action and have it happen was simply a miracle. He knew of a mechanical arm being developed somewhere on the East Coast, but never a whole suit. Mary must have found this hospital and campaigned to get them to take him. He imagined her investigating the best facilities available and negotiating his passage. The thought comforted him as he mentally instructed the suit to stand up. It breathed into life. He took several strides to the door. Karen opened it and he strode down the corridor. He didn't stop this time, but continued walking, craning his neck to see if there were any other patients on his ward. All the other rooms were empty. He heard Karen calling after him, but he ignored her. He wanted to see what lay beyond his own passageway. He turned a corner and found more identical rooms, only this time the cheeriness was replaced by gloomy dark green paint and dim lighting. He walked on down another windowless corridor and another and turned a corner to find Karen waiting like a worried parent outside his room. This was no hospital. The hum he could hear made him think he was in the engine room of some giant building.

'Now where did you go?' asked Karen, her anxiety level showing by the slight flush in her cheeks. 'I was just about to call security to come and find you. It's not very hospitable down here,' she said ruefully.

Nate slumped on the bed and looked up at her, his eyes burning with despair. She touched his forehead with the back of her hand, like a mother feeling a child for fever. He turned away. Left brain damage or no left brain damage, big questions loomed large in his mind, like where was he? And where *the hell* was his wife?

31

Fred was made suspicious by the fact that on the very morning he contacted Icor Incorporated directly, the body of Duane Williams just happened to turn up in the anatomy department of San Diego University. Even to a rookie reporter like himself, it was too much of a coincidence. But on the other hand, a big part of him wanted to believe that he had found the body and was advancing his story. As a general news reporter, he wasn't used to spending more than a day on anything and was determined to come up with something after all this effort.

He turned down a wide-berthed boulevard, lined with eucalyptus trees, and stopped his BMW at the electronic security gates. A sensor scanned the ID panel on his car.

'Fred Arlin, Welcome to San Diego University,' said an unctuous, disembodied voice. 'How can we serve you today?'

'I'm here to see Dr Rahmani.'

The barrier lifted and Fred saw the building where Dr Rahmani taught anatomy. It was like so many modern architectural edifices of the age; technocentric, with all the energy-saving devices exposed to the elements. It was shaped like the bow of a ship going into a fine point at one end, with water cascading down translucent, metallic sides as though it was cutting through waves. It was a clever idea, thought Fred, with the water acting as a coolant, while huge solar panels jutted out over the roof like giant sails.

He headed for the entrance and found a list of professors' names, but absolutely no indication as to where anyone worked. How could the best brains in the country occupy so splendid a building and not even have room numbers? Fred made his way along a corridor and found a woman sitting at her desk.

'Where can I find Dr Rahmani?' he asked.

The woman kept on writing, just to show him how annoyed she was at being interrupted. 'Third floor – take a right and a left and his office is second on the left,' she said without looking up.

Fred stared at her in a daze. None of it had gone in, but he didn't feel up to asking again. After running into a few faceless students who obliged with directions, Fred found Rahmani's office. It was empty. He looked around, leafed through a couple of printed science papers on the desk, and was about to give up when he saw a technician sprinting along a walkway in a white coat.

'Can you tell me where Dr Rahmani is?' he shouted.

'At home.'

'You're kidding. We have an appointment.'

'Ah – but did you confirm?' said the technician, who looked Korean.

'Yes.'

'But did you confirm *this morning*?' The student was clearly delighted that here was further evidence of his boss's inertia.

'I was driving down from Los Angeles this morning.'

'You'll get him at home.'

Fred called from Rahmani's office and found a man of weary indifference at the other end of the line. He noted the faint traces of an Asian accent, but plummy and over-enunciated as though he'd been to a British public school.

'I can make it in twenty minutes,' Rahmani told him without a flicker of enthusiasm.

*

'Why the visit?' said the Korean, walking into the office.

'I've come to see the body of Duane Williams. He was executed at Gamma Gulch State Penitentiary last year and he donated his corpse to the willed body programme. His lawyer told me he was here.'

The Korean looked confused. 'I don't think so.'

'His lawyer said that his body was shipped in from Phoenix.'

The Korean frowned and shook his head. 'I can take you to the storage room if you like. Maybe we'll find him.'

He led Fred to a pair of vast silver doors. A blast of cold, sweet-smelling air hit them as the man slid them open. Fred peered inside. A row of low-level lights cast shadows down a long, narrow room. Stacked on either side were mobile metal shelves like baking trays. At first Fred couldn't comprehend what he was seeing, then his eyes grew accustomed to familiar shapes and mounds: jutting hipbones, jagged shoulders, slackened arms, hands and feet all covered in shimmering crystals. The room must be harbouring at least sixty bodies. Fred looked at his own gusts of whitened breath.

'We've got a surplus right now,' said the Korean.

'What type of people donate their bodies?'

'Community-minded people, lecturers, doctors, lawyers. There's a judge over there. Judge Ramirez.'

Fred could see the ridge of a hipbone and a mound of grey pubic hair crystallized in ice.

'That would be amazing—' Fred said.

'What?'

'If Duane ended up lying next to a judge.'

'In death, we are all the same. You said this guy was a killer?'

'Yes. Why?'

'We love looking at the brains of those people. The bad boys.'

'Do you know where Duane is?'

'No.'

'You must keep a list of who you have.'

'Sure.'

'So we can just go check, right?'

'Hello, hello, hello! And what are we doing in the storage bay?'

A big, resonant voice echoed in the frosted room, making them both jump. A tall, skinny Asian man was leaning against a shelf. He was wearing a shiny orange jerkin and had thick wafts of jet-black hair which tumbled over his bulging eyes.

'Just helping your visitor out,' said the Korean with an averted gaze.

'You need *my* permission to come in here, don't you? And yet here you are with a *journalist*!'

The man fixed the technician with a guru's penetrating stare. The Korean blushed.

'You must be Dr Rahmani,' said Fred.

'The last time I looked.'

'Can you point out to me where Duane Williams is?' pressed Fred, trying to divert attention away from the Korean.

'Oh, he's not in *here*. He's in the dissection room.'

Rahmani spun around and charged off. Fred and the Korean trotted after him until they arrived at an impressive atrium. Rahmani flung the doors open.

'Don't stop for me. Carry on. CARRY ON!' he hollered.

When Fred's eyes adjusted to the brightness, he realized that several teams of students were dissecting corpses on slabs. Some of the chest cavities were pinned back. Others had femoral vessels exposed. The entire auditorium was shielded from direct sunlight by a suspended cobweb of UV-resistant mesh.

'You wanted to ask me about the willed body programme?' bellowed Rahmani. 'Well, here it is. I started all this, you know. If it wasn't for me, there wouldn't be a decent anatomy department in the whole of Southern California!'

Fred could feel the ego of the man bouncing off the walls. He looked gingerly about him. The banality of death was both underwhelming and overwhelming at the same time. Here he was in the company of at least a dozen corpses who had once walked and talked and loved and laughed and cried, and now they were reduced to slabs of meat. He had to keep checking himself to see if his legs were going to buckle.

Rahmani strode off to inspect a table where a headless corpse was being worked on, a surgical towel covering the neck. The students dutifully stood back. Fred noticed how waxen the skin looked without blood flow.

'Here's our man!' shouted Dr Rahmani.

'Where's the head?'

'He was – ah – he was—' He blustered with bombastic casualness. 'Oh – I don't know. I think the neurology department has it.'

'Can I see it?'

'There won't be anything to see now. Hungry?'

Fred could tell that the doctor was bored and tetchy, but before he could say that his appetite had completely vanished, Rahmani was ushering him towards the door.

'I have a question.' Fred was trying to keep up. 'Why would you bring Duane's body all the way from Phoenix?'

'We take cadavers from all over the country.'

'Do you know *why* it stopped off at Phoenix, at Icor Incorporated?'

Rahmani spun around, coming in close to Fred's face. Too close. 'Maybe they wanted some particular cell type or piece of tissue that they're working on. I don't know. I don't keep track.'

Damn. Fred was really looking for confirmation that the body *had* stopped off in Phoenix, but Rahmani was being evasive.

'I thought you kept a list of everyone.'

'No.'

'You *must* have a list.'

'We don't keep a list, no.' It was such a silly thing for Rahmani to lie about because it was so patently untrue. Even in lying, he was lazy. 'It's confidential,' he fudged.

'Oh, so there *is* a list.'

Rahmani looked at his watch. 'OK, there *is* a list.'

'So we could go and check.'

'Look, I'm sorry, but I don't have time. I need to prep for a meeting.'

'But I've come all the way from Los Angeles under instructions from Duane Williams's attorney—'

'Jin – will you show this delightful young man to the canteen. And no more unscheduled trips to the body store.'

After another penetrating glare, the professor cantered off, his trouser legs flapping around his beanpole legs. Fred felt a sudden fury that he had been led on a road to nowhere. He wondered why Rahmani had agreed to see him in the first place.

The resentment stayed with Fred all the way back to Los Angeles. When he arrived at his office, he could still smell the sweetened air of the dissection room on his clothes. Maybe he should let the story go. Even if it had been Duane's body, which he doubted, how could he challenge the evidence they had presented to him? And was the story interesting enough anyway?

Idly, he took out the old shoebox containing the letters from Duane to his sister Bobbie. He felt immediate guilt that he'd failed to return them as he had promised. He leafed through them and felt a tingling in his fingers when he thought that they had actually been written by a killer. But when he started to read them, he was soon bored. They all contained the same tone of self-pity and blame, admonishing the guards for their cruelty and railing against his lawyers for their inaction.

'It's always someone else's fault,' said Fred as he threw the letters back in the box. Then he noticed a disc at the bottom with the words '*me in Gamma Gulch*' scrawled on it. He inserted it into his machine. And there on the screen were images of Duane in his prison cell, goofing around for a cellmate, playing with a towel and flicking it at the camera. There were other images too: of Duane in provocative mood, reclining on his cell bed and being flirtatious. It was a poster-boy pose, displaying all of Duane's washboard stomach. Fred was stunned. He replayed the disc. Duane's torso was covered in tattoos. The body that Rahmani had shown him was completely clean. Why would they go to such lengths to mislead him? And if they were trying to mislead him, how could they be so clumsy? He didn't look that stupid, did he? Smarting from that possibility, Fred got on the web cam and called Jim Hutton.

'You sent me on a wild goose chase.'

Fred could see the lawyer's nose twitch. 'How so?'

'I went down to San Diego University and I was shown a body but it wasn't Duane's body.'

'Tell me more.'

Fred told him about the visit to San Diego, Dr Rahmani's

indifference and the disparity between the body in the dissection room and the tattooed body on the disc.

'It sounds like a good old-fashioned case of body misplacement to me, Fred. Maybe you have stumbled across a *real* story here. Forgive me for thinking that you never had it in you.'

'What shall I do now?' asked Fred plaintively.

'I'm not your college tutor. Use your head, kid.'

'Come on. Help me out here. Who contacted you about the body?'

Fred was beginning to like Jim Hutton. His curt manner and punishing rebukes appealed to Fred's hangdog need to be mocked.

'Someone at Gamma Gulch.'

'Care to elaborate?'

'I can't, but if you were misled, then so was I. And if Icor Incorporated are involved and set this whole thing up, they clearly don't want you to get any closer to this story.'

'So what do I do?' said Fred.

There was a deep breath of exasperation at the other end. 'Why don't you try getting closer to *them*?'

Fred laughed. 'OK. OK.'

He plundered the Internet with greater excitement for the rest of the afternoon. He tracked down the financial accounts of San Diego University and there it was, the bombshell he had almost been expecting. The biggest sponsor of the anatomy programme was Icor Incorporated. A thrill unfurled in his stomach. For the first time in his career, he was working on a real story. He was no fool, and Icor's arrogant attempt to dupe him was going to backfire.

PHOENIX

32

Nate tried to quell the fear rising up through his body. He told himself it was the right brain flooding his left brain with negativity, just like Karen had said, but he still couldn't figure out why Mary hadn't been to see him. Had she left him because of his injuries? Had she sat by his bedside while he was unconscious and found it all too much? He'd seen that happen in cases of spinal column injuries or strokes and secretly despised the cowards who deserted their husbands, wives or friends in their hour of need. But that wasn't Mary. There must be something going on or she would be by his side. His inability to talk was beginning to make him feel like a muzzled lunatic.

He tried to coach himself into a more optimistic frame of mind by piecing together all the good things about his marriage, like how they met. It was a story they'd talked about so often that it had taken on the texture of bedrock in the foundations of their marriage.

Nate had gone with his pal David to a whacked-out conference on consciousness in Santa Fe. David had been invited to talk about identifying the areas of the brain that became hyperactive during meditation. Nate couldn't stand the faith-healer fraternity at these conferences, their worshipful faces smiling in rapt attention while visiting neurologists deigned to talk to them, but a few days in a beautiful desert setting made the idea seem bearable. Besides, he could write it off against tax.

He dragged himself to a few lectures, including David's,

and noticed among the audience a slender woman with unruly, sexy, dark brown hair. He wasn't particularly attracted to her. She had a narrow hook to her nose, a strong, jutting jaw and horn-rimmed glasses. He categorized her as a preppie Jewish New Yorker, spiky and uncooperative, but he figured that she might be good for a distraction, so he edged his way towards her during the coffee recess. She was holed up in the centre of a small crowd and was talking animatedly, her slender hands cutting and chopping the air for emphasis.

'What did you think of the talk?' he'd asked when there was a gap in the conversation.

'What did I think?' she said, looking confused. 'About the lecturer or the topic?'

He felt immediately on the ball. 'The lecturer.'

'David De Souza? He's a total charlatan.' She looked at his nametag. 'What are you doing here, Dr Nathaniel Sheehan?'

'I'm with David De Souza.'

She laughed. He loved the freedom in that laugh. Later, he would notice how her green eyes would light up at the prospect of any mischief. But she wasn't malicious. It was just an escape route for her quicksilver mind.

'So are you two together as one?' she mocked, crossing her fingers. 'You know, partners?'

'You mean am I gay? Not unless I have a twin that I don't know about.'

He found out over the next few days, as they missed lecture after lecture and tore up their hotel rooms with their lovemaking, that far from being spoiled and difficult, Mary was passionate, generous and honest. And she was on to him immediately.

'I bet you're categorizing this as your fling in the desert,' she said to him.

'No I'm not,' he protested.

'Well, I hope this isn't going to be it.'

'What do you mean?'

'You know – you go back to LA. I get on the plane to New York. A few calls, e-mails. That's it.'

'We'll work something out.'

'No. Let's not do that. If it's gonna be some half-assed thing, I'd rather make a clean break of it now. No dishonesty.'

'Why do you say that?'

'Because I think I'm falling for you,' she said candidly. 'And I don't want to linger in that dead zone of hope. All that: is he going to call? Isn't he? What's his life really like? Am I ever going to find out? I'm done with all that crap. You should be too. You're old enough.'

Up until that moment, it had been Nate's tendency to avoid intimate conversations with his girlfriends, but he felt so proud that she'd had the courage to open up.

'And by the way,' she said, jutting her chin out in a way that would become utterly familiar to him, 'I think you have Kluver-Bucy syndrome.'

'Is it fatal?'

'Maybe.'

'What is it?' he said, grabbing her and pulling her back to the bed.

'You have a violent urge to put everything in your mouth.'

They were married within a year. And Nate hadn't really been interested in another woman after that. What deeply attracted him to Mary was her honest stance on the issues she believed in. She told him that what attracted her to *him* was his cynicism, which belied a sincere and disappointed soul. He wanted to make babies with her. He wanted to impregnate her, make her vulnerable and be totally reliant on him. But Mary had wanted to wait. She was already a respected scientist in New York and had found a good position at UCLA almost immediately when they agreed that Los Angeles was the place to live. She was too excited about her career to embrace motherhood.

She was a natural academic in the relationship, devouring every medical paper that she could find. There were piles of journals stacked six feet high in their office at home. Her passion for medicine gave her a kind of nutty brilliance. She was always looking for possibility, always looking to the future. His stance was one of seasoned sceptic, disbelieving of everything that couldn't be proven by vast epidemiological studies and fighting grimly with insurance companies.

Nate's general practice in Beverly Hills fed his habit of running a free clinic in Huntington Park. His sainthood was assured, Mary teased him. But it was always what he was expected to do. His own father had opened a free clinic in North Carolina after he retired and urged Nate to give back to society what he had got out of it.

Although many of Nate's clients were in the movies, he had no time for Hollywood. He hated standing boorishly on the sidelines of one of the world's most glamorous industries and watching the neurotic cockatrices bitch and moan about minor ailments. It was easier for him to shun the scene rather than try, like so many desperate and greedy doctors, to prostrate themselves at the altar of celebrity and watch the lawsuits pile up.

The one thing that Nate didn't respect about Mary was her interest in cryonics. When she first moved to Los Angeles, she had joined a tiny group of fanatics who believed in physical reincarnation. For her it was a hobby, something to do in a strange city. But all too quickly, she ended up as one of their main advocates. She lectured on the subject and was always on call if there was a head or a body that needed to be frozen. It was the only thing that reduced her credibility in Nate's eyes. He felt that there was something reckless in her character that drew her towards the lunatic fringes of medicine.

'Why are you even *interested* in cryonics?' he always demanded of her.

'Because it's so loopy,' she explained, her green eyes glinting, almost taunting him. She was fearless of him. 'It's my medical folly. I'm a lonely girl in a new city. I have to have something to do, or I might go out and find myself a lover.'

Nate opened his eyes. Mary's voice was as clear as if she'd been standing in the room.

'*Where are you?*' he said. '*And when are you coming to take me home?*'

33

It was Tuesday. Nate knew it was Tuesday because he'd been told by a nurse. He kept repeating the word. He wanted to see how long he could keep the day in his head. Karen wheeled in a new screen for their morning session.

'I want to introduce you to the Abacus,' she said as she placed a pair of comical-looking glasses on Nate's nose.

Tuesday. Abacus. He could sit up in bed on his own now, though he still needed the stroke recovery suit to get around.

'The glasses have special sensors built into the frames which can pick up the movements in your eyes,' continued Karen. 'A red dot will appear on the screen and that's your point of focus.'

He could see the red dot quite clearly, which was a miracle

in itself compared to his vision of two weeks ago. He flicked his eyes to the left and the dot moved to the left. Then to the right and the dot moved again. Karen tapped a keyboard and a grid of letters and numbers appeared on the screen.

'All you have to do,' said Karen, 'is allow your eyes to settle on the letter you want for more than three seconds and it will drop down to the word bar below. If you make a mistake, just move the dot to the letter "C" for cancel and carry on.'

All at once, his mind went blank. He couldn't think of anything to ask.

'No hurry, Nate,' said Karen gently. 'Something will come.'

A question swam into his mind and he moved his eye line falteringly across the letters. After a frustrating few minutes, he had his first words.

'WHAT – HAPND – ME?'

Karen grew serious. 'I'll be right back.'

Typical, thought Nate. *Go get the consultant.* No underling can deliver the big news. Karen returned with the two doctors.

'We've only just started working on the Abacus this morning,' Karen told them, 'but as you know, Nate is very quick to respond to stimuli and he has a very important question for the two of you.'

The doctors looked at the screen.

'What – happened – me?' said the male doctor, sitting down on the bed. He looked overcome, as though he didn't know quite what to say. 'Nate, my name is Garth Bannerman and this is Persis Bandelier.' He touched the blonde woman on the arm. 'We've been guiding the waking project from the very beginning. How are you today?'

Nate's impatient eyes flicked this way and that. 'HIT – N – THE – HED.'

184

The two doctors exchanged looks.

'No, not exactly. I want you to ask me questions, Nate, but first, do you mind if I ask you some? What year do you think this is?'

Nate looked quizzically at Garth. The number didn't come. He tried to concentrate.

'2006,' he punched out.

'And where do you live?' encouraged Garth.

The name took for ever. 'VENICE.'

'And where do you work?'

'BEV HILS.'

'How old are you, Nate?'

Nate's eyes darted along the row of numbers. '37.'

'Do you have any children?'

'NOOOOO.'

Nate was growing impatient. He burned the red dot on the W, moved up the grid two lines for the H and along to the left for an E, working furiously to build another sentence.

'WHER – WIFE.'

He was feeling agitated now, but not agitated enough to miss their expressions.

'You've been through an extraordinary passage . . .' Garth began.

Nate shut his eyes. He hated beginnings like that. 'I'm afraid to have to tell you . . . this is not going to be easy . . . the results came back and I'm afraid it's bad news . . .' He'd heard them all before, Christ, he'd *said* them all before!

'Your wife didn't make it to this point in time, Nate.'

This point in time. What point in time? Nate couldn't take it in. He saw Garth glancing at the others for reassurance. It was a quick look, but he knew there was a big speech coming.

'You are a living, breathing, walking phenomenon, Nate. If I can explain: the year is 2070. More than half a century ago your head was frozen or vitrified. You were shot and your wife had you cryonically frozen.'

Nate could feel a vein pulsing against the dressing on his neck.

'I know it sounds impossible, Nate, but you survived all this time. Then we developed the technology to bring you out of cryostasis.'

Nate worked ferociously to make more words.

'WHA – HAPN – MARY?'

'Mary died a long time ago, Nate. I'm very sorry.'

Nate's face turned to stone. He began scanning the letters. 'BAD JOKE.'

'No joke. I'm sorry.'

'DON – WNT – BE – HERE. PUT – ME – OUT.'

'I know it's difficult . . .' ventured Garth.

Nate's gaze flicked angrily across the abacus. 'I WN OUTTTTTTTTT.'

They sat in silence. Nate raised his hand to touch the scar on his chest.

'That scar is from all the procedures we had to perform on your donor body,' said Garth, taking each sentence slowly to make sure that Nate understood. 'In the last twenty years we have developed the kind of nanotechnology that made it possible to bring you back. We can do amazing things with the body now, Nate. We can grow new organs from a few cells, repair diseased hearts without bypass or transplant. We can grow skin and bone and vessels. We can repair brain damage and prevent dozens of diseases by genetic alteration. And we have cured cancer, Nate. Can you believe it? All one hundred cancers are curable.'

Garth knew he was going too fast, but he wanted to give Nate an optimistic picture, something to live for.

'It is a world of wonder out there and you will be able to experience it.'

The tears from Nate's eyes misted his glasses. Karen wiped them and put them back on his nose. He noticed that there were tears in her eyes too, but not in the female doctor's, with her inscrutable half-smile. Nate started to form new words.

'ARE – THER – OTHRS?'

'No. You're the first. An unexpected gift for us and we're so grateful for it.'

Nate lifted up his hand and turned it over. 'WHO – BODY?'

'Your donor died in a road accident.'

Nate began to work on the Abacus, dropping letters into the word bar. 'PUT – ME – OUT.'

Karen took his hand and squeezed it. 'I'll go get you something to make you feel better,' she said. Karen looked at Garth, who acquiesced. Nate turned his face to the wall. Garth stood up.

'I'm so sorry about Mary,' he said.

Nate felt a tentative hand of reassurance on his shoulder, but he didn't respond. He didn't want to look at anyone in the room.

34

When Nate rose from the depths of a drug-induced sleep, 'dirtied' was a word that came to him. His mind felt 'dirtied'. He knew there was devastation lying at the foot of his bed. A few more moments and it would come back to him.

Tuesday. Abacus. Mary. Dead.

Which Tuesday? The Tuesday just gone or some other Tuesday from weeks ago? Try as he might, he just couldn't remember when they told him. Time was something that expanded and contracted. There was day and there was night. Which day and which night he had no idea. He knew he'd had an operation on his voice box and now he was finding a voice. It was a croak, but at least he could make sounds.

Tuesday. Abacus. Mary. Dead.

He kept expecting a freight train of grief to hit him and send him hurtling into oblivion. But for some reason it hadn't happened and that in itself produced waves of guilt. Mary. He could picture individual features, but he still couldn't see her face and they weren't able to provide him with a photograph.

The second nightmare that came flooding back was the fact that he had been immersed in liquid helium for more than half a century. The truth of it filled him with a special kind of dread. When he was alive, his two phobias had been a fear of drowning and being buried alive. Now he knew they were strangely prophetic as he had been subjected to both.

After a few minutes of utter despair, he managed to pull himself together. Foraging for words helped. *Null – dull – mull* – that's what he was doing – mulling over the handful of words that he summoned up in his damaged brain.

Nate's mood spiralled down, so he tried to concentrate on the physical progress he was making. He reached up to touch his neck with both his hands. They shook with the effort but he managed to run his fingers over the scar. The two humps on either side of the crease still felt huge, plastic and engorged.

Ever since he'd found out his fate, he was becoming obsessed with the graft and the landscape of his alien skin. He ran his hands over the body the whole time, feeling the muscles and stroking the body hair. It was black and smooth, lying neatly in waves across the tawny skin. His own skin had been paler, the hair more tangled. He noticed too that the body had many slight indentations where the hair was uneven, as though there'd been some kind of skin graft or laser work. There was a mole on his chest, a scar by his ankle, and his feet were long and slender. Elegant even. As he assessed all these idiosyncrasies, he was overwhelmed by the notion that they once belonged to someone else. He didn't want to touch the penis. Fortunately, it had been handled by the medical staff up until now, but very soon there would come a point when he would have to direct it into the bowl himself, and he'd been horrified a couple of nights ago when he woke up with an erection. The organ was clearly functioning, but he couldn't ever imagine using it to make love.

Burdened with all kinds of guilt and strangeness, Nate turned his head away from the observation window and sank his head into the pillow. How much were they screening him right now? Thank Christ they couldn't identify what he was *actually* thinking. Or maybe they could? Who knew what kind of technology they had at their disposal?

The door to his room opened and the comforting, squat figure of Jessica waddled in carrying the bags of nutrients that would feed him for the day. Jessica was one of the sweetest nurses who tended him, a Filipino with a loving smile.

> With a slow and noiseless footstep,
> comes that messenger divine.

Henry Wadsworth Longfellow, Portland's distinguished poet, came to him from out of the blue. It puzzled Nate that he could remember every word of the two stanzas, yet he couldn't recall the word to describe his medical condition. He clung to the poem, as though he were clinging to a part of his old self.

Takes a vacant chair beside me
Lays her gentle hand in mine.

He tried desperately to remember more words as he watched Jessica change his nutrient bag. Maybe her compassion brought the poem back to him.

'Dr Sheehan – Dr Bandelier would like to see you this morning,' announced Jessica as she undressed him for a bed bath. He heard the words like an echo and nodded. He liked it that she called him doctor. It gave him some kind of authority, though inside he felt as helpless as a child.

'Tomorrow – we start to feed you by mouth,' she said, arching her painted eyebrows. 'What would you like?'

Nate shrugged. He had absolutely no appetite.

'I will make sure they give you something nice.'

Jessica nodded for him to get up. Nate pushed himself off the pillow, enjoying the newfound strength in his stomach muscles. But he wasn't ready to give up the recovery suit just yet. He was convinced that if they took it away from him, he would crumple to the floor.

He often wandered in and out of the empty rooms like a zombie. And he could still convince himself that he *was* actually dead and this was some kind of clearing house for the newly departed, his numbed flesh the proof that it was all an illusion. When Jessica had finished her chores, she escorted Nate to one of the observation rooms.

'Good morning, Nate,' said the female doctor. 'How are you today?'

Nate shrugged and sat on a chair opposite.

'I've got a *very* old toy for you.'

She handed him what looked like a blunted electric razor. Nate recognized the synthesized voice box immediately.

'Those little gadgets haven't changed much,' she added.

'When your voice gets tired, hold it up to your throat and we can carry on the conversation. But I don't want you to get *too* dependent on it, because Karen and I want you to work on your *real* voice.'

Real. Nate wasn't sure if any of this was *real.*

'Go on. Try it,' urged Persis.

'When did you tell me that Mary was dead?' voiced Nate through the box. He sounded like a robot.

'More than a month ago now, I think.'

So he'd known for weeks.

'Are you OK?' Persis asked.

'I'm finding it hard to keep track of the time.'

'Well, we're keeping a good eye on your brain activity, Nate. You're still aphasic.'

That's it! *Aphasic* – the word he'd been looking for to describe his mental deficiency. Aphasia: damage to the language centres of the brain, caused by strokes, gunshot wounds, blows to the head and other traumatic brain injuries.

'How did I die?' he asked through the voice enhancer.

'We don't have a whole lot of detail,' she said. 'We've got the basic records and a few newspaper articles. You were shot, you died instantly from your injuries.'

'And Mary?'

'She survived, and she did a remarkable thing, which got a lot of attention at the time. She decided to freeze your head immediately after the shooting. She did it right there in the ambulance. You must have had some kind of pact about that.'

'No, we didn't,' he said curtly. 'I'd like to see my file.'

'Sure,' said Persis, but he could tell that she wasn't keen on giving him the information. Why not? Was she lying to him? He just couldn't get past her inscrutable exterior.

'I was going to introduce you to the Dome today,' she said. 'Do you still want to do that, or do you want some time to think about what I've just told you?'

'Have you told me before?'

'A few times. But it's normal that you wouldn't necessarily remember the information at this point in your recovery. Shall I carry on?'

Another shrug.

Monty wheeled in a dome-shaped machine made of translucent fibreglass. He lowered it over Nate's head.

'The Dome is another scientific miracle of our age,' said Persis, hooking up the machines. 'We can tell from electromagnetic pulses how healthy your brain is, then we can stimulate activity where it's needed and make you feel better. Everyone uses the Dome. Many people have them installed at home or you can take your data into Government drop-in centres. We have almost wiped out depression, schizophrenia, mania, OCD. And it's so simple: two titanium coils in liquid helium. The rest is in the programme.'

Persis and Monty got busy behind their computers and promptly forgot about Nate for several minutes while they swapped notes and talked in a technical jargon he couldn't understand. He grew impatient. Persis looked up.

'I'm sorry, Nate, we're neglecting you. We just want to make sure that we're concentrating on the right areas of your brain. Do you want to see yourself thinking?'

Without waiting for a reply, Persis turned her screen towards Nate. He could see the outline of his skull and the 3-D image of his brain with millions of microscopic lights all gushing and stopping and flowering in different parts of the tissue. He was instantly spellbound.

'Think of some numbers,' she said.

'I can't.'

'Take your time. Thinking and speaking at the same time generates the most brain activity.'

He waited for the mental swim. 'Eight, five, twelve, eighty-three.'

Immediately, he could see tiny dots of colour tracing strings of lights across the top of his brain.

'Isn't it great?' she said. 'Now think of some music.'

He strained to think, but nothing came. 'I don't know any,' he said.

'Yes you do,' said Persis. 'We've recorded you playing Barber's Adagio in Strings in your head.'

'You have? When?'

'Many times. We mapped the musical notes and the instruments. Our programme matched it to the piece. Try to remember it.'

Nate tried but nothing came up.

'That's fine,' said Persis. 'Sometimes the conscious cortex acts like an inhibitor. It's got too much else to think about, so it shuts down access to your deeper memories. What would you say you are feeling right now, Nate?'

'Feeling? I feel – *nothing*.'

He longed to tell someone about his terror on waking up, about his revulsion towards his penis, about his objection at being brought back from the dead, but he didn't feel like communicating the most basic and intimate part of himself to the ice maiden sitting in front of him.

'You are feeling something, Nate,' she said. 'I can see that your limbic system is active.'

'Then why don't you tell me what I'm feeling?'

'I wish I could,' she said, sensing his mood, 'but we're not that far advanced yet.'

They were silent for a while as they watched the pulses flickering in his mid-brain.

'What we are picking up is that you are resisting the benefits of the Dome right now.'

'What the hell does *that* mean?' he rasped angrily through the voice activator.

'Some brains, because they are damaged, can't be magnetically altered. We call them resisters. Given that you suffered a number of transient ischaemic episodes during and post the waking, your brain tissue can't accommodate the waves effectively right now. In a few months, when your mental agility has returned, you may be more responsive.'

'You didn't tell me about the TIEs,' he said.

'We did,' she said, and casually waved a hand as though it was unimportant. 'It's just a recall issue with you right now. Don't worry, it will all come back.'

Nate watched Persis bent over the screen, the blue light flickering in her irises. He could see that she was in her element. He knew he felt a growing antipathy towards her for poking her nose into his thoughts. That much he did know. He wondered if she could see *that* in her precious brain-imaging programme.

LOS ANGELES

35

'Where are the letters?'

Fred's mind started to race. Sulky, petulant, victimized – the female voice on the other end of the line had all the hallmarks of someone from one of his crime stories, but he couldn't place it.

'I was wondering if you could return my brother's letters to me,' said the voice again.

Fred winced. He knew exactly who it was. Bobbie Williams, sister of Duane, and he'd done exactly what he'd promised himself he wouldn't; forgotten to return the precious letters of her brother.

'I could not be more sorry, Bobbie. I'll scan them and get them in the post by tonight.'

'That's not good enough, Mr Arlin. It's been more than six months. I think that's enough time to read a few letters, don't you?' Her sentence ended in a wheeze and she sucked in air.

'You're so right and I'm sorry I didn't get back to you sooner. I'll personally drive up and deliver them if you like.'

As soon as he'd said it, he regretted it. It was a good four-hour drive to San Luis Obispo. Maybe he'd drop by on his mother while he was up there, recharge his car for free and make his only surviving parent happy.

'So are we going to write a story about my brother?' said Bobbie, interrupting his thoughts. The sarcasm annoyed Fred. But he didn't react. Never react. That's the way he'd been taught.

'I'm working on it.'

'How long does it take?'

'Good question.'

Fred had made a valiant effort to sell the Williams story to *The Metropolitan* but each time he attempted to explain what he had, he became tongue-tied. Eventually, the editor just raised a hand for silence on the web cam.

'OK – I've given this story enough time. I don't think it's there, Fred. And what's more, I don't think it's ever going to be there. Sorry, but this one's got spike written all over it.'

Fred felt oddly galvanized by the brush-off. If they weren't interested then fuck them. Someone would buy his missing body story.

Taking his old wreck of a car, which he reserved for driving in tough areas, Fred wound his way up the Pacific Coast Highway to San Luis Obispo. The old highway always made him feel closer to what California must have been like in its heyday. The flagship economy of America with the eternal sunshine and easy charm that lulled its inhabitants into a false sense of security. After the great earthquake of 2012, everything changed, but there had been an enormous effort to rebuild the PCH. It was a symbol of the values that California once held so dear; liberty, adventure, experimentation. It wasn't quite so pretty now that the ocean was dotted with desalination plants all the way up the coast.

When he arrived at the kit park, his heart began to thump. A menacing-looking gang was loitering on the street corner. He nodded uneasily at them. To his dismay, he saw that there was a party going on at Bobbie's house. People were sprawled out on the ground or sitting on mutilated sofas in the front yard. Fred tripped over someone's boot to get to the screen door. Bobbie appeared. She was unrecognizable. Her weight had dropped maybe a hundred pounds since they'd last met and what was left was poured into skintight clothes. Her chins were hanging loose and her face was sallow. From where he stood, Fred could smell a sweet, burnt, rubbery smell of skeet on her clothes and in her hair. Bobbie seemed to have descended into full-blown addiction in the space of a few months. Fred looked around nervously for some kind of anchor to the sordid scene.

'Where's your husband?' he said.

'He took off,' she slurred. Her sickly almond breath reached him. 'Wanna drink?'

'No thank you.' Fred sounded prissy but he didn't want to touch anything. 'Here are the letters and the disc.'

'Thanks.'

Bobbie tossed them down on the sofa like they meant nothing. *Great.* He'd made all this effort and she didn't even care. God, he hated spending time with these kinds of people. It made his skin crawl to be around them, to pander to them, to sit on their rancid sofas and listen to their torrid tales of self-inflicted drama. A couple more minutes and he'd be out of there, never to return.

'I think I've made some progress on the story . . .' he found himself saying, but realized pretty quickly that Bobbie wasn't listening. She was shifting from foot to foot as though she was having to handle a mental white-out caused by the drugs. Then a tall guy came through the door behind her. Fred froze. It was like staring at a dead man. Drooping, sexily defined lips, hooded eyes: he knew instantly who it was. Fred closed his mouth.

'Is this the reporter?' asked the man in a deep-throated drawl.

'This is the man,' said Bobbie, sitting down on the sofa suddenly, as though someone had shoved her from behind.

'I understand you are writing a story about my brother.'

Fred swallowed. 'Your brother?'

'My kid brother, Duane.'

Fred looked at Bobbie, hoping against hope that there might be another brother beside the FBI's most wanted. 'How many brothers are there?'

'Just me.'

Fred swallowed again and tried to conceal the dunk of his Adam's apple. So this was Keith Williams, the twin brother of Duane. He recounted the man's list of despicable crimes. Keith registered Fred's fear, laughed and flopped down on the sofa himself.

'Sit,' he commanded.

Fred sat and glanced furtively at Bobbie. He wondered what had happened to make her desert her husband and get embroiled with a brother she claimed to be terrified of.

'So.'

'So?'

'Where's the story? I don't see it published anywhere.'

'I'm still working on it,' spluttered Fred. 'I know for certain that your brother's body was used by Icor Incorporated for *something*. They just won't tell me what.'

'Mr Arlin, I got some news for you. I can feel him.'

'You can feel him?'

Keith leant in. Fred couldn't help but lean in too. There was something charismatic about the man, he had to admit, in spite of his fear.

'Duane and me, we used to talk of having one heartbeat. When Duane got himself some health problems, a mess on his insides, for me it was like a small knife going in.'

He held an imaginary knife and skewered the air with such speed and skill that Fred could imagine him making the perfect assassin's wound.

'That's what I've been feeling lately, that old knife. Ain't that right, Bobbie?'

His sister swam out of her trance and obliged like an automaton. 'They were always very close and could tell certain things about each other. Even if they were apart, like when they were sick.'

'You can feel him now?'

'I can feel him now.'

'I'm sorry, but I don't quite understand.'

'You calling me a liar?'

'No. No,' said Fred hastily. 'Is it his ghost that you feel? His spirit?'

'More than that,' said Keith, unpeeling a filthy scarf to reveal a surprisingly feminine neck.

'What was your reaction when he was executed?' ventured Fred.

Keith looked injured by the question, as though he might lash out just because Fred dared to ask it. Then his expression changed.

'Tired,' he said eventually, 'tired like I never been so tired in all my life. But then, he sort of stirred in me.' Keith squinted at Fred, challenging him to contradict it. Fred nodded a little too vigorously.

'That's all I can say.'

'Have you been to see a doctor?'

'Excuse me?' said Keith, angering.

Fred raised his hands in surrender. OK, it was a stupid suggestion.

Keith twisted his scarf through his fingers, then let it coil up on the sofa like the discarded skin of a snake. 'I want you to find out exactly what happened to him.'

'I'm trying.'

'And when you do I want you to bring him back to me.'

'I don't know that I can do that,' Fred said hesitantly. He didn't want to commit to something he couldn't fulfill. 'I mean, I have no idea what state the body's in or how I would get it away from the people who technically, legally, have rights to it now.'

Fred's blood grew cold as he saw Keith's eyes ice over. For the first time, he really understood what the man was capable of.

'Your mother lives not far from here, right?'

'How do you know that?'

'There's nothing I don't know about this town,' said Keith, leaning back and scratching his stomach. Bobbie was still in a torpor, taking confused looks between them.

'What are you trying to tell me?' said Fred, a sudden stab of fury penetrating his cowardice. That the man should bring up his mother as part of some kind of threat made the conversation both frightening and ludicrous at the same time.

'Nothing. Just bring me Duane.'

With a growing horror, Fred saw images of his respectable, reserved, ageing mother as a hostage in this filthy environment. And all because her ambitious son had chosen to write a story about the missing body of an executed prisoner.

The arrogance, the conceit, the butchery of the character before him, acting as though he was king of the kit park, giving orders, intimidating with his twisted logic. Fred wanted to tell him to go fuck himself, but for the sake of his mother's future, not to mention his own, he gave Keith Williams a craven smile and promised to do what he could.

PHOENIX

36

The numbness of Nate's skin was being replaced by a kind of hypersensitivity. They told him that the new nerve endings would be more responsive for a while and that he would be susceptible to some intense bodily reactions, like itching and pins and needles, before it would settle back down to normal. The area around his neck still felt numb to the touch and he knew that the cocktail of drugs that they were giving him was keeping the pain at bay. In the mornings, he could barely move until a series of exercises loosened up the vertebrae.

Apart from the stiffness around the graft, he was in better physical shape than he had been when he was alive. But psychologically, he had no idea how he was going to get beyond the next moment, let alone the next minute, hour or day. There were no plans, no fixed points of interest, hobbies, holidays, reunions, ambitions, goals – all the things that give the human psyche structure and hope. He had no family, no friends, no support systems to make his rejuvenation worthwhile.

Karen and Monty had developed powerful feelings for him and it was to Nate's shame and confusion that he was incapable of reciprocating. He just couldn't find it in himself. The truth was that most of the time he felt outside of himself, as though he was only in occupation of the body but not really running things. Often, when he reached for something, the action happened before he thought about it consciously. It was the most peculiar sensation and made him feel that he had no free will. As a result, he was becoming overly conscious of everything he said or did, but he hadn't told anyone about it yet. He had to have some secrets.

Just as he was trying to remember if the condition had a name, Karen arrived with her bag of tricks, as she did every morning.

'OK, Nate,' she said brightly, 'today is a day of pleasure. We are going to feel joy. We are going to feel awe. We are going to feel what it is to be alive. But first, we have some simple stuff to get through. I brought my old cards in. I look at them as a kind of progress chart.'

She shuffled the pack and showed him a card with an animal on it. 'What's this?'

'Lion.' He obliged with a clear, even voice.

'And this?'

'Gorilla.'

'This?'

'Zebra. Rhino. Tiger. Elephant.'

'There you go!' she said with triumph. 'We're home. I got these cards at the beginning of my career, when most of these animals were still in existence.'

'You mean they're extinct?' said Nate.

'Why yes,' she said brightly. 'There are a few giraffes and zebras in conservancy camps. The others are gone.'

Karen produced a tiny gadget from her bag. It was the size of a thimble with a padded button at one end. 'Now, *this* is going to make you very happy—'

'You mean there are no predators left on this earth?' he said, interrupting her. 'Apart from us?'

'All the big game have gone. The viruses got the few that were left in captivity. I'm sorry. I thought they told you.'

'If by "they" you mean Persis and Garth, they haven't told me anything yet. What about the sea? What's gone from the sea?'

'Whales, otters, manatees, walruses, most sharks. There's a half-century ban on fishing while the stocks of tuna and swordfish replenish themselves, but it's doubtful they'll ever come back. The only thing that has thrived over the century is the giant squid. They like the warmer waters and are increasing in size. Oh dear – I was just about to make you very happy,' she said, wilting.

'I'm sorry, Karen. But you have to give me a moment.'

'We have preserved tissue banks of every living creature,' she said hastily. 'Everyone talks about creating an ark somewhere, but so far, no one has had the money or the incentive to do it. Maybe this project will make it possible.'

Karen rested her hands in her lap. She looked momentarily so lost that Nate felt obliged to rescue her.

'I'm OK now,' he said. 'Let's carry on.' He tried to fake a smile, to bring Karen out of her obvious sorrow, which he always felt was pretty close to the surface.

'Let's give your brain a quick scan to check that everything's functioning,' she said.

Once they were watching his brain on screen, they were both distracted. Nate was expert at controlling his brainwaves now. They had taught him how to do it and he could make the lights dance along the neural pathways at will. He was beginning to learn which thoughts would light up which areas, and it was fabulous to make his own patterns.

'Happiness is not a single state of mind,' said Karen, trying to act as though the earlier part of the session had never happened. 'It involves physical pleasure, absence of negative emotion and meaning. I know it's tough for you to achieve that state right now, but we're going to try to get closer to it today and I'm hoping that you will feel cohesion in your ventromedial cortex.'

'How are you going to do that?' said Nate.

'I'm going to stimulate your reward pathways.'

Karen pressed her thimble and something very familiar wafted over him and through him. It was the chords of an acoustic guitar filling the room with extraordinary clarity.

'Is all this sound coming from that tiny machine?' he said in wonder as the guitar's simple, melodious notes tripped down a musical stairwell.

'Yes,' she said, grinning.

'Unbelievable.'

An electric guitar joined the acoustic and now the flat, strangulated, tinny voice of someone he knew but couldn't name.

'It's *Sticky Fingers*,' he said, not even realizing he knew it.

'That's right. It was the Rolling Stones' twelfth album. Released in 1971, if my history books are correct,' said Karen proudly.

'"Wild Horses",' murmured Nate. 'I was given a signed copy of the original LP by one of my godparents. I remember the cover so well. It was the picture of a man's crotch with a real zipper. Designed by Andy Warhol. I never listened to it, but then this movie director Martin Scorsese used it in a film called *Casino*. I really got into it after that.'

'There you go. I'm so glad about my choice,' said Karen.

The kick of Keith Richards's backing vocals fell into line like a rogues' chorus – dissolute, ragged, decadent.

Karen magnified Nate's brain so that he could see lights going on in his auditory cortex. 'And here comes the waterfall of dopamine.'

Karen switched to another visual and Nate watched his own rostromedial prefrontal cortex lighting up as millions of neurotransmitters made their way along the enjoyment pathways, leapfrogging from axon to axon and locking pleasure into his consciousness. The band were meandering through the song with exquisite melancholy.

'Does it bring back anything?'

Nate let the riff wash over him. 'Wild Horses'. It was a plain old blues song, with its sprinkle of sensitivity and genius. Something *was* bubbling up from the murk. He closed his eyes. He could see his old house, a 1920s beach house which he and Mary had found in a rainstorm one afternoon on the Venice canals.

'Not yet,' he lied, because he didn't want Karen gatecrashing his precious memories.

'Give it time,' said Karen.

Nate didn't need to give it time. He was already back there, standing outside the front door of his old house. It was barricaded up when they first saw it. He and Mary had picked their way round to the side and discovered another door hanging off its hinges.

'Let's leave it,' said Nate.

'No, I want to go inside,' said Mary, wrenching the door open. The house had been derelict for decades and was clearly an old refuge for the dope-smoking hippies who languished on the canals in the 1960s. The rafters of the pitch-pine roof still oozed with a musky smell of marijuana.

'This is it, Nate,' said Mary with psychic certainty. 'We're going to live here.' As they moved through the deserted house, they counted at least twelve sleeping cubicles, each with a tiny makeshift bed. Little touches had been added to make the bays individual, like handcarved shelves and headboards. Threadbare drapes fastened by drawing pins still hung in tiny windows and piles of rotting clothing had been strewn across crocheted bedspreads. In one cubicle they'd found copies of *National Geographic* dating back to 1964. It was as though the whole commune had been evicted in an afternoon and the house had been boarded up and left standing empty. During the renovation, Nate found dozens of clay pipes, beads, artificial limbs, bicycle wheels, possums' skulls and aeronautical maps in the crawl space under the house, but never the treasure that was supposed to be buried there.

'We'll just have to bury our own treasure,' said Mary, and together they had found a watertight capsule and put all the things they cherished inside: the original passes to the conference in Arizona where they met, the photographs of their wedding and the intimate photos that neither wanted anyone else to see, a brooch belonging to Nate's mother and a diamond earring that was once part of a precious pair that Nate had given Mary on their first wedding anniversary. They wedged the canister between two wooden beams, lit a candle, burnt a smudge bundle of sage in honour of the departed hippies and made love.

'Is anything happening?' said Karen.

'Not much,' said Nate.

He'd loved that house and the canals and the giant, scarred seabirds that would swoop down for an easy catch of fish. But try as he might, he still couldn't see Mary's face.

'I see an elevated level of activity in the limbic system, Nate. To me that represents some kind of cognition,' Karen pressed.

'My house. I can see my old house,' he conceded at last.

'What was it like?'

'A beach house – in Venice.'

'Ah – Venice.'

'Why do you say it like that?'

'Like what?'

'"Ah – Venice." There was something in your voice.'

She paused for a moment, trying to think of words that would not upset him.

'It's all right, Karen. You can tell me.'

'They haven't told you anything?'

'Nothing.'

'I – it's hard to know what to tell you, Nate,' she said.

'Try me,' he said.

'Well, Venice doesn't exist any more.'

37

'I'm sorry we've been keeping you in the dark, Nate, but in your waking state, taking in too much knowledge at once is like forcing a baby to learn mathematics,' apologized Persis. 'In other words, it's completely pointless. We've been worried that you might experience some kind of information overload. But you say you're ready?'

'I don't want any more surprises like this morning,' said Nate tersely.

After the session with Karen, Nate had called up Persis and insisted on a briefing.

'OK, I'm going to give you a rundown of some historical details, then you can ask me questions. Stop me at any time. Set your own pace.'

Monty had joined them and flashed a wand-like instrument. A bank of hologramatic screens appeared in front of them. He adjusted something with his wand and the translucent screens angled towards Nate.

'I have prepared some images,' said Persis. 'Some of them will be upsetting.'

Nate tensed. Part of him was desperate to know what had

happened in the last half century. Part of him couldn't stand to have his own dismal vision of the future confirmed.

'There's so much to tell you, but I had to start somewhere, so I thought you'd want to know about the Los Angeles earthquake of 2012, which is what Karen was referring to.' Persis hesitated to gauge Nate's reaction. 'I know Los Angeles was your home.'

He nodded. Of course there had been an earthquake. It had been endlessly talked about and endlessly feared.

'I have to say that as far as we know, it's how Mary died. Her body was never recovered.'

Nate dropped his chin and stared directly at the screens.

'Are you OK?' she said.

He nodded.

'On 6 July 2012 at 2.37 p.m., the Los Angeles County Civil Defense Warning Center reported that there had been a significant earthquake in the Santa Cruz–Santa Catalina Ridge Fault Zone out by Catalina island.'

As Persis spoke in her quiet, understated way, the images blurred into a nightmare of devastation. Wood-slatted guest-houses in Avalon reduced to piles of matchsticks. Nate and Mary had spent many hot nights on Catalina, screwing on uneven beds in tiny, airless rooms.

'I know you were alive during the Great Asian Tsunami of 2004. It was a 9.3 in the Andaman-Sumatran subduction zone.'

'I remember,' he said.

'Well, this was an 8.6, the biggest the region has ever experienced. Unlike most earthquakes in the Los Angeles basin, this lasted for five minutes, and afterwards, a fifty-foot tidal wave barrelled across the Pacific and slammed straight into Los Angeles. Another one hit Hawaii six hours later.'

There was more shaky footage of a towering wall of water

bent over the city like a devouring witch. Nate couldn't comprehend how the images could have survived.

Persis was watchful of his reaction. 'Do you want me to carry on?'

'Yes. I need to know,' he said sternly.

Persis tapped her screen. Another set of images appeared: helicopters recording the mass exodus from the West Side; miles of glinting, abandoned cars on the freeways; people running inland; nurses trying to push gurneys up the street, doctors helping patients, and the elderly being deserted by auxiliary staff. Tears formed in Nate's eyes. That's where Mary would have been. In the hospital, helping others. And that's where he should have been.

'They had an hour to evacuate the whole of the West Side,' continued Persis. 'A lot of people made it. A lot of people didn't.'

So the unimaginable, the very thing that every Los Angelino secretly dreaded, had actually happened. And in the middle of it all Nate imagined the body of his wife, swirling in the broiling, filthy water. He could see her body struggling, then going limp as the water filled her lungs and finally her brain. He ached to know what had happened to her.

'It had a profound effect on the confidence of the nation.' Persis broke off. They sat in silence.

'How many died?'

'Five hundred thousand that day. More in the outbreaks that came later.'

'And Mary was among them?'

'As far as we know.'

'We lived in Venice.'

'I know. I'm so sorry.'

'But it was in the afternoon, so she may have been at work.'

'Where did she work?'

'UCLA – inland.'

'UCLA and USC were mostly destroyed by the after-shocks.' Persis coughed awkwardly as though she were having trouble saying the words. 'Seventy-two hours following the tidal wave, there was a 7.3 aftershock along the Newport–Inglewood Fault Zone and an area covering fifteen square miles of tectonic plate dropped fifty feet into the sea. As you know, the foundations of Venice and Marina Del Rey were built on the geological equivalent of gravel. You said you lived in Venice, well, you may remember insurance reports on your house. The earthquake status of your area was designated "liquefaction". That's basically what happened – it liquefied.'

He watched the screens. There were pictures of the new shoreline and the 10 Freeway going right up to a jagged overhang, then shots of concrete buildings, great monuments of engineering, twisted and contorted by the magnitude of the disaster.

'About forty per cent of the entertainment complexes were destroyed that day – MGM, MTV, Fox, Sony. The entertainment industry was snatched up by other cities and countries. Universal, Warner Brothers and Paramount are still operating, but it's a much reduced heartland of entertainment now. Los Angeles has never recovered.'

Persis checked his body monitors. 'You have a serious buildup of stress, Nate. I think we should stop.'

Nate's mouth was gaping open and closed like a dying fish. 'Let me go,' he whispered.

'I can't do that.'

'I'm already dead, Persis. There's nothing left for me here. Just help me do it. I really want to die.'

'But you've come so far. There's just a few hurdles left.

You're depressed, but it *will* correct itself and you *will* begin to feel your mood lifting.'

'I didn't ask to be brought back. I don't want to be here. My wife is dead. So listen to me. You're going to help me die. You're going to help me do it.'

'There are twenty-five people out there who worked around the clock to make sure you came through this.' Persis pointed at Monty. 'He sat up with you night after night watching over you. He talks about you like you're family.'

'It's true – I do,' said Monty.

'We worked so hard to give you life. You don't know how lucky you are to have a second chance!'

'But it's *my* life and I don't want it!' he bellowed.

Suddenly, Nate grabbed Persis's keyboard, the symbol of her power and intrusion into his every waking moment, and threw it against the wall. The components scattered. Persis and Monty stared at him, saying nothing, then Persis quietly picked up the keyboard.

'This is exactly why we held off telling you. You're not ready. I'm sorry. I should have been more firm about it.'

'Then I guess the session is over for today,' he said bitterly.

38

'How was the session?' asked Garth, as Persis came into his office.

'A disaster.'

'What happened?'

'He's just not ready to hear the truth. I told him about the earthquake and he had a violent outburst.'

'Are you OK?'

'Sure.' But she was still trembling as she sat down and inserted her disc into the machine.

'What's going on in the brain?' said Garth.

'There's an overall reduction in the anterior neocortical function, and increased function within the cingulate and frontal areas, and I picked up several micro-expressions of despair. Watch this.'

Persis replayed the last moments before Nate smashed the keyboard.

'Watch for the micro-expression that follows.'

When Nate sat back in his chair, a fleeting expression of hopelessness flitted across his face before the anger returned.

'And watch here,' continued Persis. 'He's exercising the zygomatic major and the risorius, but there's no truth to that smile. In short, we have one profoundly depressed patient on our hands.'

'Can we put him under the Dome?'

'Right now, he's a resister.'

'Why don't we give him a seratonin re-uptake inhibitor? We still carry stocks of them somewhere in the company.'

'That'll interfere with the dopamine receptors. I don't think we can risk it. And there's another thing.'

'What is it?' he said.

'I think Duane is back.'

'Why do you say that?'

'Do you remember when I questioned Duane about the murder, and he threw the sensor cap at me?'

'How could I forget?'

'Well, it felt like Nate was re-enacting one of Duane's last experiences.'

They played the tape again and watched Nate wrench the keyboard from Persis and smash it against the wall.

'I wonder if Nate had violent tendencies when he was alive,' said Garth.

'From what we know on paper, he was a doctor with a successful practice and a good heart or he wouldn't have opened up that free clinic in LA.'

'That doesn't preclude violence.'

'True. But we do know that Duane had chronically elevated levels of cortisol and odosterone for most of his life. His cellular make-up would be hypersensitive to stressful situations. And he was prone to outbursts.'

'OK, but let me be the optimist for once. Nate feels toxic in his mind as well as his body. He has no familiarity with the emotions and instincts that are bubbling up to the surface. It's going to take a while for him to get to know himself and his new body. He may display the odd symptom of Duane's chronic anxiety, but let's just say it's not going to be anything that we can't handle.'

Persis didn't look convinced. 'If nothing else, it could be bad for Nate's health. High blood pressure, arteriosclerosis—'

'We may have to medicate him to keep those impulses in check.'

'And I think we should stop telling him anything else about the world for now.'

'How far did you get?'

'Just the earthquake. That was enough.'

'They were the last generation who lived in relative peace and prosperity. He died just before everything happened.'

'Talking about things happening,' said Persis, 'don't you think we should be inviting the EIS to see the new body before we get any further down the road?'

'He still has traces of the antibiotic in him.'

'No, he doesn't. I looked at the latest tests this morning. He's clear.'

'Then I'll call them today.'

Persis gave him a look.

'OK – I've been putting it off,' said Garth, a pang of guilt hitting the pit of his stomach. He hated the procrastinator in him.

'We have to deal with it, Garth. There's already no comparison between Nate and the other bodies. How are you going to explain *that*?'

'That at long last we got everything right.'

'Not everything.'

39

Early evening was the worst. Nate would pace the room like a neurotic polar bear that he'd seen at the Bronx Zoo, marching back and forth along the bars, waiting for the ordeal of his life to end. Then, when he couldn't stand it any more, he would burst from his room and run around the block of dimmed corridors. They left his door open so that he could come and go as he pleased, but he noticed that all the exits on his floor were locked and though he'd tried to find it, there was no call button on the lift.

He waved to the nurses on duty as he jogged past their room. They waved back. They were accustomed to his nightly exercise and let him get on with it. Apart from seeing that he didn't get into trouble, there was not much for them to do. That suited him fine. He wanted to be left alone.

When he'd completed his twelfth circuit, he found Monty waiting in his room.

Monty spent at least four nights a week with Nate. They didn't talk much, but played board games and word games. Tonight, though, Nate felt curiously light-headed and chatty, now that he knew what he was going to do.

'Where is your family from, Monty?' he said after they'd reached a long pause in a game of chess.

'The Philippines. My great-grandfather came over in 1987, when there was unrest in our country.'

'How old are you?'

'Twenty-eight.'

'Do you have any brothers or sisters?'

'A brother. He's married. He works for Icor too.'

'Here?'

'No, at their headquarters in Savannah. He works for the big boss man.'

'Really. Impressive. Are you married?'

'Nooooo.' Two little frown lines creased Monty's boyishly smooth forehead.

'Are you gay?'

'Noooooo,' he said, then scrunched up his nose and concentrated on his next move.

'Do you want a wife?'

'Sometime, but I can wait.'

'Till when?'

'Forty, fifty.'

'Do you have a girlfriend?'

'No.'

'Don't you want a woman?' Nate didn't want to bully his gentle companion, but he was suddenly burning with curiosity about the sexual mores of this unknown society.

'Sure, but it's hard to get a woman.'

'What do you mean?'

Monty looked pained and shy. 'We stay away from one

another, I guess. There's been so much disease. There's just too many risks. You want to be sure.'

'Disease?'

'Nate, I've been told not to talk about the bad stuff until you're ready.'

'OK. I understand. Are you a virgin?'

Monty nodded piously.

'I don't know if I could go without a woman for that long. How long do you expect to live?'

'If the bugs don't get me – a hundred – a hundred and ten. I'm not a *genetic*.'

'What's a genetic?'

'Rich people.'

'How come?'

'They pay for genetic alteration so they have the best chance of survival. Like Persis. She's a genetic.'

'Ah,' said Nate. Of course she was a genetic, with her perfect heart-shaped face and her long, lean body.

'I wonder how different your lives are compared to when I was alive?' said Nate. He was almost enjoying himself. His voice hadn't cut out once and he hadn't had a single lapse in recall.

'Don't go talking like that, Nate – you *are* alive.'

Nate smiled at Monty. He didn't want to alert him to anything. 'Marriage is different now though, isn't that right?'

'Oh, sure. Marriage is based on a short-term contract. You can sign up for three years. If it works out, great. If it doesn't, goodbye.'

'Really? People don't feel like they need more security?'

'I guess not.'

'What about, what about—' And there it was, the blank.

'What about?' urged Monty.

'Children!' Nate said at last.

'You sign a provisional agreement for the children – so that's OK. Lot of people make it beyond the three years.'

Nate imagined what Mary would do with a short-term contract. He could see her pretending to tear it up at the merest hint of an infraction of his behaviour, just to get him riled.

'When do women have children?' he asked.

'They got a lot of time to have children. Twenties right up to their fifties and sixties.'

'Sixties! Is that routine?'

'Not routine, but it's usually OK. Every woman gets the chance to freeze her eggs early. Gives her more choice.'

'What's the success rate of in vitro fertilization?'

'Pretty much a hundred per cent. If you want a baby that way.'

'How so?'

'A lot of women, maybe seventy per cent, opt for having their babies in synthetic amniotic sacs. Especially older women.'

'Are you serious?'

'Oh, sure. Personally, I'm not surprised they don't want to have it vaginally.' His nose crinkled up.

'Where are the embryos –' and again there was a pause while Nate had to wait for the word ' – gestated?'

'In baby farms. We've got one here.'

'At Icor?'

'Sure. But they keep it very discreet. There was a big scare about five years ago when a baby farm was contaminated. Many babies were lost, so this building has got unbeatable security.'

'I know. How the hell am I going to get out of here?'

Monty looked up from the board.

'I'm just kidding.'

They played a few more moves.

'What was *your* marriage like?' asked Monty.

'My marriage?' Nate needed to savour that one. 'She was the best woman I ever had. But she was always in my face.'

Monty let out a boyish giggle. 'What does that mean?'

'You haven't heard that expression?'

'No.'

'She never let me get away with a damn thing. Which was good for me.'

'Why?'

'Before I met her I think I was, I was – ' and Nate had to wait again ' – more ruthless. But Mary was my match. More than my match. I tell you, Monty, if you ever find a girl like that, don't let her go.'

'So you were happy?'

'Yeah, I guess we were.'

'What's that like?'

'Happiness? Don't you know?'

'Not really.'

'What about the Dome? Doesn't that make everybody happy?'

'I can't pay for that.'

'I got the impression it was for everyone.'

'At a price.'

'Well, happiness for us was not very complicated,' said Nate. 'I think it's all about being occupied in the right way. We worked hard in jobs we liked.'

'I like my job.'

'See. There's something, Monty. You must get a lot of job satisfaction.'

'I guess.'

'And good friends. We went out with friends. Then most

weekends, we went on trips. It was a pretty indulgent, selfish existence when I think about it.'

'But you were happy.'

'Sure.'

'Where did you go on trips?' There was longing in the question.

'Hiking all over California, camping in the mountains or the desert. Skiing up to Lake Tahoe. Las Vegas. Mexico. Caribbean, Europe. You name it, we used to go for it.'

'I'd like to take a trip.'

'So what's stopping you?'

Monty let out a big sigh. 'We can't travel out of state without contamination checks and a visa from the Health Council.'

'You're kidding.'

'There's very little traffic between the states.'

'Don't you feel trapped?'

Monty took a furtive glance up to the observation camera and put a finger to his lips. 'Another time,' he whispered.

Nate almost felt bad when he drew the game to a close with a checkmate. But he couldn't hide the glow of satisfaction that he'd managed to hold a full conversation and beat Monty at chess for the first time since the waking.

'You're getting your smarts back, Nate. I like it,' said Monty.

'And you didn't let me win.'

'No – I didn't let you win.'

'You're a good man, Monty.'

'Don't be stupid.'

'You are. There's not a single bad bone in your body.'

Later, when Nate was lying on his bed, he felt the familiar emptiness return. The gloom and the silence pressed down on his ears and gave him the feeling of being the lone occupant of an Egyptian tomb. Cyril, the night guard, popped his head round the door to say goodnight.

'You know, Cyril, I could do with going outside. I haven't even seen the stars yet.'

'I can't let you do that, Dr Sheehan.'

'Just for a moment?'

'I'm sorry, Dr Sheehan. I have my orders.'

'Orders. Am I a – '

Cyril waited by the door.

' – a prisoner here?'

'No,' answered Cyril patiently, 'but we have pollution alerts and they told me that if you go out without the appropriate clothing, it will make you very ill.'

'I'd like to take that chance.'

'It's for your own good, Dr Sheehan.'

'Like this whole experiment.'

'I don't know about that. Goodnight, Dr Sheehan. You sleep well now.'

Nate listened to the lift doors swish open and Cyril step inside, leaving him alone except for the duty nurse who would be asleep in a matter of minutes. He waited in the dark until it was time, then looked under the mattress where he'd secreted the bottle of pills. He opened it and popped a handful. He took a swig of water and swallowed. He had 150 to get through. He'd snatched them from the drugs room during one of his jogs. He had a feeling they were some kind of opioid analgesic, but they were colour-coded so he wasn't sure. Hell – 150 of *anything* would put an end to it. He took another handful. They felt chalky and resistant on his tongue, so he took a swig of water. He glanced up at the watchful eye of the camera. He knew the nurse would be sleeping, and he'd removed his clothes with their built-in sensors, so for once he was beyond their investigation. Another handful and he nearly gagged. Then a kind of self-disgust filled him up. This was not the man he was destined to be, a suicide, but he was out of his time and he just couldn't face whatever was in store for him. His mind drifted a little, a mental slide into strangeness, and he realized the pills were taking effect. He thought of *Antony and Cleopatra*, his favourite Shakespeare play.

'*Caesar shall not live to be unkind,*' he mouthed as he lay back on the pillow, recalling the point where Octavius Caesar pretends to be merciful to Cleopatra, promising to treat her well in defeat. But Caesar's real purpose was to drag Cleopatra 'like a writhing whore' through the streets of Rome. And that's what Nate knew he would become if he lived – a macabre celebrity to be paraded before the world. He would never have any privacy and would never be able to lead a normal life. If suicide was the honourable way out for a Roman general or an Egyptian empress, then it was good enough for him. He reached up his left hand, his strong arm, and just about made it to his mouth with more pills. As he lost consciousness, he heard the whispering of Cleopatra's maid.

'*The bright day is done, and we are for the dark.*'

40

Monty fired up his electric cart and hurtled down the path towards the centrepiece of the lighting display. He was heading towards a twenty-foot-high reindeer made out of steel that he'd crudely put together in his workshop at home. He tried to make a new structure for the city's Christmas Lights Fantasia every year, but this was by far the most ambitious creature that he'd ever created. It had a barrel stomach and crazy antlers. The proportions were eccentric, the legs way too short and the tail had broken off in transit, but lit up with thousands of tiny white bulbs, the reindeer was going to look spectacular against the desert night sky. The wasteland lay beyond the mountain park golf course and the Fantasia was one of the highlights of the season. Thousands of people turned up to drive dozens of electric carts through the maze of illuminated pathways.

Monty was elated after his session with Nate. Usually, his patient lapsed into long, moody silences, but tonight, he couldn't stop talking and had actually shown Monty genuine affection. It was a real breakthrough and Monty couldn't wait to tell Persis.

'Not a bad bone in my body,' said Monty, smiling as he took his foot off the pedal. He had eighty tracks of bulbs to lay before the night was out. He knew the reason he was so determined to make this year the best yet was so that Nate could come and admire his work.

He began to gather clumps of bulbs in his arms. He leant the ladder against the steel skeleton of the reindeer and looked out over the acres of figurines. There were elves and dwarves, Snow White and Father Christmas, even steel effigies of mountain lions that once roamed free in the desert states.

He swung the first line of bulbs over the spine and was just about to coil the cable around the ribcage when he noticed a man strolling towards him. The place was deserted. He tried to assess if the man was a threat and noted that the stranger was wearing a beautiful cloth coat, a rarity in Arizona, so he figured he was safe.

'Is this *your* work?' shouted the stranger, striding right up to him.

Monty looked at the man's handsome, carved features,

slightly exaggerated in the shadows. He could have been a cartoon hero with his cocked eyebrow and square jaws.

'Sure is,' said Monty, throwing a second line of bulbs over the ribcage. They clattered down the other side. He was anxious not to stop.

'Did you make this yourself?'

'In my workshop,' said Monty proudly.

'Impressive,' said the man, nodding.

'So, what brings you out here in the middle of the night?' said Monty, raising one eyebrow, mirroring the other man's expression.

'I'm sorry – my name is Fred Arlin. I'm here on business. I came in from California today.'

'How did you get across the state line?' Monty asked.

'I got a pass.'

'What do you do?'

'I'm a doctor. I develop medical techniques for human regrowth.'

'Not at Icor?' said Monty.

'Adronium Industries.'

'Our rivals.'

'Who are *you* with?'

'Icor.'

'You're kidding.'

Monty kept on weaving the bulbs, trying to act casual, wondering what was going to unfold.

'What are you working on?' asked the stranger.

'Regrowth.'

'I don't believe it. You must know Garth Bannerman.'

'He's my boss.'

The man smacked his gloved fists together. 'We met at a conference. How's the project coming along?'

Monty felt alarm bells ringing. The question seemed too focused. Maybe the guy was an industrial spook. And as for the waking, Monty had taken an oath of silence and had been faithful to it, not even telling his parents.

'Depends what project you are talking about,' he said cautiously.

'Garth said you were working on some pretty interesting stuff.'

'We're keeping busy.'

'What do you regrow exactly?'

'Hearts, livers, spleens, eyes, skin and bone tissue. Hey, you're not trying to take away our business, are you?'

'Hell no. I just had an idle evening and I saw these lights in the distance and I was drawn like a moth to the flame. I'm here for a few days. Maybe I'll see you around. What do you do for entertainment around here?'

'What entertainment are you looking for?'

'Something to eat and drink, talk to a few people who work in the industry. I think I bore outsiders.'

Monty didn't have a social life. He didn't have much spare cash.

'Some of the guys get down to Palliachi's on Main.'

'Well, if I see you there, I'll buy you a drink. Here, let me give you an ID.' He handed a thumbnail diskette to Monty. Monty pressed play.

'Hi – I'm Fred Arlin – medical director of Adronium Industries, California Division,' said the image. 'Let me tell you about my job and the company I work for . . .'

Monty pressed pause. 'Thanks.'

'No problem. Nice to meet you.' Fred turned to go, then hovered. 'Monty, if you ever want to change sides, call me. We're always looking for new blood. You never know. There might be an opening.'

'Maybe I'll see you in Palliachi's.'

'Tomorrow night – sevenish?'

'Sure.'

This time the guy turned on his heels and strode off down the fairytale walkway, his dark outline cutting across the silver archway of bulbs. Monty had just about finished draping the haunches of the reindeer when he realized the man had called him by his first name, though he'd never introduced himself.

41

Dawn crept quietly over the desert floor, covering the valley in a pale pink gauze. The gossipy squeaks of the quails could be heard as they darted in and out of the cactus, bobbing their bonnets and diving for cover. The rabbits loped under cholla bushes before scampering back to the cool of their burrows. If Persis was up at this hour she would always watch the wildlife beyond the adobe walls of her garden. She was endlessly amused by their comic, exuberant dashes.

'Come back to bed,' said Rick softly. She glanced at her husband, whose fine-boned features looked bruised in the blue light. They'd just made love. It was a rare moment of intimacy and they'd clung to each other in the frenzied way that couples do when they're trying to revive their passion.

'In a minute,' she whispered.

'Come on.'

She smiled, and sauntered back to bed. Rick started to kiss her again, which made her feel incredibly sad. She felt almost relieved when the web cam buzzed in her office.

'Don't answer it,' he murmured, but she was already pulling away from him and heading for the door.

*

'Nate tried to commit suicide during the night,' said Garth, who looked dishevelled and unshaven.

'No!' said Persis, 'is he—'

'He's OK. Monty got to him in time.'

'How?'

'He took a bottle of folic acid from the drugs cupboard.'

'Thank God he missed the serious stuff. Who the hell left the cupboard open?'

'I don't know. I'm looking into it.'

'What about the duty nurse?' said Persis.

'He slept right through it.'

'And the nanos. Didn't they trigger the alarm?' Persis was referring to the twenty nano-computers implanted in Nate's body.

'The AV3 recorded an irregularity in his pulse, but never responded. If Monty hadn't come back half-way through the night—'

'Why did he do that?'

'A hunch, I think. He said Nate was talking too much, saying things which had a finality to them.'

'Thank God. What's his condition?'

'There's been a couple of haemorrhages in the stomach, but we can clean that up and get him back on his feet. We have to develop a programme to take him off the anguish loop. This was no cry for help. He said he wanted out and he very nearly made it.'

'I'm coming in.'

'No need. He's stable now, but I thought I should tell you.'

'I want to. This was *my* fault.'

Persis dressed, barely giving an explanation to Rick, who was sitting up and watching her.

'Slow down. Talk to me,' he said.

'Nate tried to commit suicide last night.'

'Is he OK?'

'Just.'

'In many ways, we'd be better off,' said Rick, leaping athletically off the bed.

Persis looked at her husband in astonishment. 'What?'

'We're wasting a lot of money on this guy and he doesn't even want to be here.'

'And the fact that he is a scientific miracle doesn't play a part in your reasoning?'

'Phoenix has to become viable, Persis. This whole project is meant to bring the growth accelerator into line so we can start using it commercially. He's not essential to the project any more. And when I see us spending a *huge* chunk of our budget on treating him, I'm beginning to wonder how we can justify it.'

'I don't want to have this conversation right now,' said Persis, heading for the door.

'You've done an amazing job, Persis. No one disputes that. And I'm not for a second denigrating your efforts.'

'You can patronize the staff with your platitudes, Rick, but don't waste your breath on me.'

When she reached the sleep labs, Persis found Monty whispering to Nate who appeared to be sleeping. His skin had a grey, sickly pallor.

'His jaw was clenched,' said Monty, squinting up at her. 'I could barely get the pills out of his mouth. And there was blood in the froth—'

Just then, Nate woke up and rolled his bloodshot eyes. He winced as though he was trying to grapple with the acute pain in his head.

They wheeled him to the theatre where the reconnection

had taken place. It was the first time that Nate had been allowed beyond his living quarters.

'This is where it all happened,' explained Persis. 'The reconnection.' She looked down. Nate's eyes were squeezed shut, his jaw taut under an early-morning growth of stubble.

'Nate, I want to give you a full transcranial scan. I can put you under if you like.'

'I don't care either way.'

They administered a shot, waited for his body to relax, then manoeuvred his head under a magnetic resonance imager. Persis worked tirelessly, inching over each fold of grey tissue, pixel by pixel, sending the information to Monty's computer for verification.

'I think I've found the root of his depression,' she said.

There was no response. Persis looked up. Monty was slouched over his computer and fast asleep.

'Monty,' she whispered.

He jerked awake. 'What?'

'Take a look at this.'

The image tracked over the limbic system like a satellite over a moonscape. Persis magnified the millions of pathways running up from the limbic system to the frontal cortex.

'I think his limbic system has too much power. The pathways leading up to the frontal cortex have been rebuilt, so he's generating more emotion, which is good, but there's still faults in the inhibitory pathways going in the other direction that would normally damp down that emotion. I think we have to accept that he needs more stem cell infusions.'

More costs, she thought. *Screw Rick. I'm going to do everything I can to keep him alive.*

*

When he heard that Nate had been returned to his room and was awake, Garth prepared himself for a welcome-back speech. He had no idea what he was going to say to a would-be suicide, but he had to say *something*. He found Nate being shaved by Jessica. The patient's eyes were still bloodshot and he was wearing a new expression of disdain.

'You're looking a lot better,' said Garth. 'How are you feeling?'

'Great.'

'Do you want to talk about what happened?'

'No.'

'Let's look at this as the low point, Nate. From here something has *got* to improve.'

Nate sneered.

'We care a great deal about you. And I understand how difficult it's been—'

'Do you?'

'Well, I don't know *exactly* . . .' Garth paused. He decided to call Karen. She might be able to reach him. When Karen arrived, she was out of breath as though she'd run all the way. She sat on Nate's bed and took his hand.

'Can I talk to him alone?'

'Of course,' said Garth, and withdrew from the room.

Karen fixed Nate with her intense pale grey eyes. 'I'm not surprised to find you here. I knew you were going to do this, ever since you woke up.'

Nate's expression softened. But he had no words of comfort for her. He wanted out. And as soon as they stopped concentrating, he would try some other method. The dreadful thud of blood pumping through his head caused a new wave of sickliness with every beat. It was like suffering the worst hangover imaginable.

Karen squeezed his hand. 'I think it's time to tell you something that I've been keeping from you.'

'What is it?'

Her expressive face brightened visibly as she recalled a happier time in her life.

'I had a family once – Ken, my husband, two girls and a boy. We lived in Washington while Ken was doing some work for the Government and my practice was going well. I heard about this conference in New York. They had invited practitioners from all over Europe, China, Japan. It was the biggest forum for years. I was desperate to go. I wondered if I should leave my children, but I really wanted to be part of it all. I toyed with the decision for weeks. There hadn't been a major health crisis on the Eastern Seaboard for five years and I felt that I just couldn't miss out.

'It took a while to sort out all the paperwork and get a pass to go across the state line. They make it very difficult for some people, particularly those in health care.' She swallowed. 'While I was away, dengue fever swept up the coast. My family was unlucky. We lived on Chesapeake Bay, which was very badly hit.'

Nate understood for the first time why there was so much pain etched in Karen's face.

'They sealed off the area. They do that. No one can get in or out. It's tough, but it's the only way,' she said, unconvinced. 'People are left to their fate. I waited for weeks in a hotel near the boundary. I was in constant visual contact with my family and I had to watch them go, one by one. My boy was the last to die. I had to tell him, in the last days, how to look after himself. Food is left for people to collect outside the town. I had to tell him where to put my husband and his sisters so the bodies could be collected. A guy from next door helped him. The bravery of some people. He took good care of my son.'

Her chin began to wobble and the tears that had been hovering in the rims of her eyes began to plummet down her cheeks. 'I couldn't be there for him, Nate. I couldn't touch him or smell him. I wanted to die along with them. I wanted to walk that path with them so badly.'

'You don't have to go on.'

'I'm not done,' she said. The burden of her story had deadened her normally sing-song voice.

'I thought the grief was going to kill me. So I went under the Dome. I was OK for a while. I began to do things. And a few people were very, very kind. But there was this terrible monster lurking all the time, and while I was under the Dome I felt like I wasn't dealing with it, so I didn't go under the Dome and it brought me to my knees. I had no life. No laughter. No contact that I could understand. The world seemed to be mocking me in my grief. Then bit by bit—' She broke off and wiped her cheeks with the back of her hand. 'Now I know why I was meant to survive. I was kept alive to look after you. To see you through this. And it was worth it. To be alive to help one person through.'

Nate didn't know what to say.

'You are a marvel. Look at you. A beautiful new life has been created. You're very strong and secretive and stubborn. I know that makes a man whole, but you need to reach out to us, Nate. We are here and ready to embrace you whenever you're ready. You were taken from your wife and you will always carry that loss with you, but *you* have been given back to the world. Look at the body you now have. Look at your potential. To give up is just so – wasteful! Try to cling on. You may be dead next week or next month or next year anyway. We cannot control the forces that have taken so many of us, so please, try to get something out of the time you have left.'

Karen stroked the hair away from his brow. She hugged him to her chest. He could feel her tears soaking through his surgical gown.

42

Fred pulled off his coat and sat on the bed in his dreary motel. He was desperately trying to retain every word of a conversation that he just had at Palliachi's. He'd taken a microrecorder, but for some reason, only half of the conversation had been taped, so in a state of panic, he was trying to write notes of what was said.

The restaurant the Filipino recommended had turned out to be a dive at the basement of a huge building near Icor. Its black walls, deep red musty carpet and black leather booths set around lacquered tables reminded Fred of the few places that were left open in Las Vegas. Red lights glimmered at each table and he could feel the stickiness of the carpet beneath his shoes. A cloying, sweet smell of cheap liquor permeated the room. It was an insult to his senses, but he had no choice. Palliachi's was the only lead he had to ingratiate himself with the staff at Icor and find out more about the company. He took a seat at the end of a long padded bar and waited for the Filipino to turn up.

Fred had found Monty Arcibal's name in an Icor staff newsletter during his extensive trawl of company information. Then he'd matched the name to a picture of the man smiling goofily at the camera with a bunch of local dignitaries at a previous Christmas Lights Fantasia. It didn't take much digging to find out that at this time of year Monty was nearly always on site at night. When Fred got into town, he found out where the Fantasia was held and had waited for hours in the darkness until Monty turned up.

For some reason, Monty was a no show at Palliachi's, so Fred had spent the entire evening trying not to get drunk or look conspicuous. He talked briefly to a couple of workers at Icor, but they moved away from the bar when a new guy came in.

'Hey there – you look like you had a bad day,' said Fred as the tall black guy sat down two seats away.

'You could say that.'

Fred was immediately alert. 'Then let me buy you a drink.'

'I'll have a Craif.'

'Two Craifs,' Fred signalled to the barman. It was a highly expensive protein- and vitamin-fortified drink, designed to provide all the nutrients required for a single day. Fred knew he was being taken for a ride, but he knew the gesture would guarantee him a conversation.

'What's your name?' said Fred.

'Okorie Chimwe – yours?'

Fred handed him another bogus ID. Okorie was maybe six foot five, with ebony skin. His features were refined, with a narrow bridge to his nose and a strong jaw. Fred learnt that he was Nigerian, recently arrived from Africa.

'So, why did you have a bad day?' said Fred.

'I got fired.'

Fred perked up. 'Who fired you?'

'Icor.' There was a surly, defeated demeanour about him.

'My rivals.'

'That's right.'

'What did you get fired for?'

'They work us into the grave and then there's one tiny problem and that's it.' He clapped his huge hands together and Fred watched his beautiful long fingers coil themselves around the glass.

'So what happened?' Fred ventured a second time.

'I was framed.'

'Framed? That sounds serious.'

The man said nothing.

'Why were you framed?'

'I was framed because I'm an African and they don't like us.'

'I heard that about Icor,' Fred lied, trying to find some common ground where the guy might open up. 'What division did you work in?'

'Regrowth.'

'That's my field too,' said Fred. 'I'll check with Adronium. Maybe there's a job.'

'Thanks,' said the guy. There were a few minutes of silence. Fred looked around the dreary bar.

'Did you ever get to work with cadavers?' he asked, trying a new tack. 'There's a real shortage. We can't get them anywhere.'

Okorie frowned. 'Try the prison system.'

'Is that where you get yours?'

'Sure.'

'Which prisons? I tried Angola last year, because they had so many executions, but they wouldn't play ball.'

'Gamma Gulch.'

Fred tensed but tried to look casual. 'Thanks for the tip.'

Okorie fixed him with a knowing stare. 'You don't work for Adronium.'

'Why do you say that?'

The guy clicked his tongue which made a rich, clucking

sound. 'You're not a doctor. A doctor would never ask a question like that.'

'You're right. I'm a journalist.'

Okorie nodded sagely.

'Do you want another Craif?'

'Sure. You want to hear a real story?'

'Sure.'

Fred was used to people saying they had the greatest story never told and it usually turned out to be some protracted personal dispute that wouldn't make him a single dollar. The very words filled him with lethargy, but hell, there might be something.

'What is it?'

'I signed something so I can't talk about it, but I am going to tell the world about it one day and no one will believe me.' He spoke with the deliberate, delicate intonation of a West African.

'What is it?'

'I cannot say. Not yet.'

'How did you get into the US?' said Fred.

'My grandfather worked as a diplomat in Washington. He had some friends. It took me five years. Now look at me.'

'It's better than being in Africa, no?'

Okorie drained his glass.

'So – what is the story?' pressed Fred, sounding to himself like a bad actor.

Okorie clucked again.

'Are you looking for money?'

'As from today.'

'We've only just met, but I can trust you and you can trust me – right?'

Okorie sucked in air. Fred wasn't sure if that meant a yes or a no.

'I'm trying to find a body that left Gamma Gulch about a year ago and was brought here to Icor. He was called Duane Williams. A killer who was executed. I assumed it was a routine thing, you know, dissecting for tissue samples. No big deal. Make a nice little story for a medical journal that I work for. No one, but no one, wants to talk to me about this goddam body. Then I was sent down to San Diego University where they showed me a corpse, but it wasn't Duane Williams. Now, why would they do that?'

'How do you know it wasn't Duane Williams?'

'Duane Williams was covered in tattoos. The body I saw was clean.'

Okorie had an odd smile on his face. 'I'm going to need a lot of money.'

So there *was* a connection between his story and the body. Fred leant back on his stool. *The Metropolitan* might pay him something. But they were notoriously tight. And although he had contacts with the kind of web journals who might pay more, he had to have some proof that it was worth it.

'Is it to do with the body?' he repeated. 'I have to know if there's a connection or I've got nothing. I know people with money, but you've got to give me *something*.'

Slowly, Okorie nodded. 'Yes – it *is* to do with the body and it will blow your mind,' he said, and slid off his bar stool and headed for the door. Left by the emptied second glass of Craif was a screwed-up ticket with a telephone number. Fred looked around the bar, then covered the ticket with his hand and put it in his pocket. One day, he told himself, he would learn how to be an investigative journalist without behaving like a ham.

43

Nate knew that he was being watched every moment of the day. He also noticed that one or two familiar faces among his carers, including Okorie Chimwe, had disappeared, probably fired for being asleep on the job or for leaving the drugs cupboard open. He felt bad about it, but didn't feel like defending them. He might have fired them himself if he'd been in Garth's position. And besides, he was beyond caring about anything much.

They injected more stem cells into the pathways that led from his frontal cortex to the limbic system to try to inhibit the negative emotions that were welling up from his mid-brain. The new cell growth would take several weeks. The suicide had been a plunge downward. It wasn't in his character and he detested himself for it, but he couldn't see how he was going to survive psychologically.

One evening, a few days after the operation, Persis knocked on his door. Everyone did that now as a mark of respect for his privacy. It was as though the attempted suicide had made them more aware of his separateness and that he had a will of his own.

'I wondered if you'd like to go for a walk,' she said.

'Outside?'

It was an option he'd longed for so many times, yet now that he was being offered the chance, he actually felt trepidation. He noticed Persis press her thumb on a sensor by the lift. The doors opened. How he longed for his own security clearance. When they reached the decontamination chamber, she pointed to a biohazard suit.

'My only condition is that you wear one of these.'

'Why?'

'You're still vulnerable. It will protect you from the pollution.'

'When will I be strong enough to go out without it?'

'I don't know – maybe never. A lot of people need respiratory aids all the time. On bad air days, we all use oxygen. Most people don't spend that much time outdoors, but I insist on it. I won't give up my hiking.'

She modestly retreated into a cubicle to change. He saw her put a tube on a string around her neck which emitted a small hiss when she twisted the cap.

'It's an air purifier,' she said.

The mist seemed to hover around her head. She led him up to the lobby, where they greeted Cyril who was sitting at the front desk.

Nate felt lightheaded by the time they stepped outside. He tripped down the steps and Persis caught his arm. He looked about him. The black glass tower rose up behind them, surrounded by a vast car park. Beyond that was an intimidating perimeter fence, too high to climb and topped off by coils of barbed wire.

'Some things don't change,' he said.

'Like what?' asked Persis.

'Security.'

The cars that he could see were recognizable for what they were, but formed different shapes and shadows against the night sky. Some looked quite comical, with jagged wings and slanted hoods.

'Cars run on solar power in the desert states,' explained Persis. 'The panels are moulded into the bodywork.'

'Genius,' said Nate. He could see great domes rising up above the other buildings. 'Will it look very different in daylight?'

'I think you'll be surprised by some of the architecture.

Critics call it brutal industrial, but a lot of people find it very beautiful. Most of the city is driven by solar power. We have our own power plant off the grid.' Persis looked at him intensely. 'Nate, I wanted to apologize to you.'

'What for?'

'I could have helped you with your depression. I could have given you an old-fashioned antidepressant. We don't use them much now, but we still manufacture them. I decided against it, because neuronal growth is lethargic if we inhibit it with SRIs. But I think in your case, I made a mistake and I'm sorry.'

'I don't know if anything would have changed what I did. I don't want to be here. It's as simple as that.'

'Even now?'

'Well, you're watching me all the time. So I am biding my time and hoping for a change of heart.'

'Then that's all we can hope for,' she said, and smiled. She looked out towards the city. 'You're lucky.'

'I am?'

'Arizona is one of the cleanest, safest states in the country.' As she was speaking, she swung away from the city towards the vast black gape of the desert. 'But I do miss the sea.'

'What am I going to do with my life?' he said. 'That's what I can't figure out.'

'It's a question of adjusting,' she said.

'Give me a break, Persis. You can't stand it here.'

'Yes I can.'

'No you can't. And all you had to do was move across country. I've had to travel half a century.'

'What I don't understand is why Mary did what she did, knowing you were so against it.'

'I said to her: "If I go first, don't you *dare* freeze me. When you're dead you're dead. That's it. *Bon voyage.*"'

'So you must be mad at her.'

'No, I'm not. I'm not mad at anyone. That's the trouble. I don't – feel like me. Or what I remember as being me. I'm not the me I used to know.' Nate looked down at his strange, lean body hidden under the biohazard suit. 'I feel separated from myself – does that make any sense?'

'Of course it does,' said Persis. 'We have a binding problem going on in your brain, Nate. Your circuits aren't in a state of cohesion yet. But compared to a few weeks ago, you have improved beyond our wildest dreams. I don't see any reason why that improvement shouldn't continue and you will get yourself back.'

'So everyone keeps saying. It's ironic. Mary was the one who believed the technology and she never got the chance to benefit.'

'She wanted you to live, Nate. And here you are. Why don't you try and hang on for her sake? It's what *she* would have wanted.'

They looked out at the desert and the vast expanse of sky, a huge purple-black bowl above them. In the silence, Nate felt an intense desire to get back to Los Angeles and find out exactly what had happened to his wife.

44

'I was wondering if you'd like to come over to the house for dinner?'

Garth was looking awkward, even on the web cam. The very suggestion seemed improbable.

'I think my diary's empty,' said Nate.

'Tomorrow night then.'

Nate was almost touched by Garth's attempt to be social,

but he felt a certain dread as the evening approached. After everything he'd been through, he felt introverted and shy. They gave him a different kind of biohazard suit for the trip, with a lightweight hood and a wide perspex visor for greater visibility. Nate thought it looked ridiculous, but as he and Garth made their way through the outskirts of Phoenix in Garth's capacious car, he noticed a number of people wearing similar headgear.

He strained his eyes through the prism of his visor to get a better look at the city. The buildings he could see reminded him of the huge power plant that he used to pass on the 405 to Long Beach; great cylindrical tanks surrounded by girders, towering pillars and steel rods. Like Persis said, quite beautiful in their way.

He looked up at the sky. He could see anvil-shaped cloud formations with small, jagged streaks of lightning scissoring through them.

'The clouds look angry.'

'We have a lot of dry electrical storms,' said Garth. 'Probably many more than you remember. Don't worry. They rarely do much damage. Sometimes they're quite spectacular.'

'And those huge domes,' said Nate, counting at least a dozen on their journey so far, 'I noticed them the other night.'

'Some are magnetic tabernacles. People go there to relax, meditate, relieve their depression. The bigger domes are where we grow all our food.'

'Like biospheres.'

'That's right. It's the only way to avoid contamination in the desert states. We try to be as self-sufficient as we can.'

Garth turned his car into a side road and stopped outside a massive iron gate.

'We need good security,' he said. 'We had a problem with gangs, but the National Guard has it all under control now.'

The road turned into a dirt track, more humble than Nate was expecting and lined on either side with low-lying adobe houses half-hidden behind thick, uneven walls. The car eased noiselessly to a halt.

'You have seventeen miles of power left. Time to recharge,' intoned a velvety-brown voice from the dashboard. Nate followed Garth through an exquisite courtyard full of cacti and bowers of trailer plants which filled the night air with their delicate perfumes. Beyond the courtyard, golden light shone through recessed windows set deep in the clay walls.

'Just to brief you, Claire, my wife, knows everything, but the children think you're a colleague from work. It's easier that way. When we get inside, you can take the hood off.'

They found Garth's wife in the kitchen. Nate immediately enjoyed the spectacle of Claire. Everything about her was slightly exaggerated: the cheekbones, the big, strong aquiline nose, the full lips. For some reason, it comforted Nate to know that Garth had bagged someone so heroic-looking. They kissed each other affectionately, then Claire broke away and took Nate's hand.

'We've been waiting for so long to catch a glimpse of our star,' she said, and studied him before embracing him. 'So how are you?'

Nate smiled. 'I'm OK – I guess.'

Garth grabbed some bread and a sorry-looking tomato and crammed them hungrily into his mouth. 'I'm starving!' he protested after seeing Claire's expression. The familiarity between them made Nate crave some intimacy of his own. How he longed to quibble with someone over tiny things like greed.

'It's the first course!'

'Try and stop me.'

'I apologize for my husband,' she said.

'It's a great house,' said Nate, trying to distract them from their happiness.

'Thank you. It's historic – built in 1986. Garth – could you do me a favour?' said Claire in a way that left no room for negotiation.

'What?' he said, freezing like a pointer dog, the bread poised in his mouth.

'Can you talk to Suzanne? She's not feeling that great.'

'Suzanne, my thirteen-year-old, has cancer,' said Garth, helping himself to more bread and some white, curd-like substance that Nate presumed was cheese. 'A few weeks ago some tumours showed up in her stomach and her back and her liver,' he went on casually. 'It's an aggressive strain.'

'What are you doing about it?' said Nate. He couldn't believe that there were no whispers, no trauma, none of the residue of terror suffered by his generation around the business of cancer. In his day, Suzanne's diagnosis would have been a death sentence for sure.

'You remember angiogenesis inhibitors?'

'As another false dawn,' said Nate.

'Not a false dawn as it turned out. We still use them for tumours. And monoclonal antibodies for stray cells. We tailor everything for the individual. We have wonderful machines that can process the information and manufacture personally engineered drugs within a matter of hours. I'll show you one day.'

'Well, right now she needs a hug,' said Claire.

'I'll be back in a minute,' apologized Garth, leaving Nate alone in the kitchen with his wife.

'Something smells good,' said Nate.

'We've got royalty coming.'

'Who's that?'

'Well, there's you – then there's Persis and Rick. We don't get to see them much. We're way too dull.'

Nate smiled. 'Persis's husband also works for Icor, doesn't he?'

'Rick – yes. You've not met him yet?'

'Not that I can remember. But my memory is pretty unreliable.'

'He's the boss of the whole division. That's why he shoehorned Persis on to the waking project.'

'He didn't shoehorn Persis. I was lucky to get her,' said Garth, coming back into the room. At that moment, their nine-year-old son Charlie came bounding into the kitchen, followed by Suzanne, who looked as though she had been crying. Garth put his arm around her.

'Mr Grey's gone missing and we want you to help us find him,' shouted Charlie.

'It's the family cat,' said Garth. 'He wanders off into the desert, which is a reckless gamble with his life, considering the number of coyotes who share the neighbourhood. Do you want to come, Nate?'

'Would I need to wear the hood?'

'I'm sorry – but that's a yes.'

They started up the road. The cragged outline of the hills rose up sharply before them. A couple of coyotes yelped in the distance. Charlie raced ahead. All Nate could see was his pale trousers in the fading light. A weird sense of unreality consumed him. It was business as usual and yet freakishly abnormal. Here they were, another generation, the Banner-mans, middle-class, relatively affluent, and searching for a missing cat. The ordinariness of it was overwhelming.

'Do you work on Dad's project?' Suzanne asked Nate.

'Yes,' said Nate.

'Will the project make you famous?'

'I hope not.'

'Dad, tell me again, why didn't it work with all the other heads?'

Nate saw Garth cringe in the half-darkness. 'Suzanne – can you go and find Charlie? I don't want him getting too far ahead.'

'Why didn't it work on the other heads?' she insisted.

'Because we hadn't developed a good enough growth accelerator to make the new neurons grow quickly enough between the heads and the bodies, so there was never any meaningful communication between them. Now, go on.'

Reluctantly, Suzanne darted off up the track.

'Suzanne knows about your work,' said Nate in shock. 'I thought you said—'

'She knows about the *work*,' said Garth ruefully, 'she just doesn't know it's *you*.'

'Isn't it risky to tell your children?'

'Charlie doesn't know, period, and I've asked Suzanne to keep it a secret which I know she will. She's a great kid.'

'She could tell anyone.'

'She could, but she won't.'

'You said I was the only one.'

'You are the only one who survived. But we *did* make a number of attempts before you. We used the oldest heads to be frozen, the earliest ones we could find, from the 1960s and '70s. The freezing methods were so crude back then, and the cell rupture quotient was profound, so we knew we wouldn't be able to revive them.'

'Like a practice run.'

'You could say that.'

'And the bodies?'

'From the local morgue,' lied Garth.

'I saw Mr Grey!' shouted Charlie, running up and butting into his father, 'and then Suzie came and dragged me away.'

'I did not – there was nothing there.'

'I think Mr Grey heard us,' said Garth, sweeping up both his children. 'You know what he's like. Come on – there's a feast waiting.'

When they reached the house, Nate lingered by the gate. He so wanted to carry on walking into the night until his legs gave way and he could fall face down in the dirt and let death take him. Garth saw his hesitation.

'Are you coming, Nate?'

Nate stood his ground.

'Come on. Claire is a really good cook.'

'Are you telling me Phoenix has got to show a profit by '73?' It was Claire talking.

'That's the promise I made when I came down here.'

Nate looked at the man who had just spoken. He was sitting on the stool in the kitchen. He was absurdly good-looking, with a finely tipped nose and darting, guarded eyes. Nate knew instantly who it was. Rick Bandelier – Persis's husband. Nate wondered if he was a genetic like his wife. He had an innate sense of superiority in every casual, unbridled move that he made, from pouring himself more wine without helping anyone else, to crossing his legs and swinging round when he saw them.

'Hey there,' he said, as though he was hosting the party himself.

Nate noticed Persis look at her husband sharply. He wondered if she was embarrassed by his arrogance. She was helping Claire with the supper, pouring olive oil over a straggly salad.

'Well, I'm sure your famous business acumen won't let you down,' said Claire. The remark wasn't flattering or ingratiating. It was almost challenging.

'I'm sorry – you must be Nate,' said Rick, leaping off the stool and shaking Nate's hand a little too vigorously. 'I would have come to say hi sooner, but I never seem to get the time.'

Bullshit, thought Nate. His intuition told him that Rick didn't want to be in any situation where he might be upstaged by his wife.

'I hear you're growing up fast, already out there, wining and dining.'

Nate wanted to like Rick. The words themselves sounded OK, but there was too much studied bonhomie in his style. Everything he said and did looked like a conscious effort and right now he was working on his kindly, concerned persona. 'Are they doing enough to keep you occupied?'

'I rarely get time to *think*,' said Nate.

'Well, you've been keeping the team busy. I can't remember the last time I sat down to dinner with my wife.'

'It makes a change from New York where I never saw *you*,' jibed Persis.

Nate caught the chilly look between them. Claire cranked open the oven door and pulled out a deep dish covered in a thick yellow crust. 'OK,' she said with a tight smile, 'let's eat.'

They sat in a walled courtyard under a glass roof. The smell of all the scented creepers was suffocatingly sweet.

'What is it?' Nate ventured, after being served a ladle of rubbery brown mince.

'Bobotie – a South African dish.'

'Is it meat?'

'Soy,' she said apologetically. 'We don't use much meat. A little chicken, but that's about it. We belong to a great biodome, but even they can't get much meat, so we mainly do without. The diet can get pretty boring.'

'I'm sure it's great,' said Nate, picking over the mound with his fork. He tried a bite. The texture was chewy and tasted of meat, egg custard, chutney and turmeric, all warring with one another in a mess of culinary overkill.

The conversation was polite and a little stilted. Nate tried to gauge the relationships of the people around him. Persis was quiet and watchful, smiling and willing Nate onward when he made the odd contribution. Claire was forthright, but there were a couple of little barbs towards Persis, which got stern looks from Garth. Nate wondered if Claire was jealous of Persis. And Rick seemed to be enjoying his power over all of them. But Nate could see that he was also undermined on some deeper level by the self-containment of his wife. So Persis was the enigma of the group and without knowing it, she was really shaping their behaviour.

'So what is your favourite subject at school, Charlie?' Rick asked Garth's son after a lull in the conversation.

'History,' said Charlie definitively.

'What do you like about history?'

'The plague.'

'I don't think anyone *likes* the plague,' said Claire.

'Which one?' asked Rick.

'The Eastern Seaboard Outbreak of '57.'

'Why?'

'Because of the way they organized the disposal of the bodies—'

'Charlie!' said Claire. 'The dinner table is the one place to forget. Remember the rule.'

'He asked me,' said Charlie indignantly.

'We still get plagues,' said Suzie ominously to her brother. Charlie's eyes grew wide.

'Not for a long time,' interrupted Garth, 'and they're not nearly as bad.'

The conversation was taking Nate to the brink of what he would have to face in the coming months. As he looked at everyone around the table, he wondered what colossal adjustments he was going to need to make. He thought it must be like living in Tudor times, where lives were parochial and plagues could arrive on the wings of crows or the backs of rodents. He wondered if they were more superstitious like the Tudors, believing in bad omens and the persecution of outsiders. A sudden fear began to grip him as he saw a life ahead of him where he would always be the outsider and could so easily be persecuted just for being alive. He stood up from the table.

'Is everything OK, Nate?' said Claire.

'Can I use the bathroom?'

'Sure – it's on the other side of the living room.'

He wandered through the beautifully lit rooms and inhaled the scented candles. It should have been a haven, but the stifling, heavily perfumed atmosphere reminded him of a funeral parlour. How easily, with the wind blowing in the wrong direction, this house could turn from sanctuary to mausoleum. He found a guest room and sat on the bed.

After a while, there was a soft knock on the door. It was Persis.

'Is everything OK?' she asked.

'It's all so fragile,' he said.

'What is?'

'Your world.'

Persis sat down beside him. 'Every generation has to face the reality of their situation.'

He looked at Persis's beautiful face, the tiny upward comma at the corner of her mouth. She was in the prime of her life, but all he could imagine, in his highly emotional state, was the putrefaction of her creamy skin as it peeled back in decay over the white bone of her skull. Was this a premonition? Or was his imperfect mind sending crazy, random thoughts into his consciousness?

'Shall we go back?' she said.

'Do we have to?'

'Come on. Claire fought to the front of the food line for strawberries this morning. She'll be very upset if you don't have some.'

They returned to the dinner table as a meagre pile of strawberries was being ladled by Garth into bowls. Nate felt a hum in his body, an intense desire to run, and found it took everything he had just to keep sitting on his chair and behave like a normal human being. Charlie exclaimed as a sleek grey cat walked through the room, ignoring everyone. Another thing that hasn't changed, thought Nate, as he watched the cat saunter towards the kitchen, and that was the singular behaviour of a cat in search of a good meal.

'What did you think?' said Persis to Rick as they were driving home.

'He's very alert and he's certainly getting emotionally attached to you.'

Persis laughed.

'He was watching you all the time.'

'I was watching *him*.'

'You were watching each other.'

'You're jealous! I love it.'

'No I'm not.'

'Yes you are.'

They were silent for a moment, both resolutely watching the road in front of them.

'He's an experiment, Rick. A wonderful, extraordinary experiment. And I've been with him from the beginning. So of course I'm going to look out for him and get attached to him. But that doesn't mean I'm attracted to him.'

It was always a surprise when Rick's jealousy surfaced. Persis knew that it bubbled beneath the patina of his composure. Occasionally, in the early part of their relationship, he had verbally lashed out at her for flirting, and over the years she had developed ways of dismissing other men to put Rick at his ease. This felt different though. She felt she had betrayed Nate by describing him as an experiment. Even in jest. He was much more than that to her now. How paradoxical that Rick's antennae should sharpen her own self-knowledge.

Persis looked at her husband's profile. She couldn't help feeling that his lack of support over the waking project was about more than just profit. It was as though he was trying to undermine her in some way. She came to the conclusion that deep down, he would have preferred her to fail. Competitiveness was so deeply ingrained into his psyche that he just couldn't stand to see anyone else succeed, not even his wife.

'Tragic,' she murmured.

'What is?' he said tersely.

'Nate – losing Mary. He really loved her.'

'Oh, that,' said Rick, and turned up the music.

45

'So you went to the boss's for dinner,' said Monty in a resentful tone. 'How was it?'

'Educational.' Nate didn't want to enthuse. It was clear the team rarely socialized and Monty was probably offended that he hadn't been invited. 'Monty, you know, we haven't really talked much since I tried to kill myself.'

'What is there to say?'

'I don't know.'

'You had your reasons.'

The blandness of Monty's words irritated Nate. 'So it was OK by you then?'

'Well, no – I—'

'Apart from Karen, who lost her entire family, I don't get the feeling that any one of you has a normal emotional range,' said Nate. 'What do they do to you? Is it the Dome? Does it cancel out the highs and the lows?'

'I don't know what to tell you, Nate. Maybe. But I told you, I can't afford it.'

'But what do you do, Monty, when you're not here with me?'

'I sleep mostly. Talk to my brother.'

'There must be other stuff going on?'

'I have my hobbies, my interests,' he said defensively.

'Like what?'

'I do the Christmas Lights Fantasia every year. I was hoping that you might come take a look before it's open to the public.'

'Well, whoopee. I can't wait to see that.'

'I need to go do some work,' stammered Monty, and left the room.

Nate felt guilty for being a bully. He would apologize to Monty first thing in the morning. The man had been so gentle and kind and he didn't deserve Nate's sarcasm. But Nate just didn't know how he would ever be able to truly relate to these people and their vapid responses. He hammered his body around the corridors, twenty laps if he was counting correctly.

Sometimes a minor confusion would blank out abstract con-
cepts like simple maths. At the end of it, he didn't even feel
tired. He was reaching a whole new level of fitness. In his old
life his body had been functional and he mostly ignored it,
trying to keep his weight down and his diet healthy. But he'd
been so preoccupied with his busy life that it was usually
Mary who pointed out any changes. Now, as he focused on
the hardening contours of his torso and the lean, tawny tissue
over muscle, he realized that he was beginning to feel admir-
ation. He didn't like it, but he was definitely beginning to
feel it.

'So I'm finally becoming a narcissist?' he said to himself
with grim mirth.

He decided to take a shower. He soaped the body and
thought about the donor. As much as he longed to see a
photograph of Mary, he longed to see an image of the man
who had once inhabited the body. Nate conjured up a clean-
living, respectable guy from a loving background who was
ready to take on his share of responsibility in the world. He
thought about the cruel configuration of events which had
brought the man's life to an end, a road accident, not the
donor's fault, but a side-on collision that would have broken
his neck in an instant. Nate envisioned devoted mourners at
the man's funeral and speeches that talked of the donor's
honour, integrity and generosity. He thought about the
donor's family. Weren't they curious to know what had
happened to their beloved son or brother? One day, he would
find them and thank them.

Nate looked down at his penis and began to soap it and
felt the stiffening of an erection. Maybe the guy was married.
Christ! Nate hadn't even thought about that. What if there
was a wife somewhere, grieving and struggling to look after

small children? What were the family or Icor doing to support her? That train of thought brought him back to the bizarre reality of his predicament and the erection disappeared.

He stepped out of the shower and ran his hand across the steamed-up mirror, listening to the squeaks the friction made against the glass. It was a familiar, comforting sound and he was grateful to hear it. Grateful. Maybe his mood *was* improving.

He looked at his reflection. The engorged hillock of scar tissue on his neck was receding. It still felt enormous to the touch but in the mirror, it didn't look so pronounced. There was a wispy white line in the centre of the two humps, some small snags in the tissue and a button of gristle under the skin by his left ear. His hair was already needing a trim and his eyebrows were getting bushy. The fact that they were growing at all sent a thrill through Nate. The body was actually working, the cells replicating. He was, indeed, a miracle.

He put on his robe and returned to his room, his mind drifting, as it so often did, back to Mary. She used to pluck the anarchic hairs from his eyebrows. It was part of their morning ablution ritual. He would stand there, head hung, like a patient old horse while Mary would cluck at him, put her tweezers to work and admonish him for not being more conscientious about his looks. He remembered how she loved to disapprove of him and he loved being disapproved of.

'What must your patients think?' she said to him practically every single morning. And in that instant, he realized that that's what a marriage was. It was a routine, with all the rituals of intimacy built into the language. She wasn't really admonishing him about his lack of attention to his appearance. What she was really doing was telling him that she loved him.

'I love you too,' he said, his voice cracking in the silence.

46

It was an anonymous tip-off. The Epidemic Intelligence Service got a lot of calls like that. And it was their duty to react to every single one. The skill was to sort the wheat from the chaff, the genuine whistle-blower from the grudge-bearing employee. The caller, whose voice was disguised, told them the regrowth programme at Icor had an unregistered body that had been kept alive for months.

Dr Kim Andrew was alerted to the call by a junior officer. It had come through on the confidential tip-off line, which wasn't always so confidential, but the caller had been cautious, making the connection from an unregistered line. The voice was clearly male, but it was unlikely that the EIS would ever be able to trace it. Not that it mattered. The man said the body had been revived with a bacterial infection. That was all they needed to know. Dr Andrew had given Dr Bannerman the chance to open up, but he had decided to deceive her, and now she had all the proof she needed to make sure there were no more experiments of this kind anywhere else in the state. Cryonics was just too high-risk.

The senior officer obtained a warrant to enter and search Icor and was already on her way up Tagar Avenue towards the company's Phoenix headquarters. In Dr Andrew's eyes, Icor was a monument to all the overblown grants and stipends gifted to reckless scientists like Dr Bannerman, while she had to struggle to keep her unit functioning and just this side of a public scandal. Resources were something that she never had enough of and her predicament was risible considering the responsibility she had to keep disaster at bay.

The quiet trundle of the military tanks behind and in front of her made Dr Andrew feel safe in her decision. By tonight,

Icor would be bagged and sealed, and a skeleton staff would be at work on the premises, keeping the baby farm open and the organ regrowth programme operating. With any luck she would get the Phoenix division shut down altogether. President's visit or no President's visit, everyone had to live by the letter of the law and Bannerman had flagrantly disobeyed her.

Garth had been alerted to a commotion at the gates and blanched when he saw the convoy of the National Guard coming to a halt outside. He knew instantly what it meant and with a defeated air called up Icor's lawyers.

'I don't think you've been straight with us,' said Dr Andrew, her blue eyes piercing his resolve.

'I was about to tell you,' he stammered. His mouth was dry and he tried to swallow.

'How long has he been alive?' she demanded, testing Garth to see if he was going to lie to her again.

'Five months.'

'Why the *hell* didn't you tell me? I bent over backwards to accommodate you!' She was quivering with rage.

'How can we operate in this environment? If I told you, you would have confiscated the body and shut us down. You don't have the expertise or inclination to keep the body alive. It would have perished if you'd taken it. He was an anomaly, Kim. We didn't expect him to survive – but he did. As a scientist who believes in progress, what else could I do?'

'Why would we even need to confiscate the body?' she said. Another test.

'He contracted an infection.'

'That is why this whole area of cryonic revival is so dangerous! The body comes with us and the unit gets sealed off. Sorry, Garth. I've got no choice.'

'He's completely clear now. No risk to anyone.'

'How did you achieve that?'

'He's strong. He fought it and we managed to get a supply of antibiotics from Europe that actually worked.' Garth's mind was racing. Who tipped her off? Was it one of the sacked workers? Had the Center for Disease Control traced the trail of antibiotics?

'Let *me* be the judge of that,' said Dr Andrew icily.

'Can I at least talk to him before you take him?'

'He's talking?'

'Kim – he's walking, talking, thinking. And a lot of people will be very upset if anything happens to him.'

'Well, you should have thought about that before you lied to us,' she said.

'At least keep him isolated.'

'It depends on what facilities are available.'

'Don't endanger him because we kept you in the dark. *Please.* He needs isolation. He could be susceptible to any kind of infection himself. I know the quarantine unit. People go in there healthy and they don't come out.'

'I'm not interested in your opinion of how we operate,' she said.

'Let me talk to him. Prepare him for what's coming.'

'Be my guest,' she said, mimicking the politeness of their previous visit.

'Hey, Garth. Thanks again for last night,' said Nate, getting up from the bed.

'We have a *big* problem.'

'What?'

'There's an agency called the Epidemic Intelligence Service.'

'I remember them. They were formed in the 1940s to fight polio. I came across them in Los Angeles, trying to control TB.'

'Well, their status has changed. They have much more power than they used to and somehow, they found out about you. They're not happy about the fact we didn't tell them about you, and they're going to take you to their headquarters in Phoenix and run some tests on you to see that you're clear of infection. I'm sorry, but it's not going to be a pleasant trip.'

'Why didn't you tell them – about me?'

'Because of the infection you contracted when you were revived. We wanted to wait until it cleared up and then we were going to tell them.'

'What will it entail?' said Nate.

'A thorough examination. We will try to come with you, but they may not let us.'

'Why not?'

'This is what I mean by power. They will ask you questions and you may be badly treated. They have a poor reputation in Phoenix. If they do ask you anything, say you can't remember. The less you tell them, the better. I'm so sorry, Nate. Someone betrayed us.'

Six guards in biohazard suits manhandled Nate to the decontamination rooms, with Garth and Persis shouting instructions all the way. The EIS brought a protective suit for Nate and ordered him to put it on. Persis was as threatening as her professionalism would allow, telling the EIS that Icor's lawyers would be seeking access to the patient immediately and that nothing could happen to him in the meantime. Garth stayed in the background, looking cowed. Rick was nowhere to be seen.

The masked invaders bundled Nate into a windowless

tank. No one spoke as the convoy hurtled through the streets. He heard powerful gates open, then he was dragged from the back of the vehicle and pushed into another interior. His mask was removed and he found himself in a long, windowless room lined with benches and lockers.

'Remove the suit and put it in the bag provided,' said a voice through a speaker system.

'I need to know what's going on!' shouted Nate.

'Remove the suit, or we will do it by force.'

The air was stale and smelt of musty wood and bodies, like a changing room at an unsanitary gym. Nate undressed.

'Move towards the end of the room and wait by the door.'

The door shunted open and he stepped into darkness. He felt water from above. A decontamination shower. A small light glowed at the end of the room.

'Scrub yourself,' said the disembodied voice, 'put the gown on and lie down on the gurney.'

He obeyed, thinking that to run or fight would be worse. The soap smelt of skin-peeling disinfectant. When he was done, he lay down on the gurney and heard the stiff joints of a heavy metal door. Two medics in full body suits appeared and wheeled him into another chamber.

'Look at his neck,' one said.

'A real Frankenstein.'

A circle of bright lights blinded him.

'Lie with your palms up and your feet splayed. Take three deep breaths and relax. Do not resist any penetration by the machines. Resistance will harm you.'

An octopus of robotic arms whizzed and whirred above him, their pincers, needles and blunted prods poised for attack. All at once, the arms came clamouring towards him, gripping his skin in their cold metallic forceps, finding their spot and piercing the skin to extract samples of blood. When the examination was over, the arms withdrew and waited above his head.

'Turn over, keep your legs splayed, take three deep breaths and relax.'

Nate let out a gasp as a painful jab punctured his neck at the base of his skull. There was another at the bottom of his spine. A lumbar puncture. The procedures needed an anaesthetic. He felt a cold metal prod penetrate his rectum. He bellowed in agony as the machines took biopsies.

Eventually, the voice instructed him to lie on his back and the lid of a metal tube was lowered over him just inches from his face. It was filled with a blue light. They must be giving him a full body scan. Unlike the old MRI scanners, this was noiseless and mercifully quick.

'Get up and take another shower, please.'

Nate tried to stand up. His legs felt weak.

'I can't,' he said softly. No one came. Eventually, his head cleared enough to stand. There were a dozen puncture marks on his body. His back was bleeding and so was his rectum. After the shower, he was surrounded by guards in biohazard suits. One of them, a short, squat woman, sniggered and touched the scar on his neck.

'So what's it like to come back from the dead?' she taunted.

Nate averted his gaze. She yanked his jaw round so he was looking straight at her. She had lazy, dead eyes and a square jaw which jutted out like a pugnacious little dog's.

'Welcome to the EIS.'

47

They gave him a surgical gown and shunted him into a long dormitory lined on either side with bunk beds. When his eyes adjusted to the light, he saw that every bed was occupied. He could hear coughing, like the whizz of a drill in an empty barrel. It was the unmistakable sound of the TB rattle. He could see at least two patients who were blue. He covered his mouth with his shirt.

'Who's treating these people?' he said. 'They should be in isolation.'

'This *is* isolation,' said the female guard.

They marched him along the aisle. If he wasn't ill now, he would be very soon. The door at the end of the ward opened and he was pushed into another long corridor of cells with beds, also full of sick people.

'This is yours, Frankenstein,' said another guard, and pushed him inside. 'Don't get too fond of Kevin, he's not going to be with us for very long.'

The man in the bed looked to be about forty. He was in a state of delirium and skinny as a rail. There was vomit everywhere and a dark stain in his trousers. Automatically, Nate took a pulse and felt his forehead. His temperature was at least 103 degrees.

'We can do something for this man!' he shouted.

The female guard turned round and marched back to his cell.

'And what do you think we can do for him?' she said.

Nate tried to think. 'I think it's malaria. If it's plasmodium falciparum, we can give him quinine sulphate, Doxycycline.'

'Anything else?'

'Mefloquine and an anti-emetic to stop the vomiting.'

'You think?' Her lip curled up in a mean smile. 'The malaria we got now is resistant to everything.'

She walked back down the corridor. Nate saw hands coming through the bars to get her attention.

'Carrie, I need water . . . Carrie, help me . . . Carrie . . . Carrie.'

'Shuddup,' she said lazily.

Nate looked at the man on the bed. He tore up a sheet and tried to clean him up. If it was plasmodium falciparum and the man was in the latter stages without receiving any treatment, death would come soon. Nate could see from the dark stain on his trousers that he was already in a state of renal collapse.

At one stage the man grabbed Nate's arm. He looked terrified. Nate wiped the sweat from his forehead.

'How long have you been in here?' he asked, but Kevin was too far gone. By late afternoon he was dead. Nate checked his pulse.

'Hey,' he shouted to the guards. He didn't stop shouting until someone came.

'If you keep this up – no food or water, understand?' said the woman.

'This is barbaric. You have no right to treat people like this!' said Nate.

'What's your problem?'

'He's dead. Very soon, he's going to be a danger to everyone, including you.'

'They collect at eight. Now shut the fuck up. You're giving me a headache.' She went to leave, then turned around. 'Oh by the way, the good news is, that when you came in here, you were clean.'

'Then why don't you let me out?'

'Paperwork.'

'Why am I being punished like this?'

'Like the woman said – shut up! You're giving us *all* a headache.' It was a man's voice speaking from a cell further along.

'What's your name?' asked Nate when the guard had gone.

'Hisham.'

'Why were you brought here?'

'My wife came down with a fever. They arrested the whole family.'

'Where's your wife?'

'In a different block. Women and children are split up.'

'How long do you think you'll be in here?'

'They said anything up to a month.'

'I thought this was the malaria ward.'

'Don't believe anything they tell you.'

'My cellmate is dead.'

'I've had two die on me already. You just got to wait until tonight.'

Nate looked down at Kevin's emaciated body. They *must* have invented a quinine derivative to treat malaria, surely? Kevin could have been saved if they'd got to him early enough. Nate remembered the routine that he went through as an MD, when he was called out to pronounce someone dead. This time, he simply covered Kevin's head in a blanket and said a prayer. He wondered how and when the EIS had lost its sense of basic human decency, considering that it was looking after the nation's health, and what kind of society he had come back to that would allow the agency to get away with it.

48

It was the worst job on shift. You had to be really careful suiting up. No pinholes or tears anywhere on the suit. Double-thickness gloves. Duct tape. Manny had already lost two buddies to the plague. After that he'd become extra meticulous. He trudged around the wards with the new guy. He didn't even know the man's name, but he felt too lethargic to ask. When he had to do something he didn't want to, it was as though his shoes were filled with lead and his mind was half shut down.

There were three bodies in ward six, another two from the women's ward and three from the children's block. Manny didn't bother to look at the charts as he was supposed to. He just nodded to the living dead, which is what they called the patients who were still alive in quarantine, and put the corpses into body bags. He didn't like checking the cadavers either. Detachment was helped by the suit. You could tuck your chin into your chest, keep your eyes down, and the periphery of your vision would be cut off by the visor. Then you didn't have to look at all.

Once they had the full quota, they wheeled the body bags along the corridor to the night truck.

'Not too many tonight,' said Manny to the driver.

Sometimes it could be anything up to thirty, but things had been quieter for more than a year. The lack of activity almost got Manny worried. There was another round of cuts coming and he wondered what the hell he'd do if he lost his job.

They drove through the streets to the morgue and delivered their cargo. There would be a rudimentary autopsy, to satisfy the statistical requirements of the EIS, then the bodies would be cremated before dawn. It was a neat and tidy operation. Not like the quarantine hospital. Manny wasn't the type to feel outrage about anything much, but that hospital should be shut down. Everyone said so. And yet there it was, still open. He looked at the chart on the wall. Dina was the pathologist on tonight. Good. He liked Dina. She was no-nonsense.

'Hey, Manny,' she said with her tough, slightly crooked smile. She had a freckled, cowgirl look to her, with sinewy arms. He liked looking at those arms.

'What you got for me?'

'Three men. Two women. Three children. Malaria.'

'It's getting to be quite a problem. Put them over there, will you?' she said, and left the room.

'OK – alleyoop,' he said to his new partner, and they formed a swinging motion to flip the bodies on to metal tables. There was a rustle from one of the bags. Manny and his partner both made 'ooohhhhwaaaaa' sounds. The rustle was one too many for a corpse.

'Did a rodent get in there?' said the new guy.

'Oh Jesus, I hate those things.'

They listened some more.

'Dina can handle it. Let's get out of here.'

Dina laid out her instruments on a metal tray. It was going to be a long night. Eight bodies and no one to help her. At least none of the bodies were designated infectious, so she didn't need to fire up the robot. She began to unzip the first body bag. A hand grabbed her wrist. The action was so quick and so shocking that her legs gave way.

'Who the fuck—?'

Nate peeled away the body bag and jumped to the floor, twisting the woman's arm as he went. Dina made a lunge for the emergency button, but he got there first.

'Don't even try it,' said Nate.

'Don't hurt me.'

'I'm not going to hurt you. What's your name?'

She swallowed, too stunned to say anything.

'How many security guards are there in this place? Come on – talk to me!'

'One. Just one. John. He's upstairs.'

'OK – you're going to get me to your car, show me how to drive and give me a new set of clothes. Think you can manage that?'

'You won't get far,' said Dina.

'Why not?'

'I've got fifteen miles of power left. Just enough to get me home.'

'That's all I need.'

'John will see us. On the security network. I'm the only one on duty. He'll wonder who you are.'

'No he won't. You're going to wheel me out the same way I came in.'

Dina's car was like a covered golf cart and just as easy to drive. The morgue was a little way out of town and there was no street lighting. Nate switched on the car's two tiny headlights, which threw weak beams across the uneven road. He felt a tremendous rush. To be out of captivity and driving. He ended up liking Dina. Once she'd recovered from his shocking manifestation, she had given him a full body suit, her card to recharge the car and some cash. She understood, she said, why he wanted to get away from quarantine. She even offered to give him a blood test to find out if he had picked up any malarial parasites or viruses while he was there. It came back negative. She promised she would give Nate time to escape before she reported him to the police, but he didn't know if he could trust her that much.

The outskirts of Phoenix were almost deserted. Nate's blood ran cold when he saw the silent progress of an armoured tank approaching in the opposite direction. He knew he couldn't turn around. They would only get suspicious. Four soldiers sat on the perch of the tank, monitoring the streets with search lamps. When they saw him they trained the beam on his car. He drove on, keeping his head low. Dina told him the night patrols would check the ID on the windscreen to see if the driver had permission to be out after curfew. He fully expected to be flagged down, but they didn't react. Dina must have kept to her word.

Once he was out of harm's way, Nate took a detour off the main road. The street was lined with buildings that looked like the helmets of Chinese warriors, with narrow windows for the eyes and vents for the front door. He drove down street after street of helmets, from Spanish conquistador visors to rounded American military models, bewildering in their number and style. He wondered what the hell they were. They were too ugly to be shops and too hostile to be houses.

Nate was peering so hard that he didn't notice the car. It burst out of a side street and headed straight for him. Nate yanked his steering wheel, careered across the junction and smashed straight into the front of a building. There was a dead crunch of metal. His head ricocheted. He could just hear the screech of brakes and tyres as the other car made its getaway before he blacked out.

When he came to, a group of dark figures were gathering around the car. He could hear a hiss from his suit and realized it must have been punctured. He grabbed the flap on the dashboard and snatched the air-purifier Dina had given him. He saw one of the figures yanking the passenger door open. It made a dull crack. Before he could utter a sound, a shroud descended over his eyes and he passed out again.

The next thing Nate remembered was lying in a darkened room. People were standing around him. Someone had removed his visor and his head was being supported by something hard. There was a stabbing pain in his neck and ribs. Instinctively, he began to check to see if he was injured. His mind travelled over the body and, to his relief, he found he could still feel every limb. And he could twist his neck both ways. He was lying on a sofa in some kind of a bar and there was a powerful smell of sweat and beer. He looked down and saw the air-purifier in his hand.

'Who are you?' An older guy was speaking, fifty maybe, his face covered in whiskers. 'What's your name?'

'Icor,' Nate whispered. A dagger of pain cut through his neck.

'You work for Icor? Those fuckers. I couldn't give a fuck about Icor.'

'Here – give him a beer.'

'Beer? He needs air.'

It was a woman's voice.

'The air in here is the best in town,' someone else said, and they all laughed.

'Let him breathe,' commanded the woman who walked into Nate's peripheral vision. She was young, pale as a ghost, with scraggly, scarecrow hair and filthy hands which tugged at his biohazard suit. She took the air-purifier from his hand, twisted it and put it around his neck. Then she took a small vial of powder from a necklace that she was wearing and poured out a tiny pyramid between her thumb and forefinger. She sniffed and offered it to Nate.

'It'll kill the pain,' she said. 'Then we can work out who you are.'

Nate hoped it was a horse tranquillizer, something powerful enough to jettison him out of this world. He sniffed as hard as his lungs could inhale.

'Hey, hey – not so fast!' he heard the girl say as an explosion of white firecrackers lit up before his eyes.

49

Fred hated paying money for information, but in Okorie's case, he knew he had to make an exception. The guy had said he wouldn't give him anything unless Fred came up with the cash. He could sense, even from one meeting and a couple of calls, that Okorie was as tough as they came. He had to be, to have escaped from Nigeria. And, actually, it had turned out well. At long last, Fred had got a commitment from *The Metropolitan* and a cashier's cheque to pay Okorie a part of his fee if they ever ran the story. He was finally being treated like a professional.

He hopped on the dawn airbus from LA to Phoenix and hired a bubble car to get to Okorie's house. He hated the tiny, comical car, but he just couldn't afford a bigger one. The expenses that the magazine had agreed to pay him were pathetic. They knew it. He knew it. But they knew what a break Fred was getting by being published, so they were happy to exploit him.

Fred soon found Okorie's address, a bland townhouse on the edge of the city, the colour of the sandy hills that rose up behind the estate. It was surprisingly opulent for someone who worked as a nurse. Fred rang the bell. No answer. He felt a surge of tension. What if the guy had changed his mind?

How was he going to explain *that* to *The Metropolitan*? He rang again and saw an old woman look through the curtains next door. He smiled at her. She dropped the curtain.

Fred decided to ring her doorbell. She might know where Okorie was. A little old man answered.

'I'm looking for Okorie Chimwe. Have you seen him today?'

'You're not the only one.'

'What do you mean?'

'A lot of people came by here.'

'Like who?'

'Don't know. Men like you.'

'He said to meet me here. Do you know where he is?'

'He's gone.'

'Gone – gone where?'

'I don't know but the back door's open and there's no sign of him. Looks like he took off someplace.'

Fred borrowed a ladder and climbed over the back wall. The glass doors were wide open and the modest living room was completely empty. Not a stick of furniture, an empty coffee cup or a photograph on the mantelpiece.

'Okorie?' Fred shouted weakly. 'Okorie Chimwe. It's me, Fred Arlin.'

Fred didn't really want anyone to answer. He didn't want to find an assassin in the wardrobe or a body behind the shower curtain. He tapped numbers into his wristwatch.

'Hurry up, hurry up,' he whispered. Why were they taking so long? Without even looking upstairs, he stumbled back out on to the patio.

'This is the emergency service. What service do you require?' said a sleepy female voice at the other end of the line.

'I want to report a missing person,' said Fred.

'Is it a genuine emergency?'

'I think so,' said Fred, a sense of doom descending on him. *What was it about this story?* he thought. 'Am I cursed? Why can't I nail down a single damn thing?'

50

Nate could see a curtain above him undulating listlessly in a breeze. It was covering what looked like a trailer window but thicker, with two, maybe three, panes of glass. He could hear snoring off to the side. He tried to move, but a metal collar was tied around his neck and it was tethered to something. The stiffness in his whole body reminded Nate of the accident, his rescuers and the drugs he'd inhaled. He sniffed the air and felt a scorching inside his nostrils. So he hadn't died from an overdose after all, but the substance the girl had given him had singed his nasal passages. He sniffed again. There was a smell of old clothes, fur, must, earth and something more sinister which teased his senses – dog shit.

Directly above him an oxygen mask hung down on its plastic noose. He moved his hand and felt a padded leather armrest. He must be lying on a dentist's recliner, but it was too messy to be a surgery and there was something familiar about the mask. Painfully, he rolled on to his side. Through the silvery dawn, he recognized the cone shape of the room immediately. He was lying in the first-class compartment of a jumbo jet. But this plane hadn't been anywhere for a very long time.

There were a dozen or so people asleep in the other recliners, still in their rumpled, filthy clothes. The door to the cockpit was open, revealing the tangled spaghetti of wiring where the control panels had been ripped out. All the detritus a human can produce was scattered around the cabin floor. A hollow-eyed dog looked out at him from under a chair and raised a quizzical eyebrow. Defeated, half-starved, his meek entreaty would have been enough to call animal rescue in another life.

Nate lifted himself up on an elbow and pulled back the curtain. The material came away in his hand. He brushed his palm over the dirt-caked porthole. What he saw took his breath away. Across the entire valley floor was a sea of airplanes, a century of aviation exiled to the desert and left to burnish under the sun.

There was every kind of craft imaginable, from smaller executive jets to the massive double-decker airbuses. He could make out familiar insignia on the tails: American, United, British Airways, Singapore, Aeroflot, Virgin Airways.

As he looked more closely, he could see figures hanging around the huge wheels; groups of men sitting and talking, women washing their children with hose pipes, packs of dogs, lazing cats and kids running in and out of the metal carcasses. It was like a vast, crazy gypsy camp stretching as far as the eye could see.

Someone inside the cabin coughed. Nate jumped. He realized that the suit and the air-purifier had been taken away and he was wearing a vest and shorts. He tested his lungs and was surprised to find no constriction. It was just his neck. He knew he hadn't broken it, but he had definitely sprained it. He needed a painkiller badly, but he didn't want to cry out. He must have drifted off to sleep again because when he woke up the others were joshing each other and grumbling in low voices. They looked at him with surly indifference. There must have been eight or so men and three women, all filthy, with matted hair and threadbare clothes.

He tried to figure out if there was a leader of sorts and

scanned the room for the girl. He saw her tucked into the armpit of some huge guy. They were stirring. The man was ferocious-looking with huge rust-coloured freckles on his fore-arms, and pale blue eyes. He had a face like a wounded soldier, with a handlebar moustache. Nate noticed that his swollen hands were indented by big silver rings and thought he might be a type 2 diabetic, carrying all that weight.

'My name is Dr Sheehan.' Nate directed his introduction at the big guy. 'I'm being looked after by Icor Incorporated. I need to get back there as quickly as possible. Can you help me?'

He didn't want to go back to Icor, but he didn't know what other options he had. No one said anything. In desper-ation, Nate raised his chin to reveal his neck scar.

'Someone tried to garrotte me. They nearly killed me. Icor have been healing the wound.'

'Can Icor set me up with a new set of teeth?' said someone in the cabin.

'Yeah – and I need some L385,' said another.

'If you help me to get back there, I promise you I will get all the medicines you need,' said Nate.

'You got a virus?' said the big guy, suspicious.

'No virus. I swear. I'm clean. Icor have been treating me for the injury. I just need to get back there and finish my treatment.'

There was a mechanical clunk and a buzzing started up. The crowd banged on the cabin walls and cheered, then gathered around the air vents, putting their faces close to the ducts.

Nate lay back on his recliner and prayed for the pain in his neck to go away. For the rest of the day, the gang ignored him and went about their business, while the strangest eccen-trics from elsewhere in the camp came to check him out.

Many wore lunatic clothing – Dr Seuss top hats, pink quilted dressing gowns – and one or two wore plastic false breasts tied like aprons around their chests. Some had mad, darting eyes, missing teeth and skinny, undernourished limbs. There were all kinds of tribal body painting on hands and faces. One guy had actually managed to distort the length of his neck with a string of necklaces, and Nate noticed a couple of the women had forced wooden discs into their lower lips. It seemed as though some of them were retarded or borderline autistic. That was the only way he could explain their blank faces when he spoke to them. He wondered why they had no language skills.

By the evening he was determined to establish some kind of relationship with his captors.

'What's your name?' he ventured to the big guy.

'Tony.'

'How do you keep order, Tony? Do you have guns?'

'Sure we do. They think they can disarm us and leave us to our fate, but we got guns. We don't tout them around is all.'

'Who is *us*?' asked Nate.

Tony said nothing. Later, Nate managed to corner the girl who'd helped him after the accident. He found out her name was Pearl.

'How long has this place been here?' he asked her.

'As long as I can remember.'

'How did you end up living here?'

'It's easier.'

'What do you mean?'

'When you get into trouble, they won't leave you alone. You're on the list. In here – they can't touch you.'

'Doesn't the National Guard or the police ever come in here?'

'Every now and then, to find someone. But we try to avoid that.'

'How?'

'We're the police. If someone comes along and they've been in trouble and the guard are gonna come after them, we get rid of them or they get rid of themselves.' She looked at him pointedly.

'I'm a doctor. I could be useful.'

'We've got enough doctors.'

'You do?'

'Sure, and professors and lawyers. We got all the help we need.'

'Some of the people, they didn't seem to understand me. What's wrong with them?'

She looked at him furiously. 'You know what!'

'I don't.'

She clucked. 'They got their brains fried by the Dome.'

Of course, thought Nate. Why would the Dome be a benign instrument to cure mental illness? One tweak of the programme and it could so easily become an implement of destruction.

'You mean they scramble brainwaves?'

'I don't know what they do, but people turn up gibbering and dribbling like idiots and there's nothing we can do for them.'

Nate wondered how many people existed beyond the boundaries of structured society.

'Why did you have to come here?' he asked her.

'And why should I tell you?' she said, her dark eyes turning cold.

Nate watched the comings and goings of the camp through the porthole. He noticed there were dozens of water filtration plants, yet a lot of heaving and sickness. Not surprisingly, every single person in the cabin had some form of physical defect – infected lungs, suppurating wounds, anaemia – and a couple of them probably had something more serious. Then there were the people with tics, tremors and incoherent mumbling. A couple showed all the telltale signs of psychosis and schizophrenia.

He carefully listed everyone's symptoms in his head. It was an old, old habit from his days as an MD. He made a valiant effort to keep the conversation going, to humanize the situation, and he promised them medical help if they would just let him go, take him back to Icor and deposit him outside the gates. But they weren't interested, at least not for now.

The plane was like a furnace during the day. The gang hitched themselves to spots near the air vents or fanned themselves with trays. No one respected anyone else's privacy. Most doors were gone and there was a lot of hawking and spitting and bodily functions that had to be borne by everyone. They gave him a bucket to do his ablutions in, but they weren't interested in helping him out of his chair. He wanted to admonish them for being so filthy and tell them that they were encouraging disease, but he refrained from saying anything that might antagonize them.

At dusk, the drums started up, sending vibrations across the desert floor. The gang went outside, leaving Nate chained by his neck to the chair. He could hear eating and talking under the belly of the plane, talking that turned into carousing as the night drew on and descended into shouting and fighting after midnight. It was like living among Neanderthals. He wondered how long they would keep him here without making a decision about his future.

Every morning, someone came to check on Nate's pulse,

look into his eyes and feel for swollen lymph nodes in his groin and under his armpits. The whirr of the air-conditioning bored into his brain and despondency started to grip him. He felt he had to get away somehow or he would go completely crazy.

On the fourth day, he demanded to be unchained so he could take a shower. Surprisingly, they complied and let him into the first-class toilet. Once a cradle of luxury with its unguents and potions, it was now a putrid, squalid cesspool. The stench flailed his nostrils. They told him to wait while they pumped up the water. He found a door, shored up the entrance and turned on the protesting faucet. Hot brown water oozed from the shower head but at least it was wet. While he was trying to raise some suds out of a tiny pellet of soap, the door was pushed aside. Pearl was standing there. She was ageing before her time, with a pinched little mouth and dust blown into the cracks of her skin. They had barely exchanged two words since their last conversation. He said nothing, hoping that she would lose interest and go away.

'What's that?' she said, looking down.

'What's what?'

She sauntered over and pointed to his left buttock. Nate wanted to swat her away, but he held back. 'That snake growing out of your butt?'

He twisted his torso and flinched at the stab of pain in his neck. 'What snake?'

'You got a snake tattoo coming out of your butt.'

'The tattoo. I forgot,' he said, improvising. 'I haven't seen it in a while. Can you show me? There's a mirror over there.'

Pearl considered his request. 'You're strange,' she said, then angled the broken mirror so that Nate could see his reflection. He could just make out the tip of a snake's head coming out of his buttocks, with white fangs biting down on to a cheek. Why had Icor never mentioned it? They must have known about it, though it was pretty well hidden.

'I think it's kind of sexy,' said Pearl.

Nate pulled his buttocks apart and saw the neck of the snake heading towards his anus. What kind of a man would want to carve a tattoo like that into his skin? And the pain he must have endured! Nate felt a slide of adrenaline as this new piece of information shattered the illusion of the life he had concocted around the donor body. The mature, respectable family man. With a snake coming out of his anus? Even as a joke, it was a brutal thing to inflict on yourself.

'Do you want to fuck?' said Pearl, leaning against the door frame.

'No.'

'Why not?'

They stood facing each other. The heat and the worms of her hair pleated across her forehead made Nate feel hot, confused and – aroused. If this was survival, then for the first time since his waking, he recognized that in the confines of the most basic existence, sex could play a part. He put his hand over his penis to cover himself. He felt abused and a little scared by the directness of her approach. If he'd said yes, how did she think the encounter would go? Would they just do it in the shower under the nose of Tony, who was clearly her man? She was physically filthy and he wondered what viruses he might pick up from her. Yes, he did want to fuck and his body was ready, but he couldn't do it to himself. Not yet.

'When you're physically impaired, there's not much sexual desire,' he said, searching the cubicle for his shorts.

'You look OK to me,' she said, squinting at his groin.

'Pearl, I'm sick. If I don't get back to Icor I may die.'

'We're all dying,' she said. 'And you're not going any-where. We're seeing if you're worth anything to us.'

'What do you mean?'

'Tony is not happy about you being here.'

'But you brought me here.'

'You rather we'd left you?'

'Well, no, I—' In many ways he wished they had left him alone.

'So you'd better be worth something. He's killed ten men, so don't mess with him,' she said defiantly.

Nate laughed. He actually laughed, and though the action hurt his neck and sounded strange to him, he enjoyed it. It shook him up. 'You can't frighten me with your threats, Pearl. What you don't know is that I'm one of the walking dead already.'

Pearl considered what he'd said, then stormed out. Nate leant his forehead against the mirror. He remembered some girlfriend long before Mary. What was her name? Julia. She was a British publicist with a tawny complexion and pretty but hard, nut-brown eyes. They were taking a flight to London when they got lucky with an upgrade. He took advantage of the free massage while Julia lined up the empty miniatures on her trestle table. Boy, could she drink. He remembered that about her, about all Brits. The hum of the plane and the massage made him feel horny. The masseuse noticed and shockingly whispered in his ear that she would be happy to 'pleasure him' for an extra 200 bucks. When it was over he returned to his seat and relished the joy of being fed succulent titbits by the stewardess, stroking Julia's athletic thighs and drowning in champagne. This turned out to be some kind of bacchanalian prelude to even more passion. He and Julia figured that they couldn't make sex work on their recliners without upsetting the other passengers, so they'd snuck into the toilet and stripped each other naked. What a magical fuck that had been. He wished Julia could appear through the mirror right now, hold out her hand and help him back into his old dimension. But all he could see in the reflection of the mirror were the loping figures of his inmates going about their chores and adding to the filth that was already littering the cabin floor.

51

First light revealed a grey blanket of smoke lingering over the plane park. There'd been no wind during the night to shift the toxins left by the campfires and the dozens of little lamps that hissed and spat. The air was getting to Nate's lungs and he could feel the tightness of an infection developing in his chest. He had to get back to the protection of Icor or he might do some serious damage to his body. He wondered what the life expectancy of the plane park was. There didn't seem to be any old people. His heart broke at one point when he saw through his cabin window a two-year-old boy stuck between two puddles and screaming. No one was watching over the boy or coming to the rescue. Nate shouted at the gang to do something.

'Someone will come,' said Tony casually.

Pearl approached his recliner, looking beat-up and mangy in the early-morning light.

'We're going on a trip,' she said, tying a leash to the dog collar that was attached to his neck.

'I'm not going to escape,' he protested.

Pearl yanked him down the steps of the plane. The smell hit him first, a sharp tincture of animal manure, burning rubber and charred meat. A number of pathetic farm animals were being kept under the shadows of the aircraft along with a handful of long-suffering horses. Nate's eyes watered from the campfires. He could see from the piles of ashes that they were burning everything they could find.

Pearl pulled on the leash, dragging him through the camp. Everyone stopped what they were doing to stare. Not one of them registered surprise. They seemed to know exactly who he was. When they reached a small jet, Pearl pushed him through a covered walkway. The interior door opened. The air was icy cold.

'Here he is,' said Pearl, and thrust Nate into a chair. She jerked the collar as though she was disciplining a dog. The pain brought tears to Nate's eyes. He looked around him. It couldn't have been more different from the cabin where he'd been sleeping. It was a model of sterility. Everything, the chairs, the tables and the kitchen, was scrubbed and spotless. Through a doorway walked a tall, slender man. His white hair hung down to his waist and he had pale green eyes. His skin was pale too and crusted dry. Unlike the others, who seemed to pride themselves on unstructured eccentricity, he wore casual sacking garments. His nails were long, yellow and curly. It was impossible to tell his age. He could have been anything from sixty to 105, though he moved with unusual grace. Behind him and holding on to his trousers was a girl of about seven. Nate noticed immediately that she was blind. Her opaque, milky irises scanned the room.

'So this is your special find,' said the old man to Pearl in a European accent. 'What is his name?'

'He says he's a doctor. Dr Nathaniel Sheehan,' said Pearl dubiously.

'ID number?'

'I don't have ID,' said Nate.

'Of course you do,' said the man as he manoeuvred the girl into a seat.

'626-55-0534,' said Nate, reciting his old social security number.

'That's not right.'

'I'm sorry. I suffered some kind of amnesia during the transition. That's all I can remember.'

'Transition?'

'Icor Incorporated brought me over to Phoenix for treatment after I was injured.'

'Icor have a regrowth centre here. And a foetal incubator farm. They don't have patients.'

At last, thought Nate, *someone who knows things.*

'That's true. But I'm part of a special experiment.'

'I can believe it. Still, I want to check your name against our computer. What was your address in California?' There was a frigid, wintry aura about the old man and a grandeur, as though he was used to being taken seriously.

'2521 Grand Canal, Venice.'

It was an automatic response. Nate shouldn't have said it, but his mind just wasn't sharp enough to invent an alias. Only weeks ago, he would have had trouble remembering the address at all.

The old man bristled with impatience and let his nails clatter on the table. 'It doesn't help to be uncooperative, Mr Sheehan. The Venice canals were destroyed in 2012. I was alive. I remember it.'

They sat in silence.

'Try the name and number,' he snapped at someone out of sight in the back of the plane. 'And the address. See what comes up.'

Nate could hear the thunk of a computer starting up.

Suddenly the little girl, who had been sitting quietly, grabbed Nate's hand. Her dry fingers traced the contours of his palm.

'What do you see, Colette?' asked the old man.

The little girl frowned. Shook her head.

'Colette is a true visionary. There's nothing she can't see if she looks hard enough.'

'You didn't kill her,' whispered the girl. 'You didn't do it.'

'Does that mean anything to you?' asked the old man.

'No,' said Nate.

The girl's hands travelled up Nate's chest to his face.

'Close your eyes,' ordered the old man.

Nate shivered as he felt the sandy scrape of her crab-claw fingers.

'Mary,' she said.

The hairs stood up on the back of his neck. 'What about Mary?'

'She says she's sorry.'

'About what?'

'I'm sorry, Nate.'

'Anything else?'

Colette let go and shrugged her shoulders as though she was bored. Her moonstone eyes began another restless tour of the room.

'If you are to survive in this world,' the old man said, 'you have to tell us exactly who you are and how you came to be driving along in a car that didn't belong to you.'

'I keep telling everyone. I'm being treated by Icor Incorporated. The EIS forcibly took me into quarantine to carry out tests on me to see if I had an infection. If you let me go back to Icor, I will make sure you get medicine for the sick.'

The old man laughed. 'You think that a minor republic like Icor Incorporated will extend the arm of compassion to *us*?'

'She has a *real* gift,' said Nate, nodding towards the girl, trying to change the subject. 'Mary was my wife. She died.'

The old man cupped Nate's chin with one of his nails.

'Of course she has a *gift*,' he spat, sending moist and foul-smelling air in Nate's direction. 'Who do you think we are – petty, thieving grifters?'

'No. I'm just wondering how you ended up in a place like this?'

'*This. This* – what do you mean by *this*? *This* is a palace.'

'*Your* home is, but the rest of the valley? It's tough. Especially for Colette.'

'Some of us have no choice.'

'Why not?'

'The State prefers to cast out anyone who disagrees with them. It's cheaper than keeping us in prison.'

'Why you?' he said.

'I am a lawyer,' said the old man with pride. Conceit too. 'And I am one of the few people who had too much respect for the constitution. They don't like the constitution in Washington. It's a nuisance and there are a lot of people who would like to tear it up. They're always trying to bend those principles. Those of us who like words and respect the power and sanctity of the way they are put together formed ourselves into groups. I was one of the more vocal.'

He looked at Colette and cupped her head in his gnarled old hands. 'So we have to rely on our community.'

There was a commotion from the other end of the plane and a man ran through the doorway. 'I've found something,' he said excitedly. 'The number he gave us, it matches a Dr Nathaniel Sheehan who was gunned down in LA in 2006. His last known address was 2521 Grand Canal, Venice.'

The old man grew grave. 'Who are you to use the name

of a dead man? How dare you imagine my technology won't expose you in a lie!'

Nate caught it then. The shot. The Mexican kid waving the gun. The blast in his chest. Feeling the hole and a sudden loss of pressure and a profound weakness and the futility of the fact that his life was coming to an end. He wanted so much to stand up, like all the other people around him, but he couldn't, and knew profoundly that he never would again. The full impact came crashing back all at once. He stared at the old man and the little girl before crumpling to the floor of the jet in a dead faint.

52

They were carrying Nate back towards the jumbo jet. Pearl had hold of one leg and two other creatures were dragging the rest of his body across the desert floor, his leash trailing in the dust.

'It's OK,' he said. 'I can walk.'

They dropped him.

'You did a very stupid thing,' said Pearl. 'They were trying to help you and you lied to them.'

Nate realized just how vulnerable he was, outside the loop of Icor, beyond detection and the safety net. He weighed up his future. If he told them his story, he would be exposing himself as a freak and a monster to the worst possible crowd. The very act of knowing might incite them to kill him or hand him over to some other malevolent force.

Pearl yanked at the lead and hauled Nate to his feet. When they got to the jet, they threw him to the ground, tied up his hands and knotted his leash to a pole.

'You can't leave me out *here*,' he shouted.

'You should have told the truth. You made us all look like fools.'

'I'll die without shade. What good am I to you then?'

A tired old dog was flat out and panting in the shadows of the plane. Nate strained at his collar to reach the shade himself, but the leash was too short. He looked down at the dirt and realized that he was lying in a field of bones and grime from the nightly feasts.

They left him there for the entire day. He managed to dig himself a shallow grave with his feet and pull a trashcan lid and some rubbish over himself. Whenever someone passed by, Nate pleaded for water. One man got a bowl and taunted him with it, holding it just out of reach.

'I'll tell you everything. Just let me inside,' he begged.

'We don't care any more,' said the man before climbing up the steps.

How he got through that day he never knew, but the evening came and the sun turned from white to deep scarlet as it descended over the mountains. He'd had nothing to drink and he could feel his internal organs crying out for water. The clan descended the steps with cooking utensils and bags of food. After a while, Tony lumbered up with a plate of dusky pink meat.

'You sorry now?' he said.

'Don't let me die out here, Tony.' Nate's throat felt mangled with dehydration. 'Icor have spent millions of dollars on my treatment. I'm worth a lot of money to them. I know they will pay you what you need.'

Tony looked at him curiously.

'You must need money. We all need money. Why don't

we just work on this together? Have you tried to contact them yet?' Nate used the word 'we' to demonstrate his solidarity. Tony got up and went over to where the evening meal was being prepared. Nate watched the crowd muttering to one another. Tony returned with a bowl.

'Try this,' he said.

Nate looked at the thick, brown liquid.

'What is it?'

'Beer.'

'It doesn't look like beer.'

Tony shrugged. 'It's our kind of beer.'

'There's no poison?' Nate said dubiously.

'No.'

'No hallucinogens?'

'No what?'

'This won't make me see things, strange things?'

'Drink ten bowls and you will see anything you want.'

Pearl came to untie his hands, though she wouldn't undo the leash. She had to maintain some kind of power over him. The beer tasted like pale ale with a liquorish after-burn. Someone brought him a plastic canister and he drank almost all of it, unable to stop himself. He was dangerously dehydrated and knew that he should be drinking water, but they wouldn't give him any. Very quickly, he felt bloated, sickly and crazed. A bigger crowd joined them, and a sharp-smelling stew was ladled into bowls from an enormous vat. They handed him a bowl. Nate turned over the rice with his fork and found a number of grubs among the gluey sauce. It tasted strong and pungent, like game, and he wanted to spit it out, but managed to swallow a few bites.

The temperatures dropped and the drums started up, their relentless rhythms echoing out across the valley floor. The dogs howled, fires were lit, and the dancing started. It was tribal and trance-like, with disjointed jigging and leaping and clacking of long sticks.

From his remote corner of the arena, Nate was beginning to get charged up. They came and danced around him and started whooping and shouting and leering into his face. He knew that if he tried to escape, he wouldn't get very far, so he drank more beer and watched them pound the ground. He had no idea whether they intended to kill him or barter for his freedom.

His physical recovery was remarkable, masked by the numbing effects of the alcohol. He leapt up and pranced around, the pain of the last few days a distant memory. They laughed at him, threw bones, and pushed him over and kicked him. He was an animal to them now and he felt as unreal and insane as a mad dog himself.

Two hefty figures locked arms over a rickety table. After a few rounds of arm-wrestling they dragged him over and sat him down. Nate tried to pull away, but a dozen people wrenched his arm into position, locking his hand with some huge lug opposite. Immediately the guy put the full thrust of his shoulder behind his grip. Nate did the same and felt his left arm go rock hard as he wrenched the guy's arm backwards. He ended the move with a great big roar.

He beat all of them. He couldn't believe his own strength. Maybe it was the ale. He caught a glimpse of Pearl looking at him with disdain, which sobered him up, but the next guy had already sat down. It was Tony. They gripped hands, joshing for advantage. Tony rammed his might behind his shoulder, pushing his massive body sideways. Nate couldn't hold him at first, but his arm went rigid again and they stayed like that for thirty seconds, inching backwards and forwards, hands juddering. Then Tony raised his other arm and whacked Nate across the head, sending him spinning off his chair.

Suddenly, bodies were on top of him, sitting on him and restricting his breathing and sending stabs of agony through his injured ribcage. Hands leant in and spun him over, then someone thrust their fingers down his throat and held his mouth open, cutting his lip as they poured more ale down his gullet. The challenge had been too much for Tony.

Choking on dust and ale, Nate knew he'd be killed if he didn't do something. He heaved on his shoulder and dislodged the grip of one of them, and with his left hand gave a tremendous punch, felling someone to his right. They grabbed him from all sides while Tony stood over him, ready to deliver a deathblow. With superhuman strength, Nate leapt up and kicked Tony in the chest. Tony staggered against a wheel of the plane, a surprised, almost hurt look on his face, then surged forward, head down, ready to ram Nate in the chest.

Nate grabbed his hair, yanked it back and ran with Tony back against the wheel. He gripped Tony's throat and began to squeeze.

'Can't breathe,' whispered Tony, his face turning purple.

'Can't hear you,' said Nate. The words didn't feel as though they belonged to him. He consciously instructed his hand to give way. The hand disobeyed him.

'Please – don't,' begged Tony.

Nate knew that Tony had less than a minute before he lost consciousness and a few minutes after that before he succumbed to cardio-respiratory arrest. He could even visualize the hubibone through Tony's flesh cracking.

The crowd were on him now, trying to pull him off, but he was straddled over Tony, his hand locked like the jaws of a pit bull around Tony's neck.

'Let go!' shouted Nate to his own arm. 'LET GO!'

Tony's eyes fluttered.

'Someone grab the arm!' cried Nate.

They were all pulling at his torso and his legs while someone was banging a rock down on Nate's hand, cutting his knuckles. Still the arm held firm. They tore at the fingers until finally he let go.

Nate crawled away through the dust. He looked at his hand, which was mast-hard and numb. The crowd gathered around Tony, shouting at him, slapping his face and trying to wake him up. Nate dashed over. Someone blocked his path, then Pearl leapt on to his back, kicking and pulling at his hair. Nate shrugged her off.

Tony's face was blue. Nate ripped open the man's shirt and began thumping his chest and giving him mouth to mouth, knowing all the while that it was useless.

'Wake up!' he shouted. But it was no good. The guy was dead. Nate collapsed over the body, then looked at the crowd of mutants staring at him, their satanic faces inflamed by the bonfire.

'Kill me! Go on, kill me! You'll be doing me a favour,' he shouted.

Everyone was silent, the dust roiling around them. A woman was crying. And in the middle of it all there was the lifeless body of their leader, slain.

'What do you do with bodies out here?' Nate said at last.

They carried the corpse in a canvas blanket to a raised hillock where dozens of misshapen crosses stretched out across the earth.

So this is what happens to the old people, thought Nate.

He realized, as he looked at the desperate souls who had gathered quietly around him, that they were all like children, and now that he had killed Tony they were almost subservient, looking to him for direction. Nate insisted on digging the grave himself. It was back-breaking work but he got the energy from somewhere – from remorse, from shame, from the horror of the fact that he had just killed a man in the heat of a stupid game.

53

One of the key things in the currency of being a journalist was the ability to travel. For that, a Government licence was required, and up-to-date health certificates. While everything else in Fred Arlin's life was prone to neglect, from stories to friends to his ageing mother, Fred never let his health certification lapse. He prided himself on the fact that he could get across almost any state border at any time. It was one of the few perks of the job.

He was on a flight to Arizona barely two hours after Monty had called him. He'd been more than surprised to hear from Monty Arcibal, the Icor technician he'd sought out all those months ago.

After Okorie Chimwe had disappeared, Fred had decided to drop the Williams story altogether. It was more than an embarrassment to explain to *The Metropolitan* that the main interviewee with the big story to tell had disappeared. The magazine had made it very clear to Fred that they didn't want to hear from him again. They still owed him expenses.

Fred promised himself that this was truly the last interview he was ever going to make on this assignment, and if it didn't lead straight to the pot of gold, he was going to give up his investigative ambitions for good. It was so much easier to stick to a life in reactive news. At least when the shift was over, so was his commitment and he could go to sleep knowing that his work was done.

When Monty called Fred on the web cam, he looked desperate.

'You said if I ever needed a job . . . well, I need a job,' he had said.

'What happened?'

'The company got raided by the Epidemic Intelligence Service and they had to let a lot of us go. I was one of them.'

'I'm sorry,' said Fred.

'So I'm looking.' Monty's voice cracked as if he was about to cry.

As Fred arrived at the technician's home on the outskirts of Phoenix he was struck by how modest it was compared to Okorie's. It was a small, geodesic dome in the middle of a long line of domes covering a flat plateau of desert brush. They were built to keep the elements at bay, but it was a bleak scene, like a gargantuan refugee camp of igloos that never melted.

A wizened Filipino woman answered the door, smiled sweetly and led him into the house. There was very little furniture and the few pieces they had were simple, apart from an ancient kite propped up against a wall. It was probably the family's only heirloom. Monty was sitting at the dining table.

'Can we talk alone?' asked Fred.

'Mom,' barked Monty, 'we need to be alone.'

'He's such a good boy. He's a very hard worker,' his mother said, and disappeared through a bead curtain. Her courtesy and steely determination to see her son in employment made Fred feel jaded and dishonest.

'Monty, I have to tell you that I'm not from Adronium Industries. I'm a journalist.'

Monty's innocent face crumpled with disappointment. 'Why did you say you *were*?'

'I've been investigating Icor for some time. I found out by accident that a body was transported from Gamma Gulch State Penitentiary to Phoenix. It belonged to Duane Williams, who was executed. Icor has been doing everything it can to keep me from finding out what happened to it. Hell, I don't even think it's a particularly big story, but I just got locked into this need-to-know thing.'

The young man started swaying his head from side to side. 'No, no, no.'

'What is it?'

'I can't talk to *you*.'

'Why not?'

Monty gripped his hands between his knees as though he was in pain.

'Monty, clearly something is going on. That night we were supposed to meet, I got talking to Okorie Chimwe. He said he had information. I was about to interview him on the record when he disappeared. If you tell me, I'll make sure you get paid. That's better than working, isn't it?'

Monty's face went white.

'What is it?' said Fred. He instantly liked this gentle man with his dimpled cheeks and boyish expression.

'Don't you know?' said Monty.

'No.'

'Okorie's dead!'

Monty left the room and returned with a micro-computer. He replayed the news story. Fred viewed the tiny screen. A reporter, much like himself, was standing by a huge dam and talking about Okorie's death. The reporter said it was the seventh suicide of Icor workers and talked about the sense of isolation in Phoenix since the outbreak of dengue fever devastated the population in '59. Then a spokesman from Icor was interviewed saying he wasn't at liberty to discuss why

Okorie had been let go a few weeks earlier. 'We understand that he was depressed, but we cannot give any further information at this time.'

'He killed himself,' said Fred.

'Everyone knows this guy. He was tough. And he had real contempt for Icor. I didn't like him, but he would never do that.'

'Are you telling me he was murdered?'

'I don't know,' said Monty in a terrified kind of torpor. 'I don't know, but I'm not talking to you.'

Just then his mother walked into the room carrying a tray with tea and rectangles of yellow cake.

'He can do anything. He loved his patient,' she blurted out.

'Patient?' said Fred. 'I thought—'

'He was his best friend. Every night, he goes to work and he cares for him, washes him, plays games with him and then this guy, he was taken away by the EIS. And they say – poof – bye-bye.'

'Mom, don't say another word!'

'I'm only saying what happened. I called my other son in Savannah and ask if he can do anything. I don't know if he can. He works for Icor too.'

'Mom!' screamed Monty. 'Are you stupid or something? Stop talking.'

She looked at him indignantly.

'But I thought the Phoenix division didn't deal with patients,' said Fred. 'I thought it was a centre for stem cell regeneration. That's what it says on the information run by Dr – ' He checked his notes.

' – Garth Bannerman,' concluded Monty.

'So what's all this about a patient?'

Monty looked from Fred to his mother. 'What kind of

money are you talking about?' he asked, his face a picture of anguish and shame.

54

There was a dead low, ear-rending boom and a crash that sent shards of plastic and metal shooting across the cabin. Nate, who'd been allowed back inside the plane after killing Tony, was on his feet in an instant. He scrambled around for his clothes when the trunk of a tank smashed right through the side of the plane. There was screaming and shouting and bursts of gunfire. He could hear a hissing sound and instinctively thought it was gas. He grabbed an oxygen mask and attached the tube to the nozzle of a tank that he'd spotted in the cockpit. He loosened the valve and a cool burst of oxygen shot into the back of his throat.

Everyone around him was moving slowly or sitting down and putting their heads back, their mouths gaping. Nate hoped the gas was some kind of aerosolized valium and not some dreaded superhallucinogen like BZ. He cowered in the corner, breathing hard. His ability to think was sliding. He must have inhaled some gas himself.

He saw Pearl crawling along the floor, covering her mouth with a handkerchief. He grabbed her and dragged her to the oxygen mask, but her eyes rolled up into her head. Through the dust and the chaos he noticed some of the gang were wearing masks and defending themselves with handguns. He couldn't understand why they hadn't used them during his fight with Tony. He looked through the cockpit window. A phalanx of military vehicles had positioned themselves around the plane. Up above, a mosquito craft was hovering. There was a roar of outrage across the plane park and an angry mob swept down the hills. The National Guard couldn't be making all this effort to rescue him, could they?

'For those of you who are still awake, save your lives, put down your weapons and exit the plane. You have five minutes,' announced a voice in a mechanical echo.

Nate caught the mad glance of one of the gang. He gestured for Nate to leave. Nate headed for the door, dragging the unconscious Pearl with him. There was a click at the side of his temple. Another gang member yanked Pearl back.

'I'm taking her down!' Nate shouted through his mask.

The guy thrust the barrel into Nate's face.

'It's you they want.'

Nate took one last look at Pearl and walked down the steps, his hands raised in surrender. A soldier, his head covered by a reflective visor, checked the scar on Nate's neck and rushed him to an ambulance where they gave him oxygen.

Someone from the plane made the fatal mistake of taking a pot shot out of the window and there was a retaliatory bombardment into the bulkhead. Nate couldn't crowd out the screams and the shouts of the dying inside. He watched the toxic black belches of smoke extruding from the portholes. The crowd rose up in fury and chanted a low holler of discontent, practised and ritualistic. Nate could see the reactions of the soldiers, jittery, frightened, standing square against the throng. He noticed the mosquito aircraft veer off towards Phoenix. He couldn't believe that he was responsible for all this mayhem.

They delivered him back to the sanctity of Icor within forty minutes. The neat lines of the parking lot and the clean black glass tower were a world away from the filth and the burning stench of the plane park. Persis and Garth were waiting for him. Nate could see the relief on Persis's face. She clutched his arm. Garth held back. Three guards stayed with them all the way through the decontamination process. Nate noticed immediately that the atmosphere at Icor had changed. Vast banks of equipment had disappeared and the sleep labs were empty, except for a few security guards.

'Where's Monty?' he said as they escorted him to his room.

'We had to let him go,' Garth said, all kindness and intimacy gone.

'What happened?'

'The Epidemic Intelligence Service shut down the waking programme. We had to disband the unit. It was a fight to keep the other departments open.'

'And Karen?'

'We had no choice.'

'You owe them more than that,' said Nate.

'I agree,' said Persis.

Garth glared at both of them and left the room.

'What's been happening?'

'The EIS tried to close down the whole division. But there was something punitive about their actions, so Rick appealed to the chairman of Icor and the President, who has been taking a special interest in the project. They managed to intervene, but it still wasn't enough to save the unit.'

'So what happens now?' said Nate.

'No more reconnections for the time being. At least, not in Arizona. There's talk of moving the unit to another state with fewer restrictions.'

'Where does that leave me?' he said nervously.

'The EIS found nothing wrong with you and were about to release you when you escaped.'

Nate shut his eyes and fell on to the bed. He couldn't

believe the futility of it all. And now a dozen people, maybe more, were dead.

'Why did you do that?' said Persis, a desperate look in her eye.

'I was put in a cell with a dead man! I didn't know if I'd see you again. You should have warned me what it was going to be like!'

'I thought Garth gave you a briefing.'

'A sanitized briefing. And I killed a man, Persis.'

'I know.'

'How do you know?'

'We were able to track you with our implants. We saw it all by satellite.'

'Then why the hell didn't you come to rescue me sooner?'

'We couldn't involve the National Guard or we would never have got you back from the authorities. We had to wait for Icor's security forces.'

'You mean that wasn't the National Guard who rescued me?'

'No. Icor has its own security force.'

'Since when do corporations have their own militias?'

'Icor's got interests in many countries and they need to protect them.'

'So what happens now?'

'As far as the outside world and the EIS are concerned, this rescue never happened. We've decided to keep you under the radar and give you a new identity. That way, when you're ready to go back into the world, you can make a clean start. You will have to move away from Arizona though. Maybe back to California. Or Europe.'

'No arrest? No trial for the man I killed?'

'No. The plane park is beyond the jurisdiction of the

courts. And besides, your actions were in self-defence. We have it on record.'

'But that's the thing, it wasn't quite in self-defence,' said Nate.

'What do you mean?'

'In the middle of the fight, my arm became so powerful.' He held up his left hand and turned it over. 'It locked into the guy's throat. I consciously instructed it to stop, but it wouldn't. I had no control.'

She examined his hand. 'There may be some residual damage to the corpus callosum. We'll take a look at that. They haven't confiscated all my equipment, yet.'

'Ever since I woke up, I haven't felt in control. It's almost as if someone else is running the show.'

'I don't know . . .' said Persis, faltering. For once she seemed to be all out of answers.

55

After a round of tests, they showed Nate just how many viruses he'd picked up from the plane park. He watched them dance around his cells, burst through the membranes and subvert his DNA. It was a chilling way to punish him, by letting him see the things that could be picked up in the outside world. They told him that none of the viruses were life-threatening, but that he might experience some aches and pains or weakness in the limbs and joints.

But there was a bigger issue at stake. All Nate could see when he closed his eyes was Tony's face turning blue. He knew rationally that it was not his fault and that he could have died if he hadn't retaliated, but he couldn't help wondering what would have happened if he'd had full command over the body. Maybe he would have held the grip tight enough to subdue Tony, then let the man go.

Very few people tended to him after he returned. A skeleton team brought him his meals and medicine with little or no passing conversation. He missed Monty and Karen desperately and wondered what they were doing. He couldn't bear the idea that they could be facing financial hardship after all their dedication. Nate tried to talk to Garth about having them reinstated, but Garth said it was impossible. The doctor seemed to be blaming Nate for all his troubles. Persis was resolute that the whole project should have a satisfactory conclusion. A few days after his recapture, she summoned him to the viewing room for a meeting. It was a room he had come to dread.

'We thought we should tell you as much as we can about the world, so that there are no more surprises when you go back into society,' she said. 'This is not going to be easy.'

She opened up the bank of screens. 'Do you think you can handle it now?'

'Forearmed is forewarned.' It was one of his father's favourite sayings.

'OK, we covered the great earthquake of 2012. That was one of the biggest events to shape America as it did so much damage to the Californian economy. But there are others things that have happened—'

'Let me guess – global warming,' he said.

'That's right. Much like the last century was defined by two world wars, this century has been defined so far by global warming and the oil crisis, followed by the arrival of the viruses. On global warming – I don't really know where to begin, so I just thought I'd show you a map.'

The globe appeared before them on the screen.

'This is us. Right now. This second.'

Nate looked at the world captured on the live satellite image, the deepening blue of the oceans, the brown expanse of land and the familiar white swirl of weather patterns scudding across continents. It looked as though nothing had changed.

'If I call up the same picture from the early part of the century, you can see all the areas marked in yellow that have been flooded over the last seventy years, due to the rise in sea levels.'

Nate could see yellow eating into almost every coastline; parts of the Eastern Seaboard, New York, the Netherlands, Bangladesh, the Nile Delta, all places that were vulnerable to flooding.

'The permafrost of the Arctic has almost totally thawed, forcing the Inuit south. Not that there was much left to hunt anyway. There has also been a minor change of direction in the Gulf Stream, so Britain and Northern Europe are actually cooler than they used to be, by about two degrees. There can be some pretty intolerable conditions over there: hurricanes, ice storms. It's like Siberia in some places, dry and cold, but a lot of people have chosen to stay on and are adapting. Meanwhile, other countries have suffered increases in temperature.'

Another globe appeared on the screen with red zones covering most of Africa, the Mediterranean, Asia, South America and the middle belt of North America.

'The belts of land where it's still possible to live are getting narrower with each passing year,' Persis continued. 'And a lot of neighbour wars have been fought over water. That was already on the cards in your day, I think.'

'Where?'

'In just about every country on every continent. The most

tragic are the internecine wars within the same countries, between northern and southern Spain, northern and southern Italy, Jordan, Syria, Israel, Egypt, Libya, the Sudan. The provincial wars in China are still going on, and back home, between Palm Springs and San Bernardino County. So many crucial aquifers were exploited to the point of drying up. Many of the great rivers and water supplies are in dire straits; the Colorado, the Amazon, the Nile, the Yangtze are all polluted or at dangerously low levels. Glaciers have melted, causing flooding at first, then great droughts. Skiing is a dead sport. Most ski resorts are derelict. They don't get enough snow to be viable. Some countries, like Switzerland, Austria, France and Italy, have never known such hardship. And all this has caused the sea levels to rise by more than ten inches, flooding the flat lands and low-lying basins across the globe – as you've just seen. To be upbeat for a moment—'

'Please,' said Nate.

'*Some* areas have become much wetter, and there've been many programmes to encourage the growth of vegetation that will absorb the greenhouse gases. As from three years ago, we are finally sustaining levels of CFC emissions.'

'Great,' said Nate dismally.

'Shall I go on?'

He nodded.

'As you know, cheap oil production peaked in 1979 and the supply was running out from that time. Some countries prepared while others turned a blind eye. America wasn't taken by surprise, but successive Governments ignored the extent of the problem. You know how dependent we were on oil for everything: cars, air, plastics, pesticides, fertilizers. After the Iraqi war, Saudi Arabia fell to the fundamentalists and a few years later so did Iraq, putting thirty-six per cent of the world's oil supply under fundamentalist Islamic control.

This caused the oil wars of the Middle East. A twenty-first-century crusade, if you like. All the Christian forces of the Americas, Canada and Europe mobilized and fought the Middle East for the last years of oil. China took up arms with the undamentalists.'

'Did we win?'

'No one won,' Persis said bitterly. 'After so much devastation, there was a truce, but for what? Another fifteen years of oil supply? Now we question whether it was ever worth it, to propel the world headlong into an economic crisis that we may never recover from.'

'Has anyone ever used nuclear weapons?'

'Yes. India exploded a hydrogen bomb on Pakistan in 2046. Pakistan launched a retaliatory attack the same day. They turned Kashmir into a crater. Like two children playing with the same rag doll and tearing it apart rather than letting the other one have it.'

'I never thought it would actually happen,' said Nate.

Persis hesitated. Nate nodded for her to continue.

'In 2045, the last economically viable barrel of oil was extracted. Most other sources were too small and too expensive to dredge. With the crises generated by global warming and oil finally running out, there was an economic collapse on a scale never seen before.'

'You lead your life and assume that someone else will take care of things,' said Nate. 'You fill your head with petty grievances like taxes and insurance premiums. I wasn't looking to the future. I just wasn't looking.'

'People had to change the way they lived, pretty much overnight,' continued Persis. 'Many countries had to resort to a market garden economy, farms producing and selling where they grew, people eating what they could cultivate in their back gardens. Biospheres became the main food suppliers in the desert states, running on hydrogenized fuel cells. And while we were dealing with all this, we were ignoring the onset of another great environmental crisis, the desertification of Africa. It grew out from the middle of the continent and spread to the coasts. There were famines and outbreaks and winds that brought the first of the great plagues across the Atlantic. We were at our weakest point ourselves when the plagues arrived.'

'What were they?' said Nate.

'West Nile, dengue, SARS, bird flu, even a return to the bubonic plague in the worst-hit areas. We have grown resistant to ninety-two per cent of all antibiotics, so there was very little that could be done. We suffered the highest infant mortality rate for two hundred years. The Middle Eastern wars were forgotten as countries retreated to tackle their own chaos and dispose of the dead. You will see in every city the chimneys of the crematoria rising up like church spires. When you see the smoke rising, you know there's been an outbreak. I'm sorry, Nate, but that's how it is now.'

Nate realized that he was nodding like an old man.

'The population has been severely reduced. By about two billion.'

'Jesus Christ,' said Nate.

'We think we have a sustainable population, but for how long? No one is sure. There's very little air travel. The aircraft industry collapsed as no alternative fuel source was found in time. Now a new generation of craft run on fuel cells, but you may have noticed, the craft are smaller. We shall probably never return to the great aviation boom of your era. Politicians, diplomats, businessmen still travel but there's very little immigration. Everyone closed their borders. Funnily enough, the agrarian countries which were less developed, like Eastern Europe and a few parts of South America, fared better than the countries who had all but gone through the agrarian age, like Northern Europe and North America. Much of the US is unable to produce food. The great wheat plains of the Mid-West are dust bowls, much like Africa. No one looked after their soil.'

'Is there anything positive to tell me?' said Nate.

'I was just coming to that,' she said. 'This is a period of great invention. Our solar energy programmes are second to none. We can run huge buildings like this on natural, clean resources. The railways are booming. So is shipping. They're the two major forms of transportation around the globe. We're much more conscious of our resources because we've lost so much. We are a cleaner society now and that is our greatest hope.'

'You must be mad at my generation?'

'There is a tremendous amount of anger towards your era, yes. The baby boomers are famous for their greed, their indulgences and inability to take responsibility for their off-spring's future.' She spoke without emotion or malice. But it hit right at the core of Nate's guilt. Those lectures that Mary would occasionally drag him to at the Future Society and he would sit there fuming that Mary wasn't giving him a night off: this was exactly the kind of thing they were talking about. Mary was the saner one, the braver one for refusing to turn her back on the future, and Nate had actually tried to under-mine her for it. What a shallow, greedy, devouring citizen he had turned out to be.

'Forgive me,' he said helplessly.

'It's not *your* fault,' said Persis.

'It is in a way. Mary, my wife, she knew about all this. She was a – a—' The old tic was back. He couldn't find the word.

'An agitator?' proffered Persis. 'I know there were a lot of people who did care, desperately. They were just never in a position to make a difference.'

'No, no,' he said vehemently, hating her word. It was too strong – too judgemental. 'She was a *futurist*. That's why she believed in cryonics. I used to get at her for being chaotic and not paying the bills and leaving them piled up by the front door and not sorting out her life.'

'It's a pity there weren't more people like her around when it mattered,' said Persis.

56

Garth had a premonition that Kim Andrew was going to call. So when she buzzed through on the web cam, he wasn't in the least bit surprised.

'How are you, Garth?' she said enigmatically.

'We're doing OK under the circumstances,' he replied coldly.

She had been too destructive to warrant his good humour. As soon as he could, he was going to move his entire division away from Phoenix and bring even more hardship on the area. The EIS might relish their power in Arizona and the public health record might be one of the best in the nation, but their bludgeoning tactics were damaging the local economy and Garth would make sure that *that* spin would get broadcast to the local people before he left town.

'No sign of your prodigy, I take it?' she said.

'Not yet,' said Garth decisively.

'We heard you mounted some kind of incursion into the plane park.'

'We were tipped off that he might be there,' said Garth, a

little less sure of himself. 'So we went in, but we didn't find anything.'

'That's too bad. He's getting help from somewhere.'

'I think he got over the state line a long time ago, and my guess is that he's heading for California or New York as we speak. Try looking for him there.'

'Technically, he was clear of infection when he escaped from us, so I can't put out a red alert for him.'

Garth knew full well she had no jurisdiction to put Nate on red, like other infected individuals. If they had, the EIS could employ all the security agencies available to hunt Nate down, including returning to Icor and searching the building again.

'The day you took him he was healthy,' said Garth, angering. 'You could have done all the testing you needed at Icor to keep him safe, but no, you had to do it your way. Sometimes I think the EIS creates more containment problems than it solves. And where do we stand now? The patient is on the run and I'm seeking alternative premises as we speak. And what good will that do for Phoenix? Another major medical company leaves town. Is that the result you were looking for, Kim?'

'Garth, Garth,' she said, slowing him down, 'there's a way to work with us and a way to work against us. I don't think, even now, you have understood the principles of our mission.'

'I do understand and we try our best to accommodate you, always, but we have our ways of working too and they are not always predictable. I had no idea, when we revived Dr Sheehan, that he was going to survive beyond the first few days, but based on my experience, you have become so rigid in your *mission*, as you call it, that you cannot encompass the unexpected.'

'And so you deceived us. And now we have a missing patient.'

'That's *your* fault,' he said, his face burning. 'If you didn't run quarantine like a dog pound, he might still be with us. I hear you haven't even separated out the diseases yet. You were told to do that four years ago.'

'Well we have, actually,' she said. 'And if a little more of your rampant profiteering was diverted into our operations, then we would all be better off and so would your patient.'

'Believe it or not, the waking project and the regrowth programme are barely profitable, or haven't you looked at the books lately? You spend all your money spying on decent, pioneering scientists and yet you won't divert any of your finances into proper care for the sick and the desperate. It's shameful the way you—'

She shut down communication. Garth sat there wondering if, out of spite, Dr Andrew would mount another search. It was becoming clear to him that each day that Nate was still in the building, the greater the risk of even more ignominy raining down on all of them. They would have to move Nate as soon as they could or they would all suffer in the fallout of his escape.

57

'We have a visitor for you,' Persis announced.

'My first,' said Nate.

Monty walked in. The two of them hugged. Monty's face crumpled.

'I thought you were dead,' he said.

'They got me out. Just in time. How are you?'

'I'm good. I'm good.'

Nate could tell that he wasn't. There was something stricken about the man.

'What is it?'

Monty lowered his eyes and hugged Nate again.

'I think he's glad to be back on the payroll?' said Persis.

'Well, now we can get to work on reinstating Karen,' said Nate.

It was almost like a family. A peculiar, dysfunctional family, but a family nonetheless. And Nate was at the head of it, trying to make decisions for all of them. Just like he used to. His confidence felt boosted knowing that there was an end in sight and that some kind of life could be waiting for him beyond the walls of Icor. It was a great relief to him, too, that he was actually beginning to care about people. That, to him, was the most significant part of his recovery so far.

'How's your chess, Monty?'

Monty wiped his eyes. 'Rusty. You'll beat me. I know you will.'

Persis had called Monty at home to tell him that Nate had been recaptured. He was overjoyed, but there was a claw in his stomach. He was already embroiled in Fred Arlin's story and publication was imminent. He'd signed legal documents giving permission for them to use his information in exchange for money, more money than Monty could ever have imagined. He knew he would be in trouble with Icor and that they would try to gag him for breaking his confidentiality agreement, but *The Metropolitan* had told him that if Icor were engaging in illegal practices, then his story was in the public interest and his whistle-blowing would be justified in the eyes of the law. And besides, *The Met* were going to protect him and his family.

But the magazine also said they didn't have quite enough

evidence to publish and they needed Monty to get back into Icor somehow and provide them with more proof: some kind of digital image of the first cryonic man or documents confirming the creature's existence. Monty had flatly refused at first. He didn't want to have anything more to do with Icor. They had been merciless, cutting his wages to the hour that he was escorted from the building. And he didn't want to see Nate again, knowing he was going to betray his one and only friend. But after much persuasion, Monty had relented and agreed to try to get himself reinstated in order to gather more information. In his naivety, he hoped that whatever the outcome of the story, everyone would benefit: Nate would get his freedom, Monty would get his money, and his parents would get the financial security they needed to see them through their dotage.

He put in a call to Persis. He knew that if Nate was back in the building there would be more work. Persis returned his call immediately, said how sorry she was that he'd been treated so badly and that she'd been campaigning to get him back all along. She offered him work the following day. As soon as Monty saw Nate, he realized what a dreadful thing he'd done. It was crucifying. Particularly after Nate hugged him like a father. Monty wanted to run and hide from everyone. Immediately, he put in a plaintive call to the reporter and asked him to cancel the story. He pleaded with the man, but Fred had said that it was too late. They would run the story with or without him. The more information Monty could get, the more cash he would be paid.

'You've come this far,' said Fred, 'keep going. It's going to be over soon.'

Monty clocked on at midnight feeling wretched and full of self-disgust. He hoped that Nate would be asleep so that he wouldn't have to look him in the eye. He planned to capture a few digital images of Nate while he slept, copy a handful of medical files and that would be that. His bags were packed and he already had health passes out of Arizona. It would be his first trip out of the state.

That first night, Monty told himself not to fall asleep, but he must have drifted off. At around three in the morning, he was woken up by the alarms that were triggered from sensors woven into Nate's night suit. He stared at the screens, expecting to see Nate awake and active, but to his surprise, the patient was still asleep. The heat sensors were picking up small movements in Nate's left hand. Monty switched on the observation cameras and zoomed in. He couldn't believe his eyes. Nate's fingers were creeping stealthily over the bed like a spider. Monty watched, transfixed, as the hand crawled across Nate's body and settled on his chest. It was as though the hand had a will and an intelligence all of its own. Monty peered intently at the screens, barely believing what he'd just seen. He completely forgot to capture images for *The Metropolitan*.

At around five in the morning, the sensors triggered the alarms again and Monty witnessed the exact same thing, the left hand taking another stroll across Nate's body. This time the hand went further up, checking out the contours of Nate's throat, feeling the neck graft, then crawling up to his face.

Monty was convinced that Nate was in danger, so he leapt from his chair, sending equipment flying. He burst into Nate's room.

'Monty,' said Nate sleepily. 'What's going on?'

Monty didn't know whether to tell Nate or wait to call Persis or Garth.

'Are you OK?' he said.

'Apart from you waking me up – sure. Is there a problem?'

'No – no. Nothing,' said Monty, dithering. 'I just wanted to check one of the monitors. Go back to sleep.'

He went over to the bank of monitors and pretended to give them some attention, then stayed awake for the rest of the night. By the time Persis reached work in the morning, Monty was already waiting outside her office.

'You look terrible,' she said.

'I've got something to show you.'

They watched the recording of the strange nocturnal meanderings of Nate's left hand.

'He talked about the hand misbehaving in the plane park,' said Persis.

'Have you told him yet?' said Monty.

'About what?'

'The brainstem.'

She grew stern. 'No. And we're not going to, Monty. That has to be our secret. I think to tell him would be disastrous. He has to believe he's in complete control at this stage in order to take control, do you see?'

'I think so,' said Monty with a sinking heart as he recalled the excitement in the reporter's voice when he heard the news that the first cryonic man had inherited the brain's basic motor from a condemned criminal. Not only would Nate know very soon, so would the whole world.

While Nate was shaving, he felt a strange tremor in his left hand. He shook it and brought it up to pull the skin taut around his jaw. Before he realized what was happening, the left hand had grabbed his right hand, which was holding the razor, and dragged it down, snagging his chin. Blood dripped heavily from the cut. Nate stopped breathing. It had been an involuntary action, like a muscle spasm. He threw his razor into the sink, put tissue on the wound and wandered back to his room. He took out his day clothes and began to dress. He fastened up his tracksuit. Suddenly, his left hand grabbed the zipper and ripped it open.

'What the fuck?'

He repeated the action several times, his obedient right hand fastening the clothing, the renegade left hand sabotaging the action.

'Did you see that?' he yelled at the observation mirror. 'What's happening to me now?!'

58

'I think it might be Alien Hand Syndrome,' explained Persis in her office. She flipped open her hologrammatic screen to reveal footage of Nate sleeping and his hand moving around on the bed.

'My hand did that?' he said, exasperated. 'When did you film this?'

'Last night. When you reported your problem this morning during consciousness, I wondered if it might be Alien Hand Syndrome. Do you remember the condition?'

Nate raised his right hand in exasperation and felt a downward pressure in his left. The reaction sent a shock wave through him.

'No,' he said flatly.

'AHS consists of impulsive, spontaneously self-aware, but mentally uncontrollable behaviour of the contralesional upper limb that goes against the patient's verbally reported will,' she said.

'Check,' he said.

'It's purely a motor disorder due to mesial frontal and

callosal lesions. The hand may be trying to obey you. It's had a *move it* signal from your supplementary motor area, but because the right signals are being distorted by the damage to the axons passing between your left and right hemisphere, your hand knows it should do *something*, it just doesn't know *what*.'

'It seemed to know exactly what it was doing when I was shaving this morning. It deliberately sabotaged the action.'

'Please believe me when I tell you, Nate, that there is a perfectly normal scientific—'

'Was he left- or right-handed?'

'I don't know,' she said.

'If he was left and I'm right, maybe that's the struggle we're having.'

Persis, who had been pacing the room, sat down. 'I'd love to tell you that's true. Actually, I do believe in cell memory, but his actions cannot possibly go beyond the cellular level. You may have exaggerated physical responses now and then, owing to his own hormonal production, but the body is not, at any level, *thinking for you*. It has no intellectual input into your life.'

'But I can feel him, Persis. I can feel him waking up. I know I can.'

'It's *your* brain that's waking up. Your emotional range is widening. That's what you are feeling.'

'Are you a hundred per cent certain of that?'

'Let's give you a brain scan. If I find evidence of ischaemic infarction in the left mesial frontal cortex and the corpus callosum, I'll be satisfied that it's purely a brain malfunction. And I hope you will too.'

Persis was desperate to find a logical reason for the left hand's behaviour. She felt relieved when after considerable searching, she discovered a number of lesions where she had said she would. It would have been terrifying if there were none. Then Duane would truly have been asserting himself.

'I can see an infarcted area in the anterior cingulate gyrus too,' she said.

'So where do we go from here?'

'You're on the home run, Nate. A few more symptoms may show up, and we'll pump more stem cells into the damaged areas and wait for your mind to adjust. But we're nearly there.'

Nate knew he was feeling much less depressed. That was becoming more obvious to him every day. But along with the improvement had come a frightening amount of anger and frustration with his incarceration and the people around him. And in spite of what she'd just shown him, he still believed the body was trying to communicate with him on some level. He was the one experiencing it. Not her.

'I think it would help if I knew who the body was,' said Nate. 'My gut tells me that if I know, it's going to be easier to adjust.'

Persis bit her lower lip. 'We're not so sure about that.'

'Well, I'm sure!' he said.

'You don't have to raise your voice.'

'When are you going to start listening to me? I'm a doctor. Or had you forgotten? I'm entitled to a say in my own recovery.'

The fixed, inscrutable smile, the one that was ever present in their sessions, faded from Persis's lips.

59

In spite of her obvious reluctance, Persis announced that she was going to give Nate a full briefing on the donor body the very next day. Nate was surprised at the speed of her reaction, but also relieved. It felt like a real breakthrough to have some concrete information at long last. A guard escorted Nate to the screening room and Persis called up a collage of images. In central position was a face. The man was young and handsome, with brown eyes and long brown hair. He looked clean-living and conventional enough. There was surprise in his expression and an innocence, a student maybe, untested yet hopeful, expecting there to be a long life ahead of him.

'There's tape of him. Do you want to see that?' said Persis.

'Sure.'

Persis ran her electronic pen over the computer and the man appeared on the screen fooling around with friends on the precipice of the Grand Canyon. They were dressing up to go on a hike, putting on full-face visors, checking their air-pollution meters and laughing like any young group from any era. Sun glinted into the lens, whiting out the picture, and the young man was mostly obscured. It made him seem illusive and ghostly.

'Who filmed this, do you know?' said Nate, thinking it might have been a wife or a girlfriend.

'I'm sorry, we don't.'

'What was his name?' Nate was scrutinizing every detail of the body. The footage was frustratingly jerky.

'Ian Paterson. He lived in Albuquerque. He was a scientist, coincidentally, studying for his PhD. He was killed in a road accident. He carried your gene match and his body was in pretty good shape when we—'

'And what about his life?' Nate interrupted.

'His life?'

'Was he married?'

'No. He was twenty-six.'

Nate noticed that Persis was avoiding eye contact and looking glumly at the screen.

'What's wrong?' he asked her.

'Nothing.'

'Can I contact his family?'

Nate wished he hadn't handed the choice to her. She adopted one of her pitying expressions.

'His family expressed a desire not to know what happened to their son. They were generous in donating the body as it was.'

'How can they *not* want to know?'

'They were griefstricken. People make choices.'

Nate's stomach churned at the thought of their grief. He and Persis were silent for a moment.

'There's one thing I don't get,' said Nate.

'What's that?'

'Why would someone like Ian Paterson have a snake tattoo coiled around his anus?'

'I didn't know he did,' said Persis.

'Didn't you examine me?' he asked her.

'Well, yes, but not everywhere.'

He could tell her mind was racing.

'It was pointed out to me by someone in the plane park.'

'Our society is much more hardline,' she said, a lecturing tone entering her voice. 'It's had to be for the sake of our survival. We've been under siege for a very long time and people react against the rigidity. There's a lot more body painting and markings in certain elements of society, particularly among the young. Tribal markings are a gesture of separateness, individuality. I think the tattoo was youthful exuberance. And I'm sorry we didn't find it, because it confused you. Ian was a straight A student, but he owned a vintage motorbike. He had his wild side. You should celebrate his life if you can. It was a good life and he was a good son. You can work together on this. You *and* the body.'

Nate felt relief wash through him. Now he knew who the body was, he began to relax.

'Thank you,' he said, stretching out.

'That's OK,' she said crisply, and began to close up the screens.

'Can I keep his picture near me?'

He could tell that she didn't want to give him a reason to obsess, but she assented and produced an image like an old photographic plate from her computer.

'Do you have tattoos?' he asked, smiling.

'Only dead fish swim with the stream,' she said. It was an oddly brutal remark. Just when he thought he was breaking through her impenetrable shell, he realized that he still didn't know her at all.

60

That night, Nate requested an old-fashioned pen and paper and attempted to write letters to some of the people he had known in his life. He was doing it more as an exercise in memory than anything, recounting what they did and how he felt about them. One day, when he was living on the outside, he might try to find out about them or their children, but he knew he would have to be careful if he was living under a new identity.

The process soon made him feel incredibly sad. What was the point of writing letters to people who were almost certainly dead? He decided instead to write a list of priorities for his new life. The list soon boiled down to one word, which he kept writing over and over, as though he was going into a trance:

> *FREEDOM*
>
> *FREEDOM*
>
> *FREEDOM*
>
> *FREEDOM*

From nowhere came the impulse to put the pen in his left hand. Nate sat there, head bent, meditating on the body. 'Go on, Ian,' he whispered, 'talk to me.'

The hand started to move, jerkily at first, leaving long, spidery, zigzagging lines across the page. He filled an entire page with his indecipherable scrawl. Then another. The more he wrote, the more the lines started to become cohesive. Shock ran right through him when the nib finally gouged out:

> *HELP ME*

Nate sat there looking at the words. This was no seance. Ian Paterson, the chemistry student, was in communication. Something, which Nate could never explain, snapped. A thin elastic band around his reason. He began small, by banging his meal tray against the wall, then he smashed the light fittings. After that, all self-control was abandoned. With great roars he smashed and smashed, cutting himself on the broken glass. A guard bounded into the room and tried to trounce him, but Nate lashed out, flinging the guard back through the door. More guards came, but by this time Nate was slumped in a corner, his energy spent. He snarled at them and could see with chilling clarity how much fear he could instil. They pounced on him and pinned him down, holding the cold metal shaft of a stun gun against his neck. He twisted round and saw Monty standing in the doorway. It wasn't until he witnessed the terror on Monty's face that he realized what he'd become.

After that outburst, even more privileges were denied. Nate was kept mostly in his room and an armed escort would take him to the toilet. The confinement seemed to fuel his anger even more and he felt himself losing a grip on his character. When he looked in the bathroom mirror he barely recognized the face staring back. Sometimes, he imagined the body taking over completely.

He was consumed by demented, turbulent thoughts of smashing his way out of the building and running into the desert. He tried to talk himself down by telling himself that Ian was a benign presence, that he had been a decent, sentient human being who would have understood his fate. While he was locked in this state of manic agitation, he would often give the body a chance to communicate. He would sit at the desk, head back, neck slack as though he was getting out of the way to let the body talk. Then he would breathe deeply and wait for the words to come:

BIG BIRD

PEBBLE CREEK

BOBBIE

JESUS LOVES YOU

There were many random words, but the same phrases kept coming up again and again.

Then a bombshell through the scrawl:

MY LIFE IS MINE

Nate insisted on another meeting with Persis. He showed her the crazy scribblings.

'His hormones *are* being produced so all the subsequent chemical changes impacting each cell are *his*,' she said emphatically. But you are the driver of this machine. You switch on the ignition, you decide how fast you're going to go and the direction you're going to take and the destination. You have to take charge of it now, or it will begin to spook you.'

'It's already spooking me,' said Nate, 'and you know what? For a chemistry student, he feels pretty violent to me.'

'Does he?' She looked wary.

'You saw what I did the other night. And what about this writing?'

Nate thrust the paper into Persis's face.

'*Jesus Loves You*. Who was he? A religious freak? *Bobbie*. Who's Bobbie? It's a woman, from the spelling. Was that a girlfriend? Or a sister maybe?'

'Those words are from your own memory bank. Do they mean anything to you?'

'They mean nothing to me. All I can feel is *his* anger and these words.'

'What kind of anger?'

'His anger at having someone else manipulate him.'

Persis started to look nervous. 'You're projecting, Nate. It's *your* anger.'

'That's also true,' he admitted.

'I'm going to give you a series of drugs specifically designed for the anger. I think you're ready to take that kind of thing now.'

'What are they?'

'They were born out of your generation of SSRIs. But they're much more precise, working solely on the limbic system.'

'That's fine by me,' he said gruffly. 'Don't you dare lobotomize me.'

'Why would you even say that?'

'I saw evidence of it in the plane park. People turned into mutes by the Dome.'

Persis looked rueful. 'You are a scientific miracle. That's my honest opinion of you. Why would I ever do *anything* to damage what we've worked so hard to create?'

61

The new pills worked almost immediately. Nate felt more detached and found himself calming down. The hum of hyperactivity that he used to experience on waking began to abate. Monty was still tending to him at night, but they rarely spoke these days and all the old intimacy seemed to have gone. Nate couldn't understand why his friend had changed so much. He had cornered Monty a couple of times to ask him, but Monty had been evasive and cut the conversation short. Nate wondered if it was because Monty was expecting to be fired at any moment, so he didn't feel he could trust anyone. Nate sympathized. It was hard for someone so shy to be under the constant threat of losing their job.

'I was wondering if we could go on a trip to the Grand Canyon,' Nate announced to Persis one afternoon.

She looked at him and laughed. 'Are you mad?'

'It's what – a hundred miles away? How difficult could that be in all honesty? I want to honour the body. It would give me some kind of closure with Ian. It's been such a wild ride, incorporating him into my life.'

'I'm not sure we'd get clearance,' said Persis.

'Who can give us clearance?'

'Ultimately – Garth.'

'He can send a whole army of security staff with us if he doesn't trust me,' said Nate.

'I'll see what I can do.'

Garth came to see him the following day. 'No can do, Nate. I'm sorry.'

'You said that when I'm ready, you will integrate me back into society. You haven't changed your mind, have you?'

'No – but it's different this time. You'll be called by another name. You'll have new papers. The EIS will never know about you. It's too risky to let you out of the building right now.'

'You took away Karen. Monty is so frightened, he barely talks to me. I rarely see *you*. All I want to do is go on a hike to the Grand Canyon. If you want me to recover, you have to give me hope. Isn't that what they say in the manual? I'm not going to run, Garth. I know my best chances are to stick to the plan.'

'I'll think about it,' muttered Garth.

Nate regretted that their relationship had withered on the vine. He wondered what Garth was doing up in his office, but he had to go on pushing for what he wanted or he might as well give up. Two days later, the answer came back. He could go with Persis and four security staff. He was ecstatic.

They cruised across the desert floor in Icor's aero car. The oval-shaped craft skimmed above the tops of the cottonwood trees and whooshed ahead of a few land-bound cars that were heading towards the great rift.

When they saw the red gash open up ahead, the pilot slowed down. Nate had last seen the Grand Canyon seventy years before with his parents. He felt a wave of grief at the thought of them dead. His father, Dr Patrick Sheehan, had been a hard-nosed professional and unrelenting in his criticism. 'The old bastard,' Nate used to call him, but he loved him just the same. And his mother, Katya, decent, distant and gracious with that elusive bohemianism born out of old money and never having to face the responsibility of the real world.

They had all stood on the lip of the canyon, then hiked down to the bottom and camped. It was the last time they had been together as a family.

Persis handed Nate a solar reflective hiking suit and took a pollution reading from her scanner.

'The air's good,' she confirmed, 'but you still need to wear this.' She handed him a full-face visor.

'To skinny-dip in a lake,' he said. He noticed the guards preparing for a walk. 'Do they have to come with us?' he whispered to Persis. She looked at him in a way that said yes.

They stood at the edge of the canyon and peered over. Down at the bottom, the Colorado River, a thin, blue-green strip that once meandered slowly through the ravine, was nowhere to be seen.

'Where's the river?' he asked, aghast.

'It doesn't get down this far any more,' she said sadly.

They set off along a path that wound its way down the side of the canyon. Nate was soon ahead of the pack, who had to break into frequent jogs to keep up. The guards were not fit and quickly got into difficulty. They passed a convoy of burros crawling up the trail, ridden by a group of people dressed in reflective clothing with wide-brimmed hats. Apart from the convoy, the ravine was completely empty.

'There's no one about,' said Nate.

'Tourism is something of a lost industry.'

Nate looked back over his shoulder at the guards struggling down the path.

'Why don't we let these guys off the hook? They could fly the aero car down to the bottom and meet us there.'

Persis ran back up the path to negotiate. He watched her athletic form as she spoke to the guards. They showed her how to use the stun gun, then stumbled gratefully back towards the top. Nate felt huge excitement. The gorge lay before them, so awesome, it was hard to comprehend with the naked eye. Even as he looked at it through the pollution haze, the canyon registered as a postcard in his brain. He raised up his visor, wondering if he could make the view any more real.

'Hey there,' admonished Persis. 'No ozone. Exposure of more than a few minutes can lead to cataracts.'

Nate pulled the visor down. Persis marched on ahead, her long legs refusing to succumb to the stones and shingle that gave way under her feet. He watched those long, elegant legs under the silver cloth.

'This is what I want,' he said when he caught up with her.

'What?'

'This. Freedom.'

He started to run, stumbling and tripping down the path.

'Stop!' he heard her shout, but he couldn't. It was like hacking down a black ski run with scree skittering beneath his feet. He found himself cheering and laughing and falling and rolling and getting up and running on. In the end, his lungs gave up and he stopped, gulping for air.

'That was really stupid!' shouted Persis, running up behind him. 'Sometimes you're completely juvenile.'

'I know. It must be the adolescent growth spurts.'

'You cut your knee.'

There was blood oozing through his suit. He wiped the blood and licked his finger, enjoying the iron taste. It was great to savour his own blood, feel his heart beating and run with the eagles who were circling overhead. This was being alive, not being cooped up in the basement of a black glass tower.

'It won't be long now,' said Persis, as though reading his mind.

'What?'

'Your freedom.'

They stopped at a picnic area, and Persis tried to make contact with the security detail while Nate laid out the picnic. It was paltry fare compared to the feasts that he and Mary would take on their desert hikes.

'I wish I'd brought Hunter along,' said Persis.

'Hunter?'

'We have a wolf at home. He'd have loved this trip.'

'A wolf?'

'They domesticated a couple of the breeds about forty years ago.'

'What's he like?'

There was love in her smile. 'He's my guy. Very different to a dog.'

'How?'

'They think more like us. They have a strong anticipatory factor in their logic.'

'And that means?'

'If Rick and I are sulking, it doesn't even have to be an out-and-out argument, Hunter watches us like a child might watch its parents, then he tries to distract us by starting up a game with a ball. And he's very protective. He warns me about things, a landslide on a trail, animals in the park.'

The wolf had lit up an affectionate, tender side to Persis. It also told Nate that the animal looked out for her in a way that her husband didn't.

Persis took a bite of bread and delicately picked the crumbs off her lap. She was always so ordered and neat.

'Tell me about your old life, Nate. Your daily routine.'

'I don't know. To me it was ordinary. Structured. Our passion, Mary's and mine, was medicine. I'm sure you have it too. You have to have it or you can't put up with what you do. I guess it took everything we had for a while. I don't know if that energy and enthusiasm would have stretched over a lifetime.'

'Was Mary the love of your life?' A bold question, charmingly blunt.

'She was going to be – yes.'

'Was there a lot of sex?'

'You want to know about my sex life?' He laughed. She laughed too.

'I guess I *am* curious – from a scientific point of view,' she said, blushing. 'I've always wondered how much sex lives have changed. We have very low sperm counts now. Most populations are boosted by in vitro reproduction, particularly in areas where there's a lot of pollution. If you compare sex surveys with now and then, we're not supposed to be as sexually active, though it's difficult to be definitive.'

'Is that why you haven't had a child?' said Nate.

Persis looked down the mountain. 'It's rare to get two people who are both fertile. Most couples need some kind of help.'

'I don't think our generation represented *normality* in any way,' said Nate smiling. 'We had to cope with the fallout of the sexual revolution in the 1960s. We had to deal with AIDS, busier lives, both partners working. We were a pretty distracted bunch. So it wasn't all sex all of the time.'

'What about you and Mary?'

'There was a lot of sex at first and then things changed.'

She nodded, and Nate noticed a tiny cloud in her expression.

'We used to do things to pep it up. Mary was obsessed with planning trips out of town. She loved the great outdoors. Like here. She would have loved this.'

He jumped to his feet and bellowed, 'This is for you, Mary!' The echo came back to them in the cavernous silence. 'And to Ian. Thanks for loaning me your body!'

'Donating,' corrected Persis. 'He doesn't want it back.'

Nate sat down again. 'Mary was unusual. She wasn't the least bit inhibited and she often took the initiative in sex. Even later on. She almost reminded me of a guy. I loved that in her. She could be overt and she could be sly about it, but she made sure she got what she wanted.'

He dressed his bloodied knee as his mind raced over old ground.

'She had this thing about sleazy motels in LA. They were all over the place and some of them were so bad it was hard to have a good time in them. But we'd check in, do our thing for a couple of hours and check out. Just for the hell of it. Or we'd go upscale. Our favourite place was the Chateau Marmont, a wonderful old hotel right off the Strip. Is it still there?'

'The Strip?'

'Sunset Strip? Surely you know the Strip?' He couldn't believe that she hadn't heard of LA's most famous road, but her face registered nothing.

'The Chateau was very haunted. It went in and out of sleazy, so some interesting people hung out in those rooms. We loved it. Pretty corny, I guess.'

'Not at all. Imaginative,' said Persis. 'You loved her.'

'More than my life. But I didn't keep to my word.'

'How so?'

'I made a pledge to look after her until death do us part.' His throat snagged. 'What I meant is that I wanted to see her through her own death, but I died first. That wasn't in my plan.'

'It's not your fault.'

'And I still can't see her, Persis. I can't visualize her.'

'You will. You will see her.'

Nate got up and walked to the edge of the precipice. He could run from Persis right now. Hide out. Make his own way in this depleted world.

'Don't play games with me, Nate,' she warned him, understanding. She began to gather up the picnic things. 'I don't want to lose you a second time.'

How could he not respond to that? She had trusted him and taken a huge risk by bringing him out into the wilderness and getting security to stay on the ridge.

He followed her down the path to the bottom of the canyon.

62

'Good morning, Nate.' Persis swept into his room, punctual as ever. She settled down on her chair in the corner of his room. Her arms formed an appealing contour against the chair. She stroked her skin as though she was cold. Nate felt touched by Persis's preparation for their meetings. There was always a new topic which would test his memory and bring out his character to see how he was adjusting to his new life. And often, after she'd gone, he felt his body talking to him about her, demanding that he think about her. He didn't want to indulge it, but sometimes, when he was tired, it was as if he was giving in to his body's needs and imagined her in bed, touching her, gripping her arms and kissing her beautiful face.

'This morning, I thought we'd talk about the brain,' she said.

'Again?'

She smiled. 'I was wondering if you remember about the differences between the male and female brain from med school.'

He thought for a moment. There was something. 'My hypothalamic nucleus is 2.5 times bigger than yours.'

'And my corpus callosum is bigger than yours,' she quipped back. 'I make more messages between the analytical left brain and the intuitive right brain. Therefore, I am much more in touch with my emotions.'

'You think? Then why do you work so hard to cover them up?' He laughed at her. A genuine laugh.

'It's not my job to go around emoting everywhere.'

'OK,' said Nate, 'my right brain has been the most active since I woke up, as we know. I'm more instinctive than you are right now and I know exactly what you're thinking.'

She looked sceptical. 'We gave you life. We didn't turn you into a *savant*.'

He could see by the crinkling of her forehead that she was enjoying his playfulness. He decided to capitalize.

'I'm a mind-reader, Persis.'

The blood drained from her face.

'Why do you say that?'

'I don't know. It's just an expression. I'm having fun.'

'Go on.'

'You look like you've seen a ghost.'

She coughed. 'No, no ghost. What did you want to tell me?'

'That you're hiding things from me,' he ventured.

Persis turned away from his gaze. 'And what might I be hiding?'

'I don't know. I'm not *that* good.'

'We all conceal things from each other. Sometimes it's better that way, don't you think?'

'I'm not hiding anything from you. You have seen all of me. Inside and out. Except perhaps the tattoo. But you're at an advantage. You've literally been reading my mind. Total exposure is very freeing. You should try it sometime.'

'If you remember those lectures on the brain,' she continued, watching him intently, 'men lose their brain tissue in their frontal and temporal lobes earlier than women. So without corrective stem cell work, your thinking and feeling areas are more likely to be impaired in later life. A proportion of men have a tendency to become more angry and irritable and to suffer personality changes as they get older.'

'That's right,' he said clicking his fingers, 'and women tend to have more tissue degeneration in their hippocampus and parietal areas, which causes spatial and memory difficulties. I tell you what, when you forget where the bathroom is, I'll shout at you to remind you. How about that?'

'And when would that be?' she said oddly.

Nate hesitated and almost wavered. Then a surge of confidence spread through him and he rose to his feet.

She got up too. 'I don't know.' She looked towards the observation mirror.

'There's no one watching us, is there?'

She shook her head and raised her lips up to his. He didn't know how much he'd wanted those lips, but now he was kissing them, he was desperate for her. She gave a little moan as he put his leg in between her thighs and pinned her to him. There was a knock at the door. Persis fell back in her chair. Nate turned away.

It was Garth.

'Great timing,' whispered Nate. He tried to catch Persis's eye. She was resolutely studying the floor.

'Hello.' Garth looked from one to the other. Nate felt sure it was obvious that there was something going on. 'Persis told me your trip was a success.'

'It was. Thanks for letting me go.'

'We have a benefactor on this project who has been loyal to us from the very beginning. He's longing to meet you, Nate. He has a gap in his schedule and I think it's time.'

Nate knew a moment like this would come. 'Who is it?' he said doubtfully, stealing a glance at Persis.

'The President.'

'Of Icor?'

'No – the United States.'

Nate blanched.

'I think we told you, but you may not remember, that President Villaloboz has a special interest in you. His father is cryonically frozen. He's been following your case very closely and has been helping us as much as he can with the EIS, and now he wants to meet you.'

'Is he coming here?' said Nate.

'No. We go to him. To the White House.'

Nate couldn't believe it. 'How do you know you can trust me? You've been treating me like a prisoner.'

'We think you're ready.' Garth looked to Persis for confirmation. She nodded.

'But my story will get out. How will I be anonymous then? You said yourself you wanted to keep my whereabouts a secret and give me a new identity.'

'It's a private visit, Nate. No publicity. They happen all the time and the press never gets wind of it.'

'But someone is bound to leak the information.'

'We've been very strict about the terms of the visit and the Press Secretary has agreed.'

'It sounds like I don't have a choice.'

'You want your freedom?'

'Yes.'

'I need to secure this project well into the future. It's part of your security too, Nate. We can give you a new identity, but you've seen how easy it is to fall through the cracks and be at the mercy of some very dangerous people. We need to capitalize on the President's interest while he's still in power.'

So there it was, conditional support, provided he played the game. And he had no reason to resist. He wanted more than anything to leave Arizona, and if this was the concession, then he would make it.

'There can be no more attempts to escape, no more ranting and raving and smashing up rooms. You're mentally intact now and you have to be on your best behaviour for all of us. Do you understand?'

Nate found it humiliating to be admonished in front of Persis.

'Do you understand me?' repeated Garth.

'Yes,' he said dutifully.

'Good. We take the trip to Washington on Thursday.'

63

The aero car travelled at hyper drive across the desert states, which turned from brown to green as they got closer to the East Coast. Every now and then Nate caught a glimpse of the slanted snouts of the high-speed trains criss-crossing the country. The rest was a blur. The speed and smoothness of the aero car made him feel nauseous, but he managed to control it. They veered left up the marshlands of the Carolinas towards Washington and reached the capital in just over an hour. Just as the pilot was lowering their vehicle on to the ground, the sky was filled by an enormous zeppelin the size of a small village. He was told that it was a float boat that made sedate journeys up and down the Eastern Seaboard.

He felt an emotional tug when he saw the Needle and the still, orderly lawns leading up to the wedding-cake facade of the White House. Not much had changed, except the arena had been pedestrianized and was swarming with people. Intimidating armoured vehicles shunted up and down the perimeters, while strange, echoing voices issued broadcasts in many languages. Alarms sounded constantly, adding to the chaotic, almost warlike atmosphere.

The party was ushered through the gates of the White House and shown into lavish rooms where they were told, in whispered tones, that the President would be with them in a few minutes. When the man came in with his entourage, Nate couldn't believe how young he looked. The President shook everyone's hand and made sure that he missed no one in his welcome, but he reserved a special greeting for Nate.

'Dr Nathaniel Sheehan. Our first cryonic man. How are you?'

'I'm doing fine, Mr President.'

The President took a step back and raised his eyebrows as though he was about to say: 'He speaks!' Nate realized what it was to be seen as a freak of nature. And to be treated with awe and distance.

'Tell me everything.'

'I'm healthy and looking forward to resuming a normal life as soon as possible, Mr President.'

'Come and sit.' Nate followed him over to a gilt sofa. The others hovered nearby.

'Tell me, what has been the toughest part of your journey?'

Nate thought for a moment. He decided to be honest. 'Learning that my wife and family are dead.'

He was navigating them into uncomfortable territory, but he wasn't going to skate over anything. Not after what he'd been through.

'Given the choice, would you rather not have been revived?'

Nate carefully pondered his answer. 'Well, in my case, I never wanted to be frozen. My wife did it immediately after I was shot and I'm still in the process of forgiving her.'

The President laughed. 'If forgiveness could be switched on and off like a faucet then we'd all be able to sleep at night. I hope you can adjust.'

'It's a huge adjustment,' said Garth, leaning in. 'But you're doing really well, aren't you, Nate?' He put a tentative hand on Nate's shoulder.

'Is it worth it, to be alive?' asked the President.

'I know you want to bring your father back,' said Nate, evading the question.

'We do. We do. But it's not such a big gap for him. Only twenty years.'

'Then it won't be so difficult.'

'What do you mean by difficult?'

'Adjusting to a world that I don't even know.'

'Of course. And it's not an easy world to come back to.'

'How did your father die?' asked Nate.

'Brain haemorrhage. Undetected aneurysm. Too long to get help. A shock for us all. But the growth accelerator that Dr Bannerman is developing will speed up repairs to the brain and the body at the same time. It works fast enough to recover life with less chance of decay. Did I get that right, Dr Bannerman?'

'Spot on,' said Garth.

Through the charm, Nate could detect the President's deep love for his father.

'I wish you luck,' said Nate.

'And I wish *you* luck.' The President looked moved. He grabbed Nate's hand and shook it vigorously.

'Can you feel that?' he asked. 'Can you feel my hand?'

'With hypersensitivity. When the nerve tissue regrows it's much stronger than before.'

'We're thrilled for you, Nate. All of us. Maybe one day you can tell the world about your story, but I know that under the present circumstances,' he glanced at Garth, 'you don't want to do that right now and I understand. We have lunch and a small reception waiting for you.'

Nate looked at him in alarm. He thought it was supposed to be a private visit.

'Don't worry,' reassured the President, 'it's a group of interested people. They know all about the confidentiality.'

They were led into adjoining staterooms where portraits of past presidents lined the walls. A roar of appreciation and applause went up as the President guided Nate through the crowd. He felt like an astronaut just back from the moon.

Garth and Persis stayed close by, guiding him expertly from one person to another. Nate tried to make eye contact with Persis. They hadn't really talked since they'd kissed. He wondered what she was thinking. He wanted more than anything to kiss her again. But Persis was unreachable in her stoic, public state of high alert, her hair pulled back in a severe French plait.

At one stage, a cadaver of a woman with eagle eyes grabbed Nate's hand with her talons.

'Can you show me?' she said conspiratorially.

'Show you what?' said Nate.

'The graft. Can I see it?'

All at once, Nate understood what John Merrick, the Elephant Man, must have felt like when he was stripped naked and paraded before members of the Royal College of Surgeons in nineteenth-century London. Now he too was a grotesque, with the scars to prove it.

'I'm not on show,' he mumbled, and moved on.

He caught sight of an imposing man sitting regally on an ornate sofa. He had dusty-red hair and carried tremendous authority. It was impossible to miss him. Everyone was paying court to him as he sat with a brutal, enigmatic smile on his face.

'Who is that?' Nate asked Garth.

'It's the CEO of Icor Incorporated, John Rando.'

'Rando,' said Nate. The name sent a shock wave of recognition through him. 'I knew someone by that name.' He tried frantically to retrieve a memory. 'Is he any relation to Martin Rando?'

'His son,' said Garth. 'They really are the emperors of modern medicine. It was the Randos who discovered the vaccine that prevented non-cancerous cells from turning into cancerous ones. It was a milestone in the cure for cancer.'

A heaviness overwhelmed Nate, a small ripple of dark water lapping around his sensibilities. Something was wrong with the information.

'He's been waiting to meet you.'

Garth led Nate through the crowd towards the magnate.

'I knew your father,' said Nate. 'We roomed at Harvard.'

'That's right,' said John Rando, turning a stiff neck upwards.

'When did he die?' asked Nate.

'He didn't.'

'I'm sorry, I assumed—'

'He stepped down as chairman of Icor ten years ago and John took up his position,' interjected Garth. 'But Martin Rando is still going strong.'

'A hundred and seven and playing golf,' said John Rando bullyingly.

Nate couldn't believe it. Martin Rando. Alive. He tried to picture the man. Short, no more than five foot five. Eternally restless. Plain. That same hair. Nate wondered what he looked like now.

'It's not unusual, as you know, Nate, for people to live until well into their second century,' added Garth.

'How old is the oldest person on the planet?' said Nate, reeling from the news that Martin Rando was still alive.

'People can live until they're a hundred and fifty. There's someone of that age in Japan,' said Garth.

'Why has Martin never been in touch with me?'

'Maybe he can't stand the fact that you are young enough to be his great-grandson,' said John Rando, whose smile actually turned the thin line of his mouth downwards.

Nate wanted to ask him more questions, but he felt that the door was already closing on the conversation. Perhaps Rando's thinly veiled hostility was connected to the cost of his rescue from the plane park. Or the potential problems with the Epidemic Intelligence Service. Nate wanted to mention it, even to apologize, but before he could say anything more, Garth was guiding him away.

'He doesn't look well,' said Nate, watching the old man sitting erect but clutching a cane.

'He's not. He has had a lifetime of heart problems. It's getting to the point where we can no longer help him.'

So John Rando must be looking for a body transplant too, thought Nate. Maybe this whole programme was being financed for the benefit of Icor's chairman.

Garth and Persis drifted off to talk to other people, leaving him alone to observe the scene. Everyone seemed anxious to have an audience with Rando. Even the President had to wait in line, though he tried to disguise the fact. They treated him like a Caesar, listening intently to his every word and saying things that might excite his attention. In this environment, even with the thrill of having the President in the room, John Rando commanded just as much attention.

'What was it that Plato said about democracy?'

Nate turned. A tiny, elderly man was hovering at his side.

'Plato said that all democracy leads to despotism,' said Nate right off the bat. It was something he had often quoted in his old life. 'Are we there yet?'

'Yes, Nate. We're there. Some say it's the inevitable result of what has happened to us. Others say it's been a century of careful orchestration.'

The intimacy of the old man's voice gave Nate a start. There was something utterly familiar about it.

'Who by?'

'Who do you think?' said the old man. 'I hear you're an avid reader.'

'I used to be, but I find it difficult to concentrate these days.'

'Do you like Shakespeare?'

'Yes.'

'Which play?'

'All of them. *Antony and Cleopatra. Julius Caesar.*'

'How appropriate,' said the man, looking about them as the guests meandered professionally from one group to another.

'It's always about the teachers, isn't it?' said Nate. 'I remember I had a great teacher when I read it. I guess it was the first time I began to understand Elizabethan English.'

'Would that have been at Harvard?'

'Yes, I took Lit for a semester. Just for fun.'

'And would the teacher have been Herbie Rosen?'

A chill ran through Nate. 'How do you know?'

'He taught me too.'

Nate looked at the man more closely: the long, tapered nose, the grey, watery eyes and the white wisps of hair on the dome of his head. He made some kind of connection. He'd known him, but he couldn't place him.

'Who are you?' said Nate.

'Albert Noyes,' said the man in a whisper.

'My God.'

'Keep your voice down. I'm going to say this quickly because I may not have long. There is another you. And you will find out soon enough what I mean. Also, keep asking questions about your body and where it came from.'

'What are you talking about?'

'Someone else took your intended donor's place. And

more importantly, you have a doppelgänger who is you in another guise.'

'Doctors for Justice,' said Nate suddenly. 'That was our group, wasn't it, Albert? What happened to it? And Mary. What happened to Mary? They tell me she died in the earthquake. Is that true?'

'I want to tell you everything, but I don't know when that will be possible. I had to pull a lot of favours to get here today. They're not allowing you visitors of any kind.'

'I didn't know that.'

There was a commotion which upset the genteel meanderings of the crowd. Nate barely recognized what was happening until Albert was being expertly manhandled away from him, a hand cupped around the old man's neck.

'Hey, we were talking!' said Nate, his voice rising above the chatter. All conversation stopped. Persis made her way over.

'What is it?'

'I knew him, from before. My old life.'

Persis's jaw dropped. 'Really?'

'We were at Harvard together.'

She looked more alarmed than pleased.

'He's been trying to see me.'

'I don't know anything about that,' said Persis.

Nate tried to think. Albert had been talking in such riddles, he could barely make out what the old man had said. 'He told me that someone else took my intended donor's place. What did he mean?'

'I don't know,' she said. 'We *did* look at a number of donor options when we were trying to find the right body. Could that be what he meant?'

The President strode up, his stature silencing Nate for a moment. 'What's going on?' he said convivially.

'I knew that man,' said Nate, and stopped. He realized that in this closed, mysterious society, talk of their friendship might get Albert into trouble. 'Why was he thrown out?'

'Albert Noyes? Oh, he wasn't exactly thrown out. He wasn't supposed to be here. He's one of the oldest lobbyists in Washington. And a nuisance. Gatecrashes everything. I call him the snake.'

'Why?'

'I fully expect to find him curled up in a basket under my bed one of these days. Did he upset you?'

'Not at all.'

'There really should be a statute of age limitations on lobbyists. We should retire them at a hundred. But don't worry, he understands all about the limitations of his access, not least the basic principles of discretion.'

There was an assenting murmur. The assembly was clearly anxious to return to a state of normality. Nate looked over at Garth, who raised his hands in a gesture of resignation.

64

It was a subdued party that flew back to Phoenix. Nate was consumed by the strange conversation with Albert Noyes, but something told him to keep quiet about it for now. When he got back, he sat restlessly on his bed, wondering how he could get in touch. Albert must have so much to tell him. He was trying to figure out a way that he could insist on a meeting when there was a knock on his door. He knew who it was and what she wanted.

'How come you're here so late?' he said disingenuously to Persis.

She took his hand. 'Come with me,' she said. She led him down a dark concrete stairwell to another corridor.

'What did you do with the guards?'

'Don't ask.'

They walked past more doors leading off into small, dingy rooms with two-way mirrors.

'More sleep labs?' asked Nate.

'We've got three floors of them.'

'What did this company do?'

'It's always been a medical research base. They helped to develop a lot of brain-scanning technology here.' She opened a door and a smell of stale air hit them. She turned on a low light and he saw a bare room, except for two padded chairs facing each other mounted on wheels aligned on tracks.

'What the hell is this?' he said.

'In the early days of brain scanning, it was almost impossible to record brain activity during sex because the head moves around so much. So they made these arousal chairs to monitor the brainwaves during sex.'

'How old is it?'

'It's a museum piece.'

'Does it still work?' he said, jumping into the chair. Persis pulled a lever. The chair jerked back. She took a brass brace that was attached to the headrest, pulled it over his forehead and clipped it into position. She warmed up the rubber suction pads of the electrodes, licked them and pressed them to his temple. The rubber was old but still managed to create a vacuum.

'You won't be able to get a reading from those, will you?'

'You never know,' said Persis.

'So what happens now?'

Slowly, she unzipped his suit and left the room. When

she returned, she whispered, 'It's all ready, and according to the machines, so are you.'

'How do you know?'

'A neuron in your medial prioptic area is registering fifty impulses per second and I've got eyes.'

Shyly, she took off her overalls, staring intently at him, then sat on the chair opposite.

'You can operate that button and bring me towards you,' she said. 'The electrodes will read the excitement levels in your hypothalamus.'

Nate squeezed the button. Persis's chair jerked forward on the tracks. He pressed the button again. Her chair lurched. Now their knees were touching. Slowly, Persis climbed on to his lap, loosening his clothes. She stroked his chest and kissed it, small, dry butterfly kisses. Slowly, she worked her way down. It should have been the ultimate fantasy, but something was off.

'Is there a problem?' she said eventually.

'I'm sorry, Persis. I don't think I'm ready.'

She pulled away, embarrassed. 'I'm sorry,' she said, 'I misread—'

'No, no, you didn't. But this is too weird, too soon – something.'

'For me too,' she said, getting off his lap. 'I'm not exactly practised in playing the seductress. I don't know what I was thinking—'

Persis retrieved the printout that scratchily mapped his brain activity.

'You were interested for a while. Then something happened. I'm so sorry. I didn't mean to put you on the spot like that.'

'A memento of my first failure,' he said, looking at the readout and trying to be light, but the words sounded leaden.

They got dressed in silence and walked back down the dimly lit corridor. She seemed embarrassed and anxious to get him back upstairs.

'What goes on here?' he said, dawdling.

'Nothing much now.'

Curiosity overcame him and he tried one of the doors. It opened.

'Nate, these are Garth's private labs. We really shouldn't—'

He pushed open the door and instinctively turned on the lights. He gasped. There in front of him, incarcerated in three huge tanks of fluid, were a dozen hideously distorted bodies with huge, hardened growths distending and puckering the skin.

'Oh my God, what is this?' he said, disgust mounting.

'I didn't know he still had them,' she said quietly.

'You knew about this?'

'It's what we had to go through to get to the state where we could produce you.'

'Jesus fucking Christ!'

'Don't shout, Nate – you can't let anyone know we're down here.'

'They called me Frankenstein in quarantine. It's not me. It's you guys.'

'I thought he'd destroyed the early attempts,' she said lamely, but he wasn't listening. He was recoiling from the hideously macabre effigies in front of him and the agony on their faces.

'They look like gargoyles,' he said in despair, knowing that with one twist of the technology, the same fate might have befallen him.

65

Fred stared out of his office window at all the towers, glittering like marcasite against the blue-black night. He found himself smiling. He couldn't help it. He looked down at the street fifty floors beneath him, at the people scurrying through the covered walkways, the fires of the street vendors, the bicycles and the rickshaws. It was a crazy ant warren of activity and he loved everything about it. Who wouldn't? New York was still the greatest city on earth.

Jamie Bower, the features editor, who'd been so dismissive when Fred first approached *The Metropolitan* about the Duane Williams story, waved at him through the glass partition. He wasn't being condescending now. Bower had switched from studied indifference to hanging on to Fred's every word like a grovelling intern, asking him if he was warm enough, cold enough, hungry, thirsty or comfortable in his new high-backed chair.

The Metropolitan had set Fred up with a temporary office that had a full view of Madison Avenue and he'd spent the last two days with a group of the finest journalists in the country, debating whether they had enough corroboration to run Monty Arcibal's story about the nation's first cryonic man.

It was the biggest story that *The Met* had broken in years and it was all down to Fred Arlin, a junior court reporter from San Louis Obispo. No one in New York could believe how a hick from a small college town could have come across a story like that, and Fred could tell by the unfriendly looks from some of *The Met*'s staffers that there was a lot of envy about it. What did he care? It had already been indicated to him that there was a full-time position if he wanted it.

He was slightly embarrassed that they had put another writer on the story, to 'tweak the style here and there', but he'd been assured that he would get a solo byline.

Fred had managed to find another contract worker at Icor, a physiotherapist called Harmony Dusette, who confirmed much of what Monty Arcibal had told him, and, through sheer fluke, Fred had salvaged the tape that he'd made of Okorie Chimwe before Okorie had disappeared. That very day, which was why they were working late into the night, Fred had managed to contact Chimwe's grieving mother in Nigeria, who was sending them another recording of Chimwe audition-ing for a TV show. They were getting the voice tested and within the hour should be able to match it to the voice on his tape, confirming that Fred's original recording was genuine. The match was the last piece of the jigsaw that they needed to go to print.

Fred had wanted to do his own fact-checking. He desper-ately wanted to avoid the sub-editors' relentless scrutiny. Fellow journalists had warned him about having a story pawed at by *The Met*'s editorial team. It was like being tortured. And the rumours were true. The last few days had been like a blinding search beam trained on all his inad-equacies. They pointed out his terrible spelling, his poor punctuation, his failure to be consistent in his clauses, not to mention questioning every single detail about the story. But he was good-humoured, reasonably thick-skinned, and just about wise enough to keep the end in sight.

The magazine's editor could not hide his glee about how they had managed to hide Monty and Harmony from the mighty and influential tentacles of Icor Incorporated and the other reporters kept asking Fred all kinds of questions:

'How long did you get to work on this? How did someone like you manage to pierce Icor's defences? How did you find Monty Arcibal?'

Fred had perfected a casual tone and said it had been a full-on investigation for more than a year. He omitted to tell them that he'd completely forgotten about it several times. The terrible blow, he recounted with great solemnity, was when Okorie Chimwe disappeared (he didn't tell them that he didn't even know about the supposed suicide until Monty had told him), which nearly put an end to the investigation altogether, but Monty Arcibal stepped forward just in time.

As well as feeling full of pride, Fred was aware of a certain panic. He knew he was inexperienced and he wondered if he was, in any way, missing something critical. What if it all blew up in his face and the Government revoked his licence again? That would really end his career. He *had* to be right this time.

He was worried about Monty too. He'd managed to secure enough money for the man and his family to live on for several years, but if Icor had anything to do with Okorie Chimwe's death, what would they do with Monty once the story broke?

The images and papers that Monty had provided were crucial, not only the icing on the cake but the filling too. Fred knew it had been really difficult to get them, and Monty had gone quiet on them a few times, not returning his or the magazine's calls. But he came through in the end. Secretly, Fred knew that Monty was the real hero of this whole thing. He was the one taking all the risks.

Monty was still working at Icor and Fred had sent word that he should prepare to get out as soon as the story was about to run. *The Met* were going to hide him and his family in a safe house. This was a big investment for everyone.

THE WAKING

Fred studied the skyline of Manhattan. He felt momentarily dizzy, as though he was getting vertigo. He wondered if he would ever be able to sleep again, his anxiety was becoming so acute. He saw Jamie Bower heading towards his office.

'The Chimwe tapes match,' said Jamie excitedly. 'Congratulations, Fred. We're up and running.'

66

'Is this the point where you tell me we're being watched by a group of Icor executives?' said Nate, his voice barely a whisper.

They were locked together on the narrow, rickety bed in one of the sleep labs and he was having no difficulties this time around. Persis was riding him gently and he was holding on, trying not to come. He pulled her down to kiss her, but she held back. She wanted to look at him. The thrill he felt about being inside her was more than he could bear and overrode the horror of the bodies in the tank. After he'd found them she had taken him into a room to calm him down, then one thing had inevitably led to another.

'Keep still,' she moaned.

'I can't.'

'Please.'

He could tell how hungry she was and he liked the restraint of keeping still, but right now he felt like a teenager, gauche, urgent, his body ready to arch. He thrust himself deeper inside. She groaned and pressed down. His body gave a huge, satisfying shudder, then he waited for her.

'Don't leave me. Please, don't leave me,' he said, kissing her neck, but the words sounded false and far away, as though uttered in another dimension by someone else.

She kissed his forehead. 'Of course I won't,' she said.

Nate felt lost and disoriented. He wondered how they could ever compress the years.

'What I want is to—' He broke off.

'Go on.'

All he wanted was the certainty of his old life back, the daily grind, the monotony, the schlep to the mall, the ordinariness of existence that left tiny gaps for real love. It made him gloomy that whatever he could develop with Persis would only ever exist on a level of unreality. And besides, she was married, and he'd probably just made her unfaithful to her husband for the first time in their relationship.

'I'm sorry,' he said. 'I don't want to wreck your life.'

She slid away from his embrace, as he knew she would. 'You're not wrecking my life. This was my idea.'

They dressed and made their way back upstairs. Nate found himself asking Persis about Albert and his strange encounter at the White House.

'I think Albert was talking to you about Ian, your donor,' she said cautiously as they entered his room. 'We had to search the nation for the right body. So many accident victims survive now that there just aren't enough bodies available. I'm sorry if this sounds another world, Nate, but for the longest time, the ones that were being offered to us were just too damaged. Or badly frozen. It took two years to find a match. We needed someone who was young, strong and fit, with as much genetic compatibility as possible. Otherwise we'd have taken too much of a risk, with certain cells growing at different rates, responding to different enzyme instructions, unwanted tumours, irregular neuronal growth. Like you have just seen. You have to realize, Nate, that although there've been so many advances in medicine, we don't have all the answers. We can't work all the miracles that we would like to. Not everyone lives to their full life expectancy. Look at the chairman of Icor. We want to help him, but there are no guarantees.'

'So John Rando is looking for a donor body too?'

'Yes.'

Nate looked at Persis's beautiful brown eyes in the half-light and wondered why her speech sounded so much like an apology.

'I know I've been crazy,' he said, 'and I'm grateful for everything you've done. Being out there, in the world, scares me to death, if you want to know the truth.'

She kissed him, a move which sent another jolt of desire through him.

'Please believe me when I say this,' she said, her breath sweet on his face. 'It *will* be worth it. All of it.'

Nate bent his head to kiss her again but pulled back when he noticed the telltale red light of the tiny camera in the corner of the room, its black reflective lens dilating like a pupil as it focused on their embrace.

67

The following morning, Nate could feel that things were different, even before he saw or spoke to anyone. The change was as subtle as the arrival of autumn on a light breeze. He wondered if it had got out that he and Persis had been together. He began to ruminate on the possible repercussions.

It wasn't until several hours later that anyone would give him an answer as to why they were acting so differently around him. There had been a story, one of the guards said, but the details would have to wait until the arrival of the director.

Tension crept across Nate's chest. He felt outraged. If it was a story about his visit to the White House then his instincts had been correct.

Garth and Persis arrived together. Persis was barely able to look at him.

'This is serious,' he said, responding to their demeanour.

'A story has appeared in *The Metropolitan*,' explained Garth.

'What story?'

'About you. We think they got to Monty.'

'Where *is* Monty?'

'We can't reach him at his house. It's been abandoned.'

'He would never do that to me.'

'The story includes details that only Monty knows. And pictures. And—'

'Pictures?' spat Nate. 'How did he get pictures?'

'There is pandemonium outside. The world's press are upon us and there's a number of protesters. They're very unhappy about the work we've been doing.'

Nate looked from one to the other. 'The EIS will be back, won't they?'

'Almost certainly.'

'You need to get me out of here. It's best for you too. To move me, I mean. Why didn't you listen to me, Garth? I told you it was too dangerous to go to Washington.'

'The story doesn't even mention Washington. The reporter had been working on the piece for quite a while.'

'Can I see it?'

They said nothing.

'At least give me that. I'm going to see it sooner or later.'

They started to leave.

'Don't walk away from me. How can you walk away from me now?'

Nate held back from making it personal with Persis. He sat on his bed in a daze. So the secret of his existence was out. The infamy would be instant and he would be hounded like a dog until the end of his days.

BOOK THREE

LIBERATION

Fame, that public destruction
of one in the process of becoming,
into whose building ground the mob
breaks displacing his stones.

RAINER MARIA RILKE

68

An hour later an armed guard came to take Nate to the roof where he was told an aircraft was waiting to airlift him from the building. Four of them marched him towards the lift. He was surprised to see Rick, Persis's husband, waiting there. He handed Nate a suitcase.

'Nate, you're going to be flown to California, then on to Europe. You've got all the relevant passports, health visas and money you need for the journey. You'll be contacted in Europe and looked after. Good luck.'

Rick held out a hand to shake. Nate didn't take it.

'Where will I go in Europe?'

'It's all in the case,' answered Rick, withdrawing his hand.

'Where're Persis and Garth?'

'They wanted to say goodbye, but I thought it would be better if they didn't.'

'Why?'

Rick gave Nate a look. Nate wondered if Rick knew what had happened with Persis.

'I'm not leaving until I've seen them.'

Rick motioned to the guard and there was an ugly shuffle as they bundled Nate into the lift.

'I'm sorry, but there's no time,' he said with a half-smile.

A mosquito 'copter was buzzing on the helipad at the top of the building. A crowd was lining the perimeter fence. When they spotted the guards forcing Nate towards the 'copter, a great commotion went up. The media swarmed into position and the protesters thrust their banners into the air.

Nate's gut told him it was a bad idea to get into the craft with strangers and he fiercely resisted it. He thrust the suitcase at one of them, and it dropped. The lid snapped open. Inside were a couple of books, but no formal documents for his passage out of the state. The whole operation was a sham. He summoned all his strength and began to throw punches. He managed to break free and ran to the lift door. It opened. Persis stepped out. The guards grabbed Nate.

'What's going on?' he shouted through the wind and the hum of the engine.

'Didn't Rick tell you?' said Persis.

'There's nothing in the suitcase!' shouted Nate.

With beseeching eyes, Persis picked up the suitcase and showed him a schedule that was tucked into the flap. He could see that she had been crying.

'Will I see you again?'

She shook her head. 'I doubt it.'

Without looking back, Nate got into the 'copter. As they ascended into the sky, he could see huge banners in the crowd. One read:

WHILE THE RICH GO HEALTHY – THE POOR GO SICK

Another:

WHOSE HEALTH MATTERS MORE – THE LIVING OR
THE DEAD?

Then he noticed a single huge banner, bigger than all the rest.

KILL THE BEAST!

They landed somewhere outside the city limits. Nate saw rows and rows of geodesic domes laid out in a grid pattern like a vast, sanitized refugee camp. Souped-up and almost comical golf carts, like the one he'd taken from the morgue, were parked in some of the driveways.

The guards marched him from the 'copter to a car where four other men were waiting. They were dressed differently. They had no visors and all had coarse, bloated features, as though they were from the same malevolent family. Nate had a sinking feeling that he was never going to make it to the border.

They drove down a virtually empty freeway. There were no road signs.

'Is this the road to the border?' he said.

No one answered.

'How do you know where to go when there's no signs?'

'Travel is discouraged,' one of them said. The guy was sitting next to him. He had a less mean face than the others.

'This has got to be the old 10 freeway. It goes all the way to Los Angeles, doesn't it?'

Again, no response.

'It must be the 10,' muttered Nate. 'How many miles is it now?'

'To the border – fifty.'

'Can we stop? I need to take a leak.'

They grunted and pulled over.

'Take off your shoes,' ordered the driver. 'And the hood.'

'Why?'

'Take off your shoes and the hood.'

Nate refused. A rough guy, with pitted skin, held him

while the nicer guy flipped off his shoes and unzipped his visor.

Barefoot, Nate walked away from them until two of them started after him. They were jittery and drew their guns and told him to piss where he stood.

'I can't do it with you aiming at me. I'll do it behind this rock.'

The friendlier guy followed him and stood a little way off while Nate urinated.

'What's your name?' said Nate, now that they were out of earshot. The guy said nothing.

'You know what I've been through. None of this was my fault. I'm a victim in all of this.'

'It has nothing to do with me.'

'So what's happening here? No shoes. Guns drawn. I was presented to the President last week. Why the sudden change of heart?'

The guard looked at Nate's bare feet.

'Am I going to get to California? Or do you have other plans?'

The guy looked shiftily towards the car.

'What are you – a death squad?'

The guy stared, but there was a shred of compassion in his expression.

'Give me a break, will you?' said Nate.

The guy pointed the gun at Nate's chest and motioned for him to start walking back to the car. He almost expected to feel the impact of a bullet in the back of his head. How easy it would be to snuff out his life. Nate wondered how on earth Garth and Persis could have betrayed him like this. Especially Persis.

To Nate's surprise they did reach the border, at dusk.

Soldiers directed them into a long line of traffic. It was barely moving as papers were checked and cars searched. An hour went by in excruciating silence. The men were becoming more agitated and began to talk in a Spanish dialect that Nate could barely understand. He could tell they were angry about being delayed. All he could make out was '*Adonde paramos?*' 'Where are we going to stop?'

He thought they said Blythe, a small town close to the border.

It was enough to tell him that they were going to take him over the border, kill him, dump his body somewhere and make their way back. The desert provided an infinite number of places to carry out an execution. As they neared the checkpoint, Nate could see a fifty-foot-high force field fence disappearing into the desert on either side. Search beams cast pools of dazzling whiteness across the desert floor. Night creatures scattered as the beams burnt their way over the rocky landscape. Nate realized just how serious the Government were about keeping the states separate.

The car was waved into another line of cars that were inching towards a booth full of heavily armed soldiers. One of the men got out of the car to talk to the driver in front and find out what was happening. After a long wait, a second man got out, leaving two guards in the car, one of them Nate's potential ally. Nate looked at the man's shadowy face and saw the guy motion with his eyes to the door handle. Nate understood. This might be his only chance. He conveyed a silent thanks, then leapt from the car and ran into the night.

There were shouts and shots. The beams of light were looking for him in seconds, ranging across the desert as he ran. He remembered from somewhere to zigzag across the ground. It worked, but the beams caught up with him several times and shots pinged right by his head. The bullets made ineffectual zipping noises as they hit the ground, but he knew just how deadly they could be.

Panting and scrambling, he didn't stop running for what seemed like miles. He was amazed that he could do it. Eventually he came to a halt and turned back to see the faint glow of the security terminal in the distance. They hadn't followed him. Why? Panic began to creep through him as he wondered what the hell he was going to do next. He looked down at his feet. The fear and adrenaline had completely blocked from his mind that he was still barefoot and his soles were cut and bleeding.

Suddenly, the whoosh of an aircraft came over the plain, rolling great search beams across the ground. Then he saw another craft, a doughnut-shaped surveillance plane that he'd seen in Washington, hovering low and noiseless while its vast heat-seeking detection system ranged over the landscape. Soon, there were half a dozen of them flying in diamond formation.

He found a crop of boulders and wedged himself into a crack. He knew their heat-detector sensors would be powerful enough to pick up the minutest signs of life, right down to the irises of the jackrabbits. His only hope was to be outside their range. They scoured the desert like restless, hungry beasts, meandering right and left. Nate watched them, devastated. How on earth had it come to this? He was tempted to crawl back to the checkpoint and give himself up. If his surrender became a very public event, he might be spared Icor's assassins. He had a friend in the President after all. But they'd almost certainly hand him over to the Epidemic Intelligence Service or, worse, back to Icor who would finish the job as soon as they felt safe.

The planes were beyond him now and scouring the terrain several miles away. He looked at his bleeding feet and wondered how far he would get without shoes.

When he could no longer hear the planes, he scrambled up one of the boulders to find the light from the checkpoint. He reasoned that the security post must be facing east and that the road beyond it was the old 10 highway heading west. He gathered an armful of stones and used them to make a compass on the ground to give him some clue to his whereabouts at dawn when the lights would no longer guide him. He checked his stone formation against the North Star and then, miraculously, fell asleep.

70

It was an agonizingly dry mouth that woke him up. His tongue felt huge. He began to gag, then remembered to suck on a stone to stimulate saliva. His whole body was aching and his feet hurt, but he hobbled along the force field fence towards the checkpoint. He wasn't sure if he intended to give himself up or simply take stock about his chances of escaping over the border.

He trod over bones of animals which had made the mistake of walking right into the force field's shimmering, deadly membrane. Some of the carcasses still had fur on them. He stopped short when he came across the putrefying body of a wolf. They must be back in the area.

Nate climbed up a hillock. He saw long lines of traffic forming on either side of the checkpoint and a half-dozen insect aircraft hovering along the fence. There was probably an alert out for him. He decided against going down there. He felt sure that whatever authority he ended up with would punish him or execute him. He thought it would be best to head east, find a road and try to hitch a ride into Nevada.

He came across a deserted camp with debris strewn around the ashes of a fire pit. He managed to find a single shoe. It was too small, so he ripped open the toe. For the other foot, he made a moccasin from a pair of old jeans. He grabbed some plastic bags, a knife and an old knapsack.

He stumbled across the unforgiving plain for most of the day, sucking the moisture out of cactus fronds and trying to keep track of his direction. As the day drew on, he began to imagine things. Many times he thought he saw the watery shiver of great lakes before his eyes. He knew to mistrust the mirage as it would tempt him to change direction.

As the sun was setting over the mountains, he came across a dry lakebed. It had white caking around the edges and looked like a giant clown's gaping mouth. His own mouth must look like that too, he thought, scabbed and cracked. His head was pounding and his feet were in agony. There were jackrabbits everywhere.

He cursed Icor and all the people who'd betrayed him – Garth, Persis and even his dear friend Monty. He cursed Mary too for her misguided need to fixate on some eccentric hobby. She was the one who had really landed him in this dreadful spot. If it hadn't been for her arrogance, for her interference with his destiny, he might have been at peace right now. Instead, he would probably die a second, horrible death in the middle of nowhere. How far he had come from his Venice beach house, his practice in Beverly Hills, the Sunday walks along the beach trying to spot pods of porpoises, turkey at Thanksgiving, sprinkler systems, the rusty quench of red wine during languid lunches in restaurants on Abbott Kinney.

He sat down on a small hillock and felt swept up by a

profound sadness. It was a crushing, hermetic implosion. He fell to his knees and clutched his hands and realized that he was praying. He'd always considered himself an agnostic, waiting for a sign that would awaken his beliefs, but the prayer didn't seem to be coming from him. It was coming from the body.

'Lord, help me. Please help me. Let me live.' Then from nowhere, 'Jesus loves you.' He'd written those words before. The guy must have been a believer. Nate could feel that the body wanted to get moving. Whether he'd gone quite mad through dehydration or the body was simply taking over, he couldn't tell, but there was nothing left to do. He trudged on, eventually finding a sheltered spot in the middle of an outcrop of rocks. He made a fire with sticks and grass and thanked the land for rendering them tinder-dry. From somewhere he found the energy to figure out how to build two water sills to collect moisture overnight. But every moment increased his sense of dread and profound loneliness. If only there were other human beings. A road. A car. *Something*. Hunters and their trucks. He would throw himself on their mercy and beg for a ride.

He decided to meditate on the stars to help him get his bearings and mark out another compass in stones. He had a photographic image of Nevada in his mind's eye and thought there *had* to be a road within twenty miles. There had better be. He wouldn't stand a chance of surviving another day.

When he came to the following morning, the sun was high in the sky. He drank the mouthful of water that had collected in the sills and set off. After several hours, his body felt so painful that every step sent a fresh stab of agony through his legs. He was so weak that he couldn't even look at the ground to avoid the shingle. He tripped on a rock and fell to his knees.

'I think this is as far as we go,' he said in the deafening silence that was ringing in his ears. 'Or as far as I go.'

He sat there and felt quite calm. Maybe he could drag himself on for another mile or so but he had no desire to get up. He drank the last of the water and was drifting into a kind of trance, when he saw a long, strange caterpillar coming towards him through the shimmering haze. It was such an improbable image that he wondered if it was a mirage too, but he could hear the low growl of an engine. The vehicle looked like a worm-shaped hovercraft.

Nate dragged himself to his feet and waved. The long, snaking body of the machine lumbered on past him, sounding a huge siren. Nate felt crushed, believing it was his last means of escape, then noticed the caterpillar was slowing down. He hobbled along the body of the vehicle. A mechanized staircase was descending from the cab. A short, plump man was standing at the top of the stairs in a grey jumpsuit. He removed his face visor, revealing a pug nose, baby round cheeks and disconcertingly pale blue eyes.

'I sure as hell wasn't expecting to see no one out here. What happened? Your woman dump you?'

The speech pattern was so quick-fire that Nate could barely understand it. He tried to smile and swallowed a sob. 'Something like that.'

'No kidding. I found a lot of dogs over the years, and a woman once, but never a *man*.' He looked oddly at Nate and his hand hovered over something in his trouser pocket. Maybe it was a gun.

'I'm in trouble,' said Nate, trying to sound as stable as possible. 'Some bad people left me out here to die, but I'm not a bad person myself. I need to get the hell out of here. Where are you heading?'

The man stared at him for an interminably long time. Nate wondered if he had been understood.

'You're not one of them miscreants, are you?'

'A what?'

Nate realized how terrible he must look with his bandaged, bloody feet and sad sack of belongings.

'I don't take no people like that on board.'

'What are they?'

'They are whoever they want to be and it's always bad. The "no gooders" I call 'em. You got good papers? We cross the border in forty miles. I don't want no charge for harbouring miscreants.'

Nate breathed out. 'No.'

The man looked around and scratched his head. 'I can give you water and food, but I can't take you on board, sorry.'

'Just to the border? I'm going to die out here.'

'Oh, hell – all right.' The man retreated back into his cab. Nate guessed that he was meant to follow. The man gave him a plastic-tasting patty and some water and started up the engine.

'What are you carrying?' asked Nate eventually.

'Hydrogen fluoroxide.'

Jesus, thought Nate. Not only was he heading towards certain capture, he was travelling in a moving bomb.

'Who needs hydrogen fluoroxide?'

The guy laughed and his Adam's apple bobbed happily in his rotund neck. 'Nevada cops.'

Nate tried to share the joke. 'How can I get across the border without papers?'

'That's up to you.'

Nate adjusted his feet and moaned in agony. The driver looked down.

'You sure do need help. So what do I call you?'

'Nate. And what do I call you?'

'Bony, on account of the fact that my bones disappeared when I got me all this flesh.'

Nate smiled. The little guy chuckled like a happy baby. 'I think we can get you across in the old-fashioned way.'

'How?'

'In my bench, in the back of the cab. Go get yourself back there and cover yourself up. The blanket's got my dog fur all over it, but you ain't got no choice. The border's up in about fifteen minutes. And don't say nothing cos you'll get me into a whole lot of trouble.'

Nate lifted the lid of the bench and wondered how he was going to wedge himself inside. He curled up in the foetal position and pulled the musty blankets on top of him. He could feel the sensation of the giant worm slowing down and the workings of the computerized dashboard lowering the staircase.

'You seen this guy?' Nate heard someone say. 'He went missing in the desert a few days ago.'

'Nope – ain't seen him.'

'Mind if we take a look in your cab?'

'Don't you trust me? I'm delivering to the cops.'

Nate heard a dog bark. He stopped breathing.

'You can look all you want,' Bony went on, 'but don't bring no dog on board. I got asthma. Can't have no dog in the cab.'

'You got exemption papers for that?'

'I didn't bring them with me. But don't do it to me. I'll be wheezin' all the way to Las Vegas. I only got one pill and the cops don't like me being late.'

Nate heard more barks and footsteps coming up the ladder. He heard feet scraping and then the lid lifting on the bench. He almost rose up in surrender, but something told him to stay put.

'I seen you before, ain't I?' said Bony.

'We've seen each other many times,' replied the guard, lowering the lid. Nate heard more muffled voices as the guards climbed back down the steps, then the hum of the worm starting up. After a while, Bony banged on the lid for him to get out.

'This looks like your stop. I got to get this fuel to the police.'

'I don't know how to thank you.'

Bony looked at him warily.

'What is it?' said Nate.

'They said you killed four people,' said Bony, taking a sly glance at Nate's neck. Nate pulled his collar up.

'That's not true! I escaped from four guys because they were going to kill *me*!'

Bony shrugged. 'I don't take no notice of what people say about people until I've made up my own mind, but they're calling you "the Head" and said that you killed four men who were looking after you.'

'What else did they say?'

'I don't know much of anything, but they said you are some kind of relic brought back from the dead. Now *that*'s a trip.' Bony opened up a hatch in his cab and handed Nate a pair of shoes. 'They're my size, which is small, but my feet swell up – so they might fit you. And take these,' he gave Nate a couple of purple pills, 'for those feet. You won't feel no pain. One at a time, mind. That's strong stuff.'

Nate took a pill and climbed down the steps of the cab. 'I promise you I didn't kill those men.'

'I can believe it, but there's a lot of people out there who won't, so be careful. There used to be a hospital around here somewhere. I don't know if it's even open now, but you need to see yourself right by those feet.'

'Where are we?'

'They used to call this the playpen of the deluded!' said Bony as he started up the worm. 'Las Vegas,' he chuckled, and pulled the elongated larva full of deadly gas back out on to the road.

71

Nate looked about him. He was standing on the edge of the city. All he could see was street after street of clay-brown tract housing. There were no cars, and when he looked closer, he saw that all the buildings were deserted and their windows punched out. Then he saw the monuments of Las Vegas peaking above the skyline. There was the pyramid of the Egyptian, the Eiffel Tower, the Venetian and the burnt umber walls of the Bellagio. Were they derelict too? When he died, Las Vegas had been one of the fastest-growing cities in the United States.

Nate looked around for signs of a tall building that might be the hospital and saw a terracotta block a few streets away. It was surrounded by chicken-wire fencing and heavy padlocks. Nate wondered if they had any medicines inside. He found a hut by the fence, climbed over and headed towards the entrance. The doors were flung wide open.

He wandered through the empty corridors and broke open a door to an operating theatre. All the equipment was laid out on metal trays. The blood and anaesthetic bags were clipped to their frames and there were dark red smears leading from the table across the floor. It was as if a patient had been dragged from the room in the middle of an operation.

He walked through a couple of empty wards and looked at the charts still hanging from the beds. The date on each chart was the same: 3/11/2049. There must have been an emergency evacuation. But from a hospital? That's where people usually gravitated in a crisis.

He smashed open a number of cupboards and found analgesics, bandages and antiseptic ointment. In one locker, he found a pair of shoes that actually fitted him, and some clothes. Fatigue was getting the better of him, so he lay down on a bed and instructed himself to sleep for an hour. Then he would head towards the city centre before nightfall.

Nate berated himself in the darkness. He had slept for way too long. He wiggled his feet, which were pain-free for the first time in days. The pills that Bony had given him were working wonders. As he lay there in the darkness, he thought about the body. Nate had definitely felt its presence as a separate entity in the desert, and it had urged him to keep going when he was on the brink of collapse. Without drumming it up, a kind of gratitude entered Nate's soul, an appreciation towards the body for getting him this far. His own body, he knew, would never have been able to run with such speed from those guards or kept going on that terrible trek.

He longed for water and wandered from room to room, turning on every faucet, but they were all dry. He groped his way to the entrance. The street was deserted and Nate darted from doorway to doorway. This was no place to be conspicuous. He wondered how much exposure they had given his story. If a long-distance truck driver knew that he was being called 'the Head', maybe everyone knew.

He saw a vehicle, a kind of bubble car, coming towards him. He debated whether he should flag it down and beg for water. But just as he was about to step out into the road, he changed his mind and retreated into the shadows. It was terrifying to feel hounded. He had no idea who would be his friend and who his enemy.

As he got closer to the main strip, there was more traffic on the road and people were using the sidewalks. He pulled his collar up and slipped into the crowd, hoping that no one would notice him. He avoided making eye contact, but could see pretty quickly that practically everyone was Native American. He crossed a bridge and stopped. Before him was the main strip, but instead of being a blinding fiesta of neon, tiny lamps lit up the stalls of a bustling night market. Fires burnt in tin drums and smells of overripe vegetables, barbecued meat, smoke and incense filled the air.

He walked among the vendors who were trading food, beads, blankets, rugs, bags and baskets. A couple of people eyed him suspiciously.

Something profound was missing from the scene and he couldn't quite put his finger on what it was. Then it came to him. He couldn't hear the hiss and gurgle of the hundreds of fountains slapping down on to concrete. He looked about him. All the waterways, lakes and other extravagances that had once been the Las Vegas trademark were dry. The lake in front of the Bellagio was filled in and topped out with market stalls. The only sign of water on the entire strip was a waterfall on a massive screen in front of the hotel. But it wasn't even a real waterfall, it was a digitized image.

Seeing the cartoon water made him realize how thirsty he was. He saw a couple of neon signs fizzing in the darkness. It was a small bar and casino. He stepped inside. Only one slot machine was working and an old man was pulling at the arm as if he couldn't stop.

'Is there someplace I can get a drink around here?' asked Nate.

THE WAKING

The old man motioned to another, smaller room. Nate saw a handsome Native American watching a screen from behind a bar. If the man had seen the news, he would know who Nate was. Nate wondered if he should turn right round and walk out.

'Can I get you anything?' said the barman before he could make a decision.

'I need water but I've got no money.'

The man shook his head and went back to watching the screen.

'Please,' begged Nate, all pride leaving him. 'I'm dehydrated.'

The man reluctantly got up and poured him a pitcher. Nate drank it right down.

'It's not often we get to see white people in Vegas,' the man said.

'I got into—' Nate didn't have any more energy left in him to weave a story. 'I got robbed yesterday. They took everything,' was all he could think of.

'Tourist?' asked the barman cautiously, refilling the pitcher. He offered Nate some biscuits. Nate sank on to a barstool.

'That's right.'

'Where's home?'

'Los Angeles.'

'They just reopened the East Side and the Inland Empire today, but the West Side is still cordoned. Which part are you from?'

'West Side.'

'They say the worst is over but it won't open up till next week. You got family there?'

'A wife.'

'I'm sorry. She OK?' said the Indian with genuine concern.

Nate wondered what he was talking about. It must be some kind of outbreak. 'I spoke to her yesterday – she's fine. But I've got to get home. Do you know anyone who could take me there?' said Nate. 'They'd have to smuggle me over the border. I don't have any papers.'

The man looked suspicious.

'They were taken in the robbery,' offered Nate.

'You report it to the National Guard?'

'Sure, but they said I had to wait here and I can't.'

The Indian scratched his jet-black hair, which was tied back in a plait.

'A friend of mine is coming through here in a couple of days. He's going to deliver some medical supplies to California. He might be able to do it.'

'Really?'

'Sure. Come back Monday.'

Nate wanted to ask the man what day it was, but didn't want to give away his ignorance. 'It's market day,' he declared instead.

'That's right. They come in from all over the state.'

'So what's happening with the hotels?'

'What's happening? Nothing is what's happening. And I for one am getting impatient. There's been too much infighting.'

'Infighting?'

The Indian squinted at Nate. 'Between the Shoshone and the Paiute.'

'Oh, that,' said Nate. 'I always felt ignorant about the real issues here. Can you fill me in?'

The Indian kind of snorted. 'How far back do you want to go?'

Nate remembered the dates that he'd found on the hospital beds. 'What about 2049?' he said.

'The year they blew out the Hoover dam? You must know all about the effort to save the Colorado River. You were alive, right?'

Nate shrugged, assented.

'The day they blew out the dam was the day the city lost eighty per cent of its water supply. A lot of people had already got out and the corporations were long gone, but many people refused to go. I think they couldn't believe the Government was really going to do it. It got very ugly at the end. There's tales of real brutality.'

'Against Native Americans?'

'Against anyone who was still here.'

'So it's under Native American control now?' ventured Nate.

'What's wrong with your memory? That's right, no investor would touch the place for years, but the Indian tribes of Nevada kept asking the Government for the land and eventually it was given back to us in '57. We said we would rebuild it in five years. And here we are, thirteen years on, and look at us. Nothing – not a single fountain rains down on the dirt and all we do is talk.'

He got up and flicked off the screen. 'But our time is coming. Don't believe what they tell you. The Shoshone and the Paiute will make Las Vegas great again.'

'How do you manage for water now?' asked Nate.

'We get our supplies from California. But that's one of our biggest problems. We can't sustain a resort until it's sorted out.'

'What's your name?'

'Thomas. Hey – you got anywhere to stay tonight?'

'There is somewhere I can go but . . .' Nate's voice trailed off.

'You can sleep upstairs if you like.'

'I appreciate that.'

Thomas shrugged. 'Hey – you're in a bind.'

72

For the next two days, Nate kept a low profile in the bar, giving Thomas a hand when he needed it.

'You know, you should stick around,' said Thomas. 'I could do with the help.'

'I need to get back to my wife,' said Nate.

'Do you want to call her? You can do it from here.'

For a split second, Nate didn't know what to say.

'She's – I haven't got any money.'

'Don't worry. You got a code?'

'No – I—'

'It's OK,' said Thomas, his face softening. 'I think I know who you are.'

'You do?'

'You're the first cryonic man.'

'Was it on the news?'

'It's all over the place. But – hey, I'm on your side, man. I don't know what I'd do if I was brought back from the dead. They can do some pretty wacky things in medicine now, but this is really something.'

'I did have a wife before. They tell me she's dead. I've had to deal with that as well as everything else.'

'I'm sorry,' said Thomas. 'It's none of my business, but did you kill those men?'

'No. I think Icor assassinated them.'

Thomas looked at Nate's body, doubtful. 'You say you aren't a killer?'

'No. Why?'

'Go look it up. It's on the computer.'

Thomas took Nate to his tiny office and gave him a keyboard. A big flat screen was alive with a thousand different images.

'I don't know how to use this,' said Nate.

Thomas pulled up a dozen news images and there, in a tiny box, Nate could see his own face looking back at him.

Thomas pulled up the image which filled the screen. The still frame of Nate's face switched to moving footage of a crowd outside Icor's headquarters. He strained to listen to the commentary.

'*Ever since the story about the world's first cryonic man has been made public, Icor's headquarters in Phoenix have been under siege. That this hybrid could have been created at all, is being condemned as grotesque and unlawful. Icor's scientists have said that many companies are on the brink of the same innovation, it's just that the programme's medical director, Dr Garth Bannerman . . .*'

The picture cut to a wobbly shot of Garth escaping the compound in his car and being pursued by reporters.

'*. . . happened to get there first. But of course, the biggest question being raised today is how Icor managed to track down the body of killer Duane Williams to use for this experiment, and how much they paid Gamma Gulch State Penitentiary for the cadaver. Williams's family say they were never told about the destination of the body, only that he had donated it to medical research . . .*'

The words didn't make sense. And now there was a picture of someone else on the screen, a mugshot of a man with a curved, down-turned mouth and sensual, drooping eyelids, which was replaced by a moving image of the same man being escorted in chains through a top-security prison. Nate could barely take in what he was hearing and seeing.

'. . . *Duane Williams was convicted of murdering a young woman, Jenner Sommers, in San Luis Obispo in 2064. The girl was known to him and his family. He took her down to a deserted creek near the kit park where they lived and raped and sodomized her and left her for dead. She was found by her brother. Duane Williams himself was picked up near the scene by the police and later condemned to death and executed at Gamma Gulch State Penitentiary on 25th May 2069. Gamma Gulch aren't talking, but we do know that either at the point of death or sometime later, Icor Incorporated removed Williams's head and attached the body to another head that was cryonically frozen more than sixty years ago. That head belongs or belonged to a Dr Nathaniel Sheehan. We know about Dr Sheehan because he became something of a celebrity in Los Angeles when he was put on display at the Pasadena Cryogenesis Research Institute where he was being kept . . .*'

The picture changed to a hideous image of Nate's distorted and severed head floating in liquid helium. He looked down at his body. Everything matched: the muscular physique; the tawny skin; even the sinewy contour of the arms and wrists and the spatula-flat fingernails that he had just seen in handcuffs on the screen and that he himself could now feel and touch.

Ian Paterson, the cheerful chemistry student with a wild side, was obviously a complete fabrication, and Nate finally understood that he was, effectively, walking around with the body of a killer.

All the work he had done to accept his body was wiped out in an instant. All the lies they had told him – the file, the pictures, that trip to the Grand Canyon – were in honour of someone who probably didn't even exist, and the tragic, sordid tale of Duane Williams would live on in him for ever.

He leant over and put his head in his hands. He thought he was going to be sick.

'Are you OK?' he heard Thomas say through the blood pumping in his ears.

'They're liars!' Nate bellowed, and made a rush for the door. Thomas stopped him in his tracks.

'Hey, you need to calm down,' he said, pushing Nate back into the chair. 'You don't want to draw attention to yourself.'

Nate sat there in a stupefied torpor.

'My friend is going to be here at three, and if he agrees, he will take you to Los Angeles,' said Thomas.

'How could they do this to me?'

'I don't know, my friend, but they did it and hey, you *are* alive.'

Thomas's friend, who was carrying medical supplies to California, was three hours late and insisted that they start out straight away. Nate stayed out of earshot as he watched Thomas negotiate his passage. It was agreed that he would be taken across the border, but he would have to be dropped at the edge of the city because of the curfew.

'It's better to travel at night. The guards on the checkpoint get sleepy,' said Thomas, giving Nate a firm handshake. In his palm was a roll of money.

'I can't take this,' said Nate.

'It's all I can spare. It might get you a place to stay for a couple of nights.'

'I don't know how to thank you.'

The two men hugged.

It was almost a full moon and the desert was bathed in a silvery glow. They overtook strange vehicles and huge lumbering convoys of freight that ran on separate roads parallel to their own. Unlike Thomas with his trusting, easy-going manner, the driver was surly and silent. Nate was still reeling from the news bulletin. Ever since he'd seen it, he'd felt wired. He kept trying to relax, but he just couldn't get the dreadful news of his body's identity out of his mind. Or Persis. How could she make love to him knowing who the body belonged to?

'I am a killer,' he kept saying to himself. *'That's why I murdered Tony. Who knows what I'm capable of?'*

As they got closer to the border, the driver told Nate to get into the hold. He squeezed himself into a gap between the cab and the container. It was narrow and smelt of urine and was clearly used on a regular basis for just such a purpose. The guards looked in the back of the vehicle, which was loaded up with medical supplies, and let it go through.

The driver pulled over to allow Nate back into the cab. He was wearing a mask. He handed Nate a mask and gruffly told him to put it on.

Nate was dropped, as agreed, just outside Los Angeles. He wanted to thank the driver, but the guy just drove off without looking back and Nate felt the snub increase his sense of desolation.

Dawn was breaking and the purple-grey light of a Los Angeles morning gave him the illusion that he was on familiar ground. He found a ride to Barham Boulevard and headed for the Hollywood Hills. He'd pictured himself getting to a high point, maybe Runyon Canyon, and taking in the lie of the land before making his way to the coast. He wanted desperately to connect with his old haunts. He thought if he did that he would feel closer to Mary and then, if there were any records left, he would look up her documentation and finally piece together what had happened to her and any friends who might be alive.

He tried to flag down passing motorists. The electric cars and trucks made their silent, fumeless progress, but no one stopped. Maybe the health alert was making everyone nervous. Finally, an ancient pickup truck spluttered to a halt and the passenger door creaked open. A diminutive man wearing a mask and a cap smiled at him. 'You're lucky I saw you. Where are you heading?'

'Runyon Canyon.'

'Where?'

'Runyon Canyon. Off Mulholland Drive. Is there a park up there now? I haven't been there in quite a while.'

'Some parts of Mulholland are accessible. I can drop you.'

The driver was frighteningly reckless, swerving in and out of other cars.

'Don't they have any traffic violations?'

The man just laughed and increased his speed. Nate clung to the dashboard. In no time at all, they were zipping past Universal Studios which, apart from its sad and shabby appearance, looked pretty much as Nate remembered it. He recalled Persis's words, that the entertainment monoliths in Studio City were still open for business. He wondered what product they were pumping out now. There was enough real drama in the world to fill any number of development slates. The man dropped Nate at the corner of Mulholland Drive and Cahuenga Boulevard, right next to the 101. Although it was rush hour, there was very little congestion.

Nate took the left-hand fork in the road and began to climb up Mulholland Drive. The tarmac quickly turned into a dirt track. Nate couldn't believe it. Mulholland was once the main artery through the hills and he was approaching what used to be some of the richest real estate in Los Angeles.

He had a photographic memory of Mulholland. He knew it because he had a number of friends and patients who lived up there and he often made the trip in his SUV. Right now, he was heading towards the house where his old friends Mark and Julia Freeman used to live. It was situated down a tiny lane which opened out on to a flat platform of land where they had built a ranch house. As he walked, he remembered many a glass of chilled white wine being drunk on the Freemans' deck while looking out over the spectacular views of the San Fernando Valley. What tidy, happy couples they all made, participating in the insouciant, ordered prosperity of their lives, taking gifts of wine and flowers to dinner parties which would end at ten, maybe eleven if the conversation was stimulating enough. By the time he died, it was dawning on all of them that children would be the special ingredient that would make their lives complete. Or perhaps stave off the crisis of purposelessness. None of them had heard the rumble of disaster so close to home.

'And where are you now?' he said to himself as he looked at his dirty clothes. He came to the entrance to the lane. Except there was no lane. A little way up he could see the edge of the cliff, but no house. The great earthquake must have done its damage inland too. Further on he saw a sign:

ROAD CLOSED

A landslide seemed to have taken a sizeable chunk of Mulholland Drive down the hill. He found a trail over the top of the gap. He searched the hillside for other houses, but whole streets off Mulholland appeared to be missing.

As he came around a row of bushes, Nate stopped and caught his breath. The entire city was laid out beneath him.

He tried to focus. The skyline had utterly changed. All the greenery, which to Nate was the essence of Los Angeles's beauty, was gone, including the avenues of spindly palms. Many of the buildings seemed to have parched grass roofs and strange, Moorish irrigation systems. And dotted right across the city were blunted chimneys coughing up plumes of smoke. They must be the crematoria that Persis had talked about.

He trudged on and found specks of ash fluttering in the air, clinging to his clothes and his hair.

He came to a familiar bend in the road. It was the old entrance to Runyon Canyon. How many times he had parked the SUV near the trailhead and headed down the hill! He and Mary used to pride themselves on being able to do the entire circuit in under twenty minutes. Eavesdropping had been one of their favourite pastimes as they marched, though it irritated them to hear all the selfish '*me, me, me*' conversations of writers frustrated with directors and producers frustrated with writers; all the participants of Hollywood's passage of crea-tives taking their daily constitutional and letting off steam. And the view to end all views was now sullied with the smoke of the dead. How symbolic that it should come to this.

The sign to the entrance of Runyon Canyon was battered and the path, once trod by thousands of feet, was covered with brambles and weeds. Nate was determined to get to the lookout point and hacked his way through the bushes, then spotted the giant's bench where people used to perch. How remarkable that it should still be there after all these years! He pulled at some weeds that were wound around the seat and climbed on. Now he had a full view of the West Side. To his horror, he could see exactly what Persis was talking about. The sea was breathtakingly close. After taking it all in, he scrambled down what was left of the trail, tripping over stones and weeds as he went.

When he got to the top of La Brea, he slowed down to take stock. Gone was the old Spanish apartment building on the corner of Franklin Boulevard with its elaborate frescoes and modest balconies. Gone the modernist duplex, a block further down. Gone that tacky statue of four silver nymphs holding up the roof of a gazebo on the corner of Hollywood Boulevard, and all the other landmarks that he had taken for granted on his descent towards Venice.

There was more traffic on the roads than on the freeways, an oddball assortment of electric cars, scooters, rickshaws being pulled by masked bikers. It was chaotic and disorganized and everyone was masked. Nate put his own mask back on. He was astounded by the number of pedestrians. It was so unlike the LA that he used to know, where the sidewalks were the domain of the poor and the destitute. A mile further down La Brea, Nate arrived at the junction of 3rd Avenue. He felt a flutter in his body and a scorched feeling behind his eyeballs. He had at last reached the old site of Trader Joe's and the point of his own death.

Miraculously, the building was still standing, although it had a different name, and there in front of him was the parking lot where he had been shot. Nate leant against a wall and gave himself a moment. He wondered about his killer, a kid of no more than fourteen, dead probably, and Mary screaming at the kid, and now both of them were nothing but a speck of dust, if that.

He stood for a while and understood for the first time the peculiar, inexorable continuity of life from birth to the snuffing out of a spirit as the last breath is drawn. Unconsciously, Nate had a hand cupped protectively over his heart. Tears welled up in him but he sniffed them away. It wasn't far now.

73

Although the city streets were teeming with life, there was a tension that was palpable. Nate looked down an alley and saw a number of people in biohazard suits loading body bags into a truck. It brought home to him what a health alert really meant. It clearly wasn't something you could conceal from the public, though there seemed to be no panic. Perhaps people had become used to the danger. Or the worst was over.

It wasn't much further south that Nate began to hear a disconcerting sound. It was the hiss and crash of waves. He'd only just passed Wilshire Boulevard, once fifteen miles inland, and yet he was getting close to the Pacific. He could see the road blocked off by a high wall and assumed that it might be the memorial park that Karen had talked about back at Icor.

He carried on until he reached the wall and found a gate. Inside, there was a long landscaped strip of land like a promenade, though there was no elegance to the fence separating the cactus garden from the jagged coastline. It looked as though a huge crane had gouged out great chunks of cliff.

There were bronze statues of people dotted all over the park. Nate read the plaques and absorbed the details of the individuals who had mounted heroic rescues during the great earthquake of 2012. There were remnants of buildings too, their steel frames contorted and mangled where they had collapsed on their foundations. And in the far distance he could see the old 10 freeway come to an abrupt halt where its concrete elevations had been severed. Nate got as close as he could to the edge of the cliff and saw through the waves that the freeway was still intact underwater. As he peered into the

Pacific, he could see more detail. The tectonic plate had sunk in one piece.

'Your first time here?' someone said over Nate's shoulder.

It was a homeless man, unmasked, with matted hair and grime worked deep into rutted wrinkles. In the middle of his face were tiny dark eyes, darting and busy, summing up Nate as a potential giver or taker. There were no people sharper than the homeless. Nate had had to deal with so many at his free clinic in Huntington Park and he'd often seen them completely burnt out on adrenaline and overuse of their wits.

'You lose an ancestor down there?' said the man.

'Yes.'

'If you're a descendant, you can go see 'em, you know. Can you dive?'

'I did learn a long time ago.'

'They got it all mapped out. The streets and everything, Culver City, Mar Vista, Venice, Marina Del Rey and all the shipwrecks. You can't disturb nothing cos it's a national monument, but lots of people go down there to pay their respects.'

'How do I get there?'

The man gestured to some steps. Nate peered over the cliff and saw a long jetty where dozens of craft were bobbing in the waves.

'See them fellers over there?'

Nate followed the man's bent finger and spotted two or three office blocks rising up through the ocean.

'Someone wanted to turn them into an attraction, but it was dedicated as a memorial so no one gets permission. Home to the seals now.'

They both watched, silent for a moment, as the sun melted deep orange into the metallic blue surface of the ocean. Nate resolved to return the following morning to make the dive.

'Is there a hotel around here?'

'Not any place *you* want to stay. Better places up on Sunset.'

Sunset Boulevard. The resonance of that name. The Strip, where Nate and Mary used to check into the Chateau Marmont for illicit nights of passion, even after they were married. He hitched a lift on a public tram that rode all the way back up to Sunset and found that the hotel was still standing. He walked right into the lobby. It was tatty and threadbare, with huge cracks in the walls and ceilings. The central chandelier in the reception was perilously tilted. There was a tiny light on in the reception area, so he presumed it must be open. Sure enough, a sickly-looking student with pale skin and jet-black hair handed over a key.

The Chateau had retreated into the wilderness years of a century before when it was a honeypot for junkies, dealers and addicted movie stars. Shifty figures were loitering around in the lobby and along the corridors.

He was shown to a dark little room with peeling wallpaper. He lay down on the bed and wondered what lay in store for him. He thought he ought to try to reach the President somehow, through a third party, maybe Albert Noyes. Nate believed that it was the only way to secure his safety. But first, he had to know what happened to Mary.

There was a screen in the corner of the room and a touch pad on the bedside table. Nate managed to find a news station. The newscaster was standing up and moving around casually to different sources of news footage. Nate's own face didn't appear in the bulletin. Maybe they had forgotten about him already.

He ordered some food and struggled to stay awake. When he heard the knock on the door, he could barely get up from the bed. He opened it. His instinct was to slam it shut again. Persis was the last person he expected to see.

'Did you bring Icor with you?' he said, scanning the room for an escape route.

'No – I defected from the company when I heard what happened.'

'How did you know to come here?'

'You talked about this hotel. I thought that if you had, by some miracle, survived, you might make your way here.'

'How long have you been here?'

'A few days.'

'Won't they be tracking you with credit cards?'

'I have cash.'

'And why should I trust you?'

'Nate – I'm a scientist. I joined the company three years ago from NYU. I didn't know what Icor was capable of, or my husband—' She broke off. 'I knew that you weren't predisposed to kill those men, unless you were under some kind of significant threat yourself.'

'If some other death squad within Icor killed that security detail, you could be in danger yourself,' said Nate.

He sat on the bed. 'I don't think any of you thought beyond the waking,' said Nate finally.

'It's true,' she admitted. 'We didn't think it would work. And when it did, we had no back-up plan. I think later we hoped you would accept and adapt.'

'Accept and adapt,' laughed Nate. 'You lied to me. You cannot accept or adapt to a lie! And now, I'm not only a freak, but I have the body of a killer! Accept and adapt. Your language is ridiculous.'

Persis inspected the lank and drooping curtains and made an unconscious face of disapproval.

'Did you ever meet Duane before he was executed?' asked Nate.

'Yes.'

'What was he like?'

'Mentally impaired. His hippocampus was undersized. There were numerous lesions in the prefrontal cortex and the amygdala was overreactive—'

'What was *he* like?'

'Classically segregated. I saw at least three personalities—'

'But what was *he like*?'

She breathed out, frowning, thinking. 'He had a presumption that women would respond to him, so he flirted with me, his stock way of relating to the opposite sex. But he had no inner confidence, so there was deep hostility and mistrust. He had a serious loathing of his mother, which was justified. She had been sadistic and then deserted him. He may have despised me too. I think I represented to him his warped view of womanhood and authority.'

'What did you talk about?'

'I did a number of tests and asked him to recall his childhood.' She stopped and, surprisingly, tears formed. 'He was pathetic and yet he had courage.'

Nate shook his head. 'I don't get it. I don't understand how you could get to know him then do what you did.'

'There was nothing I could do to *save* him.'

'But in your mind, somewhere along the line, you must have wished him dead, Persis, so you could carry out your experiment.'

She looked at him.

'Did it ever occur to you that he might be innocent of the crime?'

Persis shook her head. 'I did have a crisis of morality about the purchase of all the bodies,' she said, 'but I guess I was ambitious enough to overlook it.'

Each new piece of information seemed to make things worse between them.

'What about your husband? What does he think about you defecting and coming here? Does he even know?'

She went over to the window and looked out over the misty, polluted city basin. 'When I resigned, I kind of walked out on the relationship too,' she said.

'Well, I hope it was worth it. Because right now, Persis, I can't protect you. I can't even protect myself.'

Too weary to battle on, Nate showered, then offered Persis the use of the bathroom. They circled each other like strangers, not touching, and when they had eaten, they lay back on opposite ends of the bed. There were no more words to be said and although he was actually stirred by her presence, he couldn't be further away from her emotionally. They were from two different worlds, and Nate had no idea how he would ever be able to be intimate with anyone again. Besides, he had a plan mapped out for the following day and his plans didn't include the woman lying next to him.

74

At first light, Nate lifted himself off the bed, dressed quietly and left the room, taking one last glance at Persis, not sure if he would ever see her again. He took an early tram to the coast and returned to the jetty where the boatsmen were emerging from their craft and getting ready for the day. He eyed up the crowd and headed for the friendliest-looking guy.

'What can I do for you?'

The man's face was cracked and aged from salt water, his hair bleached almost white.

'I want to dive down in the canals today – the Grand Canal. I lost a relative there.'

'No can do today. There's a blue alert.'

'Blue alert?'

'A whole army of cephalopods came in from Hawaii five days ago and they've settled in the bay. There's nothing happening till the weekend.'

Cephalopods. Nate remembered it was the term for squid. 'Why would that stop you?'

'They caught one up in Malibu and it was thirty metres long. Size like that and they can drag me out to sea. Happened to me once. I don't want to risk it again.'

Nate couldn't imagine the size of such a creature.

'You mean giant squid.'

'That's right. They've brought the few remaining sharks with them too. There's a feeding frenzy going on down there. I'm sorry.'

Nate looked out to sea. He noticed that there were buoys laid out in a grid pattern across the surface marking up all the streets that had been so familiar to him. He hadn't anticipated having to wait. He was wondering what to do next, when someone ran along the jetty shouting: 'The nets are up! The nets are up!'

'Never thought they'd get it together that fast,' commented the boatman.

'What's happening?' said Nate.

'It means my name is Joe and you just got yourself a ride.'

Joe's boat was a long, shallow-bottomed passenger ferry that reminded Nate of the old vaporettos that operated in the real

Venice in Italy. It glided with a low hum. No chugging and spluttering of diesel fuel as they followed the signs to Venice. Every now and then they slowed down to look at an office building that was half submerged, with seals reclining fatly on the concrete platforms. Joe brought along a young diver called Carlos, who didn't say much. Joe was the storyteller. He told Nate that the Coastguard were working round the clock to drive the squid out of town and raise the nets, leaving the submerged city clear of danger. Without being prompted, he explained how the giant squid were the life force of the ocean now. Squid had benefited from global warming more than any other species. Their predators had been wiped out by overfishing and their biomass was increasing with every degree of temperature change. Enormous specimens had been washed up on beaches from New York to Tasmania. The largest ever recorded was 150 feet long.

'They might be able to save us if we could eat them, but most of them are so toxic, we can't even use them for food,' said Joe. There were more stories of ships being dragged along by the deadly tentacles of the squid and smaller boats being engulfed altogether. They clearly left the mark of fear on everyone.

According to the signs, they were cruising over Lincoln Boulevard, so were less than a mile away from Nate's old house.

'Where do you want to dive?' said Joe.

'Grand Canal.'

'Good, because we're getting pretty close to the nets and I don't want to take the boat outside them today. Any particular house you interested in? The roof of every house is numbered, so we should be able to find it. The history too.'

'You have the history?'

'Sure, it's a nice touch for the visitors.'

'What does it say about 2521?'

Joe tapped the detail into a computer. He waited a moment. 'It says the house was occupied by a doctor—'

'Mary Sheehan?'

'That's right. And her son.'

'Her son!' said Nate, his voice rising above the waves.

'That's what it says here. And here we are!'

Nate was in turmoil as Joe put the engine into reverse thrust. A son. Their son. Mary had been expecting their child when he died. Why had he never remembered before?

Joe lowered a remote camera into the water so that they could take a closer look at the house. Nate peered into the blue depths on a screen. The misty, distorted blur of an old beach house bobbed into view, its number emblazoned across the roof. All the windows were missing and long fronds of seaweed drifted through cracks in the stucco. But the steel frame, which they had spent so much money installing as part of the retrofitting, was still standing.

'Are you sure you want to dive?' said Joe. 'There's a big shelf near here. You can get a strong undertow.'

'Where the beach used to be?'

'That's right. You a strong swimmer?'

'I was. Is the pier still standing?'

'Sure, but that's right up by the nets, so you won't get to see that today.'

Joe stalled the engines and dropped the anchor.

'OK, go get yourself suited up. Carlos will take you down.'

Nate was given a quick lesson by Carlos.

'We're lucky,' he said. 'It's going to be empty. No one likes to dive when the squid have been through.'

'Do you?' asked Nate, wondering if he was about to entrust his life to a risk-taker.

'I like to bait them. That's what I like to do. If one or two got left behind, we got hot prods and they don't like these things one little bit.'

The diving equipment hadn't changed much, except that the gaseous mixture they used gave them more time underwater and the communication device melded into Nate's mask sounded as clear as a land line. When they were ready, they sat on the side of the boat and flipped backwards.

The light and the warmth quickly faded as they sank down the rope. Street lamps lit up the ghostly network of the old canals. Its dark blue-grey hues and chilled stillness made it look more like nineteenth-century London in fog.

Nate could make out the dip where the canals had once been and saw a series of ropes along the paths so that divers could follow the grid as if they were taking a bizarre afternoon stroll. He began to drag himself along the rope towards his old house. Carlos motioned for him to look to the left. A pod of dolphins were streaking along.

'They jump over the nets,' he said.

'Do they ever get caught up in them?' asked Nate.

'We got a special detection system that releases them if they do.'

After much exertion, Nate came to his old gate. He ran his hands over the wrought-iron ivy that was woven around the bars. It had been a huge expense at the time, but Mary had insisted on installing something impressive to ward off the tourists who walked through the canals on the weekends. He tried to scrape the barnacles off the plate with their house number and a picture of a gondola. He tugged at the handle, but it was rusted shut, so he swam over the top and into his old backyard.

He was surprised to see the enormous pine tree still standing, petrified and swaying gently in the current. They had always condemned the tree as a nuisance but couldn't quite bring themselves to chop it down. It was one of the biggest trees on the canals and absolutely nothing would grow under it. Nate touched the gnarled trunk and peered up through the tangle of branches, remembering the peacock-green hummingbird which perched on the same tiny twig every morning.

Then he went cold. Hovering fifty feet above him was a huge mass of pale flesh with its phantom, suckered arms floating listlessly in the swell. It was a giant squid and the body, though distorted through the mask, looked to be more than twelve feet long. He looked around for Carlos, who had already seen it.

'Come on,' said Carlos, more serious now, 'I don't think he's seen us. Let's get to the house.'

The back door was missing. Nate signalled to Carlos and made his way through an archway to his old bedroom. He almost expected to find their antique brass bed, but the room was barely distinguishable from the undulating plant life. He swam upstairs and felt his body tensing. It was pitch dark except for his headlamp, which cast a creamy beam over the encrusted shapes and fossil-like fissures. He oriented himself on the landing and turned right towards the kitchen, which used to look out over the canals. He broke off bits of sediment from the antique stove. It was an O'Keefe and Merritt and they'd trucked it in from Hollywood. It had taken four men to install it.

Even in the darkness, he could see in his mind's eye the view that had once entranced them. The house faced two canals with wooden Japanese bridges arching steeply over the water. Apart from the weekends, it was always tranquil, with the odd canoe floating past. Nate's face began to smart from the salt of the tears inside his mask.

'Are you swimming with me, Mary?' he whispered.

'What was that?' said Carlos.

'Nothing,' said Nate. 'I was just remembering the view.'

'You know, I'm not really happy about that squid. There may be others. I think we should be getting back.'

'I thought I would find something to take back with me, you know. A plate. An ornament. Something.'

'You're not supposed to salvage anything. There's been a lot of illicit diving,' said Carlos. 'There's a couple of official memorial sites where they nailed everything down. But the rest of the houses are empty.'

'Wait a minute – I – my relative always talked about leaving a chest in the crawl space under the house,' said Nate, remembering. It was 'the love missile' that he and Mary had buried together. 'Maybe it's still there.'

'Not another treasure story,' said Carlos. 'You know, we discourage people from getting into small spaces.'

'I'm sorry, Carlos, but I'm going down there. I didn't come this far to go back empty-handed. I accept full responsibility for the consequences.'

'Well, I'm taking my baton out and putting it on full charge. I advise you to do the same.'

Nate paddled back down the stairwell to the ground floor. He came to the trapdoor at the bottom of the stairs. He found the brass ring and tried to tug it, but it was rusted into the socket. He took out his knife and scraped hard around the buckle. He used his left arm to crank open the door. It broke free, sending swirls of sediment into his face. He flippered down into the crawl space and looked around. All he could see was the concrete and steel foundation posts and a lot of silt. Something vibrant and muscular slithered past his side. Nate's heart stopped. It was an eel, which wriggled up through the trapdoor past Carlos, who kicked it with his flipper.

'We really need to go,' said Carlos, jittery now. 'Did you get what you came for?'

'No, not yet,' said Nate, scraping hopelessly at the sand. 'It was buried here, I know it.'

'You've got two minutes.'

They plunged their arms into the sand and fumbled around.

'OK – time's up,' said Carlos.

'Wait,' said Nate, grasping at something hard. 'I think I've found it.' Desperately, they both ploughed and gouged at the sand until they dredged the capsule from its burial ground.

'Well, this is a first,' said Carlos. 'OK – now come on.' He kicked at the water and headed towards the trapdoor.

Nate was trying to find the best way to carry the canister when he saw Carlos heading back towards him.

'What's wrong?'

'Is there another way out of here?'

'Why?'

'Look.'

Nate shone his beam towards the trapdoor and could see a finger-like tentacle feeling its way down the stairs of the crawl space.

'It's trying to get in here,' said Carlos. 'I don't know if it's gonna fit through the trapdoor – but if I know squid, it's going to have a damn good try.'

'Will the baton work?' said Nate.

'I don't want to use it while we're trapped. He could squirt his ink in here and disorient us.'

Nate watched in horror as the ghastly creature slumped and heaved at the hole, pressing its suckers and arms through the gap.

'I remember there was another door which opened out into the garage.'

'Then let's go!'

They dragged themselves through the crawl space, squeezing past a forest of half-rotted beams until they came to a low cupboard door. Nate gave it a mighty shove. It came away and they slid through the opening. The garage doors were missing, so they swam straight out into Strongs Drive. The street was lit by lamplight. They crouched under Nate's old back porch.

'We're a little off track, but I don't want to go back. I'll radio Joe to move directly above us and drop the line,' said Carlos. 'You got your baton on?'

'No,' said Nate. 'I dropped it.' In the panic of escaping, he'd left his baton in the crawl space.

'Shit!' said Carlos.

He opened up a signal. Joe came on the line.

'Joe, we got an emergency. There's only one baton between us and a squid is in the vicinity. Is any other craft around?'

'Not a one.'

'OK – can you manoeuvre directly above us and drop the rope? We'll have to be hoisted together.'

'Wait for my signal,' said Joe.

After a few minutes, the rope with the weighted end came tumbling out of the darkness. Carlos caught it.

'Nate – hang on to me. I'm the only one with a weapon, so if the squid comes at us, help me get to it with the prod. Joe – start pulling!'

The rope shot up and Nate almost let go of the canister. He saw his old house disappearing beneath him. They were no more than thirty feet below the surface when Nate caught sight of a dark blue shape undulating towards them. Before he could even catch his breath, the sea creature was up on them, encircling them in its grotesque, tentacled grip. Nate swung round to give Carlos the chance to lunge at it with the baton. Carlos stuck the prod right in the creature's eye. It recoiled, but its tentacles wouldn't let go. Nate could feel his lungs being squeezed of air, then he saw in horror the repulsive parrot's beak of its mouth closing in on his midriff. He thrust the metal capsule into the squid's beak, jamming it open. They broke the surface and were winched on deck in a tangled mass of limbs and tentacles.

'Oh, God – oh, God!' spluttered Carlos as he plunged his baton into the squid's head again and again.

Joe was on them in a second, ramming shock prods into the creature's flesh. The squid quivered violently and its mouth snapped and crushed the outer wall of Nate's canister.

After a frenzied, murderous hacking, the squid gave a deathly shudder and released its grip.

Nate and Carlos sprawled out, grabbing for breath, while the slippery creature lay dying beneath them.

'I'm never going out again so soon after a warning,' said Joe, dragging the rubbery corpse away. 'Remind me of that statement, will you, Carlos?'

Joe pointed to the dented metal capsule still lodged in the squid's beak. 'Looks like that thing saved your life.'

'It's what I came back for,' said Nate.

'I need a drink,' said Carlos, rolling over and coughing.

Joe got a crowbar and prised the capsule from the squid's calcified beak. 'Well, go on – open it!'

Nate yanked the lid open. The interior was dry and dusty. The first thing he picked up was a crumpled old linen shirt. He knew at once where he'd last seen it and for a moment he was back in the parking lot of Trader Joe's and he and Mary were arguing about nothing in particular. She walked away from him, her hands thrust deep into the pockets of the same shirt. And he had no idea that he had just a few minutes left to live. He ran his hands over the dried blood matted into the linen. His blood. Then he pulled out a photograph. And there it was. A picture of Mary's face, whole and not in the fragments that his mind had tried so hard to piece together these past few months.

There were dozens of pictures of her, of them at their wedding, on trips together and sharing all the secret, intimate moments of their married life. As he pored over each new image, he felt that his life was being given back to him. And Mary. Now that he could see her whole, with that strong jaw, those mischievous, defiant green eyes, he finally felt the full torrent of his grief. He found a new set of photographs. On the envelope it said *Patrick Sheehan, born 4 November 2006*. The baby was swollen and immobilized by the swaddling he'd been wrapped in. Nate kissed the baby's face. His son.

Oddly enough, he felt relieved that Mary might have enjoyed motherhood without him. He wanted her to have had a good, positive and happy life. That's all he'd ever wanted. Under the photos were cuttings of stories about his own death and the tussle between Mary and the police to keep his head cryonically frozen, the hunt for the murderer and a much later cutting saying a kid from Chihuahua in Mexico had confessed to the killing. He said that he did it for an uncle who had turned up dead in Los Angeles. Nate realized that he had clutched the shirt so tightly to him that it had disintegrated in his hands.

He wept then, wept for the trauma that Mary must have gone through and for the tragedy of her life cut short. And the passion that must have driven Mary forward, her passion and love for him. Look at them now, still separated by time and dimension – they would always be separated. Nate had never found the religious conviction that anything was waiting for him on the other side, and his own death had proved him right. There was never any tunnel or blinding white light or a deliverance of his soul into a better world. It had been a void of nothingness, of suspension, and the darkness of it crushed him.

He looked at the photographs of his son and he wept for him too, for the loss of never having known his father. He wondered if the boy had survived the earthquake or perished along with his mother.

Nate was so consumed by the find that he didn't see how close they were getting to shore. He felt a sponginess at the bottom of the capsule. He pulled away the lining and noticed an envelope tucked behind it. All at once, the envelope was both mysterious and utterly familiar. He opened it and took out some scientific documents. They were a series of memos, printouts and e-mails, and a batch of research notes. They belonged to a man called Dr Lew Wasserstrom from Caltech.

With salty fingers, Nate took a cursory glance through the documents. They were all there. He didn't need to read them. He remembered it all.

The boat veered to the left, jolting him back into the present. Joe was closing in on the jetty and to Nate's horror, a crowd was waiting for them.

'What are they doing here?' he shouted to Joe.

'I radioed ahead. You fought a giant squid. You're going to be famous!'

Nate could see that as well as a few journalists and onlookers, there were a number of the National Guard in the crowd.

'Listen, I don't need this,' he said desperately.

'Come on. It's good for business.'

'Carlos saved us. He can be filmed. Let me go quietly – *please.*' There was real desperation in Nate's voice. Joe looked put out.

'Carlos – that OK by you?'

'I guess.'

Joe pulled the boat into line with the jetty. Nate watched furtively from inside the cabin as a dozen hooks gouged into the flesh of the squid and hauled its body from the deck. Carlos was quickly surrounded and bombarded with questions. Nate's blood went cold when he heard him say 'we' a number of times. Sure enough, someone asked how many divers were down there and Carlos answered that there were two.

'Where's the other diver?' he heard one reporter ask.

Joe quickly said they'd dropped him off at another boat. But now their curiosity was up. Nate clambered up behind the throng and was about to break into a run when a little boy turned to him and said, 'Hey – it's you.'

A few people turned. Nate said, 'The squid is on the jetty over there.'

The boy said, 'You were on the news.'

Nate heard someone shout, 'It's him!'

Nate didn't wait to hear any more, but sprinted along the jetty and up the steps. Someone tried to trip him. He stumbled, recovered and ran on, holding the precious documents to his chest. He was faster than most people, but he could hear a stampede coming after him. He was nearing the edge of the memorial park and the high wall. He had no chance of climbing it and turned to be met by a heavy thwack on the temple and a sharp kick in his side.

'Smile for the camera, guys. I am filming your every move.'

The searing pain on the side of his head let Nate know there was blood in his eyes. A red curtain was blotting out his sight. He blinked. A man was talking. Through the film of blood he could see his precious photographs and papers scattered across the park. He cared more about them than he did about himself.

'I am going to file a serious complaint against you. I saw what you did. What's your name, officer?' said the stranger.

'Fuck you.'

'Legally, you're bound to give it to me.'

'I said fuck you.'

'I'm David Parks. Attorney at law. And you just made the biggest mistake of your career. This man is my client and I was due to meet him in the park.'

I wasn't meeting anyone, thought Nate in a daze. *Who is this guy?*

The guard spoke, almost spitting with hatred. 'It's that doctor. Look at his neck.'

'You got the wrong guy. The scar is from strangulation in an attempted murder case against my client. You must release him immediately. I am personal friends with Dick Murray, the district attorney, and I promise you, if you touch me or this tape or this man again, you will be in more trouble than any of you have *ever* experienced.'

Miraculously, the guards released Nate. He felt nauseous from the blows.

'You should be ashamed of yourselves,' said the lawyer. 'This was not reasonable force and you know it.'

'What's your name?' barked the guard close to Nate's ear. For a moment, Nate couldn't remember who he was.

'I warned you once,' said the lawyer.

'Fuck you. Get out of here,' said the guard decisively, and Nate scrambled around, retrieving his precious photographs and documents. The man with the camera marched him from the park to an awaiting car.

'Get in. Don't look back,' he hissed. Nate noticed the man's hands were shaking as he pulled out of the parking space.

'Thank you,' spluttered Nate as they drove along.

'It still works when you film them committing an *actual* crime,' said the man.

Nate noticed the harness with the tiny camera attached to the man's chest. 'So who *are* you?'

'My name is Fred Arlin. I'm actually a reporter. I broke your story.'

'Stop right here.'

'What?'

'Stop the car! I'm getting out.'

'But I saved you.'

'You ruined me! They're after me because of you!'

The reporter looked oddly disconcerted, as though it hadn't even occurred to him that this might have been his fault.

'How the fuck did you find me?' said Nate, wrestling with the door handle. Fred slowed down the car.

'Wait, look, I've been trying to find you since you escaped from Phoenix. I heard you were spotted in LA. Then they said you'd checked into the Chateau Marmont.'

'Who said?'

'I got a tip-off from the police.'

Nate wondered if Persis had played any part in the disclosure.

'By the time I got there you'd already checked out, then I heard there was a giant squid in the bay and thought I'd cover it for the local news. And there you were! Amazing, huh?'

'You ruined my life! Such as it is.'

'Let's go somewhere and talk, Nate. I think I have a lot of information that you'd be interested in. More than that, I think I can help you. And you need help – am I right?'

'I didn't kill those men.'

'I know you didn't.'

'How do you know?'

'I may be slow-witted, but I'm beginning to appreciate the capabilities of Icor Incorporated.'

76

They headed for the old Pacific Coast Highway by driving across the Santa Monica Mountains at the Topanga Pass. When Nate saw the sea he felt an ancient swell in his chest. In spite of the water desalination plants dotted across the horizon, it was still glittering and beautiful. They found an old shack that sold beers and chips, there being no fish to catch or eat, and found a place where they could talk.

'Did you ever meet Duane?' asked Nate.

'No. I was out of favour at work, so they assigned me to cover his execution. It was no big deal as a story. He was just another criminal on the list. Then I got to thinking – what happens to Duane's body now? I knew he'd donated his remains to the willed body programme, but what does that actually mean these days? I thought I'd follow Duane's trail to the frontiers of medical science, to see what happened to him. So I started the investigation in my spare time –'. Nate was already becoming aware of the reporter's ego. It was as though he was telling his story to some imaginary chat-show host. '– so I tracked down the pilot who'd flown Duane from Gamma Gulch to Phoenix and found out the journey ended up at Icor. That's when things really started to get interesting. I contacted Dr Garth Bannerman and he cut me off. From that moment on, I knew that something was up. Then a really strange thing happened—'

'What was that?' said Nate, feeling like Fred's patsy interviewer.

'Duane's lawyer, Jim Hutton, called me up. He said that Duane's body had turned up in the anatomy department of San Diego University. I went down there and they showed me a headless corpse, but it wasn't Duane.'

'How did you know?'

'The body had no tattoos. Duane had a lot.'

Nate looked at his arms and the almost imperceptible indentations where they must have removed them.

'So Icor was trying to distract me by showing me a bogus, headless corpse, claiming it was Duane. I thought: why would they spend so much effort doing that if they had nothing big to hide? But I had to wait for months for a break in the story – which came in the form of Monty Arcibal.'

'Monty,' said Nate. 'Of course. You found Monty.'

'Monty found *me*! He contacted me after Bannerman fired him and told me the whole story.'

'How is he?'

'I don't know,' said Fred. 'We're waiting to pay him, but he seems to have disappeared. His mother's beside herself. And his brother.'

Nate felt anxious about this piece of news. Maybe Monty got scared and left the state. He was right to be scared.

'Well – congratulations,' said Nate bitterly. 'It seems like the only one to benefit from all of this is *you*.'

The reporter looked crestfallen.

'Tell me more about Duane,' demanded Nate.

'I've got copies of his letters from Gamma Gulch Penitentiary to his sister Bobbie, if you want to read them.'

Nate felt divided. Part of him wanted to see Duane's handwriting, to find out if it bore any resemblance to the crazy notes that he had written back at Icor, while the other part of him didn't want to personify the body. It was tough enough to accept the fact that it had once been that of a murderer.

'Just *tell* me, if you know, why he murdered that girl.'

'It's not a happy story, Nate.'

'I'll hear about it sooner or later – so it might as well come from you.'

'Duane was badly abused as a child: beatings, shootings in the family home. In later life he had memory difficulties and he always claimed he was never present at the murder, though the DNA evidence confirms that he was.'

'What DNA evidence?'

'Blood on his clothing. Skin, hairs. It was conclusive.'

The words felt like needles jabbing Nate's flesh. 'Fred – I need to hear something good about this man. Was there anything redeeming about him? Anything at all?'

'I can take you to see Bobbie, his sister. She lives not far from here.'

'Bobbie?' The word sounded a distant echo. It was the name he'd written down in the wild jottings when he let the body speak. It proved to Nate that cell memory was more than hormonal checks and balances. It was an absolute truth.

'What good will seeing Bobbie do?' said Nate.

'I don't know. Give you a sense of someone who loved him. She cared enough about her brother to turn up to his execution. It might help.'

'Will you report on it?'

'I'd like to.'

'I don't want you to.'

'Then I won't.'

Two hours later, they were entering the kit park where Bobbie Williams lived. Nate didn't know how this particular piece of the jigsaw was going to fit in with his plans, but he wanted to meet Duane's sister. He believed that if he talked to her, she would somehow hold the key to his forgiveness.

The kit park was a sorry sight, like a rundown trailer park, with temporary houses lined up in rows. On the street corners, gangs of men looked the car over.

'Is this where the miscreants live?' asked Nate as Fred's BMW glided past them.

'Yes,' said Fred.

Nate could sense the level of their threat by how nervous the reporter was becoming.

'It's funny, San Luis Obispo was one of the safest towns in the state when I was alive.'

'Not any more,' said Fred, staring straight ahead, as if some sideways glance might incite a riot. They pulled up outside a squalid, low-lying house. Nate saw an emaciated figure emerge from behind the screen door.

'That's Bobbie,' whispered Fred, gathering up his things. 'When I first met her, she was as big as a house. I think she's addicted to something. Some of the drugs we've got now just tear people apart in weeks. I think it's crazy to get involved in that scene.'

'Always was,' said Nate, following Fred. When he got close to Duane's sister, he could smell a sweet, rubbery smell on her clothes and saw Bobbie's yellow, pitted face. He could tell instantly, without even examining her, that she was being ravaged by some kind of meth amphetamine derivative. She smiled, showing browning teeth, and grabbed Nate's hands and pulled his arms apart to inspect the body, then clutched him to her.

'It *is* you,' she said.

Nate didn't know what to say, except to peel her gently away from him. Then he saw fear pass across Fred's face. Before Nate could even turn around he felt a hand across his throat and something sharp dig into his ribs.

'Be still,' said a low, cracked voice right by his ear.

'You told me he was out of the state,' Fred said to Bobbie.

'Well, she lied,' snapped the voice.

Fred started to speak, his chin wobbling. 'Keith – I did everything you asked me to. I found Duane's body and I came here on trust so that Nate could talk to Bobbie. So I'm just going to leave—'

'Stay where you are!'

The man spun Nate around. Nate waited for his arm to react, but it felt like a lead weight.

'Did you ever feel me?' said Keith.

'Feel you? Who are you?' demanded Nate.

'This is Keith Williams – Duane's twin,' explained Fred.

'I knew you were alive!' said Keith. He ripped open Nate's shirt and inspected his chest and arms and down his back. 'What happened to all your tattoos?'

'I guess they had them removed,' said Nate.

'Get in the house,' Keith said to all of them.

Nate noticed a gun tucked into the waist of Keith's trousers. Once inside, he began circling them like a cheetah and Nate had the strangest sensation that he was looking at himself. Their hands were identical, with long, tapered fingers and flat, spatular nails, and they both had muscular chests and long, slim legs. Keith's face was handsome, with wide, sensual lips, though battened down with resentment. How powerful the twins could have been, had their natural parents not made them face violence so often, so young! Nate knew exactly where his adrenaline bursts and tearaway impulses came from. He could sense the exact same energy in the man looking back at him.

'You didn't feel me at all?' Keith demanded truculently.

Nate shook his head. 'I had so much to recover from when they woke me up.'

'How does it feel to inherit a maniac's body?'

Was Keith trying to frighten Nate or denigrate his brother's memory? He was as slippery as an eel and Nate wasn't sure how to play it.

'I don't think Duane was a maniac.'

'I was right all along – wasn't I, sis?' said Keith.

Bobbie nodded.

'I was right. I could feel you. I *knew* you weren't dead. Didn't I say that – Fred? Didn't I tell you there was something wrong? Goddamn.'

'Yes you did,' muttered Fred.

Nate wondered what was going to motivate Keith. He could sense there was going to be action of some kind. Keith was winding himself up, as violent men do to justify their impulses. The knife was still glinting in his hand.

'Well, well, well – my little brother.'

'I thought you were twins?' said Nate.

'I came out first.' He was circling him again now and Nate

fully expected to feel the cold slice of the blade in his side at any moment.

'All the times I protected you. All the times I had to tell you: don't do this and don't do that. But you couldn't keep anything in your head for one single second.'

'It's not Duane now,' said Nate.

'I could have been rich if you hadn't held me back. I could have been out of this country and in some other place with a new life if you hadn't—'

'He protected us too – remember?' interrupted Bobbie.

'Shut the fuck up! I'm talking here.'

Bobbie crumpled on to a sofa, clearly sickened by the level of aggression she had to tolerate from her brother. Fred was looking down at the floor. Nate was watching the knife in Keith's hand and realized that, physically, they were probably a match. He just had to kick the knife out of the equation.

'You got all the help. You got all the medical treatment. Someone was always looking out for *you*. No one ever looked out for me!'

'Tell me about the murder,' said Nate. 'I heard that you were in on it too.'

The question was pinned there, between them, like a red flag. Nate knew it would inflame Keith, but he wanted to draw him out, to see at what point he could tripswitch Keith's rage and brace himself to go for the knife.

'He put you up to this?' said Keith, nodding at Fred.

'No, I didn't,' exclaimed Fred.

'It's my own mind,' said Nate.

Keith lunged and Nate jumped back but felt the blade clip his side. They all heard it then. It was a kind of roar, almost imperceptible above the city sounds, then like an entity in itself.

'Fuck,' said Keith, withdrawing the knife and leaping like

a dangerous animal over bits of furniture into another room. Nate's sixth sense told him something deadly was approaching. With each passing second the noise got louder. It was the roar of an approaching mob.

'I know who it is,' said Bobbie. 'It's the Sommers family. The brothers are home. One of the lookouts must have told them that you were here.'

'See what you created, Fred?' shouted Nate. 'You irresponsible piece of shit!'

Fred started to shake uncontrollably. 'I didn't take the decision to use a condemned man as a donor body. Icor are the villains! Why don't we just get out of here?'

Keith ran back through the room, a soldier of misfortune, opened up a cupboard and began to position guns so he could go from one window to the other.

'Do you know how to use this?' he said, tossing Nate a rifle.

'No.'

'Well, Duane did.'

Nate grabbed the gun, panic rising in him. To be torn apart by an angry mob, to feel the initial blows and see the hatred in the throng was more than he could bear. He ratcheted back the loading system. It seemed as though it was ready to fire.

Fred ran to the back of the house. 'They're coming along the back alley. There's no way out!' he screamed, his face a mask of terror.

The mob were crowding around the front yard. Keith didn't wait. He smashed a window with the muzzle of his rifle and let off a few ear-splitting rounds into the sky. People screamed and scattered.

There was a second or two of silence. Then a voice: 'We got no quarrel with you, Bobbie. It's Duane we want.'

Keith roared with rage and fired into the crowd. Then all hell broke loose. Shots pelted through the walls, catching Keith in the leg. Nate dived behind a sofa. Bobbie was cowering behind another sofa. Nate fired a few rounds. The thin walls took a terrible battering. Keith got another hit in the shoulder and he let off a round in the house, the bullets ricocheting off the walls and pipes.

Someone screamed. It was Fred. Nate wondered if the reporter had been hit. The crowd was chanting, 'Give us Duane. Give us Duane.'

Then there was a lull. Nate tried to look for something to stop the bleeding in Keith's shoulder. He made a tourniquet out of a dishcloth. Keith gripped his hand.

'I'm going out there. I'm going to be Duane. It'll take them a moment to realize. Meanwhile, you take the car and save my sister.' Keith handed Nate some bloodstained keys. 'Let Bobbie drive. She knows the streets.'

It was as if Keith had been waiting for this moment all his life and wanted, in his own warped way, to be remembered as a hero.

'I don't know how many of you are still alive in there – but we want what we came for,' bellowed the voice.

Nate knew it was now or never. Keith clutched him with bloodied fingers.

'I did it,' he whispered.

'Did what?'

'I killed the girl. Duane tried to save her, but it was me. He pulled her out of the mud. That's all he did. We're identical twins. We share the same DNA. The cops used Duane as a lure to get me to surrender. But they underestimated me, so they killed him. For revenge.'

Nate's head was swimming. Fred had been right. It was a dreadful, sordid tale.

'I hope you don't feel this,' said Keith, and he crawled to the door and dragged himself outside, leaving a trail of blood in his wake.

Nate grabbed Bobbie and Fred and smashed through the backyard. The crowd scattered when they saw Nate's bloodied clothes and the rifle. There was a burst of gunfire from the front. Nate felt it in his chest and he knew instantly that Keith was dead.

Bobbie was sobbing as she started the engine and smashed through the garage doors which went spinning off their hinges. Keith had been right to let Bobbie drive. She rode the car through the back streets like a bronco, reversing and screeching the tyres until they ended up on a dirt track which led right out of the kit park and into the hills.

When they were out of danger, Bobbie pulled the car off the road and they spilled out and collapsed on the ground.

'Has either of you been shot?' said Nate to both of them.

'I think so,' said Fred, wincing.

'Not me,' said Bobbie.

Nate crawled over to Fred and inspected a singed corner to his expensive jacket. His skin was barely grazed.

'You'll live,' said Nate.

Bobbie began to cry.

Fred said, 'Anyone want a prop?'

Bobbie took one of the blue pills.

'What are they?' said Nate, refusing.

'I don't know – but they will make you feel a whole lot better in a matter of minutes.'

Fred took a pill and sat motionless, his eyes closed, as though he was meditating. Bobbie did the same. After a few minutes, Fred said, 'I really need to call the office, see what's happening.'

Nate walked away from the others and lay down on the

grass. All he wanted to do was go to sleep. He felt as if he would never be able to lift his limbs again. It must be the death of the twin that was so enervating. Maybe he should take one of Fred's pills. He looked down at the kit park below them. Smoke was rising from Bobbie's house.

After a little while, Fred marched up to him.

'Do you know somebody called Albert Noyes?' he asked almost cheerfully, as though he'd been through nothing more traumatic than a picnic.

'I met him in Washington. Why?'

'He's been trying to reach you. He wants me to take you to him. He has something important to tell you.'

77

'– and all I did was play a minor role in a story that turned out to be critical of the Government. I didn't even *write it*, for crissakes. And for that they revoked my licence. I couldn't work. I couldn't travel. It took me three years to get my licence back. But if you make a big splash like this, it'll get you whatever position you want and it'll be much harder for them to do it again. I'm a public figure now – virtually.'

Fred had been rambling on about his career for hours. Nate couldn't believe how he could talk with such blithe self-indulgence, considering what they had just been through. The pill must have been some kind of dopamine enhancer. Nate still felt crucified, but he didn't want to get doped up and cloud his judgement.

They were able to watch a news bulletin on Fred's wrist-watch. It said that Keith Williams had been slaughtered by the mob and that so far there had been no arrests and Dr Nathaniel Sheehan was still at large. They waited until it was dark when the tanks of the National Guard finally rolled out of the kit park, then Fred went to retrieve his car still parked near Bobbie's house.

They dropped Bobbie off at a friend's. They were just about to leave when she grabbed Nate and stroked his arms. 'I hope I see you again,' she said innocently. There was no sense of grief for the loss of her brother, no sense of fury or fear that her house had just burnt to the ground. It all seemed to have disappeared from her consciousness. Nate pondered how long Fred's wonder drug would last and whether Bobby had access to a supply to see her through the next few weeks. She was going to need it.

Now he and Fred were heading out on the long drive to Washington on Route 66. Fred said it was a dead road and no one would think of looking for them there. Nate looked across at his strange companion. He could throttle the man, with his fake tan and expensive haircut, but Fred was his only passport out of California and driving was probably their best chance of getting through security.

'Tell me exactly what Albert said to you,' demanded Nate, interrupting Fred's stream of consciousness.

'Just that he had to see you. He has something very important to tell you. He said a meeting was imperative and that you couldn't call him directly.'

There were few vehicles on the old highway. It was even more derelict and abandoned than Nate remembered. He last drove down it in the late 1980s, a road trip he took just before going up to Harvard. Even then, the famous highway had long passed its usefulness. Now it looked like a spectral monument to the twentieth century, with strange ghost towns and huge painted signs and murals fading in the dust.

They stopped for a night at an ancient motel which had

been built in the 1950s and was haunted by a strange, nocturnal couple. They were grim company but provided Nate and Fred with a barren little room and clean linen. The next day, as they got closer to the border, Fred took a detour which he said would lead them to the most remote security checkpoint in the state.

'Won't that be too obvious?' said Nate.

'There's one thing that doesn't change over time,' said Fred.

'What's that?'

'The capacity of most people to be moronic. If they even question me, which I doubt, I'll say I'm doing a story in Nevada.'

A crop of rocks rose up before them.

'OK,' he said, growing serious. 'I've done this only once before, but there will be more security this time because of the health alert. You get out before we reach the checkpoint, climb over those hills and bypass the first security detail who will open up the trunk and look under the car. Go to the restroom near the recharging bay. I'll drive over and park, then, when no one's looking, you get in the trunk and we go on through the second barrier where they will check my ID. If they've changed the routine, I have no idea what we do.'

Nate did as he was told. Fortunately, there was an odd assortment of trucks and cars parked up and recharging their batteries and Nate was concealed as he made his way through the vehicles.

They drove on, repeating the routine in state after state. Fred was right, the guards were not as alert as Nate had expected them to be.

'You have to realize, Nate, America is a big country,' said Fred pompously.

'I know, I used to live here – remember?'

'What I'm saying is that not everyone is out looking for you.'

'It only takes one,' said Nate.

Between Arkansas and Tennessee, Fred got cocky and Nate could hear him vaunting his recent successes to one of the guards.

'Yeah – that story. That was me. I wrote it,' said Fred.

'You seen the guy?'

'I wish. They say he's a monster, but I don't think so.'

Nate was furious. There was something completely hare-brained and unprofessional about the man.

'I'm putting a good spin out there!' protested Fred when Nate challenged him about it.

'What if that guard thinks twice, wonders why you're on this obscure road, making this strange journey, and decides to raise the alarm?'

'He won't, he won't,' said Fred dismissively.

Nate shook his head. If this man represented the cream of American journalism, then the profession had taken a few more steps into the trashcan.

All through the journey Fred was being contacted about the story, but he agreed not to report on the latest develop-ment, at least not until Nate had found out what Albert had to say. Nate had the notion that once they reached Washing-ton and he had made contact with Albert, he would seek some kind of asylum. It was a long shot, but his only hope.

Albert Noyes refused to meet them at his house, but suggested they rendezvous in Franklin Park. Nate remembered the parks of Washington as beautiful, orderly and pristine, laid out in the formal French style with fountains, wide gravel avenues and benches. The park was still tidy, though a little battered around the edges. They sat at the allotted bench and waited for Albert's arrival.

After an hour they spotted a tiny man hobbling towards them and leaning heavily into a cane. Nate remembered what a nimble, bustling figure he had been when they were working for Doctors for Justice. He hoped all that spent energy had amounted to something. 'I did an information trawl on Albert,' said Fred. 'He's the oldest lobbyist in Washington and he has something on everyone. That's how he survives.'

Albert clutched Nate warmly, using the weight of Nate's body to deliver himself on to the bench. His skin was deathly pale and his forehead was perspiring.

'Are you OK?' said Nate. Compared to the time they'd met in the White House, Albert looked much frailer.

'I'm almost done in this life,' he said once he'd caught his breath. 'This feels like the closure I've been looking for.'

'You've got a way to go yet,' said Nate.

'Give me a moment,' Albert replied, working to fill his ancient lungs. 'Nate – you may remember that Mary was expecting a child when you died.'

Fred's ears perked up.

Nate felt his heart begin to pound. He had that much influence over the body at least. 'I'm desperate to know what happened to him. Can you tell me anything?'

'Your son, Patrick, is not well.'

'You mean he's alive!' said Nate, stunned. 'I assumed—'

'I've always done what I could, but it's not been easy.'

'Where is he?'

'Not far from here. I always thought it was safer to keep him close to the hearth of his enemies than in some wilderness where it would be more difficult to help him.'

'What do you mean?'

'Patrick followed after you. He was one of the key agitators for health reform. But that made it very difficult. The Government effectively cut him off from formal society.'

Nate recalled the strange figure he'd met in the plane park telling him the same thing.

'Why didn't you tell me about him when I saw you in Washington?'

'It was hard to talk openly. I knew that everything we said was being overheard so I tried to tell you in code, but I'm afraid I didn't make a very good job of it. Then, when I even got close to the subject, I was ejected. You saw it.'

'Why were you never exiled, Albert? That's what you were fighting for too.'

'I am very good at finding Achilles' heels and I have always ensured my own safety in the royal court of Washington.'

'Is that what they call it now?'

'Yes. But it *is* my home. I know I was written off as a threat years ago, but I've still got my pass.'

'Are we being watched now?'

'No. This bench is at an optimum point where two SRDs do not quite have the trajectory to cover the whole area. Someone told me about it years ago and I have used it as a meeting place ever since. There are several points in the city like that.'

'Is there anything you can tell me about Mary?' said Nate.

The old man laid a hand on his arm. 'The last anyone saw of your wife was when she was headed back towards Venice to help evacuate a nursing home.'

There was so much to take in. Albert seemed to sense it and kept quiet. Fred stood up, walked away and stared meaningfully at an empty fountain.

'What happened to my son? How did he survive the earthquake if Mary died?'

'He was being looked after by a nanny. She took him inland. I found him staying with friends of yours in the Hollywood Hills. Bob and Kate.'

'Bob and Kate,' said Nate, remembering.

'Patrick was very traumatized. We all were. I decided to leave Los Angeles after that. So many of us did. I went to live in New York and placed Patrick with Mary's sister.'

'Lisa,' said Nate. Lisa was a hearty, more voluptuous version of Mary. There was the strongest bond between the two sisters. He felt great relief that Lisa had raised Patrick.

'Is *she* still alive?'

The old man shook his head. 'No. She died a while ago, Nate. I'm sorry.'

'Albert, I found the information about Martin Rando. We were working on it. Do you remember?'

'Those damned documents,' said Albert. 'I searched high and low for them after you died. How the hell did you come by them?'

'I went diving to see my old house. They were locked up in a capsule that Mary and I kept in the crawl space.'

'Do you have them now?'

'Yes.'

A resigned, hopeless expression flitted across Albert's face. He smiled. Nate knew what that look was about. All those wasted years of watching Martin Rando create one of the biggest medical corporations in the world. It cannot have been easy for the old man.

'What do you want to do with them?' said Albert eventually.

'I want to finish what we started.'

'Things have changed, Nate. I doubt that anyone would be interested.'

Nate felt anger rising in him. 'You were the one who

drove *me* on – remember? Is the world so cynical that corruption goes on right under everyone's nose?'

'We never had enough evidence to bring charges against Rando. *We* knew he had Dr Wasserstrom assassinated, but we couldn't prove it then and I doubt we could prove it now.'

'My dad told me that after the Second World War, a handful of Jews spent the rest of their lives hunting down Nazis. Even when they were in their mid-eighties, they kept on going until they'd tracked down every single Nazi war criminal they could find and brought them back to Europe or Israel to stand trial. That was *justice*.'

'No – that was vengeance. It's a different thing.'

'And justice! It was the name of our group. Doctors for Justice – you haven't forgotten that; have you?'

Albert breathed a heavy sigh, shivering as he exhaled. 'I was never as brave as you were. I think that's why Rando had you killed.'

'What? I was shot by some kid. He confessed.'

'It was an organized act, Nate,' said Albert flatly. 'This is a century of murderous intention. How could I or anyone like me hope to topple it?'

'Martin had me murdered?'

'Of course he did! You were trying to ruin him.'

'*We* were. Did he try to kill you too?'

Albert looked away. 'No.'

'Oh.'

They sat there, trying to figure it out.

'Are you compromised, Albert?'

Albert said nothing.

'My God, then why didn't you give up on my son after all these years?'

'I have what I believe in here,' he clenched a small, ineffectual fist against his chest, 'and then there's the way to survive. How you and I started out, what we used to believe in, that's what your son represents to me. But if you want a *life*, you have to give up on some of those ideals. It's not a new story.'

Albert's ancient face puckered into folds. He was the picture of abjection. The only thing that linked this centenarian with the diminutive, implacable force field of half a century ago was the long, aristocratic nose.

'What kind of compromises did you make?' asked Nate quietly.

'I never betrayed you. Or your son. But I found myself in a spot much later on, and I did agree with Rando to let the matter drop. I knew he could eclipse me at any moment. So we came to a kind of agreement.'

'And Dr Wasserstrom's murder went unchallenged and the Randos became the emperors of medicine,' Nate sneered, mimicking the President's praises.

'I always hoped that someone else, just like you, would come along and prompt me for information and I would tell them everything, but they never did.'

They sat there in silence, listening to the whiny hum of aircraft buzzing overhead.

'I'm looking for immunity from Icor,' said Nate eventually. 'Can you do anything for me? Get a message to the President?'

'Not a chance.'

'Then who can?'

'Go be with your son, Nate. He may not have long. He has been neglected and is in a very reduced set of circumstances. I tried to get a pardon for Patrick so many times, but I was never successful. With President Villaloboz, I might have one more chance. Please don't blame me when you see Patrick. I did what I could for him.'

Nate relented and clasped his old friend, hugging his feeble bones. 'I know you did,' he said, 'and thank you.'

The old man pulled away, ashamed.

78

Nate and Fred made their way through Albert's neighbourhood. Many of the old brownstones were still standing, but dilapidated.

They found the rundown apartment building on the edge of town. Squares of rusted, battered tin were nailed to the outside walls, making the oblong box look as though it was clad in a metallic patchwork quilt. They climbed an outside staircase. Each step felt heavy. Nate hadn't recovered his energy since Keith had died and wondered if he ever would.

They came to a door and knocked. A tiny Hispanic woman answered and introduced herself as Rosa. The interior was dark and smelt thick with must and decay. She gestured towards a bedroom. Nate flung back the curtains, revealing the body of an emaciated old man. He was mumbling incoherently. Nate felt his forehead.

'He's running a fever.'

As he grew accustomed to the light, he began to take in the face. His oyster eyes were watery and the lower lids were drooping like a bloodhound's. The nose was open-pored and misshapen. His lips were dry and there were deep lines leading down to the delta of his mouth. It broke Nate's heart to see his own son in such a deteriorated state. He was only sixty-five but sickness made him look ancient.

Nate pulled back the blanket.

'How long has he been like this?'

'I don't know,' said Rosa, embarrassed.

'He's got a urinary infection. Have you got a catheter?'

Rosa gestured to a drawer. Anxiously, Nate rummaged around and found what he needed.

'Can you help me over here?' he said to Fred and together they gently lifted Patrick and removed the dirty bedding.

Nate took the old man's pulse, which was weak, and felt under his arms and his jawbone and around his stomach and groin. The lymph nodes were elevated but not tumorous and the stomach was distended, probably through lack of nutrition.

'Patrick, if you can hear me or understand me, I'm going to insert a catheter. If you can just relax . . .' Nate began to use the swab. Expertly, he lifted the penis, pulled it forward and inserted the tube into the meatus.

'What kind of world is it when someone is left to suffer like this?' said Nate as he waited for the urine to appear in the tube. There wasn't much and what there was had blood in it.

'What's the problem?' said Fred, averting his gaze.

'He's got pyelonephritis – a kidney infection. And an enlarged prostate blocking the urethra by the look and volume of the urine.'

Nate inflated the balloon into the bladder, then pushed it in further by a hair to avoid tension in the neck of the bladder.

'He's dehydrated and needs IV. Do you have anything like that, Rosa?'

Rosa disappeared into the kitchen and returned with more equipment.

'Have you been giving him any antibiotics – trimethoprim – amoxycillin – floxin – Noroxin – Cipro?' With each name Rosa shook her head.

'OK, Fred – there's bound to be a whole different generation of antibiotics that I don't know about. I'm going to give you a urine sample, and you're going to take it to a lab somewhere and get it analysed, and then they're going to give you some antibiotics and we're going to administer them. Do you understand? Get them to tell you how to administer them, if there's another way they use now.'

'I hate to tell you this, Nate, but antibiotics are a thing of the past. They don't work any more.'

'OK – I'm going to write down a detailed list of his symptoms and I don't want you to come back until you've got the medicine he needs.'

'If Patrick is a dissident, there's nothing I can do. I'll lose my licence if I'm caught helping him.'

'Fred, you said yourself that you broke one of the biggest stories of the decade. And that story is *me*. This man is my son. He needs my help. Go out there and do something useful. I don't care what tactic you employ. Just do it!'

'OK – OK.' Fred took one more look at the old man and left the apartment.

Nate spent the rest of the day cleaning. It was like performing a penance; washing windows, bleaching surfaces, scrubbing floors. Rosa said very little and watched him without helping, occasionally raising her hands in a gesture of hopelessness. Patrick slept for most of the time. Nate reckoned that his fever might be receding.

It was impossible to believe that the man in the bed had once been the baby Nate had made with his wife. He tried very hard not to dwell on what he had missed – that he had never been around to protect his child and let him feel all the confidence and security of a father's love.

By late afternoon, Fred finally returned with supplies.

'How did you get them?' said Nate with relief. At one point, he'd wondered if he was ever going to see the journalist again.

'I found a diagnosis centre in Bethesda. I said that my uncle was here on a business trip and that he'd fallen ill with an old problem and couldn't leave the hotel.'

'See, you have got some initiative. And there was I writing you off.' For some reason Nate felt compelled to goad Fred, partly because he seemed to invite it.

'He does have a kidney infection, but he's got cancer too,' said Fred. 'Of the prostate. They said he should get treatment immediately.'

'I thought so.'

'I don't know what we can do. Any hospital is going to check his papers and refuse treatment.'

'That has to go against the constitution, surely?'

Fred shrugged. 'They gave me some medicine and tried to explain to me what it was, but I couldn't take it in. It has a thirteen per cent chance of working on the infection.'

'You're kidding.'

'Those are good odds.'

Nate inserted an intravenous drip into Patrick's arm. It was getting late. Rosa made a gesture of food going into her mouth, left the apartment and returned with some bread and soup. Through Rosa Nate learnt with his rudimentary Spanish that Patrick often had spells of incoherency and that the bouts of delirium were getting longer. Nate wondered if the cancer had spread to the brain. He was determined to get his son some decent medical care as soon as possible.

They prepared to bed down for the night on the floor in the living room. Fred was clearly repulsed by having to stay in such squalid surroundings.

'We could go check into a hotel,' he said.

'I'm not leaving until I sort out his problems. And neither are you.'

Fred sat gingerly on the floor. 'Nate, I couldn't help overhearing your conversation with Albert in the park about Martin Rando. Can you tell me anything?'

Nate thought for a moment. 'I will tell you, because I may need your help. But I have to be able to trust you, Fred. This is very sensitive information. Can I trust you?'

'I think so.'

'There was this scientist called Dr Lew Wasserstrom who had been working closely on creating a vaccine that suppressed two crucial cancer genes present in most forms of breast cancer. At that time he was closer to a cure than anyone else. Then all of a sudden, he was found dead in his car. There was a slight bruise on his temple and another on his wrist, and a pipe leading from his exhaust to the interior of the car. There was an uproar at the time. He was the last person anyone had expected to kill himself. The police opened up an investigation but could find no evidence of foul play. I belonged to a group called Doctors for Justice back then. So did Albert Noyes. We traded information—'

'Like what?' said Fred.

'We exposed doctors who were practising illegally. We used to shame HMOs for casting patients adrift half-way through treatment or expose companies that were trying to suppress medical studies that would be bad for business – that kind of thing.'

'What's an HMO?' said Fred.

'Health Management Organization. They were the major insurers and they paid moronic underlings to decide who got treatment and who didn't. Very few of them were qualified to make those decisions. It angered a lot of doctors at the time.'

'You must have had plenty of enemies.'

'We did. The Internet was just coming into its own as an

alternative source for the kinds of truth the mainstream media would never publish. Doctors for Justice used the Internet to make sure our information was circulated. Anyway, we were asked, unofficially, by a senior director at Caltech to look into Dr Wasserstrom's suicide to see if we could come up with any evidence that a crime had been committed. Just before I was shot in Los Angeles, I was given evidence that Dr Wasserstrom had been murdered.'

'What was the evidence?'

'Dr Wasserstrom had been approached with an offer of a limitless research grant to carry on his work, provided he resigned from Caltech and handed over part-ownership of any future discovery to Martin Rando. Wasserstrom refused. Not long after that, his body was found. In our minds, it was a classic case of attempted coercion followed by murder. The evidence was given to us by his assistant. She had copied e-mails from Martin Rando requesting meetings with Wasserstrom and making boastful promises of how lavish his life would be if only he would resign from Caltech. The assistant also gave us printouts of Wasserstrom's research, copies that she'd kept illegally, because she said that Wasserstrom's note-keeping was chaotic and she didn't want it to go astray. So at one point I had one of two copies of a possible cure for breast cancer in my hands. That's what those precious documents are.'

'And the memos were sent by Martin Rando,' said Fred.

'Yes. It turned out that I didn't have the only copy of Wasserstrom's work. Martin Rando had also stolen a copy. He was my old college room-mate. So it was beyond difficult.'

'And now look at him.'

'His greatness was created on the back of murder and theft,' said Nate. 'Caltech couldn't catch up with the research once Wasserstrom was out of the picture, so Rando and Icor Incorporated must have taken up the science and developed their own vaccine.'

'You know, I cover a lot of court cases. It's still going to be hard to pin this on him.'

'I know,' said Nate.

'I'm not sure what I can do with it,' said Fred. 'I'd like to help – but—' Fred's head hit the pillow. He was instantly asleep.

79

Sleep wasn't so easy for Nate. All night he drifted in and out. He was anxious about Patrick and when dawn came, he went in to check on his son. The old man's forehead was damp and cold, a sure sign that the fever had broken. Nate was startled when Patrick opened his eyes.

'Who are you?'

'I'm – a relative,' said Nate stupidly. He couldn't bring himself to say anything else. Patrick didn't seem to comprehend.

'Can you sit up? Do you think you can manage that?'

The man blinked. His eyes were bloodshot. 'I don't know. It's been a long time since I was able to do anything.'

Gently, Nate swung Patrick's legs over the bed and guided him into an armchair. There was an indentation of the body pressed into the upholstery. Nate imagined, with great sorrow, his son sitting for days on end with nothing to do but look out of the window.

'A relative – what relative?' The information had clearly sunk in.

'My name is Nathaniel Sheehan.'

'Sheehan,' he repeated, confused.

'That's right. And your name is Patrick Sheehan.'

A nod.

'Son of Mary Sheehan – and—'

'Did Albert send you?'

'Yes, he sent me here to find you, Patrick. This may be an impossible thing to believe right away – but I am your father.'

This time Patrick got it. He started to tap at his forehead as if he was knocking on the door of his memory. 'You must excuse me. I did know you were coming. Albert told me. So much gets lost.' He looked weak and hopeless. 'I lost you after Ma died.'

'What do you mean?' said Nate.

'Ma kept you in the Pasadena Cryogenesis Research Institute. Some time after she died, it was purchased by Martin Rando.' His thin lips clamped together with scorn. 'I tried to retrieve your remains, but Martin put up a huge fight. He made things very difficult for me, so in the end . . .' His voice trailed off.

'I'm so sorry that I wasn't there for you, Patrick,' said Nate.

'You were. You were. Ma drew such a vivid picture of you that we always had you with us.'

'I feel like I abandoned you.'

'You had no choice.'

'And you – did you have any children?'

'No. I worked in politics all of my life, mostly for Albert, but some of the work we did was not appreciated and I was eventually exiled from all state business. I was cut off from everything: work, insurance, credit, health care. It's very hard to live a normal life after that. But I was lucky. I had Albert.'

Nate felt tremendous guilt that he had created a rebel in his son.

'Tell me about the earthquake and what happened to Mary.'

'Didn't Albert tell you?'

'I'd like to hear it from you, Patrick, everything you remember.'

Patrick's watery eyes scanned the room as though he was collecting his thoughts from the walls. 'It was the strangest day. Windless and static. Dogs were wailing. All the things you're told that happen before an earthquake, but you only recognize them in retrospect. I felt a huge boom and a long rumble. Ma was at work and called us on the phone and screamed at Laura to get me out of the house. Laura was the nanny. She said a tsunami was coming and that we had one hour. It was chaos. So many people screaming and crying, abandoning their cars. The police were taking women and children up to Will Rogers State Park. We ran up Lincoln Boulevard and were picked up by the police. We got hit by the wave in the police car. It came right over us and water was pouring in. I remember it like it was yesterday, that terrible brown water gushing in, but the car stuck to the ground and the wave passed on by us. We didn't know it at the time, but we were right at the very edge of the wave. The aftershock was worse. But by then I was staying with Bob and Kate in the hills. We never saw Ma again. She must have drowned—' He broke off. 'Albert took me to New York to live with Lisa.'

'Was that OK?' said Nate. 'I always loved your aunt.'

'Yes,' he said. 'And I always had you. Ma made me understand who you were and what you stood for.'

'It ruined us!' said Nate. 'Albert thinks I was murdered deliberately because of the information I had on Martin Rando, and right now, I don't know if it was worth it, to miss you growing up.'

'What was it that Martin Luther King said?' asked Patrick. '"Our lives begin to end the day we become silent about things that matter." Tell me, could you have done anything different?'

'Your grandfather sowed the seeds,' said Nate. 'He ran a free clinic in North Carolina. "Everyone deserves a basic level of care," he said. What Albert and I were witnessing made us crazy. Health Management Organizations and insurance companies acting like the judge and jury over who lives and who dies. Drugs costs were exorbitant. Chronic conditions were not being covered. Many doctors took advantage of the system and grew rich, but I saw healthcare as the biggest betrayal of the American people.' Nate was lost in the fog of his ancient rebellion.

'I tried for so long to get you back so you would be safe,' Patrick repeated, cupping his head in his hands.

'Was Mary a good mother?'

'She was. But I wanted her to be closer. I know now that she had a lot to hold together. She loved me, but I was only six when she died – barely a man myself,' he said, the merest hint of a smile on his lips.

'You had a lot to hold together too,' said Nate, instinctively stroking the old man's cheek. 'I'm going to take care of you. I have some business to finish first but then I'm going to return and fight for your pardon and medical treatment.'

Patrick's hand closed over Nate's. 'Thank you,' he said.

Nate found Fred shaving in the bathroom.

'I'm going to leave you a copy of my files on Martin Rando. I want you to guard them with your life. They will, hopefully, be another chapter in your story, and with the money I know you will earn, I want you to pay for my son's hospital treatment. You're going to get Patrick to an oncologist today. Get Albert to help you. Get *The Metropolitan* to pay for it. Get a false ID. I don't care what you do, but you *are* going to do it or you'll have me to contend with when I get back.'

'And where are you going?'

'To Savannah.'

'And how do you intend to get there – on foot?'

'Train.'

'It's impossible to get on a train, Nate. They'll pick you up straight away.'

'Not if I travel as Fred Arlin.'

80

Finding the address was the easiest thing that Nate had done since the waking. Fred's health certificates were up to date, and with a haircut, his collar turned up and a cap pulled low over his brow, Nate could pass for Fred in any crowded station. He took a high-speed train down to Savannah and laughed with derision at the idea that Martin Rando, his old adversary, was living in such a sepulchral part of the world. He was alive, but he had chosen to live in a city that felt closer to death than any other place that he had ever visited.

He decided to head straight for Rando's estate and stopped the taxi near the boundary. There would be no surreptitious climbing of walls or creeping through the undergrowth only to be picked up by the militia Nate knew would be guarding the estate. His plan was simple. He would march right up to the gate and declare himself. He believed the audacity of the gesture would guarantee him an audience at least.

The gates, as expected, were heavily guarded and he was quickly surrounded.

'I believe Martin Rando would like to see me.'

They bundled him into a waiting truck. Nate saw everything in slow motion after that, from the breeze fluttering through the fronds of the Spanish moss to the crows that ducked and leapt from their perches making squawks of protest as the vehicle sped up the long gravel drive towards the house. They rounded a bank of rhododendron bushes and a huge nineteenth-century plantation mansion loomed up out of the dense vegetation, moon-silver like a ghost among the blackened foliage. It was a place that could exist only on the exploitation of others, from the slaves who picked the cotton to the patients fed stolen medicine by Icor Incorporated. It had a sinister luminescence, with Doric columns and tall, melancholy windows. It was a mausoleum and had been ever since the first foundation stone was laid.

'You're lucky not to be dead,' said one of the guards as he dragged Nate towards the house.

'Am I?' said Nate. He stumbled and fell. But he realized that the man was right. He *was* lucky. Not to be dead.

They pushed him through the door. Nate saw a couple of people scurry away like insects caught in a shaft of light. His gaze travelled up a long museum-like hallway. He saw superb pieces of furniture, specially lit, but no flowers, rugs or lamps that would make the place homely.

The bodyguards showed him into an anteroom, which looked as sterile as an operating theatre.

'Anyone who wants to see Mr Rando has to shower, scrub and change. The suits are over there.'

Nate complied. After he'd showered he was escorted into a beautiful drawing room. He looked around and identified a number of Impressionists on the walls: Monet, Pissarro, van Gogh.

Nate began to hear his own blood pulsing through his ears. He tried to remember when he had last seen Martin Rando face to face. Maybe it was that reunion in New York.

Who was there? Ken, George, Jack, Carl, Casper and Guy. It was a boys' night out and Martin positioned himself, as always, in the background, smiling savagely and trying to maintain the smug mask that hid his burning resentment of others who had more social grace. Martin thought himself to be the cleverest of the gang, which he was, and the hurt vindictiveness he held in him scared all of them, though they never talked about it openly.

Nate remembered being afraid of Martin's appetite for power and not actually liking himself while he was in Martin's company. He became more boorish, to fend off Martin's arrogance and ruthlessness. And his usual last resort was to lord it over Martin when he got lucky with a woman. Martin would despise hearing about Nate's sexual exploits, but couldn't help asking. Rando was so short and so plain that in most situations women would look straight through him. Women were always at the heart of the competitiveness between them.

Nate's reminiscences brought back those juvenile emotions, easily wrapped in meaning by the young body he now occupied. For the first time since Keith had been killed by the mob, Nate could feel the body stirring. He could tell that it wanted to smash things, upend tables, rip apart the opulent drapes. Nate made a tremendous effort to keep himself in check. He knew he had in him a warrior he could unleash at any moment.

Nate saw a short man walking down the corridor past cavernous ballrooms where orchestras had once played. He knew instantly that it was Martin. His gait was upright and his walk almost sprightly, the only sign of his years a slight stoop in the shoulders.

Someone scuttled out of a side room. Martin stopped to

talk to him, tilting his head to listen. He patted his subordinate on the shoulder, paternal, gentlemanly, setting an example.

Finally, he was standing in front of Nate. He was 107 years of age, a little older than Albert Noyes. The nose was distended, the mouth purple-lipped and indistinct, but the eyes . . . they had in them the glint of green that was immediately familiar to Nate. He remembered those eyes fixing on him for way too long after Nate had stopped talking when they had shared rooms at college.

'How did you get to be you?' Martin had asked him once. There was a kind of freshman's worship in the statement, but hostility too.

'Do you remember where we last met?' said Martin, as though reading Nate's thoughts. The voice was light and from the back of the throat – strangled, impatient.

'1998. The reunion in New York.'

'That's right. Who chose that dreadful bar?'

'Carl.'

'I think it was my only time in the company of lap dancers.'

Nate waited for more.

'All those women parading their bodies, leading you chumps around by your dicks.'

So the barbs would fly again and Martin would adopt the stance of moral piety over Nate and his friends to dignify his own lack of sexual success. So long ago and yet it still rankled.

'Things change—'

'No they don't,' cut in the old man bitterly, 'people just get older. Like our shadows, our wishes lengthen as our sun declines.'

Nate looked at Martin's hands, small, strangely translucent and damp. His hair was strange too, like a tangled mossy plant, a wig maybe, but probably not in these times, and dusty-red, just like his son's.

Nate remembered seeing photographs of the world's oldest people and being enthralled by age of that magnitude; the plate-sized liver spots, the purplish blotches and warts crawling over the skin as though they were breaking down the epidermis and turning it into a rugged, warped map of each passing year. He had had a few centenarian patients on his books and would go to see them. Some of them were remarkable, like broken-up little birds with knobbly talons and useless, atrophied legs. But the spirit shone out of them like a beacon. And here was Martin Rando, spry and supple where all the joints could be regrown. And yet some kind of profound disintegration was taking place. Flesh that wasn't supposed to be alive had a deathly preposterousness about it and a smell of something foul being kept at bay.

Nate could see that ageing had become a dastardly thing, yet to cheat it was to live in its shadow and be thwarted by its daily, inexorable march. Martin was neither human nor where he should probably be – in the ground. He was in limbo, on borrowed time and at the expense of the millions of people he had trampled over to get to where he was.

Martin settled on a huge gilt throne, which dwarfed his diminutive frame. 'Talk to me, Nate,' he demanded. 'Here we are, generations on. You, this extraordinary achievement, possibly the most significant of all Icor's achievements. Me, still alive, clinging on by a thread. All I can offer you now is my genius.' He laughed. It was creepy and challenging. 'You came to see me. So what do you want?'

'I want to know if you ordered my execution.'

'That's right. You got shot,' he said casually.

'The murderer was working for *you*.'

'Was he?' Martin was talking as though he was bored, as

though the matter was of so little consequence that he could barely muster the breath to respond. With his insouciance, whether it was sincere or an act, he was like a cunning little animal, totally self-absorbed and totally focused.

'I had proof of your links with Dr Wasserstrom when I was shot. The kid who shot me was not acting alone.'

Martin motioned for Nate to sit on a couch opposite him.

Six feet away from his old adversary, Nate could feel the power of the body stirring. He breathed and soothed it, told it to keep calm.

'You see this house?' said Martin. 'This house is a complete fabrication. A house exactly like this used to stand here, but it was destroyed by Hurricane Hilda in 2045. So I rebuilt it. It's mostly resin-cast and entirely hermetically sealed in case there's an outbreak. Fabrications are easily formed and easily upheld. I've learnt that in my many years on this planet.'

'Did you?' pressed Nate.

'What do you want to hear? That I did it, that I didn't do it? What difference does it make now?'

'It must be strange,' said Nate.

'What?'

'To live outside of morality.'

'I don't remember your morality coming into play when we were at Harvard.'

'What are you talking about?'

'All those hearts you broke. You didn't seem to have much of a conscience about that.'

'For God's sake!' said Nate. 'We were kids.'

'That's right, you played the field, then just at the right moment you found undying love. How simple and neat. What was her name?'

'I think you know her name.'

Martin looked into the distance, pretended to think and shook his head. 'Some things escape my mind.'

'Did you find someone?' asked Nate, knowing full well that Martin had not the faintest idea about love.

The old man picked at a thread on his armrest and let his gaze wander to the window. 'Four times.'

'Did you find your *grand amour*?'

'And a lot *mour* besides.' Martin looked around the room. 'When we were at college, you could have done anything you wanted.'

'But I did do everything I wanted.'

'But there was this skew in your make-up, this desire to turn everyone else's happiness to shit. Where did that come from?'

'I think it's more pertinent to know what happened to *you*, Nate. And seeing as we're talking about morality, what did you have in your *character* that made you think you could destroy a friend's career? The arrogance still astounds me to this day. To think you wanted to put your pathetic, misguided idealism above *me*!'

'You murdered Wasserstrom and stole his work, putting back the cure for cancer – how many years?'

'We were all working towards the same goal. Wasserstrom just happened to be ahead of the game. And I didn't kill him by the way. He killed himself.'

It was pointless pressing for a direct confession so Nate changed tack. 'I'd like to know what happened to me after Mary died.'

'The cryonics industry collapsed and I bought up every frozen cadaver I could find in America. It became a hobby. You came into my hands sometime in the thirties. I can't remember exactly when. They found you and a few others in a garage outside San Francisco. Some technician kept you going after his company went bust. Can you imagine how I felt when I found you? I had to look at you, see how you were doing, so from then on, you were always on display. I could have switched off the machine at any moment, Nate. And so many times I thought about doing it. Knowing your obvious hatred of me.'

'Why didn't you?'

'It was odd. I just couldn't let you go. You were part of me. Part of my past. I'm like that. I can never let people I care about go.' He was smiling now, thinking he was being charming, expecting Nate to believe him.

'You were the best example of freezing that we had in our collection. Mary—'

'So you *do* remember her name.'

'So I do. Mary always kept you in liquid helium. So much better than nitrogen. There was much less decay, and nano-technology was coming on line. We owned so much of the technology by then that if it worked, it was going to make us *the* only provider in the global market. I thought you were part of our future, but you and the others were a drain on our resources too. Then I hit on this idea. If I put you on display, I could make a little money out of you and you could pay your own way. So I turned you into a celebrity. You were quite famous for a while. All those freaks were happy to pay to see "the Head". Having you around was fun for me. My old college room-mate in a display case. And my betrayer. Because I know you wanted to betray me, Nate. Ever since you met me. You couldn't stand it that I was destined for great things.'

Nate didn't say anything. He wanted to hear the old man out.

'Mary was long gone by then, so there was no one around to protest your dignity. Except your son. He became a nuisance for a while but we took care of that.'

'I suppose you were responsible for his social exile,' said Nate with disgust.

The old man leant forward, his lips peeling back over his strangely white teeth.

'For years I was the *only* one who believed in physical reincarnation. The *only one*! Everyone said I was a fool, but now look at us, sitting here and talking like old friends. When I was jaded, in the middle years, I used to come and see you, to try to get some feeling going. Sometimes it actually worked.'

He was off in his own world now, his thoughts scattered and meandering, the classic signs of sociopathy, ducking and hiding from any form of truth.

'What was interesting to me was that I didn't feel hatred for you at all. What I felt for you was pity. And I was grateful for that. I think it was one of the most sincere responses that I have ever had about anyone. You were my emotional barometer. And you alone could change the temperature. Those dead periods of your life are terrible, just terrible. Worse than being in pain.'

'Why didn't you come to see me in Phoenix?'

'I don't travel. It's not that I'm not capable. I can't risk infection. There's only so much prevention a body can take in a lifetime. It's a quiet life for me now.'

Hearing the words of poison dripping like black tar from Martin's lips made Nate ache for his lost self and his wife and son. This man before him had taken all their lives and ripped them apart.

'I'm going to expose you, Martin, properly this time, just like you discredited me and my family.'

Martin laughed a wheezy laugh. 'You think people even care, Nate? I've survived the condemnation of continents. I can live out an ancient accusation that I might have had an unprovable link to a murder that happened sixty years ago.' He sat back and smiled. 'So,' he said, folding his hands on his lap, 'what do you want from me?'

'I want you to go on TV and confess.'

He laughed. 'You're such a schoolboy. People don't care. Why did you always make your life so difficult?'

'Your killing of Dr Wasserstrom cost thousands of lives and caused real suffering, and all because you couldn't bear to come in second.'

'You may be right.'

'I have lodged my evidence elsewhere.'

'Really,' said Martin, making a face, pretending to be scared. 'And what evidence is that? I suspect it's nothing more than a few ancient papers that I was looking for a very long time ago and a collection of e-mail messages from an unstable, hysterical assistant. Listen, I'm going to do you a big favour. This world isn't for you. Your time was then and this is now. We've done enough to ensure the public is terrified of you and outraged by your existence. It was me who called in the EIS by the way.'

'Why did you do that?' said Nate. He couldn't comprehend the twisted logic of it. To put a division of his own company in jeopardy.

'Once you were alive and fully conscious, I have to confess that I felt almost nervous. You were the one loose end that I never cleared up, and there you were, with a lot of hate locked up inside you and a lot of memories about to be recovered. So what better way to dispose of you than to put you in quarantine? I had it all worked out with one of the guards. Place you in the wrong cell and you'd be gone in a matter of days. But you escaped. So I decided to be patient. I knew that your road would lead back to me somehow. And here you are.'

'There must be more people than me who would like to see you dead,' said Nate.

'Oh, I'm sure of it. People can't bear to see other people being so successful.'

'It's not that—'

'I'm told that after the waking you wanted to die and even tried to take your own life. Say I'm a king who could grant you that wish. Because I can arrange it for you. Like I said, this whole project has been a resounding success and thank you for your participation. But we have euthanasia now, so let me make it easy for you, comforting even. We can make it so sweet; play music, run a film, do whatever you want and you can just fade away.'

At that moment, Nate wanted to live more than ever; to rush headlong into the prevailing wind, to feel the sting of a blizzard on his cheeks, to gulp at the shock of diving into cold water, to feel the clamminess of a body after sex. To be totally and utterly alive. And to outlive this fake human being who was rotten inside and out.

He pounced on Martin then, his left arm gripping Martin's throat. Rando's eyes bulged in disbelief.

'I have her,' spluttered the old man, his arms clawing feebly at Nate's face.

Footsteps and crashes could be heard from another part of the mansion.

'Who do you have?' shouted Nate, loosening his grip.

'Mary – I have her.'

Nate let go of Martin's scrawny neck.

'But she died in the earthquake.'

'All roads lead to Mary,' rasped Martin.

Nate felt the spasm of an electric shock crack through his shoulder blades. Someone prodded something into his thigh. He collapsed. His body went rigid and a constriction around his chest let Nate know that his heart was pretty close to stopping.

One of the bodyguards helped Martin back on to his throne. 'I'm fine,' he spat. 'Why the hell didn't you come sooner?'

'Sorry, Mr Rando.'

'You should be!' he said, slapping the man, who tolerated the feeble blow like a chastened dog.

'What do you mean?' said Nate, who was being held by two guards.

Rando coughed and rubbed his throat. 'After you died Mary turned into a harridan, campaigning for ludicrous reforms that would have decimated the health industry. She also made it very clear to me that she knew about Wasserstrom, so she must have found the documents. She tried to get the case reopened, implying it was murder. She even pointed the finger at me at a couple of public meetings, accusing me of murdering *you*. She made sure all her actions were very public so I would find it harder to get to her. But by then, most people thought she was nuts. A bereaved widow is easy to discredit. We were watching her for the longest time, hoping to get an opportunity. I almost gave up. Then an act of God helped us. We found her just before the tsunami hit the coast.'

'You killed her?' demanded Nate, breathing to ease the pain in his chest.

Martin smiled.

'Where is she?' Nate asked with growing despair.

'Downstairs,' Rando said almost lightly. 'They all are.' He turned to one of the guards and winced. 'Show him.'

'Are you sure, Mr Rando?'

'Of course I'm sure!' he barked.

Nate was marched along the cavernous corridor and down some concrete steps, Rando following. The electric shock they had given him was making his heart fibrillate. Two glass doors opened and icy air hit him. It took a moment for Nate to comprehend what he was seeing. It was a catacomb of brick arches that disappeared into the darkness. There were row upon row of glass-fronted ice cases containing dozens of bodies. In others, there were disembodied heads. Nate could hardly bear to look.

'I told you I could never let go,' said Martin. He walked up and looked at a woman, her body modestly covered by some kind of cloth. 'This is Lek, my son's first wife. She committed suicide on the estate half a century ago.'

Nate wondered what miserable life Lek had suffered in the midst of the Rando clan.

'Don't tell me any more,' said Nate. He couldn't bear to hear any more contamination. 'Just point out where Mary is.'

'Row J – half-way down.'

Nate shook off his captors and ran down the aisle, checking each upended coffin. He scoured face after face, wondering if he would even be able to recognize his wife. And then he saw her, as though asleep, her lips blue and slightly parted. He greedily scanned her face and body for all the imperfections that made her whole, the spidery scar on her cheek and the precious mole on her neck, and in those tiny blemishes, he recaptured in his mind all her loveliness, her bravery, her power. The detail was hers exclusively, as was her soul. No one could replicate Mary. No one. He leant his forehead against hers, the glass between them. He could hear footsteps on the concrete and the guards surrounding him. At this moment, it made no difference. They were alone.

'Your killer's over there,' said Martin behind him. 'The real body donor.'

Nate didn't want to leave his wife, but he had to see it. He walked over to the head of Duane Williams and saw the handsome face, also at peace, the finely bridged nose and the drawn-down lips with all the thwarted potential that he'd seen in Keith. He saw the signs of a tough life, too, and a scar at the corner of his mouth. Nate wondered if his body would have any cellular reaction to the proximity. But it remained quiet. Then he saw a familiar profile in another case. It was Monty, his eyes half-open and his face wearing that sweet, permanent half-smile. Monty in life was glad to be where he was. In death, he looked pretty much the same. So Icor's murderous bloodbath was complete.

'We will be altering this young guy's genetics so his body can be used for my son. He was one of your nurses, wasn't he?' Martin's voice was almost careless, as though he was making a benign social inquiry. Beyond all comprehension of the horror. Nate remembered going to the Holocaust Museum in Washington and looking at an exhibit of photographs cataloguing the cold-blooded killing of gypsies to test their bodily reactions to the bends. The sheer madness of it was beyond his comprehension. What else was there to say? All logic was irrelevant.

'I do want to live,' said Nate quietly.

'Then we did our job,' said Martin. 'And you have made a complete recovery. So why did you come here?' he asked. There was a glimmer of genuine surprise in the old man's expression. 'You might have been able to hide out and have longer.'

'I thought I could do something.'

Martin looked at Nate curiously, then turned and walked back up the steps.

'You know the difference between us?' Nate yelled.

'Tell me,' said Martin.

'The difference between us is that I've been there and you haven't, and I want to live, but I'm not afraid of death. And your time is coming, Martin. Can you feel *that*?'

The old man kept walking.

They manhandled Nate then, expecting resistance, but Nate felt completely calm.

'It's OK – I'm not going to do anything,' he said.

They dragged him deeper into the catacomb until they came to a small room where there was a gurney with straps to hold him down. Nate must have transmitted some message to the body. It mustered all its strength to resist being strapped in, but there were ten men hovering just to make sure the second execution of Duane Williams was completed. The body, heroic to the end, stood no chance.

Nate tried to bargain with his captors. 'Do you really want to live out your lives under this man's dictatorship?'

The guards said nothing.

'You're no better than slaves, which is how this house was built in the first place.' They ignored him and busied themselves with the task ahead.

'He is robbing you of your right to a decent life. He is sucking you dry and coercing medicine and altering the course of history to suit his own insane desires. He has no right to such power. No man has the right to such power. He is beyond the law. Is that really going to benefit you? You can kill me and put me in that gallery of his, but is that what you want to tell your grandchildren? That you were the servant of a murderer whose morality has disintegrated so far that he believes he can kill whoever he wants?'

Someone pulled the strap tight, cutting into Nate's wrist.

The body was fighting on its own now, veins standing out as it yanked against the stays.

Nate remembered some ancient research from Death Row about depression being rife among the guards who had to work there. He figured that at least one or two of his captors would be unhappy with the brutal, murderous acts that they were forced to commit.

'Years ago, Martin Rando killed someone who was due to make a breakthrough about cancer, suppressing the progress of medicine because it was different to his own work and likely to get there first. For years Martin killed people by denying them that cure. I found out about it. I was on my way to expose him and he had me killed. Shot in a car park with my pregnant wife watching me die. He would do it to any of you in a heartbeat. Don't think he has any intentions other than serving himself in this life. How well does he treat you day in, day out? I saw him slap one of you. Do you think he's worthy of your loyalty? Maybe you had mothers or fathers or grandparents who died of cancer. They could have been saved if it hadn't been for his greed.'

'Shut up,' someone growled.

Nate wasn't going to be silenced.

'He has no loyalty to you. And yet he expects total subservience,' he said, fixing on the guard closest to him.

'I said shut up.' The guard cuffed Nate, opening his lip.

'See this man for who he really is. *He*'s the one who should be dead.'

Nate looked around him. They dimmed the lights. The straps were cutting into his flesh.

'Let me live and I'll tell the world about this. You can put a stop to this. I was born in a century with two world wars where millions of people died at the hands of tyrants.

And you are the foot soldiers making it happen all over again.'

Nate heard the whirr of a machine start up in another room. Were they going to gas him or inject him or infuse him? He heard a hiss. It must be gas. His body, in its last magnificent gesture of defiance, tried to grab at the stays. Nate gave way to the body's last burst of strength and felt the burn of the stays cut deeper into his flesh. A vile chemical smell reached his nostrils. Slowly, he relaxed. He was done.

81

Fields of blinding, verdant greenness. A Swiss mountainside, manicured as smooth as velvet. He stroked the nap of the grass and felt its damp freshness. The sun's rays were glistening on every blade and there were white fluffy clouds in the sky, shaped like unshorn sheep. Was this a dream? No landscape was this perfect. Had he travelled through the light and arrived in heaven? The place he never believed existed? Up beyond him were snowy mountains.

'Nate, Nate.'

A voice was calling him and he turned to see that he was on the edge of a precipice looking down into a ravine thousands of feet deep. A few pebbles gave way under his feet and they tumbled, echoing into the abyss. He leapt back. Maybe he could just jump and all would be well.

'Nate?'

That voice again, more urgent, and he was in the grass, the long, fecund grass right in front of his eyes. But there was no snow or fluffy clouds. The sharp smell of mulch hit him. This was the Deep South, and he was lying on some kind of recliner and could smell the earth close to his head.

'Nate.'

'Am I in heaven?'

'Savannah.'

'Where Martin Rando lives.'

'Three miles away.'

An Asian woman he didn't recognize was leaning over him.

'Am I alive?'

'Yes.'

'What happened?'

'They were going to kill you, but my husband, Napoleon Arcibal, has been working undercover up at the Rando house for a year. He stopped your execution. You gave some speech apparently – it persuaded enough guys for Napoleon to make his move.'

'Arcibal?' said Nate. The name sounded familiar.

'Monty Arcibal was his brother.'

'So he was working at the house, knowing Monty's body was in the basement?'

'They'd only just taken delivery of Monty,' she said, tears welling up in her eyes. 'Napoleon was so upset he nearly blew his cover, then you showed up. He was planning to raid the house in a matter of days. You just happened to speed things up.'

'I did?' said Nate. All he could remember was passing out.

The woman looked fearful and Nate realized he was in some lush, southern garden.

'So where is he?' he asked.

'He's up at the house. There's a lot of clearing up to do.'

'I bet there is.'

'They executed Martin Rando instead of you.'

'Who did – your husband?'

'With the help of the FBI.'

'Thank God,' Nate said, feeling utter relief spread through his body. He looked at the bandages around his wrists.

'And you are?'

'Carmen Arcibal. Napoleon is my husband.'

'And Monty was your brother-in-law,' said Nate.

'Rando's hated around here. Hated. I'm so glad you put an end to it all.'

Carmen gave him something to eat and Napoleon arrived shortly after. He barely spoke and was extremely jumpy.

'I'm sorry about Monty,' said Nate. 'I loved him too.'

He grunted. A silent, wilful man, contained but grappling with powerful emotions. So different from his gentle, appeasing brother.

'And how can we make your day?' he said eventually.

'I want an immediate pardon for my son, Patrick, who has been in exile for most of his adult life. I want him to get proper medical treatment for his cancer and then I want something else.'

'I think I know what that is,' said Napoleon.

Although he had no trust in Garth Bannerman, Nate recognized that the doctor was just another pawn in Icor's now crumbling empire. And Persis too. Besides, what either of them knew or didn't know was irrelevant right now. Nate just wanted to see if there was any chance of reviving Mary. Garth was possibly the only man alive who could do it. Nate requested that the doctor be flown in from Phoenix immediately.

'Did you know about Mary being here?' demanded Nate when Garth arrived. It was the one question he had to know the answer to.

'I knew that Rando brought all the cryogenically frozen

collections across the country to Savannah, but I was always told that Mary wasn't among them,' said Garth.

'You mean you asked?'

'Yes – after you asked,' said Garth. 'You were given a raw deal, Nate,' he added, 'and I for one am ashamed.'

'So am I,' said Nate.

'They were the only group prepared to fund me through the problems with the EIS and they had the cash to give me the freedom to do what I wanted. And a lot of political clout. Not many scientists get that lucky.'

'There was a price to pay though, wasn't there?'

Garth nodded. He ran the tests on Mary's body while Nate waited in the cavernous ballroom upstairs and watched the various agencies remove the other corpses from the house. There was a moment when John Rando arrived with an entourage of bodyguards and lawyers to gain access, but he was told to keep away and that charges would follow. Nate wanted him to be arrested on the spot and couldn't believe what kind of system was in operation that could keep him from being incarcerated immediately. He was told that an arrest was imminent, providing they could link Rando Junior to the catacomb of corpses.

It wasn't long before Garth had an answer about Mary's fate.

'I'm sorry, Nate. We can't do it. There's just too much necrosis.'

Nate said simply, 'I'd like to say goodbye all the same.'

They laid Mary out on a slab and gave Nate thermonuclear gloves so that he could touch her frozen corpse. He stroked her cheek, gingerly at first, then pulled the cap off her head and arranged the hair around her face.

'My darling girl,' he said, and could almost see her sitting up and smiling at him and allowing him to lead her away from the tomb. He cupped her head in both hands and imagined himself doing that in the deepest act of making love. It was like cowering over a stone effigy in a church vault.

'You were so brave. Who will know the courage it took to be you?' he said, blowing softly into her frost-white hair.

I will, he thought, sliding his gloved hands through her stone fingers. 'I will,' he said, and then he let her go.